Lynda Page was born and brought up in Leicester. The
eldest of four daughters, she left home at seventeen
and has had a wide variety of office jobs. She lives in a
village near Leicester. Her previous novels, *Evie*,
Annie, *Josie*, *Peggie* and *And One For Luck*, are also
available from Headline.

'Lynda Page creates strong characers and is a clever
and careful storyteller... She has the stamina not to
alienate you as a reader and to keep the story going on
a constant flow of purpose and energy... A great
writer who gives an authentic voice to Leicester... A
formidable talent' *LEI*

Just By Chance

Lynda Page

HEADLINE

First published in 1996
by HEADLINE BOOK PUBLISHING

First published in paperback in 1996
by HEADLINE BOOK PUBLISHING

10 9 8

ISBN 0 7472 4856 7

Printed and bound in Great Britain by
Clays Ltd, St Ives plc

HEADLINE BOOK PUBLISHING
A division of Hodder Headline PLC
338 Euston Road
London NW1 3BH

For my grandson, Liam Patrick John,
born 21st November 1995

You were hardly ten minutes old when I held you in
my arms. Your large blue eyes looked straight into
mine and from that moment on, I was sentenced to do
your bidding

I promise to be the best grandmother I possibly can. To
cheer the loudest and allow you to stay up late – in fact,
to let you do everything you really shouldn't. But then
isn't that what a grandmother is for?

I wish you a wonderful life – health, happiness and
fulfilment

With all my love, your devoted grandmother

ACKNOWLEDGEMENTS

The Pearson family of Burbage – Vivienne, Geoff, Ivan and Brenda. Thank you for the information on the building trade, the welcome into your home and the cups of tea.

All 'my' lads in Network Services, LCL Cable Communications Leicester (now Diamond Cable). I have never laughed so much. I sometimes wonder how we managed to keep the department running so efficiently.

My friends – in no particular order, Mary Gwynne, Rosemary Bailey (Rosie) and Cheryl Hodgeson – for still being my friends.

My sister, Sue McGowan, for your unwavering duties as promotions officer, I am truly grateful.

Chapter One

Elijah Penny, desperate gaze fixed rigidly on the rotting wood of the cottage door, pounced as the latch lifted and the tall, thin frame of his daughter Matilda struggled through, carrying an armful of logs.

She jumped and gave a frightened cry as he grabbed her roughly by her shoulders, fingers digging deep as intended, and threw her bodily across the room. The logs scattered as she landed with a thud against the ancient wattle wall. She fought for breath. Although used to her father's behaviour, this attack nevertheless had taken her by surprise. She'd been hoping he would sleep for hours yet, considering the state he had stumbled home in just before dawn.

Before she had time to gather her wits her father was upon her. Grabbing her arm, he wrenched her up and thrust his contorted face into hers, his foul breath and bodily stench from weeks without washing causing her stomach to heave.

'Yous bitch!' he shouted hysterically, arms flailing wildly. 'You've bin through me pockets.'

Fighting fear, she raised her eyes beseechingly. 'I ain't, Dad. Honest, I ain't. You spent what you had last night on gin.'

He raised his hand and struck her hard across her face. The force of the blow sent her reeling and again she landed against the wall. 'Liar,' he spat, advancing towards her. 'I

1

know you've bin through me pockets. Now gimme it back or I'll thrash the livin' daylights outta yous.'

Cradling a painful cheek, she fixed her tortured eyes on this man who was her father: tall and with hunched shoulders; gaunt and unshaven, greying hair long and straggly; the clothes on his back threadbare and dirty. A nervous, trembling individual, entirely dependent on alcohol. And for a man with only one good leg, he was agile enough when he chose to be.

His bloodshot eyes darted uncontrollably. At this moment he was frantic with fear that there was no money to buy the gin. He had never cared a damn for how his daughter earned that money or for what hardship they both suffered as a result of his drinking. As long as he got his gin that was all he was concerned about.

And despite it all, Eli Penny was a man his daughter tried desperately to love, because he was her father and because he was all she had.

Somehow Tilda's fear of his brutal hands and harsh tongue was momentarily forgotten. 'I'm the one who earns the money, Dad. You don't do a stroke to bring anything in.'

His face blackened like thunder. 'And how can I?' he erupted. 'I'm a cripple, remember.' He pounded his fist against what remained of his thigh. 'If yous hadn't run off in the woods this would never have happened. It's your fault, remember. All *your* fault I'm like this.'

She flinched, flattening herself against the wall as he drew back his hand, intending to strike her again. 'Don't, Dad,' she pleaded. 'Please don't. You can't beat outta me what I ain't got.'

Hand poised, he glared at her with loathing. She reminded him constantly of times he strove hard to forget. She was there like a thorn in his side, continually jabbing at his memory. He wanted to scream at her now, tell her to go, get out of his life

2

for good, leave him in peace, but he couldn't. Much to his annoyance he needed her. Apart from anything else, without the pittance she brought in he would not be able to purchase the harmless-looking liquid that got him through the day, and if he beat her too hard, which at this moment was his deepest desire, she would be in no fit state the next morning to make even that pittance.

He abruptly lowered his arm and turned from her, cleared his throat and spat the phlegm into the fire. It hissed, sending a cloud of smoke racing up the chimney. Forcing memories away, he turned back to her, his eyes malicious. 'What's in my pocket is mine, do yous hear me? Mine. What right have yous to go through me pockets? Good God, have yous no shame – stealing off yer own, father?' Rage filled him. He was desperate for a drink and knew she had removed his means of getting it, despite her denial. He lunged again, grabbing her arms, and shook her so hard her head wobbled loosely. 'Yous must have some. How much did yers get down the market today?'

A few coppers, just enough to put a bit by for the rent, and pay for a small bag of flour for bread and a piece of fat, barley to help supplement the pan of vegetable soup continuously simmering, meal for the chickens, and what was left, together with the vegetables still in the small plot of garden at the back of their dwelling, might get them through the week if she was careful. But she could not tell him that. He would dismiss the fact that they needed to eat, take all she had and purchase a jug of gut-rotting gin to drink under his favourite tree deep in the wood. He would then stumble his way home and fall asleep on his rotting straw mattress in the corner of the room. It always amazed her, that, no matter how drunk her father got, he always managed to find his way home.

Her throbbing cheek was causing her head to ache and she momentarily shut her eyes. Ever since she could remember her father had always had a liking for the drink, but over the years that liking had become a desperate need – now, without his daily ration, he was an ungovernable monster. He was surely drinking himself to death and she felt powerless to stop it. She could fully understand his need to ease his torment. It must have been an unbearable shock, coming back as he had done from the brink of death to find himself maimed. His world must have collapsed. She longed for him to talk to her about it, to help her understand and appreciate his feelings and, in doing so, afford her an insight into how his tortured mind worked. But her father was not an approachable man, not the kind who would listen to reason or take advice from anyone, especially from the daughter he so obviously despised. Eli's selfishness had allowed the anger at his own situation to grow out of all proportion and there was nothing she could do about it now.

Conscious that he was ready to strike again, she braced herself, wanting to get it over with. She was bone weary, having been up that morning before dawn to trudge the two miles down the squelching muddy lane to stand in a biting wind in the tiny village square, hoping that someone would purchase the eggs her nine hens had laid, several frost-bitten turnips and some bundles of kindling. She had managed to sell them but not at the price she had hoped to get; she had practically had to give them away. The locals' sympathy for her situation had long ago worn thin, and besides they all had enough to cope with, trying to feed themselves, let alone worry about some outsiders who inhabited a near-ruined dwelling deep in the woods.

After buying the provisions, she had wrapped the remaining coins carefully inside an old piece of rag. This now weighed down the pocket of her threadbare serge dress and she felt sure her father sensed it was there.

Beads of anxiety formed on Eli's brow which he wiped away with a sweating palm. 'Don't hold out on me, girl. Yous must have something.' He thrust a trembling hand towards her and shook it impatiently. 'Come on, hand it over.'

Her blood ran cold. 'I told you, Dad, there's none left.' Please God, she thought worriedly, don't let him find the change in my pocket. She suddenly realised how stupid she had been. She should have hidden the money outside.

'And I don't believe yous.'

She stared at him, legs shaking. It would be so easy just to hand over the coins and be left in peace, but she couldn't because in so doing she would make her father suspicious, which could result in the discovery of her savings – five shillings, mostly in farthings – hidden in a rusty tin under her straw shakedown. It was all she had to show, painstakingly gathered, from years of hard work. There was so much she could buy with the money, so much she needed, but she kept it because its presence gave her comfort; with those few hidden coins she felt she wasn't quite destitute.

He glared at her. 'Well, in that case, I'll just sell the hens.'

'No, Dad, no,' she cried, alarmed. 'If you sell them we'll have nothing.'

He gave a cruel laugh. 'Look round yous, girl. We've nothing anyway. A few hens ain't gonna make no difference.'

She watched as he turned and stumbled towards the door, mind racing frantically for means by which to stop him because she knew without a doubt he meant what he said. 'I'll get a job, Dad.'

He stopped, turned, and glared at her mockingly. 'Job! And who'd employ yous, eh?' A sarcastic grin split his face. 'Face it, Tilda, yer not exactly the employable kind, now are yous?'

She stared back, humiliated, then her hackles rose. 'Mr Wilson the butcher said he'd think about it,' she blurted out before she could stop herself. 'He's a job going whilst his wife has the baby, and I applied.'

She bowed her head. The job offer on a card in the shop window had leapt out at her as she had passed and she had stopped abruptly, retraced her steps and stared at it. A thrill of hope had shot through her. She desperately wanted to get the job. It would be an answer to all her problems. Not only would a regular supply of money coming in lighten her load considerably, the thought of doing something worthwhile and actually mixing with people on a daily basis would make her day so much brighter. And even if the job was only for a short time it would afford her the confidence and experience needed to apply for other things.

She had paced the mud path at the side of the shop for an age, summoning up the courage to venture inside. Mr Wilson had stared in surprise when she had asked after the post, but on realising her application was serious had hurriedly interviewed her, which she'd found rather daunting, hoping anxiously that her answers were correct. Afterwards, ushering her outside, the small rotund man with his ruddy complexion and sparse hair had told her he'd discuss it with his wife and let her know.

Now Tilda raised hopeful eyes to her father and bit her lip anxiously. Her voice lowered to a whisper, she continued, 'He did say he'd think about it so I must stand a chance.'

Eli narrowed his eyes in disbelief. He lunged over to her, grabbed her arm and yanked her close, pushing his face into hers.

'And think's all he'll do, girl, 'cos he ain't gonna put someone wi' a face like yourn behind the counter, let alone yer other affliction. Why, yer'd be enough to put folks off their food!'

Tears stung the back of her eyes and instinctively she grabbed hold of the bottom of her shabby cardigan sleeve and pulled it over her withered left hand. She didn't need to be continually reminded of her plainness or her disfigurement. She had lived with this knowledge for all her sixteen years and would continue to do so for the rest of her days.

So hurt was she by his callousness she didn't see the glint suddenly appear in his eyes. Before she had time to stop him, he had pinned her up against the wall, thrust his hand into her pocket and pulled forth the coins so carefully wrapped in the old piece of rag.

Triumphantly he closed his fist and flung back his head. 'So, yous weren't holding out on me, eh?'

For a moment she thought he was about to beat her senseless, but thankfully he thrust her away. 'Your mother was right about yous. "The Devil's own" she used ter say. Reckoned yous should have bin drowned at birth. The shame of yous was what killed her.' He fixed his eyes scornfully on her withered arm, then slowly raised them to her horrified face. 'Well, he certainly left his mark on yous, didn't he, eh?'

With that, he turned from her and lumbered out of the door, a dull thud echoing from his wooden leg as it hit the stone slabs.

Tilda's body sagged. 'Oh, Dad,' she whispered, devastated.

Chapter Two

Twilight was fading. Dark shadowy fingers crept slowly across the walls and stone-flagged floor. Tilda stood by the window cradling a tin mug of hot water. She vehemently wished the water was strong-brewed tea with two heaped spoons of sugar, but there was none of either and hadn't been for a long time. She tried to remember when she had last had a cup of tea. She tried to remember the last time she had not had to worry about lighting a candle so as to avoid sitting in the dark. She couldn't.

Her view consisted entirely of the eerie shapes of trees and bushes swaying in the wind, their branches reaching out towards her like arms. She shuddered, raised her eyes and scanned the sky. It was darkening rapidly, a bank of black storm clouds rolling towards her. The night promised to be a very wet and windy one. Tilda shivered. It had been a long hard winter. March had arrived and yet hardly a sign of spring had shown itself so far.

Sighing heavily, she tilted her head, fixing her blank gaze on an ancient oak tree just abreast of the dwelling's boundary. The latest confrontation with her father was weighing heavily on her mind. His harsh treatment of her was nothing new. She had suffered his beatings and cruel remarks since she could remember. It wasn't the first time nor would it be the last that he would harshly remind her of how she herself was entirely to blame for his own predicament and her mother's sudden departure and subsequent death, which had all happened when Tilda was barely five years old. She felt she should be hardened to his cruelty after all these years but somehow, today, his words had touched a part of her she had not realised existed. If she likened her newly awakened feelings to a deep cut from an axe, she felt she would have bled to death, so devastated, so worthless, did she feel.

'The Devil's own.' The words jangled loudly inside her head. Surely her own mother had never said that? He must be lying. No mother would say that about her own child. If she herself was ever lucky enough to have a child, she would love and cherish it, but most importantly never leave it, no matter what. No person was responsible for the way they were born. Their own burden in life was to live with their disfigurements. Others' ignorance made that burden such a terrible load to bear.

How different things could be, she thought sadly, if her father would show her just a little compassion, maybe even love. She sighed heavily again. That was an impossible wish. No matter what happened in the future she would always have to bear the knowledge that neither of her parents had wanted her nor could even stand the sight of her, and despite all she was supposed to have done this knowledge was what she found the hardest to endure.

She turned from the window and slowly made her way over to the makeshift table, easing herself down on to an uncomfortable wooden stool. She winced from her injuries. Hardly a day passed now when she wasn't nursing some pain or other. She had tried everything to avoid her father's beatings, even going so far as to leave the precious money for his gin on the table where he could see it, but nothing worked. He still found a reason to have a go at her.

To her mind, her father was his own worst enemy. He wasn't

the only man around who had lost a limb. The Great War, now nearly six years over, had brought about appalling disfigurements far worse than he had suffered. But unlike others who tried their hardest to get on with things, Eli had capitalised on his injury, managing somehow to make even strangers feel responsible. He had taken all that was offered, seeing it as his right, and given nothing in return but ungrateful abuse. Over the years the villagers sympathy for their situation had faded and was now practically non-existent.

Memories were long and it was too late now for Elijah Penny to redeem himself even had he wanted to. Tilda knew deep down in her heart that if she and her father mysteriously disappeared one night, no one would mourn their departure.

The wind rose sharply. She heard it whistling through the gaping holes in the walls of the adjacent room which had long since ceased to be used. This wattle cottage, surrounded by dense woods and accessible only down a long muddy track, had been home to Tilda and her father for the past eleven years. It was a long way from the nearest sizeable town of Ashby de la Zouch, and two miles from a village close to the Leicestershire–Derbyshire border.

The cottage was virtually beyond repair, the ancient wooden framework too rotten to support new plaster even if they had been able to afford it. Tilda tried, as she had done many times, sitting alone at the table, to picture the families who had once lived here. It made her happy to visualise them as boisterous, close-knit people, eking out a living as best they could, all moving on when better times arrived.

Her eyes travelled around the darkening room. Apart from the makeshift table she was sitting at, it was devoid of any other furniture. There had never been any money to buy anything decent. Three planks of wood had been precariously nailed on the wall by the window, on which stood several pieces of chipped crockery and a handful of utensils. The cottage did not possess the luxury of a sink. A sawn off barrel kept in the outhouse served as a wash tub for bodies and clothes, a bucket by the door for pots, water being collected from a stream nearby.

Tilda knew the cottage to be poor by any standards but it was her home. The roof, at least in the kitchen-cum-living area, staved off the rain and the draughts were kept mostly at bay by paper and old rags.

Putting down her tin mug, she rose to pick up a large wooden spoon and stir the pan simmering gently over the open fire. Her stomach growled painfully in hunger. Even the thought of the thin soup made her mouth water.

She raised the spoon to her lips and licked it clean then wished she hadn't as her hunger pangs heightened. She dare not have anything more tonight. Unhooking the pot from the spit, she rested it on the slab by the hearth, leaving the soup to cool and hopefully thicken overnight. She stacked the fire sparingly with logs, made her way back to the table and sat down.

It was at such times during the long evenings that she felt her loneliest. Evenings should be spent surrounded by family members and loved ones, all chatting happily about daily events as they went about their tasks. Tilda had never known what it was like to be a part of such a gathering and doubted she ever would.

Drinking the last of her water, she pushed away the mug, folded her arms and fought to raise her spirits. Feeling sorry for yourself got you nowhere. So, her life was not particularly pleasant. Each day a constant uphill struggle to acquire the means for survival. That problem was faced by many, not just herself. Like herself, many others had just one thing that kept them going and that was hope. Hope that one day something would happen to change matters. It was all they had. If she gave up now, her very existence would have counted for nothing. And surely, even with all her burdens, her crosses to bear, her life must count for something?

She managed a smile that lit up her plain face and brought a sparkle to her large pale blue eyes. After her chores tomorrow she would tidy herself as best she could and pay another visit to Mr Wilson the butcher. Even though, according to her father, she hadn't much hope of getting the job, at least Mr Wilson could see she had been serious about the application which in turn would help bolster her dignity.

A loud hammering on the door made her jump.

'Who's there?' she shouted, alarmed.

She frowned with concern on receiving no reply. Callers to the cottage were not a frequent occurrence; someone knocking this late in the evening most untoward.

Rising hesitantly, she made her way over and inched open the door. On spotting her visitor, her frown disappeared.

'Eustace!' she exclaimed. 'You didn't half give me a scare.' She ushered him inside and shut the door.

Tilda stared down at her visitor. Seven-year-old Eustace Sprocket looked a sorry sight. His taut skin barely covered his bones, as his threadbare clothes barely covered his thin body. He wasn't a handsome boy. A large nose dominated his small face; intelligent tawny eyes were deep-set beneath a prominent brow, and the heavy spattering of freckles that covered his cheeks were just a shade too brown to be an adornment. He had a wide mouth that, when he smiled, showed several missing teeth. He was desperately in need of a few substantial meals and a bit of love. He got neither from his guardian, a deeply religious spinster aunt who had reluctantly given him a home after her widowed sister had died from influenza three years previous. Mildred Bilson had only done so for fear of what the villagers would say if she didn't. In their eyes she had done the right thing, and they conveniently turned a blind eye to her subsequent treatment of him.

The last three years of Eustace's life had not been pleasant. Mildred had practically made a hobby out of conjuring up ways to humiliate and torment the very life out of her nephew. For such a seemingly devout Christian, Tilda thought, Mildred's actions were unforgivable. Eustace was a very caring and considerate young boy, worthy of anyone's affection, and one day, Tilda thought angrily, Mildred Bilson would regret her decision to treat her nephew so badly.

Tilda had lost count of the number of times Eustace had tearfully told her he'd been locked in the dank, pitch black cellar for hours on end. Of how many weals she had bathed from the thrashings he'd received. The food she herself had gone without because she knew he was ravenous. And none of these punishments had been truly deserved. Tilda felt positive Eustace's mother would be turning in her grave could she have known of her sister's harsh treatment of him.

Now she looked at him with deep concern as light from the fire fell across his face.

'Does your auntie know you're out?' she asked softly.

He shook his head. Then tears filled his eyes, overspilling to pour down his face. He threw his arms around her waist and buried his head against her. 'I've run away, Tilda. I ain't goin' back. I can't take no more.'

Her arms flew around him and she hugged him fiercely. 'Oh, Eustace,' she whispered. 'You have to go back, you know you do.'

'I can't, I can't,' he wailed. 'Please let me live wi' yer? Please, Tilda, please?' He raised his head, eyes pleading. 'I'll do anythin'. I'll 'elp ter feed the chickens, dig the garden. I'll come ter market wi' yer. And I won't mind yer dad. I'll keep outta his way. Please don't send me back, Tilda. Please don't?'

She swallowed hard, fighting emotion. She would give anything to grant Eustace his request. To have him to live with her and to care for him was her greatest wish. The child needed someone like herself as a replacement mother. She had nothing to give him save love, but knew that was all Eustace asked for. Lack of food and other creature comforts were of no importance to him. He just wanted to be with someone who wanted him, and in return would have given his soul in gratitude. No child deserved to be treated like Eustace, but she knew it was a fact that many other children were – some worse, if that were possible.

She raised sad eyes to the ceiling. It was a crying shame Mildred Bilson couldn't open her heart and see what qualities her young nephew possessed. With the right care and guidance he would grow to be a fine young man, one to be proud of.

Tilda's first encounter with Eustace had been one bitterly cold evening as she had trudged home from market. She had been cold, tired and desperately hungry, praying that her father had not woken and eaten the remains of the rabbit stew which was all the food they had left at that moment. Her visit to market that day had been a total waste of time. No one had been buying.

Eustace's pitiful cries had alerted her, thinking at first it was an animal in distress. On investigation she had been shocked to find a little boy huddled under a bush, the clothes on his back hardly suitable for a summer's day, let alone mid-winter. Gradually coaxing him out, it was a great shock to discover his reason for being there. He had not long moved in with his aunt and still trying to come to terms with the loss of his mother yet after he had wet the bed Mildred Bilson had locked him in the cellar for over two days with no food or water. When she had finally let him out, no doubt fearing awkward questions which she would have difficulty in answering, Eustace had gobbled down the bowl of cold lumpy porridge smothered in salt she had reluctantly thrust before him, and at the first opportunity had run away.

Greatly saddened by the young boy's plight, Tilda had taken him to the cottage, given him her share of the rabbit stew, and comforted him the best she could before walking him back down the icy rutted path to leave him at the edge of the village. She had warned him sternly that he had to return or his aunt would get the authorities out and then he really would be in trouble. It was the last thing Tilda had wanted to do but she'd had no other option. Despite the obvious fact that Mildred Bilson did not want the chore of guardianship of her nephew, Tilda's father, she knew without asking, wouldn't give a lame dog a home, let alone a poverty-stricken young boy.

It was not to be the last occasion she was to find Eustace on her doorstep; soon it became a regular occurrence. But from the very first time a bond of friendship developed between them which in turn became the salvation of them both. Eustace needed Tilda's warmth, kindness and strength to help him cope with his dismal life until the day came when he was old enough to fend for himself. For Tilda, Eustace was her one true friend. He didn't see her plainness or deformity. He loved Tilda just for being herself.

She sighed deeply and fixed her eyes tenderly on him. 'You know you can't come to live here, Eustace, so it's no use keeping asking.' She pushed him gently from her and cupped his face in her hands. 'I bet you're hungry?'

He shook his head.

She stared at him, surprised. He was always hungry. 'Why not, Eustace?'

He sniffed loudly and wiped the back of his hand under his nose. ''Cos I ain't,' he replied in a choking voice.

She frowned. Something was dreadfully wrong. 'What is it, Eustace?'

He lowered his head and the tears flowed again. 'She's sendin' me down the pit and I 'ate the dark, Tilda. I can't go, I can't!'

She sank down on the stool, eyes filled with horror. Surely the woman wouldn't do that to him, however desperate she was for money? Mildred Bilson knew how terrified he was of the dark. She had locked him in the cellar enough times and listened to his pitiful screams. Tilda fought the urge to march down to the village and give Mildred a piece of her mind. But that would do nothing to ease his plight and no doubt result in further harsh punishment. Worse, it would give away his refuge which, fingers crossed, they had so far managed to keep secret. Suddenly a thought struck her.

'You're not old enough, Eustace. You can't go down the mine 'til you're fourteen. She's just trying to scare you.'

He lifted his head. 'Honest, Tilda?'

She nodded. 'Honest.'

'But she said . . .'

'I don't care what she said, Eustace. You're only seven. You're not allowed by law. And no employer in his right mind would risk jail for the sake of taking you off your aunt's hands. Even if she paid a fortune, they wouldn't.'

Eustace's grubby face, still streaked with tears, lit up. 'Honest, Tilda. Honest?'

She smiled. 'Honest.' She rose, lifted the pan of soup and hung it over the fire. Wiping her hands on her coarse apron, she turned to him with a broad smile on her face. 'I bet you're hungry now, ain't you?'

He nodded vigorously. ''Ave yer got enough?' he asked.

'I've always enough for you.' She turned from him and stirred the pan. She would go without any amount of food for Eustace's sake.

A while later she sat opposite and watched him eat. The bowl of soup quickly disappeared. When he'd finished he pushed the bowl away and wiped his mouth with the back of his hand.

'Ah, that were grand, Tilda, thanks.'

'My pleasure,' she replied sincerely.

Eustace looked across at his friend, his eyes shining. 'I love you Tilda. I'm gonna marry you when I grow up.'

She tilted her head, her eyes tender. This would be the only proposal she was ever likely to receive, but regardless of Eustace's young years, she knew he meant every word. 'I'll wait for you then,' she replied, hiding a smile. She leaned her arms on the table. 'But for now, I'm afraid you'd better be making tracks.'

He raised his eyes forlornly. 'Do I 'ave ter?'

She nodded. 'It's very late. I'll walk with yer to the edge of the woods.'

'Another few minutes?'

She smiled. 'All right.'

Chapter Three

Eli awkwardly shifted his position under the tree. He did not feel the bitter night air chilling his bones or the frozen ground prodding sharply into his bony buttocks. He was oblivious, lost in his own inebriated world. He slumped sideways and fought to right himself, cursing loudly. Once upright, he raised a billy can to his lips and gulped down the last of the gin.

Deep in the woods he was totally alone and that was the way he liked it. The rest of humanity could fall victim to the plague for all he cared, except of course for old Ma Whittle. God forbid anything should happen to that old witch, he needed his regular supply from her illicit still. It was the only thing that kept him going.

He raised the can once more, found it empty and threw it away in disgust. It bounced off a protruding tree root and came to rest with a clatter against a small rock. The noise echoed loudly and he listened with a smile as the sound broke the silence. A rustling close by caught his attention. He smirked. It was only a March hare. Frightened by the unexpected noise it had popped its head up through a clump of fading primroses. Eli and the hare momentarily locked eyes then the hare was gone, but Eli's eyes remained fixed on the flowers, wafting eerily in the cold night wind.

How he hated the sight of primroses. If it was up to him he

would have all the plants uprooted and burned. But that was impossible, the woods were filled with them. If it wasn't for the fact that there was nowhere else to go that would afford him solitude, he would never venture here at this time of year.

Primroses conjured up a vision of Eileen. She had adored all flowers but primroses had been her favourite. At the opening of the very first blooms she would rush to the woods, gather handfuls and fill the cottage, and that would continue until the last of the flowers faded and bluebells took their place.

He grimaced hard, his eyes narrowing. He didn't want to think of Eileen. Thoughts of her awoke an intense rage, a hatred so deep it seared his very soul. So strong was his passion he could almost smell it. He would never, ever forgive her for prolonging indefinitely his life of exile. The corners of his mouth twitched. The only good kind thought he held about Eileen was that she had been a good-looking woman. But her looks were the last thing on his mind at the moment of their meeting.

He leaned back against the hard bark of the tree and shut his eyes. Helped by all the gin he had swallowed, his thoughts drifted. Back in time he travelled, back to when this sorry mess had all begun.

The ditch was deep, the bottom filled with stagnant slimy water, but the grasses grew high. It was deep enough, the growth high enough, to afford him cover. Eli wasn't quite sure where he was or how far he'd travelled. All he knew was that he'd been dodging through fields and keeping close to hedges for over a week. He was exhausted and starving, but thankfully, for the moment at least, he'd escaped capture.

His mother was right, though. He needed to keep moving, get as far away as possible. Being caught by the police was not his greatest fear. Being caught by relatives of Jimmy McCraven was.

He shivered violently, the icy wetness of his trousers chilling his young bones. How he wished he was in bed in the dilapidated tenement listening to his father's drunken snores. If he'd been just a little more careful that's where he would be still, dreaming about building an empire. Instead he was running for his life.

Not that he was sorry for what he'd done. Jimmy McCraven had deserved to die. Attempting to muscle in on Eli's turf was to his mind a killing offence if ever there was one. He'd stuck the knife in deep and twisted it hard, watching in satisfaction as the blood of his arch rival spurted forth. It had pleased him immensely to see the shock and horror filling Jimmy's eyes as he had drawn his last breath.

He'd do it again, given the same circumstances. He was only sorry for the fact that, unbeknown to himself, the murder had been witnessed by men who would put their own sisters on the street if the price was enough for a pint of best and a packet of fags. That was lax on Eli's part. He should have waited, held back, but as usual anger had got the better of him and because of his own lack of control he had no doubt that now the underworld of Glasgow, aided and abetted by the McCraven clan, would be scouring the area for him, hell bent on revenge. Them and the police. And he knew who worried him the most.

He rubbed his numbed hands. That was all in the past. He had to think of his future, and the most immediate need was to get out of this icy cold ditch before he caught something terrible. He also needed some food in his stomach. How to achieve this was the problem. He had no money apart from a few coppers and his sodden muddy clothes were conspicuous to say the least. He looked every inch what he was, a man on the run.

A noise from above alerted him and he froze. Slowly he crawled up the bank and parted the grasses. Above him on the roadside, her back to him, a woman sat on a stone, a fraying carpet bag at her feet. Elbows resting on her knees, she was staring out across the fields. Suddenly his own boot slipped on the wet mud and he fell back, landing on the far bank with a thud. A stone struck his back and before he could stop himself, he yelped in pain.

Alarmed, the woman jumped up, spun around and looked down.

'Who's there?' she cried. She bent down and picked up a large stone, holding it aloft. 'Come out before I brain you.'

He clenched his fists. There was nothing for it. He would have to identify himself before she did as she threatened. After all he'd gone through he didn't fancy ending his days in a ditch through the actions of some stupid woman.

'Hold on,' he pleaded, clawing his way upwards. He reached the top of the roadside, stood upright and held up his hands in mock surrender, grinning broadly. 'I'm innocent, honest.'

His eyes quickly scanned the area. Stretching as far as he could see, in all directions, were fields and trees. There was no sign of any other human being. He breathed a sigh of relief and turned his attention to the woman still holding the rock aloft menacingly. Well, woman was stretching things. She was seventeen at the most. Her clothes were shoddy, the boots on her feet coming apart in places. He raised his eyes to her face, his own registering surprise.

She was pretty now, with a promise of better things on maturity. Large pale blue eyes stood out against the blackness of her hair, curly tendrils of which were escaping from under a battered straw bonnet. She had an aura of innocence never witnessed in a woman from the Gorbals. It was clear she presented no threat to him but he was nevertheless aware of his own vulnerability, exposed to view on the open road. Once again his eyes darted. He suddenly had visions of swarming policemen coming at him from all directions. But one thing he was sure of: this woman was English. He had managed to travel farther than he'd thought.

'What are you looking for?' she asked, frowning deeply.

'Eh?' He turned his attention back to her, mind racing frantically. 'Oh, er ... the group of men I was with. I seem to have lost them.' The lie slipped out easily and prompted the next. 'On our way to ... er ... London, yes, that's right, looking for work.' He screwed up his face, apparently perplexed. 'I cannae understand where they've gone or how I managed to land up in the ditch for that matter. I do remember we had a good dram or two last night, though.' He tilted his head, eyes narrowing mischievously. 'But that ain't a braining crime, surely?'

She stared searchingly at him for a moment, then tutted loudly and lowered her arm, dropping the stone to the ground. Looking for work wasn't a crime, she herself should know that. And he did look an honest type. He was certainly good-looking. She noticed his clothes.

'You're soaking. You really ought to get out of those wet things before you catch pneumonia.'

'Yeah, I ought.'

At this moment catching pneumonia was the least of his worries. He had to get off the open road. But he had to do it in such a way as not to arouse her suspicions. There was always the possibility of her being questioned later and pointing the police in his direction.

He watched in surprise as she stooped to pick up her bag.

'Come on,' she ordered. 'There's a stream across those fields. I'll help you get cleaned up.'

Immensely relieved, he followed her. They walked in silence

through several fields of ripening barley. The sun was high, its rays warming. The air smelt pungent, a mixture of grasses and early-summer wild flowers. Such smells were alien to him. Smoke and grime, though, had never smelt as good as this and for an instant he felt glad to be alive, then fear for his dire predicament crowded in on him.

'How d'yous know about this burn?' he asked, breaking the silence.

'Burn?'

'Er . . . water.'

'Just do,' she replied flatly.

He grimaced and dug his hands into his sodden pockets. Suddenly an idea sprang to mind. If the police had tracked him this far they wouldn't be looking for a man and a woman. She must be on her way somewhere but if he could somehow coax her to stay with him for the interim it would afford him precious cover, and he could always offload her when she had served her purpose. It was worth a try.

'Are yous on your own?' he asked casually.

She stopped abruptly and turned to him. 'Why?'

'Just asking.'

She gulped then lowered her eyes. 'You could say that.'

'So yous weren't waiting for anyone then?'

She raised her head. 'Why?'

'Just asking,' he repeated, trying to keep the annoyance from his voice.

She pursed her lips haughtily. 'If you must know, I've just lost my job.'

'Oh?'

She took a deep breath, eyes flashing angrily. 'I was kitchen maid-cum-dogsbody for a farmer a few miles from here. Only the boss took a fancy to me and his wife didn't like it. So she slung me out. I can't go home 'cos I've no home to go to.

I know about the stream 'cos I spent last night sleeping next to it. Now, anything else you want to know?'

He shook his head. 'No.'

'Good. It's just over there.'

She marched ahead and he trailed after her.

Sitting on the stream bank, an old petticoat dug out from her carpet bag covering his modesty, he watched the girl hang his clothes over a tree's branches. He found himself impressed by her skills. After the short space of time it had taken him to scrub the grime from his body farther upstream he had come back to find that not only had she cleaned his clothes, she had also gathered some logs and lit a fire.

The clothes secured, she moved towards the fire and put on more twigs. Reaching for her bag, she opened it and pulled out a parcel, unwrapped it and produced a small loaf and a chunk of cheese. She broke a wedge from each and handed them over.

'Thanks,' he said appreciatively.

'Well, unless you've anything hidden up your sleeve, that's it. That and a few shillin' was all the missus gave me afore she kicked me out the door.'

He smiled. 'Better than nothing, though.'

'Yeah, I suppose.'

She looked over his near nakedness and smiled. The sudden smile lit up her face and again for an instant he saw a glimpse of beauty to come. 'I ought to know your name, in the circumstances,' she prompted.

'Yes, I suppose yous ought,' His thoughts raced. What was he going to call himself? 'Elijah.' Elijah . . . now why had he come out with that?

She giggled. 'Elijah?'

He scowled. 'What's wrong with it?'

'Nothing. Only you don't look like an Elijah.'

'Well, tell that to me ma. She happened to like it.' His voice faltered. 'Well, if I had a ma, that is.'

She looked sympathetic. 'Oh, you haven't family either?'

'No,' he lied.

He gathered the petticoat around him and rose abruptly, yanking his trousers off the branch.

'They're still damp.'

'They'll do.' He slipped behind a bush and pulled them on.

She turned her back, settling her gaze on the flowing waters ahead. 'Elijah what?'

Buttoning up his shirt and slipping on his jacket, he picked up his meagre belongings. 'Elijah . . .' He looked down at the few coppers in his palm, all he possessed in the world, and thrust them into his pocket. 'Penny,' he answered, slipping out from behind the bush. He held out his hand. 'Elijah Penny.'

She turned, took his hand and shook it. 'Eileen Calister.' She gazed up into his eyes. 'It's strange us meeting like this. Just by chance, really. Me losing my job and you your friends. Fate, do you reckon?'

The corners of his mouth twitched. He didn't believe in nonsense like that but it wouldn't hurt to humour her. 'Yous could be right.'

She turned from him and walked towards the stream where she squatted on her haunches and trailed her hand absently through the clear cold water. She was thoughtful. Meeting this man could be her salvation. A couple of hours ago she had sat on the roadside deep in despair, wondering what God had in store for her and if she could cope with any more. She really felt she had had enough. Losing her job through no fault of her own had been the final mishap in the long line of hardships she had endured throughout her life.

Orphaned at the age of five, with no relatives willing to take her in, she had landed in the poor house. Inside the cold stark walls for nine long years, she had suffered the strict regime and harsh punishments handed out for the slightest misdemeanour by cheerless individuals hell bent on misery-making. Most of her short working life had been no better. Employers, knowing her orphan status and well aware how much she needed her job, had worked the skin off her fingers for little reward.

Landing the job at the farm had been her one joy. The farmer was strict but fair with his staff, his wife fat and jolly, loving to cook and see those around her appreciate the delicious foodstuffs she produced. The more they ate, the better she liked it. She was decent to work for, realising her staff needed sleep too. Eileen felt her life was fulfilled and had envisaged spending the rest of her days working for this lovely couple. That was until the master began to cast an eye in her direction. His wife might be fat and jolly but she was no fool. She knew her husband well. But it wasn't her husband she blamed for the flirtation but Eileen herself, and lost no time in harshly chastising her and sending her packing.

Eileen supposed she had been lucky, though. The farmer had cast an eye but his wife, thank God, had seen to it that that was all he had done.

She raised her head and glanced the length of the stream. She breathed deeply, savouring the sweetness of the air. How she loved the countryside and wished she need never leave it. To live and work again in the grime of a town gave her no joy, but needs must. Wherever she could get work, she would try hard to make the best of it. But one thing was for sure: enjoying the warmth and beauty of her surroundings would not pay for food and for a fleeting moment she regretted sharing the bread and cheese with Elijah, as desperately hungry as she knew he had been. A smile touched her lips. Maybe, though, in a roundabout way he could repay her for her kindness.

She stood up, brushed down her long black cotton twill skirt and turned to face him. He was sitting on the bank, chin resting on his knees, staring into space, and for a moment she wondered what was on his mind. Come to think of it, he had been rather jumpy when she had first come across him. She mentally shook herself. Just my own fancy, she thought.

As she studied him she felt a warm fluttering inside her stomach. Elijah Penny was a good-looking man. She liked tall men. Only four inches over five foot herself, height in a man made her feel protected somehow. Dark hair which she preferred to blond, and his dark hooded eyes had an air of mystery, as though he was hiding a secret. Instead of giving her a warning, Eileen's inexperience saw this as an added attraction.

She walked towards him, stopped abruptly, folded her arms under her nicely developing bosom and took a deep breath. Best get her proposition off her chest before she lost her nerve. 'Could you do with a companion? Just until you catch up with your friends. I wouldn't be a burden.'

Eli turned his head and looked up at her blankly. 'Eh?'

She took a step backwards, embarrassed. 'Forget what I said,' she blustered.

He stood up, running his hand through his hair. 'How can I forget what yous said when I never heard in the first place?' How could he have heard? He had been back in a dark street in Glasgow staring down at the man he'd murdered. His throat dried and he swallowed hard. He could feel the creeping shadows of Jimmy McCraven's relatives closing rapidly.

The look on his face made Eileen frown in concern. 'Whatever's the matter?'

'The matter? Nothing,' he said abruptly. 'Just thinking, that's all.'

'Oh,' she replied, too polite to probe.

'So?'

'So what?'

28

'Yous asked me something?'

'Oh, yes, I did.'

Hesitantly she repeated her proposition. It was harder the second time round. Somehow she felt she was begging. 'I don't like the thought of travelling on my own, never knowing what shady characters are lurking nearby. Only 'til the next town, I mean. Then I'll get out of your way. Although,' she added wistfully, 'I like the sound of going to London. Is that where you're headed still?'

He cocked his eyebrow in surprise. London? Yes, he had told her that lie when they had first met. He rubbed his chin thoughtfully. On mulling it over, it didn't seem such a bad idea. He dug his hands into his pockets and turned from her, eyes absently scanning the fields beyond, well aware she was watching his every move with bated breath. London? Surely the police or Jimmy McCraven's relatives wouldn't think to look for him there? He'd managed to evade them this far. If they kept off the main roads and only stopped when absolutely necessary he might just pull it off. His eyes lit up. London was the place to go. A wanted man could get well and truly lost in London. But more to the point, London was the place for a man like himself to fulfil his dreams . . . with the right kind of people to help him along.

He turned back to her. 'I suppose yous can tag along, if yous want.'

The rain poured down in torrents as it had without let-up for the last two days. Eileen was soaked to the skin, desperately hungry, her body so tired it screamed for rest. The soles of her boots were near non-existent, the feet inside blistered and bleeding.

For three long weeks they had walked, only stopping for short snatches of sleep before Eli would insist they set off again. He was stumbling ahead of her now like a man possessed down a mud-clogged track to the side of a field. She wiped rain from her eyes with the back of her hand. This field was not the first they had tramped through in pouring rain; the sodden hills they had just climbed over would not be the last. At this moment Eileen wished with all her heart she had never begged to be allowed to accompany him.

She had thought their journey would be at a leisurely pace, stopping en route to work for food and shelter. How wrong she had been. Most of their food had been begged from kindly souls showing pity for their predicament, she herself being given the embarrassing task of doing the begging; the rest, having left her in some deserted spot, Eli would return with, to her mind miraculously, since she knew he had no money. After the first couple of times she began to suspect that maybe he stole it, but dare not challenge him just in case she was wrong. For shelter, if they had not come across an isolated barn or outbuilding, the heavens were their roof and she would pray it did not rain.

Suddenly she stumbled, falling heavily. She lay for a moment, stunned. It wasn't the first time she had fallen but this time was the final straw. Caked in soggy mud, the rain beating down on her relentlessly, tears of desolation rolled down her cheeks. 'Eli!' she cried despairingly. 'Eli, Eli!'

He stopped, turned, and looked back at her angrily. 'Get up,' he ordered crossly.

'I can't. Please, Eli, I have to rest.'

He held his arms wide. 'Where? Yous tell me where?'

'I don't care where, Eli. A hole in the ground. Anywhere. Just somewhere to lay my head.'

Suddenly she saw it. 'Look.'

He turned and stared in the direction she was pointing. At the end of the field was what appeared to be a shack. He sighed with annoyance. This was no time for stopping, he had wanted to cover another few miles before they took a break. He turned his head and stared at her. Taking this woman along was proving to be a bad mistake, she had slowed him down considerably. He pursed his lips. Well, maybe not a mistake. After all, he was still a free man. Turning from her, he made towards the shack and disappeared from view.

She sat motionless and waited.

Finally he emerged. 'It'll do for the night.'

Her body sagged in relief. 'Thank you, God,' she whispered.

Eli stared down at Eileen, cuddled against his side peacefully sleeping. Several hours ago they had made love and the act of doing so had made him feel good.

It wasn't the first time; that had happened several nights after their journey had begun. That first seduction had been easy. He had known from the start she was attracted to him. What had pleased him, though, was the fact she had still been a virgin. Not that it had mattered to him. He had only used her body to satisfy his own. As the weeks passed he felt a certain fondness for her, but not love. Eli had never experienced true love. When he did it would be for a woman of quality, not a penniless orphan like Eileen despite her good looks.

When he got to London, where the threat of the hangman no longer shadowed him, when he'd made his fortune, then he would be ready to meet the type of woman he envisaged marrying. He would settle in a fine house, servants at his beck and call, maybe have children. He would be respected. He had it all planned out. With each step he had taken, boots clogged with mud, soaked to the skin, starving and exhausted, across hills, in valleys, through deep dense woods, he had planned his future down to the minutest detail.

He was going to make money, lots of it, and he didn't care how. But however it was, it wouldn't be legal; he'd never earned money legally in his life and wasn't about to start now. Then he would live as he'd always dreamed of doing as he'd lain on the bug-infested mattress, listening to warring parents and screaming babies in the adjoining tenements, his stomach gnawing him painfully from lack of food.

His eyes scanned Eileen and a hint of a smile touched his lips. It was time to say goodbye. She had served her purpose. It was time for them to part. He eased gently away from her and awkwardly rose from the hard earth floor they'd been sleeping on. It was still dark, he'd barely slept three hours, but it would have to be enough. He wanted to be well away from her before dawn.

It was approaching six o'clock in the morning and the small market town was just beginning to stir when Eli crossed its boundaries. He was humming to himself, pleased. In the three hours since he'd left the shack he'd covered quite a distance and in his pocket was his means of survival for several weeks at least.

Opportunity had presented itself as he had rounded a bend on a deserted country road and a house had loomed before him. People really should not leave windows open or valuables on display. The watch and several pieces of jewellery, which he would tell the pawnbroker had been left him by his longlost aunt, should raise a tidy sum. He smiled to himself. He'd had enough of walking. He'd catch a train. Third class, he didn't want to be rash, but it would be luxury to what he'd endured these last few weeks. And he'd have a bath. There must be a bathhouse somewhere in this Godforsaken place? He didn't want to arrive in London looking like a tramp.

He frowned as a thought suddenly struck him and he stroked his eight-week growth of beard. He hoped he didn't look bad enough to arouse the pawnbroker's suspicions. Nonchalantly he shrugged his shoulders. Lady luck had been on his side for quite a while now, there was no reason for her to desert him just yet.

Later, lying back in the slipper bath, he sighed contentedly as the hot soapy water lapped over him. He had scrubbed every inch of his body and felt clean and relaxed. Any time now the barber would come in and shave off his beard and cut his hair. Next port of call was a tailor's. Mentally he picked himself out a suit – not expensive, he hadn't money to burn just yet. A shirt, tie and shoes, not boots. He exhaled slowly and savoured the thought. At this moment he felt he was in heaven. These country folk, he thought, really hadn't a clue. The goods had been pawned so easily. He'd spun the broker such a convincing sorry tale that Eli could almost see tears in the man's eyes as he unsuspectingly swopped the stolen goods for money.

He looked towards the door and tutted, annoyed. Where was that damned barber promised by the wizened old man at the front desk? Sighing in exasperation, he picked up the morning edition of the *Daily Sketch*, left on the chair by the previous occupant, and shook it out. It had been weeks since he had seen a newspaper; while he waited he might as well take this opportunity for a read.

He scanned the front page. Nothing much had changed. He turned a page. News from abroad did not interest him. The advertisements for clothing did and for several moments he studied them. He lowered the newspaper and looked again towards the door. He'd certainly give the barber a piece of his mind when he condescended to arrive. He shook the paper out again and turned the page.

The headline leapt out and his eyes bulged in horror.

SCOTTISH MURDERER STILL AT LARGE

Beneath the headline was a rough, artist's sketch. There was no mistaking that face – Eli would recognise himself anywhere. His face paled alarmingly as he quickly read the paragraph following and all his bravado, the feeling he'd cheated the hangman's noose, drained away.

> Douglas Smilie, wanted for the brutal murder of James McCraven, is rumoured to be somewhere in England. Several sightings have been reported as far south as Northampton...

Eli scowled. Northampton? He had never heard of Northampton, let alone been there.

> ...Police have advised the public not to approach him. Detective Inspector Mottle, in charge of the case, states: 'This man is dangerous and could be armed. Any sightings should be reported directly to the nearest police station.' Inspector Mottle is certain it is only a matter of time before Smilie is caught.

Beads of sweat poured from his face as he read on:

> The police are not Smilie's only concern. Relatives of McCraven have vowed...

A loud knock sounded on the door. Eli jumped, so alarmed a wave of water sloshed over the side of the bath. Through the door shuffled an elderly man as wide as he was tall, carrying a box filled with the tools of his trade.

'Oot!' Eli cried, shocked by his sudden appearance. 'Oot, oot!'

The barber froze, staring at the man in the bath as though he was mad. Oot? What did he mean by that? He must be a foreigner.

Eli thrust out his arm, sending another wave of water

34

slopping across the floor. 'Oot,' he'd ordered savagely.

'Oh, out?' The barber hurriedly retraced his steps. 'Sorry, sir,' he mumbled. 'Wrong room. My apologies. Enjoy yer bath.' As he shut the door, he grimaced. If ever a man was in need of a shave and haircut, that man was.

Eli was trembling, his appearance the last thing on his mind. He had to get out of here, quick. He didn't even dry himself off before pulling on his clothes. As he left he ripped the report from the newspaper and stuffed it in his pocket.

He had no other choice at that moment but to return to the shack; once there he hoped to gather his thoughts, formulate some kind of plan. The journey back was fraught with fear that he would be recognised but thankfully he was not.

Eileen spun round to face him when he burst through the door. She was so filled with joy to see him that she did not notice his agitated state.

'Oh Eli,' she cried. 'I thought you'd left me.' She rushed over and threw her arms around him burying her face in his chest.

He pushed her roughly away. 'Can a man no' go for a walk—'

'A walk. Eli you've been gone for hours. I didn't know what to think. I didn't know what to do.' She wrung her hands. 'I . . . I was so worried.'

He stomped across the room then turned to face her. 'Has anyone been here?' he demanded.

'Here? No, why? Oh, only the farmer . . .'

He leapt over and grabbed her arm. 'What did he want?' He shook her. 'What did he want, Eileen?'

She eyed him alarmed. 'Just wanted to know what we were doing here. That's all.'

'And what did yous say?'

She flinched at his savage tone. 'Just said we took shelter for the night.'

'Nothing more?'

'No.' She eyed him worriedly. 'Eli, what's wrong?'

'Nothing,' he spat. 'But in future if anyone asks after me just keep your trap shut. I don't like people knowing my business.'

As she stared at him her lips tightened. 'He did ask if we were looking for work,' she said softly. 'He needs a man, Eli, and he said if you're interested—'

'Farm work!' he erupted. 'Me?'

'It is work, Eli. Work of any kind isn't to be sneezed at. If you took the job he says we can have this house.'

'House!' He flung his arms wide. 'It's no more than a shed.'

'Oh, it's not that bad, Eli,' she coaxed. She moved towards him and tentatively laid her hand on his arm. 'It wouldn't hurt to stay here for a while, would it? We . . . you could still make for London. But you'd have some money in your pocket. I could fix this place up. I could make it quite homely,' she enthused. 'I could dig a patch of garden and grow some vegetables. Maybe get a couple of chickens. He's a nice man, the farmer. I think you'd like him. Think about it, Eli. It wouldn't be forever.'

He stared at her hard, turned from her and ran his fingers over his beard. Eileen, in her innocence, was handing him a solution. This was just the cover he needed. The police or Jimmy McCraven's relatives would never dream to look for him here. The passing of time dulled people's memories. Other events would happen in the interim to fill their thoughts if he himself did nothing in the meantime.

He inwardly smiled. Dougie Smilie, a lowly farm worker. It was laughable. But if he kept a low profile, and his beard and hair long, hopefully he'd not be recognised. Several years hiding here with Eileen, however much he resented it, was better than the alternative.

'I'll go and see this farmer,' he said grudgingly.

'You will!' Eileen gasped.

She watched as he headed for the door. Her delight at his decision was far more than she dared show. She would need to put down some roots, make some sort of home for the baby she had suspected for a week or so now was growing within her.

The sound of terrified screaming split the air. Eileen spun round and her jaw dropped in horror at the sight of Eli storming out of the shack. In his outstretched hand he held their four-year-old daughter upside down by one leg. The child was screaming hysterically.

'Can't yous control this wean?' he shouted, incensed.

She dropped the armful of wet washing she was pegging out, rushed forward and wrenched her distraught daughter from his grasp. Turning her right way up, Eileen hugged her protectively. 'There, there, poppet,' she soothed. 'Daddy didn't mean to hurt you.'

Eli thrust his face into Eileen's. 'I did! I told yous when it was born that it was *your* responsibility. Yous should have done what I said and got rid of it. It's nothing but a bloody menace.'

'Oh, Eli, please, she's just a child.'

He clenched his fists and stuck one under her chin, pushing her head back. 'Yeah, the Devil's. Now I'm telling yous, keep her out my sight. She makes me feel sick.'

Eileen's shoulders sagged despairingly as Eli turned and marched back towards the shack. 'Aren't you going to work?' she called after him hopefully.

He stopped abruptly in the doorway and turned to face her. 'Does it bloody look like I am? You stupid woman!'

Eileen glanced over at him, mouth set grimly. He looked in dire need of a good wash from head to foot. No, more than a wash – a scrub with a hard brush. His grubby threadbare long johns were sagging at the seat: there were holes in the knees. She had just about given up trying to get them off him. She wondered if he realised that he smelt. He was far from pleasant to get in beside of a night on their straw shakedown.

Eileen sighed forlornly. Falling in love with Eli had been easy and giving herself to him had seemed the most natural thing in the world. When she had told him she was pregnant she'd thought he would share in her delight. After all, they had far more than some couples: a home in which to raise the baby, albeit a run-down shack, but Eileen was working hard on improvements; Eli had a job and his employer was not a mean man – in fact he and his wife had been more than generous towards them. The only hard part had been keeping their unmarried status a secret. Eli was against a union, wouldn't even talk on the matter. This had hurt and bewildered Eileen but at least he hadn't abandoned her, for which she had been eternally grateful.

Her pregnancy had not been easy, when the baby had finally arrived the marks it carried were of no consequence to Eileen. On her part she felt total love. But not so for Eli. He could hardly bring himself to look at his child. Eileen did her best to coax him into fatherhood, but he wanted no part in it. It was her child. She had decided to have it and against his wishes. He supplied their daughter with food, what more did she want?

His utter dismissal of his daughter hurt Eileen beyond belief and as the years passed the situation did not improve. Her life became a constant battle to keep the child away from him, doing whatever she could so as not to arouse his temper.

Try as she might she could not fathom his glaring resentment of all around him. He was like a caged animal desperate for freedom. But, why was he so discontented when he had so many things men would envy? She dare not voice her fears or ask questions, she did not relish the threat of his fist. She had already made that mistake more than once before and she had learned her lesson.

'But, Eli, Mr Ruddle'll be expecting you,' she said keeping her voice light.

His face reddened angrily. 'Yous listen to me and listen good. I ain't naebody's lackey. That Jonas Ruddle must think I'm an idiot, working my guts out for the pittance he pays. I've had enough. I'm no' working any more unless I get a decent wage. Got that? Now, I'm going back to bed and I dunna want disturbing so keep *her* quiet!' Without further ado he turned and marched back inside the shack, slamming the door behind him.

She hugged the still weeping child even closer and kissed the top of her plain little forehead. 'There, there, my darling. Daddy didn't mean to hurt you, really he didn't.'

'He did,' sniffed Tilda. 'He's always doing it.' She raised her eyes and looked straight into her mother's. 'Why doesn't he like me, Mam?'

Eileen stared at her beloved child. How could she ever tell Tilda of her father's true feelings when she didn't understand them herself. All she hoped was that her own love made up for the lack of her father's affection.

Brushing aside Tilda's question she kissed her tenderly on the cheek. 'Have you fed the chickens?'

Tilda shook her head.

'I thought not,' Eileen playfully scolded. 'No feed, no eggs. No eggs, no what, Tilda?'

Tilda wiped her hand under her nose and grinned. 'No food for us.'

'That's right. Now run along. Then you can come with me to gather sticks for the fire.'

She smiled as her daughter turned to go. 'Eh, just a minute, you've your dress tucked in your breeches.' She caught hold of her daughter and straightened her clothes then frowned quizzically as she heard something rustle inside her pinafore pocket.

'What's that?'

Tilda stared at her blankly. 'Nothing, Mam,' she said defensively.

'Tilda.'

'It ain't nothing, Mam. Just some paper. I found it, honest. I was gonna put it in my treasure box.'

Intrigued, Eileen eyed her. 'Can Mammy see it?'

Tilda thought for a moment then nodded, delved into her pinafore pocket and pulled forth a folded yellowing piece of newspaper.

Eileen carefully examined it. As she read, a deep puzzled frown formed on her brow. 'Where did you get this, Tilda?' she asked. When she received no reply she raised her eyes. Her daughter, head bowed, hands clasped behind her back, was digging her toes into the dirt and watching them uncomfortably. 'Tilda. Where did you get this?'

She raised her head guiltily.

'Tilda, please tell Mammy where you got this?'

'Daddy's pocket,' she whispered, so low it was hardly audible.

'Pardon, Tilda? I didn't hear you.'

She rubbed her disfigured arm guiltily, then pulled down her sleeve to hide it. 'Daddy's pocket,' she repeated louder.

Eileen stroked her chin thoughtfully. Eli's pocket. What was he doing keeping a newspaper cutting reporting a murder? Admittedly it was to do with Glasgow, his home town, maybe that was the reason. She realised Tilda was still staring up at her and smiled reassuringly.

'Go and feed the chickens, darlin'.'

'Will ... will Daddy hit me, Mammy?'

Eileen took hold of her daughter's hand. 'No, I'll put it

back before he misses it. But don't go through his pockets again, there's a love, or next time he just might,' she warned. There was no 'might' about it, she thought. Should Eli find out either of them had been near his pockets, both would receive a beating to within an inch of their lives.

She watched absently as Tilda went to fetch the bowl of chicken feed then disappeared around the back of the cottage to complete her task. For a moment Eileen's heart swelled with love for her little daughter, then her thoughts returned to the piece of newspaper in her hand and she studied it again. Several things were niggling her. One was the date. The report said the murder had taken place around the time she'd met Eli. The second that the murderer was still at large. The third . . . Her eyes stared at the artist's impression. Suddenly she jumped as the shack door opened and Eli loomed.

'I cannae sleep. Get me some food.' His eyes travelled to the piece of newspaper. 'What's that?' he demanded.

'Oh, er . . . nothing, Eli,' she said, screwing up the paper inside her hand.

'What do yous mean, nothing,' he hissed, advancing towards her. 'When I ask a question, I want an answer.' He caught hold of her arm and wrenched open her hand, grinning sarcastically. 'Yous shouldna keep secrets from me, Eileen. I dinnae like secrets.' He thrust her away and unscrewed the piece of newspaper. His face paled alarmingly, then blackened in thunder. 'Where did yous get this?' he demanded savagely.

At the sound of his tone Eileen stepped back, fear suddenly filling her. Her mouth opened but no words came out.

'I said, where did yous get this?' He caught hold of her arm and pulled her close. 'And you'd better answer me, woman.'

'I . . . I . . . found it.'

'Found it?' he spat. 'You liar! You've bin in my pockets. I've told yous never to touch my pockets.' He let go of her arm and brought his hand crashing down across her face. The blow knocked her to the ground and she screamed out in pain.

Stunned by the blow, Eileen stared up at him, terrified. Many times she had been on the receiving end of his fists, nursed countless injuries, but never before had she seen quite such a look in his eye. Why was he so incensed about an old newspaper report? Her mind raced frantically as he loomed above her. Then suddenly the truth hit her with such force it took her breath away and she gasped for air. He was so incensed because it was about himself. *He* was the man the paper talked about. That was the only answer. The artist's impression. Without his mane of hair and thick beard, the face was Eli's. It was the cold look in his eyes now that clinched it for her.

She momentarily shut her own eyes as an overwhelming feeling of doom settled upon her. Their whole time together had been one living lie. He had used her. That was all she had ever been to him, a shield to hide behind. Her love for him had meant nothing. The police had been looking for a single man, not one travelling with a woman and subsequently eking out a living in the depths of the countryside with a supposed wife and now child.

The fine thread between love and hate suddenly snapped as all the suffering she had endured through simply loving him boiled over.

'It's you,' she blurted. She raised herself up on all fours, staggered upright and backed away from him, wagging a finger. 'You're a murderer, aren't you, Eli? You are aren't you? You used me. You used me and our daughter for cover to save your own precious neck.'

A wicked grin spread across his face. 'So what if I did? What if I am this murderer you accuse me of being? What do yous propose to do about it? Go to the police? Well, yous do and I'll kill yous too!'

He began to walk towards her, face contorted in anger, an insane glint in his eyes.

Terrified, her eyes darted. To the side of her was a fallen branch. She snatched it up and waved it menacingly. 'Don't come near me, Eli, I'm warning you . . .' From the corner of her eye she spotted Tilda appearing around the side of the shack. Fear for her daughter's life was her only consideration. 'Run, Tilda, run,' she screamed.

Thinking this was just another row between her mam and dad, Tilda fled towards the shack, rushed inside and slammed shut the door.

In the momentary distraction, Eli seized his chance. He grabbed hold of Eileen's wrist and wrenched the branch from her. She eyed him in horror, seeing the murderous look on his face. He was going to kill her. She froze. If Eli did away with her what would become of Tilda? Eileen had no doubt he would kill his daughter too. She sprang into action, kicking her legs and beating her free hand against his chest.

He just stood and laughed. 'Don't fight, Eileen. Yous are no match for me.'

She shrank in terror. 'Eli,' she wailed. 'I'll take Tilda and go. You won't hear from us again.'

His eyes filled with malice. 'Oh, and yous expect me to believe that? I've just spent the last five years of my life watching my back. I don't intend doing that any more. This is your own fault. Yous should never have gone through me pockets.'

His raised the branch and brought it crashing forward, smashing Eileen on the side of her skull.

She dropped like a stone, her head hitting the hard ground with a dull thud. Blood gushed forth, staining the dried earth, settling into a pool.

He stared down at her lifeless form, the sudden shock of what he'd done quickly replaced by intense anger. Blast the woman!

She should never have gone through his pockets. She had only received her just deserts.

He took several breaths, fighting to put his thoughts into some semblance of order. He knew that whatever plan of action he decided to adopt he would have to get away, he couldn't stay round here. Whatever plausible story he concocted, a death however it happened would result in an investigation by the police and could eventually lead to his true identity being revealed. Then he'd hang for sure, and these last five years of lying low and putting up with poverty would have been a total waste of time.

A noise in the distance suddenly startled him. Across the fields he could just make out the figure of Farmer Ruddle herding the cows towards the milking sheds. Eli blasphemed under his breath. In a very short while his absence from work would be noticed and Ruddle would come looking to see the reason why.

His throat constricted as he seemed to feel the hangman's noose about it. He shuddered violently, filled with dreadful foreboding.

A plan. He must have a plan of action, and quickly, but in the interim he needed to hide Eileen's body to give himself a little more time. Grabbing her legs, he dragged her across the piece of ground past the side of the shack towards a hedge where he rolled her in the ditch and hurriedly covered her with dead undergrowth, hoping she wouldn't be found for quite a while. He stood over it for a moment and smiled. It was ironic that Eileen should end up this way. A ditch had figured prominently in their meeting too.

It was in his mind to leave there and then when he suddenly remembered Tilda. He deliberated for a moment, then decided the child could prove useful in his initial getaway as Eileen had five years before.

Inside the shack he cold-bloodedly told his distraught daughter that Eileen had deserted them – he'd tell her she was dead later – and that he himself had lost his job, so it was better to move on. The child was young, and she would soon forget her mother's existence. Tilda had angered him greatly by screaming and wailing. While he had held her in a vice-like grip he had been painfully aware that precious moments were ticking by. It took all his strength to stop himself from doing away with her also. He had to keep reminding himself that he needed her for the time being.

Finally he managed to calm the child enough to gather the minimum of possessions and set off.

Once again his life was uprooted and he was back on the run. As before he kept to isolated pathways, only stopping when absolutely necessary. He planned, when he was well out of the district, to abandon the child, be rid of her once and for all; he liked the thought of being unencumbered again. But Tilda proved to be the asset he'd envisaged. The few people they did encounter felt sorry for their plight and gave them both food and shelter.

After several days of travelling, upon descending a hill on the Derbyshire-Leicestershire border, he spotted a deep dark wood stretching before them and knew the time for getting rid of the child had come. He was far enough away from their last abode and from his planned destination of London to fear she could do him harm. All people would think was that Tilda had been abandoned. She would not be the first child that it had happened to.

Leaving her sleeping under a bush, he stole silently away, never once glancing back. He was free at last and the feeling was good. He had waited for just this occasion for the past five years. He rushed recklessly onward, not heeding where he was going, his mind filled with thoughts of finally being able to build his long dreamed of empire. He saw the money he would have and the luxuries it would buy, the women . . .

The rusty mantrap sprang shut before he knew what had happened, its jagged metal teeth biting deep. His blood-curdling screams of agony filled the air as he looked down and saw the mangled remains of what had been his leg. Blood gushed forth, and as it flowed he could feel his life ebbing. This was it, his end had come. By his cunning and connivance he'd avoided capture and escaped the hangman's noose only to end his life in this miserable way.

Gasping for what he thought were his last breaths, the pain so intense he didn't think he could bear it much longer, Eli shut his eyes and screamed Tilda's name. He didn't want to die alone, the thought terrified him, and he'd sooner have the child he detested by his side than no one at all. Miraculously he heard her respond – 'Dad, Dad' – but her voice sounded older. It didn't make sense.

Without warning the pain abruptly stopped and he thought he had died. He lay there waiting – waiting for what he wasn't quite sure but frantic with fear that the Devil would appear and pull him downwards to the depths of hell. The likes of hell had never bothered him before but now he was unexpectedly faced with the prospect of spending eternity in the company of Satan, he was terrified witless.

When nothing happened he gingerly opened one eye. It was dark, pitch dark, and he was soaking wet and freezing cold. He opened the other eye and stared frantically around. Then his body sagged with relief. Thank God. Oh, thank God, he wasn't dead. Too much gin had caused his recurring nightmare, the one he continually fought to forget – and yet how would he ever, with his wooden leg a constant reminder?

He felt around for the billy can; he desperately needed a drink of gin to calm his jangling nerves. Then he remembered he had drunk it all. He grunted angrily then froze, shocked. Through the trees a shadowy figure emerged and for a split second he thought his nightmare had returned. He sneered in relief, realising it was only his sixteen-year-old daughter, Tilda.

'Wadda yous want?' he snarled.

She arrived breathless. 'I heard screaming. It woke me. I thought you were in trouble, Dad.'

'Well, I ain't in trouble so yous can clear off.'

Ignoring his remark, she took a deep breath. 'It's so cold, Dad, and you're soaking wet. Please come home else you'll freeze to death.'

'Home? Is that what yous call it?' Home to him would always be Glasgow, a dingy tenement where he'd shared the bug-infested accommodation with his own precious family. Family that due to one stupid mistake and its aftermath he would never see again. He struggled to rise. His efforts proved fruitless. His good leg was stiff, his back aching, and he collapsed.

Instinctively Tilda moved forward and grabbed his arm in order to help him. He pushed her roughly away and she stumbled, just managing to keep her balance.

'Piss off. I can manage.'

She flinched, filled with hurt. 'Dad, please . . .'

'Piss off, I said.'

Sighing sadly, she turned and made her way back through the woods.

As she disappeared from view Eli's eyes narrowed darkly. The nightmare he'd just experienced still sat heavily and the aftertaste it had left he knew from experience would stay with him for days. His mouth set grimly. He knew what had caused it. It was her. Tilda. She was a constant reminder of past mistakes. But he couldn't let her go. He needed her. A man with one leg whose only trade was murder and theft was practically useless in an everyday environment.

By rights he should be grateful to her. She had saved his life. Whilst he had lain helpless, the rusty mantrap embedded in his leg, she'd woken, found him and gone for help, running fearlessly through the dark eerie woods until she'd reached the village.

He had been carried to the half-ruined cottage and there had lain for several weeks on the brink of death. When he had recovered sufficiently to realise what had happened, he'd wished wholeheartedly he had died. To Eli a man without a limb was no use to anyone, let alone himself, and he took his loss hard.

Reluctantly he'd waved goodbye to any plans he had had for a wealthy future. Returning to the shack was out of the question. A new hovel would now become his home. He was a condemned man. Condemned for life to be a pitiful cripple, reliant on his daughter and the charity of the villagers. For a man such as himself it was like being condemned to purgatory.

Gritting his teeth, he adjusted his cumbersome wooden leg and awkwardly rose. Tilda was right, damn her. If he stayed out any longer he would freeze to death, and he wasn't ready for that, not just yet. Death didn't frighten him. Dying would be a blessed release from the life he was now subjected to. It was fear of what and who he would face in the afterlife that frightened Elijah Penny the most.

Chapter Four

A nervous Tilda paced the dried dirt path to one side of the small row of shops in the village centre. All around her busy daily life was in progress. Wednesdays were nearly as crowded as Fridays. People living farther out travelled in, either walking, by cart or the new omnibus services, to do their midweek shopping, purchases mostly being made from the huddle of market stalls surrounding the village green.

Usually at this time of the morning Tilda would have been standing on the fringes of the stalls, hoping to sell her eggs, seasonal vegetables and bundles of kindling – in summer she added to this bunches of freshly picked wild flowers which she would rise well before dawn to gather – but today she had abandoned her post for a few minutes in order to check the outcome of her interview. She was desperate for the news to be favourable.

As she paced to and fro she was conscious people were looking at her curiously as they entered the butcher's, and she calmed herself. If she wasn't careful someone might just remark on her to Mr Wilson and that wouldn't look good. Inwardly she scolded herself. If she thought she was capable of performing the job then she was capable of the simple task of entering the shop and enquiring after her success.

Taking several deep breaths, she brushed down her threadbare black twill skirt, straightened her equally ancient blouse, tucked several loose tendrils of hair behind her ear and walked boldly forward, hoping the fact that she was shaking would not be noticed.

The shop was packed and she quickly tucked herself unobtrusively behind a large woman carrying an enormous laden basket. Very rarely having the money to warrant a visit to the butcher, Tilda spent the first few minutes of her wait staring around, envisaging the meals she would be able to prepare should she have enough money. Above the wooden counter several unplucked chickens hung grotesquely by their necks from large metal hooks. On the back wall hung a side of beef, parts of it missing where Mr Wilson had hacked chunks off. He was at the counter now, chatting to a customer as he wrapped a piece of tripe in brown paper and handed it over. Tilda gulped. For no reason the man suddenly looked formidable and she wanted to run, but an abrupt departure would have looked conspicuous and caused more talk than if she stayed and faced her fate.

Finally she was facing him. Wiping his hands on his large white apron, stained by splattered blood, he smiled broadly at her. For an instant her hopes were raised. He wouldn't be looking so pleased to see her if she hadn't got the job, then it suddenly registered he was asking what she wanted.

She gulped and cleared her throat. 'I've ... er... come ... er ...' Suddenly she was aware that the chattering in the shop had ceased and they were all looking at her. Instinctively she pulled her sleeve over her withered hand and fought to stiffen her shaking legs. Taking a deep breath, she straightened her back and raised her chin.

'I've come to enquire if you've made a decision about the job yet, Mr Wilson?'

He stared at her blankly for a second. 'Oh, yes, the job. I'm afraid it's gone, me dear.'

'Gone?'

Mr Wilson picked up his cleaver and with one swing chopped a bone in half. 'Hetty Cobbley starts Monday.' Picking up the bone, he proceeded to wrap it. He lifted his head and noticed the look of acute disappointment on her face. His brow knotted. 'Look, I'm sorry, Tilda, but Hetty's mam needs the money.'

So do I, she wanted to say to him – desperately. But the prospect of this job had meant far more to her than the money it paid. Her bottom lip began to tremble, tears to sting the back of her eyes. Her dismay at this rejection heightened by the fact that everyone in the shop was witnessing her defeat. She raised her head, fighting to keep her dignity. 'Thank you for considering me, Mr Wilson. I'm much obliged.'

He smiled, relieved, and pushed the wrapped bone towards her. 'Take that.'

She stared down at it then raised her eyes. 'I don't take charity, Mr Wilson. I work for what I get.'

He cleared his throat, feeling suddenly uncomfortable. He picked up the parcel and walked round the counter. Taking her arm, he steered her aside. 'Look, Tilda, I couldn't take everybody on that applied fer the job. I had to make a decision, weigh up all the odds so to speak, and Hetty Cobbley won. It was as simple as that.'

She looked him in the eyes.

His face filled with shame. When he'd weighed up the odds about who should get the job, Hetty had won because she was a pretty young thing with a bubbly personality. Her plain features and deformity had been part of the reason why Tilda had lost out, but not all. Everyone knew what a hard worker Tilda Penny was. Secretly most of the folks in the village admired the way she stood by her father, working her fingers to the bone mostly to pay for his gin. A lesser person would have walked out long ago, leaving him to his own devices. They all knew how he beat her and made her life a misery. But they, like himself, had turned their backs, not wanting to get involved. They had all, in one way or another, felt the sting of Eli's evil tongue over the years and didn't relish unnecessary contact.

Mr Wilson grimaced thoughtfully. But that was all in the past. Eli Penny was old before his time. The shock of losing his limb so cruelly and the heavy drinking had taken their toll. The man couldn't be more than forty yet looked nearer seventy. He never came near the village now, preferring the solitude of the woods. If he kept drinking the amounts they all knew he did, then surely it wouldn't be long before he left this world. His brow furrowed deeply. When that did happen, where would it leave Tilda?

He suddenly realised he had made a mistake. Taking Tilda on would have been a far better decision than choosing lazy Hetty. And as for Eli – the passing years had removed any real threat he might pose. But it was too late for retraction. His wife had been adamant that Hetty should have the job, and his wife was not a woman to cross. Not that he intended to admit as much in public.

Himself not a man to mince words, he took a deep breath and looked at Tilda. 'There's no denying you're no great shakes in the looks department but that wasn't an issue when who should have the job was being decided. The truth of it is – well, it's yer dad, see.'

'Dad! What's my dad got to do with this?'

'Everything, Tilda. I run a business. I couldn't risk yer father coming down and causing trouble, as he would, I've no doubt. Yer dad's a law unto himself. A meaner man I've yet ter meet.' He smiled sympathetically. 'I stopped feeling sorry fer him a long time ago, Tilda. What happened to him was awful, but worse has happened to other men and they ain't made others suffer unjustly. The villagers bent over backwards to help when the accident happened and all we got in return from him was abuse. Since then he's never lifted a finger to help himself, just taken from anyone daft enough to offer – with no thanks either. All he does is drown his sorrows in Ma Whittle's gin. And we all know what yer father's like when he's full of gin.

'Look, I know he hasn't marauded through the village for a while now, but I ain't willing ter take the chance.' He thrust the wrapped bone in her hand. 'Besides, if I had given yer this job, Tilda, yer dad would 'ave only used yer wage for his drink. You know that as well as I do. I feel we've acted in your best interests. Now tek the bone, there's a good gel.'

He turned from her and bustled back behind the counter. 'Yes, Mrs Crumley, what can I get yer? Weather not bad today. Looks like spring's finally on its way.'

She stared at him for a moment, mortified, then stiffly turned and headed for the door, conscious that people were whispering now and no doubt about her. Probably saying she was a fool even to have applied for the job in the first place. Mr Wilson was right, though, going on past performances, her getting that job would have afforded her father ample opportunity to come down looking for trouble, and he would have demanded she hand over her pay, so in the long run she'd be no better off than she was now. Regardless, the feeling of loss sat heavily on her. It was she who had applied for the job and she who had been turned down. And she wasn't her father.

Outside the shop she hurried around the corner and pressed her back against the wall. Suddenly she saw her whole life in slow progress before her, filled with the daily struggle to put food on the table and little else. On reaching the end of that long dark road she would die. She wouldn't have achieved anything, made no mark on the world, left nothing for anyone to remember her by.

She squeezed her eyes tight. Doing something with her life

had never seemed important before. At the end of each day, if she had made enough money for food and a little to put towards the rent, and of course her father's gin, that was all that had mattered. Now, for some inexplicable reason, the daily struggle for survival was not enough. She wanted more. Getting that job would have been the starting point.

She absently grabbed hold of her withered hand and stroked it. Her father was right, she hadn't a hope in hell of ever getting the chance to do anything. Nobody in their right mind would want somebody like her.

A hand touched her shoulder and she jumped.

'There you are, Tilda. I was hoping I'd catch you.'

She turned abruptly and came face to face with Rosamund Dunrummy, the pretty young wife of the village doctor.

'Did I scare you? Sorry,' Rosamund continued, and smiled sweetly. 'I wonder if you could spare me a few moments, dear? I couldn't help overhearing what transpired in the butcher's and I have a proposition you might like to hear.'

Tilda stared at her. 'Me?'

Rosamund pursed her lips. 'Well, there's no one else here, is there? Now come along with me. I'll make you a nice cup of tea and we can discuss it.' She held a large basket towards Tilda, laden with her purchases. 'Would you take care of this for me? I've just to pop into the draper's to get some embroidery silks. You can wait for me outside.'

Tilda obediently took the basket. 'But I've to get back to the market. I've left my own basket . . .'

'Oh, don't worry about that. It'll be all right. Now come along.'

Rosamund's slight figure, encased becomingly in a fashionable blue calf-length woollen suit, a matching fur-edged pill-box hat complete with feather perched on her head, turned and marched ahead. A bemused Tilda, feeling decidedly shabby, trotted after her, mind filled with thoughts of what the doctor's wife could possibly want with someone like herself, plus the worry that she had hardly made any money today and if she didn't hurry the best of the customers would be gone.

Once she had seated her in the parlour of her house, Rosamund left Tilda and went off to make the tea.

Sitting amongst such finery Tilda felt clumsy and awkward, afraid to move in case she disturbed anything but savouring every minute, fully aware that this would likely be the only time she would be asked inside such a lovely home, to sit in such a beautiful room.

Presently Rosamund came back bearing a tea tray on which sat a silver tea set and two china cups and saucers.

'I made Earl Grey. I hope that's all right for you? I can never get Darjeeling in the village. Have to wait until we take a trip into town.'

Tilda nodded appreciatively, hoping the fact she hadn't a clue what Rosamund was talking about wasn't apparent.

The tea poured and handed over, Rosamund sat back in her chair and surveyed her visitor. Shame, she thought. Some people were born to be pitied. This girl certainly had her burdens to bear. Still, her husband was always telling her good deeds paid dividends when it came time to meet their maker, and she was hopefully going to add to her list when Tilda jumped at her proposition plus the fact that her sister would be eternally grateful to her for solving her domestic problems, and that was points in anyone's book. Rosamund wanted her sister on her side when the time came to persuade her own husband to move on. Her sister's husband had contacts in high places.

'Tea all right?' she asked.

Tilda nodded. It was the first tea that had passed her lips for such a long time it tasted like nectar. If this was Earl Grey then she wanted pots and pots of it.

Rosamund set down her own cup and crossed her shapely legs. 'Now, Tilda, as I said, I couldn't help but overhear what happened in the butcher's. I take it you're looking for a job?'

Tilda's jaw dropped, then her eyes sparkled eagerly. 'Yes. Yes, I am.'

Rosamund smiled, thinking to herself that it was a pity that Tilda didn't have more to smile about. When she did her plain face was transformed. The girl would never be classed as pretty but was certainly passable when she smiled. It was her eyes that did it. Such lovely large pale blue eyes. They were her redeeming feature. For a moment Rosamund envied her, visualising her own small brown ones. 'Well, I might be able to help you there. My sister is looking for a maid. More tea? Pass your cup over.'

Tilda willingly obliged, trying to control her impatience, wanting only to hear more about the job. Maybe it wasn't such a bad thing that she had lost the one at the butcher's after all. This one sounded much more promising.

'Now where did I get to? Oh, yes. My sister needs someone with a good head on their shoulders. Someone who'll get down to it, so to speak. Someone like you, Tilda, who doesn't mind hard work.'

'Oh, I don't mind hard work, not at all.' Tilda carefully put down her empty cup on a silver coaster on the walnut side table next to her and eyed Rosamund anxiously. 'I've never been a maid before, though.'

'That's not a problem. Mrs Witheringshaw, that's my sister, will train you up.' She eyed Tilda's clothes. 'And you'll get to wear a uniform. Her husband's a doctor too. A big practice and his patients pay their accounts on time – and with money, not bags of potatoes or coal.' A note of envy filled her voice. 'They've a big house with large grounds. We could have had all that but my dear husband found his calling here.' She sighed heavily. 'Not that I mind,' she said tritely. 'I just hope one day he'll come to his senses before we ourselves land in the poor house. Promissory notes don't pay the bills, do they dear?'

Rosamund suddenly remembered she was addressing a lowly creature who lived with her drunken crippled father in a tumble-down residence in the woods. 'Now, my sister really does need someone reliable,' she said briskly. 'You can't get maids these days for love nor money. Young girls are more interested in getting married or working in a factory. The Great War has changed everything. And not for the better, I feel. Before it happened young girls knew their place. But now...' She shook her head disapprovingly. 'I ask you, what sort of career can you find in a factory. Noisy dusty places. No fit place for young girls. And as for getting married ... well, they soon find out the hard way when the babies come along and money's tight. My sister lost her last three maids that way. Spent precious time and money training them up just for them to leave and get married. She told me herself, the next maid she takes on will be someone who will stay with her. So that's why I thought of you, my dear. You're just the kind of person my sister needs, and she'll make allowances.'

Tilda frowned quizzically. 'Allowances? I don't understand.'

Rosamund's eyes filled with pity. 'For your hand, my dear. My sister won't mind that in the least.' She smiled broadly. 'Well, it's not as though it stops you doing anything, does it? I expect your other hand is twice as strong to make up for it. Like a blind man, I expect. They have good hearing, so I'm told, to make up for their loss of sight. Anyway, you'll like it in Bristol. Do you good to get away from this place. It'll be the making of you, my dear. Mark my words.'

Tilda stared at her as the full impact of her words sank in, and slid her withered arm beneath the folds of her skirt. So that was it. Rosamund Dunrummy had only considered her because there was no threat whatsoever of her ever getting married or being offered another job. A hard lump of misery stuck in her throat. She doubted Rosamund even realised how hurtful she had been.

Tilda wanted to jump up and give sweet little Mrs Dunrummy a piece of her mind; tell her that she might have a withered hand and be plain faced but that didn't mean to say she hadn't a brain inside her head and wasn't capable of doing more than the most demeaning kind of jobs. It was painfully obvious that Rosamund Dunrummy had never gone without anything in her life despite her moans about her husband's lack of income, and Tilda doubted if she had ever been made to feel worthless as she had just made her visitor feel.

Humiliated, Tilda lowered her head. Her day, one that had begun with such hope, was turning into a nightmare and she wasn't quite sure what to say to redeem the situation, something that would give her back her self-respect. At this moment in time she felt she had none worth salvaging.

Rosamund broke into her thoughts. 'So I'll arrange with my sister about an interview?'

Tilda raised her head. 'Pardon?'

Rosamund tightened her lips in irritation. 'Have you been listening to me, Tilda? I said, I'll arrange an interview. My sister is coming up to see me in a couple of weeks.'

'Coming up?'

'Yes. From Bristol. My goodness, girl, whatever's the matter with you? Here I am, offering you the chance of a lifetime, and you've gone all vacant on me.'

Tilda took a deep breath. 'Your sister lives in Bristol, Mrs Dunrummy?'

'Yes.'

'Then I'm sorry, I couldn't even consider it.'

'You couldn't? Why?'

'I couldn't leave my father.'

Rosamund stared at her, greatly surprised. 'I would have thought you'd have jumped at the chance to get away from him?'

'Would you? Then I'm afraid you were wrong. If I abandoned him he would have no one.'

'In my opinion he doesn't deserve your loyalty. From what I've heard and seen he hasn't exactly been a good father.'

Tilda's eyes filled with anger. 'He's still my father when all is said and done.' She rose abruptly. 'Thank you for considering me, Mrs Dunrummy, but I'm afraid I'll have to turn down your offer.'

For a moment Rosamund was struck speechless. How dare this girl refuse her kind proposal. Who did she think she was? 'I really think you should take time to consider, my dear,' she said sharply. 'After all, offers like this don't come very often.'

Tilda smiled knowingly. 'For girls like me, you mean, Mrs Dunrummy? Poor unfortunates with no prospects other than cleaning up other people's muck?'

'Well, really, Tilda! If I'd realised you were going to be so ungrateful, I would never have approached you in the first place.' She rose and walked to the door, pulling it open. 'It's the best offer you'll ever get.'

Tilda followed her. 'I've no doubt it is, and I thank you, but as I've explained, I cannot leave my father. He wouldn't manage without me. I do hope your sister gets someone suitable, though. If it's as good an offer as you said it is then she shouldn't have any trouble.'

'Oh, she won't!' Rosamund bristled tartly. 'Queuing up, they are. It's just that my sister is choosy, that's all.' She narrowed her eyes. 'It was a mistake on my part to think that you would fit the bill. Good day.'

Tilda opened her mouth to retaliate then thought better of it. 'Good day, Mrs Dunrummy,' she replied softly.

The front door was shut firmly behind her. On the step Tilda stood for a moment and took several deep breaths. She wanted to cry. A tear wobbled precariously on her lower lid but she quickly wiped it away. She wouldn't give Rosamund Dunrummy the satisfaction of seeing she was upset. She knew the woman was peeping at her from behind the lace curtains. Straightening her back, she raised her head and forced herself to walk jauntily down the path. She would cry later in private back at the cottage when no one was around to see and ask the reason why.

She arrived at the gate at the same time as Dr Dunrummy. He looked at her in surprise then frowned, his handsome young face creasing in concern.

'Matilda Penny, isn't it? Have you come to see me?'

'Er . . . no, doctor. Mrs Dunrummy wanted a word, that's all.'

'Did she? Hmmm, not putting on you, I hope. Are you all right? You look upset.'

'No, no, I'm fine. Just . . . er . . . got something in my eye.' Tilda spoke hurriedly. 'I managed to get it out but it's still a bit watery, that's all.'

'Well, if you're sure.' He searched her face. Despite what the girl said he was unconvinced. Her eyes were full of tears. He had a strong suspicion what was troubling her. It was her drunken oaf of a father, it had to be. Being relatively new to the village he had seen neither Penny visit his surgery but had heard of them all right. By the sound of it, this girl had a sackload of troubles and more besides. He smiled sympathetically. 'Look, my dear, this is really not the place to speak but should you ever need anyone to talk to or help in any way, come and see me. We doctors are not just here to administer medicine. Well, this one isn't anyway.'

Tilda smiled wanly. 'Er . . . thank you, doctor. But there's nothing I need to see you about. I'm perfectly well.'

Dr Dunrummy sighed. 'I wasn't referring to your health, Tilda.' He took out his pocket watch and looked at it. 'I have to rush, I'm late for the surgery. Just don't forget what I've said.'

'No. No, I won't. Thank you again, Doctor.'

He turned to leave her then looked back. 'By the way, what did my wife want to see you about?'

'Pardon? Oh, about a job. A maid for her sister.'

He raised his eyebrows anxiously. 'And did you accept?'

'Er . . . no. I didn't.'

He smiled, relieved. 'Thank goodness.' He leaned over and whispered in her ear, 'Between you and me, my wife's sister is a tartar. You'd have hated the job, my dear.'

He patted her shoulder, turned and hurried off down the path.

What a nice man, thought Tilda, and what a contrast to his wife. She suspected the handsome doctor, in one way or another, had burdens of his own to shoulder. And after what he'd told her, thank goodness she hadn't accepted the job.

By the time she arrived back at the market stall most of the customers had gone home for dinner.

Molly Green, the owner of the second-hand stall, who she had asked to look after her basket, smiled as Tilda approached.

'How'd you get on, love?'

She lowered her head. 'I didn't get it.'

The sadness in Tilda's eyes was not lost on the older woman who was sympathetic. 'Ah, well, never mind. There'll be other jobs.' She eyed the brown paper parcel Tilda was carrying. 'Been buying?'

'This? Oh, no. Mr Wilson gave me a bone. It'll help make some good soup, but I'd sooner have had the job.'

Molly grimaced and patted her arm. 'It's his loss, lovey, remember that. Anyway I managed to sell the eggs and a couple of bundles of kindling,' she said, handing over the money. 'Not many folks buying today. I hardly did much meself. Still, there's always Friday.' She picked up a wooden box and started to pack the clothes and other items and load them on a hand cart.

Tilda stared down at the money in her hand and sighed heavily. 'Thanks, Molly.' As she had said, there was always Friday. But these coppers in her hand would hardly see them through today, let alone until Friday. Unlike the other market traders, she would have to come back again tomorrow and take a chance of some trade.

As Tilda prepared to leave Molly beckoned her over. She was holding out a dress. 'Eh up, wadda yer think of this?'

Tilda put down her basket and fingered the blue material. The dress was beautiful, the sort she'd always longed to own. She had never had anything new. The clothes she wore now had been mended and patched for so long she couldn't remember at this precise moment where she had actually got them from. Oh, yes, she could. Several years ago two ladies from the church had thought her a worthy cause and called upon her with a bag of items she suspected even the poorest in the village had refused. 'It's lovely, Molly.'

Molly beamed. 'It is, ain't it? Got it with a bundle of other stuff from a chap whose wife passed away. Right bargain I got an' all. So?'

Tilda looked blankly at her.

Molly beamed. 'Would you like it?'

'Me? Oh, Molly, I'd love it. But I couldn't possibly afford it.'

'Who mentioned money? I didn't,' she said, thrusting the dress at Tilda.

Her jaw dropped. 'But I couldn't possibly...'

'Yes yer can. As I said, I got a bargain. More than made me money back on selling the other stuff that came with it. Now tek it before I change me mind.'

Tilda clutched the dress to her chest. 'I'm sorry, Molly, I can't.' With a great effort, she thrust the dress back. 'But thank you so much for the offer.'

Molly grimaced thoughtfully. A widow herself, with six growing kids, and having had to work hard all her life, she knew what it was like not to have much. But even at her worst times, she herself had fared better than this girl. She suspected Tilda had never had anything decent to call her own.

Molly had been working this market for the last two years and whatever the weather this young girl standing before her would trudge through the woods to stand for hours, hoping to sell her meagre wares. Many times it had hardly been worth the effort but still she would return. And Molly had heard about the father and the dreadful conditions they lived in.

Her own standard of living wasn't great but it was a damned sight better than this girl's. A thought suddenly struck her. It was Tilda's pride that was preventing her from accepting the gift. She might be desperately poor but she was proud. It suddenly became very important to Molly that Tilda should have this dress. The girl needed something to restore her confidence after losing that job she so obviously wanted and needed.

An idea struck her. 'I'll do you a deal.'

'Deal?'

Molly bent down and retrieved two bundles of kindling from Tilda's basket. 'These in exchange. I'm desperate for kindling and you've done me a favour 'cos I nearly forgot to get some.'

'But...'

'Done.' She spoke firmly to close the subject. 'I'll see you Friday then. Now I must get cracking else the rest of me brood'll think I've done a runner. Now where's our Cyril? Cyril!' she bellowed at a young boy playing with some other children on the village green. 'Get your arse over here and help me pack up or we'll never get 'ome.'

Tilda stood speechless for a moment, watching Molly pack away her stall. A warm glow spread through her. Molly's kind act had done more for her than Molly herself would ever realise. After the dreadful blows she had suffered today, this woman's kindness had given her back her faith in human nature. Obviously not all people thought her worthless. She wanted to rush to Molly and hug her fiercely with gratitude, but knew she wouldn't want that. It would only embarrass her.

Folding the dress carefully, Tilda put it at the bottom of her basket and piled the unsold kindling on top. 'See you Friday then, Molly.'

Molly waved goodbye, and, hitching her basket comfortably on her good arm, Tilda walked slowly back through the village, not really wanting to get home, knowing what was facing her there.

The warmer weather had brought barefooted children out into the street and huddled groups of them were playing games of football and hopscotch or just sitting on the grass verges expertly tossing small stones they called 'snobs'. They were all giggling and laughing, happily lost in their childhood games, and Tilda suddenly had the urge to join them and lose herself for several moments.

She had never had a childhood to speak of. Not a carefree one, where she was able to make friends and play games. Hers, as far back as she could remember, had been filled with trying to make a living in order to support herself and her father. After school, whilst her classmates had loitered outside the school gates, planning their nightly exploits, she had had to rush home and tackle chores. Her father had worked then for Mr Williams the blacksmith. But even the kindly giant with his florid red face from years of bending over his furnace had eventually admitted defeat and asked her father to leave. An even-tempered man such as himself could only put up with so much and her father's nasty remarks, bad timekeeping, shoddy workmanship and drunkenness had finally worn even his patience thin. Tilda had been barely ten years of age when the burden of the family's finances had fallen on her shoulders.

She passed by a row of grey slate miners' cottages, nodding a quick greeting to several women sitting on their doorsteps peeling potatoes, then on towards the railway station, skirting the back of the coal yard, and towards the edge of the woods. Inside them stood the ancient cottage where her father would frantically be watching for her return, his hand already outstretched for the money. Tilda's shoulder's sagged despairingly and her steps slowed.

A rotting tree trunk lying at the side of the path looked inviting. She parked her basket, sat down and put her head in her hands, staring absently at the decaying undergrowth at her feet where the warm spring sun had yet to reach. Suddenly the thought of the years stretching endlessly ahead filled her with dread. She had to do something. Think of something that would make life better for herself and her father. It would have to be she who did it; her father, she knew without asking, would not be interested. He had sunk so low into self-pity she doubted he even knew what time of year it was. As long as he got his daily ration of gin, that was all he cared about.

She raised her head and smiled as she noticed tiny buds of green forming on tree branches and bushes. Mother nature had rested, awakened and was now tackling her work. In a few weeks' time Tilda herself would be seventeen years of age. Time, she thought, that she woke up and did something to improve her life. She had no one else to turn to. No one to offer help or advice. Whatever it was she did would have to be thought of and accomplished by herself. Like Mother Nature, she was on her own.

How? How would she go about it?

A sparrow flew down and began to peck near her feet and for several moments she watched it. Then a smile spread over her face. That was it. That was what she would do. The only means at her disposal was the cottage and the tiny parcel of land around it. What if she cleared more ground and expanded the garden? Growing more vegetables would give her more to sell. She could also enlarge the chicken hutch. Somehow she would acquire more chickens. Offer to work in exchange for them perhaps? It was worth a try.

Optimism grew as she formulated her plan. The clearing of the ground would be backbreaking work, preparing the soil for growing laborious, but the idea was a start and there was no telling where it would lead. And she had five shillings hidden inside her tin. Five shillings that would buy seed to sow in the newly reclaimed ground.

A new sense of purpose grew within her. She had a goal to reach, something to aim for, a real reason for rising in the morning. She smiled. And in future, when she went about her business, she had a lovely dress to wear. That dress would make all the difference to people's perception of her. Maybe they would see her differently, dressed in something decent. Later that night, when she was sure her father was well out of the way, she would take it from her basket and try it on. Her excitement mounted. She couldn't wait.

Her ears suddenly pricked. A dull thud-thud-thud was coming towards her. Her feeling of optimism and goodwill was rapidly overtaken by dread. The sound was her father's wooden leg drumming against the path. He was coming to look for her.

Quickly she took the money she had made at market from her pocket and added it up. It totalled four shillings and ninepence. Quickly calculating her needs, she snatched off her holed boot and hurriedly put two shillings inside the well of the heel. It was uncomfortable beneath her foot but at least the money was hidden and hopefully safe. She still had a bit to put towards the rent and the food to be bought.

Grabbing up her basket and steeling herself for the worst, she headed down the path.

Spotting her as she rounded a bend, her father attacked her head on.

'Where've yous been?' he cried, grabbing her shoulder. 'I've been waiting fer yous.'

'I . . . I hung around the market hoping to catch any late shoppers . . .'

'Aye, aye,' he erupted impatiently. 'Just give me me money.'

Meekly she handed over one shilling and ninepence.

He stared down at it. 'That all yous got?'

'No.' She eyed him apprehensively. 'I made a bit more. But I need that to put towards the rent and buy food.'

He looked at her aggressively. 'You ain't holding out on me, are yous?'

'No, Dad, no. Honest, ain't.'

'Huh. Well, I suppose this 'ull have to do.'

She stared at her father. He looked awful. He had obviously not long risen from his bed and hadn't been near the water barrel for days to clean himself up. 'Have you eaten, Dad?' she ventured.

'Aye, I've eaten. Some of that muck left in the pan.'

'Dad,' she began, then clamped her mouth shut. She desperately wanted to tell him of her decisions, wanted to share with him her plans for their future, hoped that maybe he might even help. But she knew he wouldn't be interested.

'What?' he snapped.

'Nothing,' she replied softly.

He stared at her, then narrowed his eyes maliciously. 'Did yous get that job?'

She lowered her head. 'No. No, I didn't,' she whispered.

He laughed, a dry chesty cackle. 'Told yous, didn't I? But yous wouldn't listen. Naebody's ever gonna take yous on, girl. Naebody, do yous hear? You're too bloody ugly.'

A rush of tears filled her eyes. 'He gave me a bone for soup,' she said before she could stop herself.

His lip curled. 'And that's all yer worth, Tilda. A bloody bone.'

He turned from her and stumbled away down the path. She wouldn't see him again until morning.

It was too late to stop his words from hitting home. As usual they cut deep. Sighing deeply, she straightened her back and resumed her journey. As she rounded the bend near the cottage a little figure came running to meet her.

'Tilda!' Eustace shouted. 'I've bin waiting for yer. I hid 'til I saw yer dad go out.'

She put down her basket and gathered him in her arms. 'Oh, Eustace,' she exclaimed joyfully. 'How glad I am to see you.'

'Are yer, Tilda? Are yer?'

She smiled broadly. 'Yes, I am.' She held him at arm's length and ran her eyes over him. 'My, you look smart.'

He stared down at his clothes. They were shabby, but far more presentable than the ones he normally wore. 'Me auntie made me put these on 'cos her cronies from the Church came ter visit. And I've had me tea. Sandwiches and cake. It were grand, Tilda, grand.'

She shook her head. 'Let's hope they visit often then, eh? Does your auntie know you're out?'

'Sent me packing herself. Said I was getting in the way.' He pulled a little black Bible from his pocket. 'Told me to study this.' He opened the book at the Ten Commandments while she looked on.

'And have you?'

He nodded. 'A bit whilst I was waiting for yer 'cos she'll ask me questions.' He looked up at her with a worried expression. 'But I don't understand it.'

She ruffled his hair. 'Neither do I. But I tell you what, let's get inside and we'll go through it together. See what we can make of it, eh?'

'Oh, thanks, Tilda,' he said gratefully. 'She might not lock me in the cellar then, eh?'

Tilda controlled her anger. 'No, she might not.'

She released him, picked up her basket and took his hand.

Settling Eustace to read his Bible, Tilda quickly did her chores, then as she spooned her soup, tried to interpret the Ten Commandments, hoping her understanding of the words was correct. The last thing she wanted was for Eustace to be punished for her mistakes. Inwardly she fumed. How callous of his aunt to expect a lad of his tender years to understand the Bible and explain its meaning when many educated adults couldn't.

The task of the Commandments' deciphering done to the best of her ability, Tilda made him close the book and put it safely in his pocket. She was just about to enquire if it was not time for him to go, not that she wanted him to, but she dare not make him late, when she remembered the dress.

Excitedly she jumped up from her stool. 'Eustace, I've something to show you. I got a present today and I want your opinion.'

'My opinion,' he asked.

She smiled warmly. 'Yes, yours. Wait here. I won't be a minute.'

Grabbing her basket, she went into the back room, the one with the gaping holes and leaking roof. Several moments later she returned.

He gazed at her in awe. 'Ah, Tilda, yer look beautiful.'

69

She held the blue calf-length skirt of the dress out wide. 'It's a bit on the big side but I can hopefully alter it.'

'You can, Tilda,' Eustace said, nodding in agreement. 'You can do anythin'.'

She beamed over at him. 'Thank you, kind sir.'

He pulled a wry face. 'You won't want ter marry me now, will yer, Tilda? Not now you've got that dress. You look like a princess.'

She rushed towards him and threw her arms around his neck, hugging him tightly. 'Oh, yes, I will, Eustace. You're not going to get out of our arrangement that easily.'

'I don't want ter,' he said shyly, his eyes filled with devotion.

Chapter Five

Months passed. Every spare minute of Tilda's day was spent clearing more land around the cottage. As she'd expected it was back-breaking and laborious, but inch by inch the earth was exposed. Flopping into bed bone weary of an evening, she would remind herself over and over why she was doing it. This reclaimed land would secure her a better future.

Eustace, God love him, whenever he could steal away would come and help her, provided her father wasn't around. Between them they dug up roots, cleared dense rotting under-growth, moved large stones and dug deep in the hard ground beneath. It was early-November before Tilda finally gave way before the hardening ground and laid down her tools, but satisfaction filled her. Over winter, the frosts and snow would break down the soil and come spring it would be ready for planting.

The small garden was now nearly twice its original size. That meant twice as much seed could be sown, twice as much produce would be grown, twice as much money would be coming in. Her eyes shone brightly. It was a start, and come spring when the ground softened and the planting had been taken care of, she would begin again and reclaim some more.

Tilda stared in fascination at the Christmas tree, at the gaily coloured twinkling baubles and wide scarlet ribbon bows, at the prettily wrapped boxes beneath, and a pleased smile touched her lips. She envisaged the tree standing in a house, a family surrounding it. She felt the happiness that filled them all, the anticipation of the children desperate to unwrap the parcels and see what Father Christmas had brought them.

She took a deep breath and the smile slowly faded as loneliness filled her. She would never be part of such a gathering.

Her eyes once again strayed to the parcels beneath the tree and for a fleeting moment she wondered what it would be like to receive such a package, feel the anticipation of opening it and the thrill of finding out what was inside. It wouldn't have mattered to Tilda what the present was; to her the thought that someone had bothered to buy her something would have been enough.

A child standing nearby was examining a brightly painted toy car and Tilda visualised Eustace and knew how much he would have valued such a toy. She doubted his auntie would even think to buy him a gift for Christmas and felt saddened. She wished wholeheartedly she had the money to buy it for him.

A hand touched her shoulder. 'Are you buying, miss?'

The voice was harsh, toneless, and she swung round. 'Pardon?'

A pair of faded hazel eyes in a wrinkled face scanned her disdainfully and she shuddered under their scrutiny, very conscious of her own shabby apparel. All around folks were busy purchasing their Christmas shopping off the well-stocked counters, shopping bags bulging with parcels, pushing and shoving each other as they fought for the attention of the harassed shop assistants.

Tilda eyed the floorwalker warily. She had had a good morning at the market, managing to sell all of her bundles of kindling and the holly and mistletoe she had collected from the woods. She had money in her pocket, more than she had

had for a very long time, but none to spare for anything other than the most basic of items. Any left over would need to be put towards the buying of seed for the newly dug ground that at this moment was lying under a thick layer of frost.

The only Christmas present she had bought was a jacket for her father from Molly's second-hand stall, the half crown it had cost painstakingly paid over several weeks. Her father, she knew, wouldn't thank her for it but his other jacket was so old it was no protection against the harsh cold winter and she did worry for his welfare. It was a wonder he hadn't caught pneumonia before now, lying around as he did in all weathers, drinking his gin.

She felt the eyes of the floorwalker boring into her as he waited for her answer and suddenly she regretted venturing into the store. She had walked the seven miles to town on a whim after the village market had finished, telling herself she wanted to see the Christmas decorations, but knowing the real reason was the fact that she didn't want to go home and sit in the dark all by herself.

Normally she would never enter such a store but the tree had caught her eye through the window and like a magnet she had felt drawn towards it. Before she'd had time to check herself she was standing before it marvelling at its beauty.

The floorwalker cleared his throat. 'Excuse me, madam, I asked if you were buying? If not I suggest you leave, you're getting in the way.'

Tilda flinched. The emphasis on 'madam' was not lost on her, nor the look of distaste in his eyes. As always she was being made to feel small and insignificant, being judged by her plainness, deformity and shabbiness. She tightened her mouth. She wanted to put this obnoxious man in his place, tell him she had as much right as any of the other people to be in the shop, whether she was buying or not. She knew, though, such words would be lost on him. Only people who looked as if they had money in their purses would be afforded any kind of courtesy here.

A vision of Eustace and the car came back to mind and before she had time to check herself or think of the consequences her mouth opened.

'I'll thank you to know I am buying. I was deciding, that's all.'

His eyes widened in disbelief.

'I want one of those cars, please,' she continued. 'And I'd like it wrapped.'

'It's one and sixpence,' he replied sharply, his whole manner indicative of the fact that he seriously doubted she had the money.

Tilda gulped. One and six would buy their Christmas dinner of a small piece of oxtail plus the potatoes and sprouts which her own garden had stopped providing, and maybe two stale mince pies. Oh, God, why did she have to go and open her big mouth? She was about to say she had changed her mind when fierce pride flooded through her. Suddenly she was fed up with being looked down on – being made to feel worthless. What did it matter what she looked like? She deserved the same courtesy as anyone else. She lifted her chin haughtily.

'Is that all?' she said, smiling sweetly. 'I thought they were dearer than that.' Just in time she stopped herself saying she'd have two, just to drive her point further home.

'Oh,' he mouthed. 'I'll see to it then, madam. Right away.'

Tilda sauntered jauntily down the street that led out of town, smiling to herself. Her pride had cost her dearly. Christmas dinner was now severely in doubt but she didn't care. The astonished look in the floorwalker's eyes was worth every penny, but more importantly she had a present for Eustace and that fact gave her more pleasure than anything. She couldn't wait to see his eyes light up when she gave it to him. The present was also a nice way by which to express her gratitude for all the help he had given her in the garden. And of course for his friendship, though that to Tilda was priceless.

It was almost dark when she approached the cottage. The sky was clear, stars beginning to twinkle. The icy air held a threat of another layer of thick frost come morning. A full moon shone brightly, illuminating the trees with an eerie halo. From a distance the cottage looked empty and uninviting, but to Tilda it was preferable that way to finding it occupied by her father and having to face whatever mood he was in.

Standing on the stone slab in front of the door she raised her hand, prepared to lift the latch, when a noise from inside alerted her. She froze, her eyes fixed on the door. There was someone inside. Her heart thumped, then she breathed a sigh of relief. It would be Eustace. She remembered the present and hurriedly hid it at the side of the cottage, intending to retrieve it later. A broad smile on her face, she lifted the latch and walked inside.

Her eyes were drawn towards the newly lit fire in the grate then jumped to the figure across the room, illuminated by moonlight streaming through the tiny window at the side. It was far too tall to be Eustace and a blind panic filled her. As she entered the man spun round and for several moments each stared at the other in shock.

Tilda's surprise momentarily turned to fright, then anger mounted at the audacity of this stranger's entering her home uninvited. She took a step forward. 'Who . . .' the words died on her lips as she suddenly noticed he had something in his hand. It was her tin. The tin in which she kept her savings. Money she had painstakingly gathered for years and which was going to be used to secure her future. This man was stealing it!

Her eyes darted round. Propped against the door was a twig

broom and she snatched it up, waving it menacingly towards him. 'Put that down!' she cried. 'Put it down now!'

The man looked at the tin, then back at Tilda.

'Put it down,' she shouted again, incensed. With no thought for her possible danger, she advanced several steps. Her mind was filled only with the fact that this stranger had her tin and she was not going to allow him to take it.

The man saw the broom heading for him and hurriedly put the tin on the floor, then raised his hands in surrender. 'Look,' he said, in a thick Scottish brogue, 'I thought this place was empty. I thought it was derelict. I'd nae idea anyone lived here 'til I got inside.'

Broom still poised, Tilda stared at him. That could be true, she supposed. The cottage would give that impression. But it still did not excuse him. 'Well, it's not,' she said icily. 'And you've no right to be here.'

He looked around him. He'd seen some sparse living conditions in his time but this had to be the worst he'd come across. Despite that he had to admit the place was clean. Usually people this poor were filthy with it. But noticing the lack of dust and dirt had been the last thing on his mind when he had entered. He had been too glad to come across the dwelling as he had, just by chance, cold, ravenously hungry and desperate for sleep. To find it wasn't quite so bad as he'd first envisaged, and on further investigation contained items to make his stay a bit more comfortable – the old shakedown complete with several threadbare blankets, logs stacked outside to make a fire and some old cooking pots – had come as a nice surprise. Then to find the tin with just about enough money inside to pay for some provisions had been an added bonus. The fact that the cottage was inhabited was staring him in the face but he'd been too exhausted for it to register.

He shifted uncomfortably on his feet. He could easily have

taken the tin and anything else he wanted for that matter. The girl posed no threat. Where he came from it was an inborn instinct to steal, a way of life. His widowed mother had shown no remorse when she had sent him out to scavenge whatever he could with a stern warning not to come back until his pockets were full. Thieving didn't come easy to him but the alternative was starvation. But to take from those in the same or a worse situation was not his way.

'I'd better leave,' he muttered.

She lifted her chin defiantly. 'Yes, you'd better.'

He skirted around her, making for the door.

As he came abreast of her Tilda saw the tiredness in his eyes, could tell by his movements that he was exhausted. His face was gaunt. He looked as though he hadn't eaten a decent meal for weeks.

He paused by the door and turned to face her. 'I'm sorry.'

The apology was most unexpected and, taken aback, she stared at him. Then compassion for his situation rose within her and instinctively she opened her mouth to offer her hospitality. Then she remembered she had caught him red-handed with her precious savings and her mouth snapped shut. She wanted this man out of her house as quickly as possible.

As he turned to depart his legs suddenly buckled and he grabbed hold of the door for support.

Instinctively she dropped the broom and rushed towards him, sliding her arm under his in support. 'You'd better sit down for a moment.'

He pulled his arm free and righted himself. 'I'm fine,' he snapped.

She took a deep breath, hoping she wasn't about to make a dire mistake. This man was on the point of collapse and she couldn't turn him away, it wasn't in her nature.

'When was the last time you ate?'

He shook his head. 'I cannae remember.'

She sighed resignedly. 'Well, I can't offer you much but you're welcome to what I can give you. Then you must go.'

His eyes filled with gratitude. 'Thank yous.'

She guided him towards a stool and sat him down. Hurriedly she cut several slices of bread and handed him one. He snatched it from her and gobbled it down, then eyed the other slices, mouth watering.

Ignoring his hungry eyes, she turned her back and set about making a pan of soup. The loaf of bread had to last two days. It wouldn't last two minutes if she let him have his way. The soup simmering gently, Tilda tidied the table and set out two chipped bowls, conscious he was watching her closely as she went about her tasks.

'What's wrong with your arm?' he suddenly asked.

Her head jerked up. 'Pardon?'

'I asked what was wrong with your arm? Did yous have an accident?'

Instinctively she pulled down her cardigan sleeve to hide it and took a deep breath. 'I was born like this. It's withered,' she said softly, almost apologetically.

'Oh.'

His nonchalant tone startled her and she stared at him.

'Yous should count yourself lucky,' he said matter-of-factly, his eyes once more travelling to the slices of bread. 'I've seen many with worse than yous.' He tore his gaze away from the bread and looked at her. 'Want a piece of advice? Stop covering it up. People notice more that way. We all have to be grateful for what we've got and make the best of it. Yous should do the same. Yous could be a lot worse off than just having a withered arm, believe me. It's better than not having one at all.'

Her eyes widened. Others had always made her feel a freak because of her deformity. But this man was right. Her arm

78

might be withered but that fact didn't stop her from doing anything. Its weakness was a hindrance but something which was compensated for by her other arm being twice as strong. She pressed her lips together. It was just a pity that others did not share his views. They saw her deformity and plain features and that was where they stopped. Any other qualities she possessed went unrecognised, and she did not envisage that situation ever changing. One man's enlightened attitude did not change a whole society's.

She wiped her hands on her apron and abruptly changed the subject. 'Supper shouldn't be long.'

He smiled. 'It smells good. I could eat a horse.'

'You maybe could but you'll have to make do with a bowl of soup,' she replied sharply, then instantly regretted it. This man had just, in his way, been very kind to her. It was wrong of her to repay him by rudeness. She stared at him thoughtfully. 'You're a long way from home, aren't you?'

He scowled at her. 'What do yous mean by that remark?'

'I just mean that you're Scottish. I didn't mean any offence.'

'Oh, I see. Yes, I am that. And proud of it.'

'So's my father.'

His eyebrows rose in surprise. 'Is he! Where from?'

'Glasgow.'

His already drawn face paled alarmingly. He slowly rose, placed his hands flat on the table and leaned forward, his gaze riveted on hers. 'Glasgow? What part?'

Tilda stared, his sudden change of attitude bewildering her. 'I . . . I don't know.'

'Yous don't know?' he challenged. 'Why don't yous know?'

'Because . . . because I don't. My father's not the talkative kind.'

'What's his name?' he demanded.

'Why . . .'

79

'Just answer me. What's his name?'

Tilda backed away from the table, frightened by the murderous look that now filled his eyes. 'Elijah,' she stuttered.

'Elijah what?'

'Elijah Penny.' She backed away even further. 'And I'm Tilda. Matilda Penny.'

'Penny,' he repeated under his breath. It was nothing like the name he was hoping to hear. He ran his eyes over her. The name was hardly apt. She didn't look as though she had two halfpennies to rub together. He thrust his hand inside his jacket and pulled out a yellowing, tattered piece of paper. He thrust it towards her and, trembling, she advanced and took it.

Confused, she carefully opened out the paper and studied the faded artist's impression of a young man. She raised her head and looked at him blankly.

'Does it remind yous of anyone?' he snapped.

She shook her head. 'No. Should it?'

He reached over and took it back, sighing heavily as he sank down on the stool. 'I was hoping it might.' He sat in silence for a moment then raised his eyes to her again. 'Do any other Scots live around here?'

'Not that I know of. Why?'

He folded the paper and put it back in his pocket. 'It's a long story and I really don't want to talk about it.' He gave an unexpected smile. 'I'm sorry if I upset yous.'

She stared at him, confused by his sudden change of mood, then tightened her lips. 'Upset? Frightened, you mean. Are you like this with everyone you meet or just people with Scottish connections?'

He gave a sheepish smile. 'As I said, it's a long story and I don't want to talk about it.' He took a deep breath. 'Will your father be back for supper? Be nice to have a crack with a fellow Scot.'

'No,' she said sharply, annoyed that he had changed the subject, and feeling strongly she deserved some kind of explanation for his outburst. 'Besides, my father's not the talkative kind, and whether you're a fellow Scot or not he won't appreciate finding you here when he does come home.' She eyed him coldly. 'You'll be long gone by then. And let me tell you, I'll be checking around to make sure nothing of mine has gone with you.' She turned abruptly, walked over to the fire and gave the soup a vigorous stir. Taking a sample on her wooden spoon, she tasted it. It was delicious.

A while later she sat opposite and watched as he ate. Although she was hungry, her own bowl remained practically untouched. She wished she hadn't offered her hospitality, his outburst had unnerved her. All sorts of possible reasons were racing through her mind. Her eyes narrowed. She didn't like this man and couldn't wait for him to finish his food and leave. And by the looks of it that wouldn't be long, he was shovelling it down quick enough.

She judged his age to be around the early-twenties. He wasn't good-looking, his vivid green eyes were too close together and his nose too long, but then neither was he ugly. She supposed some women would be attracted to his leanness, wanting to feed him up and mother him or maybe run their fingers through his thick thatch of bright red hair. His clothes had seen better days. They were not so bad as the ones she wore, but then she supposed if he had travelled from Glasgow, for whatever reason, then even the smartest dresser would by this time look shabby.

He pushed away his bowl and wiped the back of his hand across his mouth. 'That was much appreciated.'

She rose to her feet. 'I expect you'll be wanting to get off,' she said, choosing to ignore the fact he was fighting to keep himself awake.

He stood reluctantly, gathered his bundle of belongings and

walked towards the door. Pulling it open, he peered out into the cold dark night. He turned, tilted his head and grinned at her cheekily. 'I presume there's no chance of a bed for the night?'

'You presume right.'

He nodded resignedly. 'Well, thanks for the food.'

She watched as he walked out of the door and shut it behind him, then a dreadful feeling of guilt surfaced. If anything happened to him during the night it would be her fault for turning him away. It was too late now to get any lodgings, even if he did have the money, and unoccupied shelter was practically non-existent in this area. Without further thought she rushed to the door and yanked it open. She could just see him disappearing into the darkness. The wind was icy sharp and she shuddered. Her father was out in this, sitting under his favourite tree drinking gin. But then, he was used to it. Years of the habit had hardened his constitution when a lesser man would have caught pneumonia and died long ago.

A vision of a corpse propped against a tree sprang to mind and a feeling of dread filled her. She already carried the blame for her mother's death and her father's loss of a limb. The thought of any more on her conscience was not to be borne.

'Mister,' she shouted. 'Hey, mister.'

The man stopped and turned back to her. 'Aye?'

She took a deep breath. 'You can sleep in the back room. It's full of holes and the wind and rain come in but it'll be better than the open. Only for tonight, mind. And you'd better not let my father know you're there. He wouldn't be pleased, I can assure you.' As he joined her she locked her eyes with his. 'And I'm warning you...'

'Warning me?'

She shuffled uneasily on her feet. 'Yes, you know what I mean.'

He looked at her for a moment. Was this girl really warning

him off from seducing her? He fought to hide the smile that threatened. To say she was ugly would be doing her a grave injustice, but she was definitely plain. Some man might find her appealing but definitely not him. 'Don't worry, I promise I won't lay a finger on you or touch any of your belongings.'

Is wasn't me I was worried about, she thought. That fact hadn't crossed her mind. But finding her belongings gone in the morning had. 'Good. We understand each other then,' she replied gruffly.

She showed him into the dilapidated room at the back and handed him a thin blanket from her own bed. She looked guiltily at the hard floor, then raised her eyes to his. 'I hope you sleep well.'

He smiled. 'I'm that tired I could sleep on a clothes line. Goodnight.'

'Goodnight.'

She made to shut the door then paused. 'By the way, I should know your name in the circumstances. After all, you know mine.'

'Yes, I suppose yous should, considering.' He held out his hand. 'Ben. Benjamin McCraven.'

Chapter Six

An hour before dawn, in the freezing cold room, Ben unwound the blanket and rose stiffly. It was the first night he'd slept undercover for quite a few nights and the roof, such as it was, had been welcome, as had the young woman's hospitality, even though he knew he didn't really deserve it after she'd caught him the way she had. Still he was grateful, and more than likely so would she be when she rose to find he had gone. She didn't like him and he couldn't blame her.

He yawned loudly. He'd hardly slept a wink. What with the icy wind whistling through the holes in the roof and walls, and also the problems that replayed on his mind, sleep had been a long time coming and when it had it wasn't restful. Ben hadn't had a decent night's sleep for over a year since he had discovered the truth about his father's demise. His mother had just died and he had been going through her things.

The words on the yellowing piece of paper hidden inside a locked tin box had stunned him senseless before a lust for revenge had gripped his soul and he realised he wouldn't rest until his father's murderer was, in one way or another, brought to justice. He just prayed that after all this time the man was still alive and Ben himself could make him suffer for the torment his mother had endured; not only the loss of the man she had loved but the harsh life she had been forced to live, struggling to raise her son and grieving for the ones who would never be born. But that was not all. Ben himself had been denied his father. Jimmy McCraven had been no angel, Ben knew that from what people had told him, but when all was said and done he hadn't deserved to die in a stinking back street with a knife in his chest like a slaughtered pig.

Relatives had tried to dissuade him from his quest. Duggie Smilie was as cunning and evil as they came and had remained undetected for the past eighteen years, they argued, but Ben had stood firm. He would not rest until this man paid for his crime.

For over a year he had travelled aimlessly, criss-crossing the country, working when he could, taking what he needed when no other option was open, but always enquiring and following any lead, however small. This he would continue to do until his objective was fulfilled. Then and only then would he feel free to return home.

Gathering his things, he stole to the rotting window and as gently as possible eased it up, hoping it did not disintegrate and wake the young woman. His stomach growled in hunger and the noise it made echoed round the room. He slipped his hand into his pocket and fingered the few coins in the bottom. Hopefully he had just enough to buy some breakfast and it looked as though he would have to find some kind of work very soon if he wasn't to starve. During the night a heavy frost had settled on top of the one left unmelted the previous day and, shivering, Ben turned up the collar of his jacket, hunching his shoulders against the biting wind. For a moment he regretted leaving the thin blanket and hard stone floor and prayed that the nearest village or town wasn't too far away.

Suddenly his strides ceased as a sound reached his ears. He strained to distinguish the noise, then grimaced. It sounded as though someone was banging a wooden stake against the hard earth. He shrugged his shoulders. Must be a madman to be out working at this time in the morning. For the life of him he couldn't think what they could be doing.

He resumed his journey. As he rounded a bend the noise grew louder and he stared in amazement to see heading towards him a dark eerie shape. As it advanced the outline became clearer and Ben relaxed and gave a wry smile. So that was the noise he had heard. It was a man stumbling along on a wooden leg, and by the looks of him he was very drunk.

Without warning the man tripped and fell flat on his face. Ben dropped his belongs and rushed towards him. He held out his hand.

'Yous all right, mate?' he enquired. 'Here, take my hand.'

Without lifting his head, Eli grunted, 'Piss off.'

Not deterred by the nasty rebuff, Ben tried again. 'Ah, come on now. I'm only trying to help. You'll freeze to death if you stay down there. Come on, take my hand.'

Eli's body stiffened in anger. 'Didn't yous hear what I said? I dinnae need your help. I dinnae need anyone's help.'

The hand was abruptly withdrawn. 'Suit yersel'.'

'I fucking will. Now piss off.'

Frowning angrily, Ben retrieved his belongings and resumed his journey. Before he rounded a bend he stopped, turned and surveyed the man still struggling to rise. Long greasy hair and an even longer straggling matted beard so that his features were obscured, but even without the verbal abuse he'd received Ben would have known he was not a pleasant man. The fact radiated from him. He screwed up his nose. Ungrateful bastard, he thought, pitying any poor person who had him to contend with. Then a thought struck him. Could this possibly be the father of the young woman who had given him shelter? He sincerely hoped not. The poor lassie had enough on her plate without that sorry specimen of a human being to cope with.

Shaking his head disdainfully, he turned and continued his journey.

Ben was right, Tilda was mightily relieved to find he had gone when she gingerly opened the door to the room at the back just after the break of day. And not only because she didn't like or trust him but because her father had returned in a foul mood, waking her up with his cursing and swearing, and the presence of the stranger would only have made matters worse.

Tilda deduced that her father must have fallen over on his way home; causing his wooden leg to become dislodged. In his drunken state he hadn't been able to fix it back on, had had to drag himself the rest of the way down the icy rutted path, and wasn't pleased about it either. His clothes, which had been bad enough before, were in a terrible state and she desperately tried to think of a way she could get them off him and at least try and clean them up a bit. A tramp looked better kept and smelt nicer than he did. Shame filled her. What must people think of her for letting her father carry on this way?

Her offers of help were refused with abuse and fearing his wrath would only be vented on herself once he restored his wooden leg, she hurriedly gathered her wares and set off for the village, praying his mood would have mellowed when she returned later in the afternoon.

It was at this time of year the Pennys' finances were at their worst. Produce from the garden had dried up and she was solely reliant on what she could gather from the woods and what her chickens laid, though two of those had recently died from old age. Cutting back to accommodate shortfalls was extremely difficult and sometimes nigh on impossible. Tilda fought to feel optimistic. Hopefully this time next year things would be better now that the garden had been expanded.

It wasn't a normal market day and standing on her own on

the village green would have been humiliating but for the fact it was something she had done for so long she had learned to live with it. Her eyes scanned the huddle of shops across the road. There weren't many people about today. Several of the shop-keepers were busying themselves cleaning windows or sweeping paths in front of their premises. Her gaze reached the local hostelry and widened in surprise as through the door walked the man to whom she had extended her hospitality the previous night.

He spotted her, paused for a moment, then sauntered over. He looked at her in some embarrassment. It was obvious to Tilda that he hadn't expected to bump into her again.

'So this is what yous do for a living,' he said, a cheeky grin on his face. 'Sold much?'

How much she'd sold was none of his business, thought Tilda. 'It's early yet.'

He glanced around him. 'S'pose it is.' He scratched his ear. 'Look ... er ... thanks for what yous did last night.'

'Think nothing of it,' she said flatly.

He stood for a moment, angered by her dismissive attitude. He made to walk away then stopped. 'Do yous happen to know where there's any work going?'

Her head jerked around. 'Work?' she repeated, surprised.

'Yeah, work.' His eyes narrowed. 'Don't look so shocked. Whatever yous might think, I wasn't stealing from yous last night.'

'Weren't you?' She pursed her lips. 'I happen to think otherwise so we'll leave it at that, shall we? Anyway, what kind of work are you looking for?'

He shrugged his shoulders. 'Anything, really. Just something that'll pay enough to see me on my way.'

She thought for a moment. 'You could try Mr Williams the

blacksmith or Mr Griffin the local odd job man. You might be lucky.'

'Oh, right, I will.' He tipped his forelock. ''Bye.'

''Bye.'

Tilda watched as he strode across the green. If he did find work she doubted he'd stick it for long before he was caught stealing and carted off to jail.

Taffy Williams straightened his broad body and eyed the man before him. He picked up a cloth and wiped rivulets of sweat from his face and naked upper torso. 'As it 'appens I do have some work.' He lumbered over to the furnace and placed his large booted foot on the end of the bellows to pump in air. The fire inside glowed white, the heat it threw out hitting Ben like a blow. Retrieving a molten red piece of iron from the fire with a pair of long tongs, Taffy laid it flat on his anvil and, picking up a hammer, began to beat it flat – all the time sizing up Ben from the corner of his eye. 'I won't be taking on just anyone, though.'

'I don't mind hard work,' Ben replied with conviction.

''Tain't the hard work,' Taffy said, shaking his head. 'It's the staying power I'm concerned about. You young lads can't seem to stick at anything for long, specially ones like yourself just passing through. I blame the war. Nothing's been the same since the war.' He turned over the piece of iron and resumed beating. 'I've got to be careful who I take on see. I've landed some overflow work from the nearby foundry and if I do a good job more will come my way. It's at least six weeks' work and whoever gets the job I'll need to be assured he'll see it through.' He sniffed, stopped his hammering and wiped his large hand under his nose. 'I've had six lads come and see me since word got round and none was worth the time I spent talking to 'em.' He looked Ben up and down. 'You don't seem the type to me neither.'

His last words were spoken as a challenge and Ben's back stiffened. He resented the fact that the blacksmith was judging him by others' shortcomings. Mind you, he thought, six weeks seemed a long time when the most he'd ever stayed in one place since leaving Glasgow was two days. Six weeks? He quickly mulled over the prospect of staying in this village for that length of time. He suddenly remembered the last winter he'd spent on the road. Many nights he'd slept out in the open, the cold so intense he was surprised to wake up in the morning. Six weeks would see him well into February, and if he was careful with his wages for the remainder of the winter he'd be able to afford the odd night in cheap lodgings. As far as his quest went, six weeks was nothing when he considered that Duggie Smilie had gone to ground over eighteen years ago. In reality time spent here wasn't going to make much difference. An idea presented itself.

'Give me the job and I'll do yous a deal.'

Taffy thrust the piece of flattened metal back into the furnace. 'I ain't in the market for deals,' he replied flatly.

'I think you'll like this one.'

Taffy withdrew the metal and turned to face him. 'All right, I'm listening.'

'I'll work like a navvy, that I promise yous. All hours if yous want. Yous give me somewhere to sleep, three decent meals and a shilling or two for a pint on a Friday. The rest of my wages yous pay me when the job's finished. If I don't work out or I leave, you've lost nothing.'

The blacksmith stared at him thoughtfully then nodded. 'Seems fair to me. Okay, done.' He walked over to Ben and extended a large hand. 'You can start right now.'

Several days later Tilda was shocked to see Ben beavering away as she walked past the blacksmith's. She stopped for a moment and watched him before continuing on her way. She was pleased he had found work, everyone deserved the chance to earn some money. She just hoped the blacksmith had locked any valuables away.

On Christmas Day, dressed in the new blue dress which she had carefully altered, Tilda sat down to eat a solitary dinner, her father snoring loudly on his shakedown at the other side of the room. Christmas Day was no different from any other to him and his present, wrapped in a piece of old newspaper, lay unopened at the side of the fireplace. There was no evidence of anything for Tilda but then she hadn't expected there to be.

Her dinner consisted of a small piece of oxtail, boiled potatoes and green cabbage. Once it was eaten, she toasted the air with a mugful of water.

'Happy Christmas, Tilda,' she said softly.

She stared wistfully into space as a picture of Eustace opening his present filled her mind. She wished she could have been there to witness the event. If his joy was anything as much as he had shown on receiving the gift-wrapped parcel, with her stern warning that it was not to be opened until Christmas morning, he would be ecstatic. He had taken the parcel from her and stared at it for several seconds before rushing to her and hugging her fiercely.

'Ahh, Tilda thanks, thanks! I don't care what it is, I'll treasure it forever.'

Love for the little boy had filled her being. She had smiled her pleasure, kissing the top of his head. And then surprise had filled her own face as Eustace had delved inside his pocket and thrust something towards her.

'It ain't much, Tilda, but I want you to 'ave it.'

It was a picture ripped from a magazine advertisement for a holiday. It showed a train puffing its way through the countryside, people hanging out of the windows waving.

'I'm gonna go on a train one day, Tilda. I'm gonna go and see the world.'

'I believe you will,' she said, smiling with conviction. 'And you'll write to me from all those faraway places, won't you Eustace?'

His brow had furrowed deeply. 'No, I won't write.'

She frowned too, hurt. 'You won't?'

'No, 'cos you'll be with me. I ain't going nowhere without you, Tilda.'

She'd smiled broadly, eyes tender. 'We'll see, young man, we'll see.'

Her father grunted loudly and turned over, and as she looked across at him the episode with Eustace was abruptly wiped from her mind. Sighing deeply, she placed her elbows on the table and rested her chin in her hands. In just over a week's time a new year would dawn and she wondered if 1925 would treat her better than any other she had lived through.

Chapter Seven

Tilda was feeling justifiably pleased with herself. She had just purchased some seed for the garden. At home, in a box in the back room where her father never ventured, she'd carefully stored cabbage, turnip and carrot seeds, and the parsnip ones she had just bought she would now place alongside them. Next week, provided she made enough money at the market, she was going to see a local farmer to buy a pile of manure. She smiled to herself. Bit by bit her plans were coming to fruition.

For a mid-winter's day the weather was surprisingly mild and the watery sun had brought quite a few people out. Tilda was wearing her new blue dress and had washed her long dark hair in rainwater from the tub outside, brushed it until it shone like silk, then knotted it at the back. She felt good; in fact could not remember ever before feeling like this. Maybe it was the dress or maybe it was the fact that she felt she was actually in the process of achieving something worthwhile.

She stepped lightly towards the village green, swinging her basket on her arm. The church bells rang loudly and she smiled. One of the Adkinson girls was getting married and Tilda was going to watch the proceedings over the wall. She was looking forward to it, and to seeing many of the villagers dressed in their best. The bride was a pretty young girl, the groom a handsome young man, and she couldn't wait to witness their joy as they stepped from the vestry after taking their vows.

Suddenly her steps slowed and her joy was replaced by anger. Marching towards her, long skirt flapping, was Mildred Bilson. Several feet behind her, Eustace was struggling to carry a sack on his back. It looked heavy, far too heavy for a little lad of his age to contend with.

Tilda fought the urge to rush over to Mildred, give her a piece of her mind and make her carry the sack, or at the least share the burden with her nephew. But she dare not. The aftermath for Eustace would far outweigh any pleasure to be gained from putting Mildred Bilson in her place.

Mildred stopped and turned abruptly. 'Get a move on,' she barked at Eustace. 'We ain't got all day.'

Tilda watched helplessly as he flinched, thinking his aunt was going to strike him, but then realised, as did Tilda, that Mildred would never do that in the open where people could see her. Actions of that nature were kept for behind closed doors. Instead she grabbed his arm and yanked him hard. 'Come on, I said.'

As they approached Tilda pretended to search through her basket. As Eustace spotted her, his eyes lit up and his mouth opened to address her. Her heart thumped rapidly, knowing his innocent acknowledgement would betray their friendship. She gave a quick shake of her head and glared at him in warning. Thankfully he quickly realised the predicament he was just about to get them both into. His mouth snapped shut, his head bowed and he passed her by. Luckily for them both Mildred noticed nothing amiss.

As they turned and disappeared down an alleyway between the shops, Tilda sighed heavily. The incident had pained her deeply and she knew without doubt that the feeling she was experiencing would be shared by Eustace. It was a dreadful thing, she thought, that two people who held such a high regard for one another should have to hide their friendship in this way. It wasn't fair.

After taking several deep breaths she continued on her way.

By the time she got to a good vantage point by the church wall a small crowd of village women had gathered also to watch the proceedings. Standing several yards away, Tilda thought wistfully how nice it would have been to be invited to join them and be included in the friendly gossip. Putting her basket down, she leaned her arms on top of the wall and fixed her eyes on the vestry door, waiting for the young couple to emerge.

By village standards this wedding was a grand affair. The father of the bride, a brewery drayman, must have saved all his life to give his daughter such a send off, Tilda mused knowing his wage couldn't have been a high one. A horse and carriage, decked out in ribbons and winter greenery, stood patiently waiting to take the couple back to the wedding feast, and he'd even gone to the trouble of paying the local chimney sweep to put in an appearance to bring the couple good luck. Tilda smiled. The sweep looked funny, hovering by the church door, a brush several feet taller than himself positioned across his shoulder and wobbling precariously. Several late arrivals gave him and his sooty brush a very wide berth.

After they'd waited for quite a while a few of the family finally emerged. The mother and father of the bride checked around to make sure all was in order before the bride and groom came out. Mrs Adkinson smiled proudly over at the gathering by the wall, nodding a greeting. Her gaze travelled round before coming to rest on Tilda. Her smile faded. Beckoning her husband over, she spoke to him at length. He looked across. His wife then gave him a hefty push and he strode towards Tilda across the grass.

As he approached he nodded and smiled at the people close

by, then stopping several feet short of the wall, whipped off his hat and ran his hand across his slicked down hair. 'Mornin',' he said gruffly, looking over Tilda's left shoulder.

She turned and looked behind her, thinking he was addressing someone there. There was no one and she turned back, pleasurably surprised at the thought that Mr Adkinson, with all his other important duties, had taken the trouble to walk across and pass the time of day with her. A broad smile lit up her face. 'Good morning to you too. Lovely day for a wedding.'

His eyes travelled upwards and studied the sky. 'Yes, yes, it is that. Lovely day.' His gaze fixed upon her and he took a deep breath. 'Shouldn't you be getting home then?'

Her smile slowly faded and she looked puzzled. 'Sorry?'

'I said, shouldn't you be getting off home?'

'Home! Well, yes, after I've watched the wedding.'

He pursed his lips and leaned closer. 'Go home now, Tilda, there's a good girl. This ain't the place for the likes of you today.'

She stepped back in shock. 'The likes of me?' she whispered.

He sniffed in exasperation, took several steps forward and put his hand on the wall, leaning over. 'I don't want no trouble, Tilda.'

'Trouble?' she said, aghast. 'I'm not causing any trouble, Mr Adkinson. I'm only watching the wedding.'

He pressed his hat back on his head and clasped his hands tightly. 'I ain't bothered meself but it's the wife, see.' He rocked uncomfortably on his feet. 'She . . . er . . .' He scratched his ear. 'Well, she's got it into her head that you being here will bring ill fortune, and we don't want that, do we? Not today. My daughter needs all the luck she can get, marrying that Jack the Lad, believe me.'

Tilda's jaw dropped in shock. 'I would bring bad luck? But I don't understand.'

He stared at the ground intently. 'Me wife reckons you must 'ave been born under an unlucky star and she don't wanna take no chances.' He took a deep breath and raised his head. 'Well, you've only got ter look at yer, Tilda. The good Lord must have had a day off when you were created.' He leaned over and patted her hand. 'I don't mean to be unkind, really I don't, but it's the wife, see. This wedding's got her all het up and if anything goes wrong...'

'It'll be my fault,' Tilda cut in, swallowing hard to rid herself of the lump that was forming in her throat. 'That's what you were going to say, wasn't it?' She fought to stem the flood of tears that threatened.

He stared at her pityingly. 'Well, you don't seem to have much luck, do you, Tilda, so me wife must be right.'

She raised her chin defiantly. 'Yes, she must, mustn't she, Mr Adkinson? If Mrs Adkinson says my presence is a bad omen then she must be believed.'

'Now there's no need for that,' he said crossly. 'You're just making matters worse. It is in your own best interests to leave, really it is.'

'My interests? And how would you know anything about my interests, Mr Adkinson? You don't know me so how could you? To the likes of you I'm just a plain deformed woman who lives in a hovel with her crippled father. I've no feelings, have I? You can say and treat me just as you like because to you it doesn't matter.' She grabbed her basket. 'Don't you fret, Mr Adkinson, I'm going. After all, I wouldn't want your wife having to suffer agonies in case I brought bad luck. I wouldn't sleep soundly.'

'You're looking nice today, Miss Penny. New dress?'

Both engrossed, neither had seen Ben approach from behind a gravestone. He unexpectedly winked at Tilda and then fixed his gaze on Mr Adkinson.

'Ah, just the man I want to see. Can yous spare me a minute?' Without waiting for an answer, he addressed Tilda across the wall. 'And I'd like to speak to yous as well. I won't keep you a minute. What I have to say to Mr Adkinson won't take long.'

'I can't, I'm sorry,' she said urgently. 'I've got to get home.' The last thing she wanted to do was hang around here.

'No. Please wait. I'll nae be a minute, I promise yous.' He took a bewildered Mr Adkinson's arm and firmly led him out of earshot. Tilda, fighting tears, looked on wondering what he could possibly want with her.

Tucked well behind a large gravestone, Ben let go of the older man's arm and faced him. 'Mr Adkinson, isn't it?'

He puffed out his chest importantly. 'Yes, that's me. What can I do for you, sonny? And yer'd better make it quick, I've a wedding to get back to.'

'Nothing.'

'Nothing!'

Ben's smile vanished as his eyes narrowed menacingly. 'I just wanted yous to know that I heard every word yous said to Miss Penny and I didn't like what I was hearing.' He thrust forward his face. 'Who the hell d'yous think you are, yous mealy-mouthed bastard? That poor girl's got enough on her plate without yous rubbing things in. She ain't a dog, yous know, she's a person. She deserves the same respect as yous gave that fat old bag without the teeth who's standing by the gate. Yous haven't asked her to move on, have yous? Yous stood talking to her early on. And dinnae deny it 'cos I saw yous as I was working this morning. Miss Penny's only doing the same as her, watching the wedding. What harm is there in that, eh?'

Mr Adkinson bristled indignantly. 'Now you look 'ere, sonny. You gotta understand, 'tain't me, it's the wife . . .'

'Oh, I see,' Ben cut in. 'Always do the wife's bidding, do yous?' He shook his head in disgust. 'Meself, I cannae stomach a man who's under the thumb. Do everything she says, do yous? If she asked yous to jump in front of a train, would yous do that?'

'No, 'course not.'

'I didn't think so.' Ben's voice lowered menacingly. 'But yous'd upset a defenceless girl who's never done a day's harm to anyone – and all because your wife insists.'

Mr Adkinson took a stance. 'Now you look here, this ain't nothing to do with you. And if you've got any sense, you'll keep yer nose out.'

'You're right there, it ain't nothing to do with me. But I'm making it my business. I dinnae like seeing innocent people bullied by bigots like you.'

'Who are you calling a bloody bigot? Damned foreigner, coming down here like yer own the place! You should get back where yer belong and stay there.'

'Oh, should I now?' Ben thrust his face even closer. 'A pity yous English never did that instead of swarming across our lands, raping our women and killing anything that moved.' He stabbed a finger in Adkinson's chest. 'You had guns, we Scots only had our bare hands. Unfair advantage, wouldn't yous say? Just the same as now with yous throwing your weight around bullying that poor girl. Well, I'm not going to let yous, mister. Say another word to her and you'll have me to deal with. And be warned, I ain't nice when I'm roused.'

Mr Adkinson's face turned purple. 'Is that a threat?'

'Oh, yes,' Ben replied matter-of-factly. 'Most definitely.'

'Oh!' the man exclaimed, shocked, his purple tinge fading rapidly. He glanced around anxiously, not sure what to do next. At heart he was a coward, and what was worse, he knew the young man facing him knew it too. 'I ... er ... best get off. The wife ... she'll ... um ... be wondering where I've got to.'

Ben forced himself not to laugh. 'Good idea. I'm going to join Miss Penny and enjoy the rest of the wedding. Yous don't mind, do yous?'

Mr Adkinson gawped, a vision of his wife springing to mind. He didn't know what terrified him the most: Ben's threat or his wife's wrath for failing to do her bidding. 'Er ... no ... no, not at all,' he stuttered, hurrying away as fast as his legs would carry him.

'Nice doing business with yous, Mr Adkinson,' Ben shouted after him, and couldn't resist adding, 'Give my best to your wife.'

As he approached Tilda the church clock struck one and he glanced up at it sharply. 'Oh, God, I'm late. I'd best hurry or I'll get the sack.'

He made to hurry off but Tilda stopped him. 'Just a minute. What did you want to see me about?'

He looked at her blankly. 'Eh?'

She exhaled, annoyed. 'You asked me to wait.'

'Did I? Oh!' He ran his fingers through his thick red hair and blew out his cheeks, his mind filled with the promise he'd made to Taffy. Hard work and no sloppiness, and that meant being on time. If he didn't hurry his promise would be broken, and his pay, something he'd worked hard for the last five weeks, would be in jeopardy. 'I can't remember what I wanted yous for.' He shrugged his shoulders. 'Sorry. Look, I've got to go. See yous.'

Stunned, Tilda's jaw dropped. She felt a complete idiot but raised her chin defiantly. After all, what else could she expect from a man who was nothing more than a thief?

She turned her head and looked across towards the church. The congregation, including the bride and groom, were crowded together, having their photograph taken. From what Tilda could see, the bride did look pretty. So when all was said and done, she'd seen what she'd come to see.

Oh, to hell with Mr Adkinson and his wife. For someone who had suffered far worse taunts from her father, Mr Adkinson's words had been minor in comparison, nothing she hadn't heard before. With a great effort she forced the whole incident to the back of her mind. She would not let it upset her any more. She now had a purpose in life and would concentrate on that. Turning on her heel, she straightened her back and hurried off down the path.

Lying in bed later that night, Ben pulled the covers under his chin and snuggled down. He was bone tired, desperate to sleep. And it was well-earned sleep he'd be getting when it finally washed over him. The blacksmith was certainly getting his money's worth out of Ben McCraven and he knew it. But Ben didn't mind. Truth be told he was enjoying work with the big Welsh giant. He was a fair man and expected Ben to labour only as hard as he himself did. And the home comforts were welcome. Mrs Taff, as Ben called her, was a jolly woman, a good plain cook who kept her house spotless. There were always clean sheets for his bed at the end of the week.

He'd miss all this when he left. Ben stretched his long legs and gave a long loud yawn. In two days' time his job here would be finished and in a way that suited him fine. He found, much to his annoyance, that he was getting used to being in one place, beginning to feel quite settled in fact, and it had been a struggle to refuse an offer of permanent work when Taffy had approached him with it. Staying in any place was not on his agenda. Now he had money in his pocket to see him through the rest of the winter his search for Duggie Smilie could be resumed. Getting on with the living of his life would begin only after his main priority was resolved to his satisfaction.

As he dozed, relaxed and warm on the verge of deep slumber, a picture of Tilda unexpectedly filled his mind and remorse pricked his conscience. He hadn't given the girl another thought since the incident earlier that day, and if he was truthful, in his own way he had treated her as badly as Adkinson by asking her to wait and then leaving her flat to rush back to work. But then, he assured himself, he'd had no choice, and besides he'd only asked her to wait so she would see the rest of the wedding once he'd put that bigot in his place. And he'd achieved that all right.

He tossed and turned for several moments, trying to block thoughts of Tilda, but they refused to budge. He fumed inwardly as he settled himself unsuccessfully for the umpteenth time. For a girl he couldn't give a damn about, she was certainly occupying enough of his energies. It suddenly occurred to him why – he felt sorry for her. After all, she had a lot to put up with in more ways than one. He raised himself and plumped up his pillow then tried again to get comfortable. It was no good feeling sorry for her. It wasn't in his power to do anything for her, even if he wanted to. Which he didn't. In two days he would be leaving.

A thought suddenly struck him. There *was* something he could do. Taffy had a stack of old horseshoes in his yard. He'd select a good one, give it a bit of a spit and polish, and take it to her. Might just bring the girl some luck. Well, you never know, he thought. Stranger things have happened.

Sleep took him there and then, before he knew it, it was time to get up.

Chapter Eight

'Please don't hit me, Auntie, Please, please!' Eustace begged, cowering in the corner, his thin arms wrapped around his head for protection.

Mildred Bilson loomed over him, her hand with its long claw-like fingers raised ready to strike. 'Hit you? I'll knock you into next week, you thief!'

She brought her hand down hard across his back, the force of it knocking his head into the sharp corner of the wall. He yelped in agony, a lump the size of an egg forming on his brow.

He fought for breath. 'I wasn't thieving, Auntie. Honest I wasn't. I was 'ungry.'

'You're supposed to be hungry. That was what the punishment was all about. I warned you, if you didn't study the Bible I'd punish you. And you never did, did you? You never read one word. You deliberately defied me.'

'But I did, Auntie. I read it all.' He took several sobbing breaths. 'I don't understand it. And you ask such difficult questions.'

'Difficult,' she spat. 'A two year old with half a brain would understand what the Lord meant when he said, "Judge not, that ye be not judged. For with what judgement ye judge, ye shall be judged: and with what measure ye mete, it shall be measured to you again." But you . . .' She narrowed her beady eyes menacingly and bared her tiny sharp teeth. 'You haven't got a brain, have you, Eustace. 'Cos you're stupid. A stupid imbecile, that's what you are. You deserved to be punished. Deserve to be flayed alive. A saint, I am, for taking you in. And you repay me by stealing bread from my table. Your mother, God rest her soul, would turn in her grave if she could see how you've turned out. If she wasn't dead already she'd die with shame, she would!'

She stared down at him with loathing as she placed her hand inside her skirt pocket and slowly pulled something out. She dangled it in front of him. 'Where did you get this, Eustace?'

His eyes travelled upward, coming to rest on the object in question. His jaw dropped, throat tightened and his heart thumped rapidly. It was the treasured toy car Tilda had given him for Christmas. It had been hidden safely in his bedroom, only taken out when he was absolutely positive the coast was clear.

'Well, Eustace, answer me. Where did you get it?' She curled her lip. 'I'll tell you shall I?' she continued smugly. 'You stole it, didn't you? Like you stole the bread.' Hand still outstretched, she turned and marched towards the fire. 'Tell me the truth or I'll throw it in.'

'No, Auntie, no!' he shrieked 'It's mine. Honest it is.' He tugged her skirt, eyes raised beseechingly. 'Please don't burn it, please don't.'

'Well, tell me then. Who gave it to you?'

He sank to his knees defeated. He could not betray Tilda. His love and respect for her would not let him do it. If his aunt learnt of their friendship she would put a stop to it and that he could not bear. He would take any amount of punishment his aunt doled out to keep their secret.

'I . . . I stole it,' he whispered.

Her face darkened angrily. This was not what she wanted to

hear. She had a feeling in her bones that he had a friend somewhere, someone he turned to, someone he regarded very highly. That someone had given him this toy and she meant to find out who this someone was. She had thought of several possibilities which had turned out to be mistaken, had even considered the young doctor's wife who had quickly been discounted. That madam wouldn't give away the drippings off her nose let alone buy presents for an orphaned boy. But regardless, she would get it out of Eustace. And she knew just how.

'Pardon, Eustace, I didn't hear you?'

He raised his head defiantly. 'I stole it,' he shouted. 'I stole it. I STOLE IT.'

'That's what I thought you said.' Her eyes widened maliciously. 'And I don't believe you. Someone gave this to you, didn't they, Eustace? You're going to tell me, boy, and I don't care what it takes. You're going down in the cellar with the demons, and you'll stay down there 'til you do tell me.'

He screamed out in terror. 'Oh, no, Auntie. Please, not the cellar! Not with the demons!'

The corners of her mouth twitched pleasurably as she pointed her long bony finger towards the cellar door. 'Now.'

Eustace pressed himself into the corner. 'No,' he said, shaking his head savagely, eyes bulging in fear. 'No, I'm not goin'. I'm not, I'm not.'

Temper boiling over, she grabbed his shoulder, thrusting her face into his. 'The demons will surely get you this time. They don't like lying little boys. They eat them for breakfast. Cut their gizzard out and fry it with onions.' She licked her lips. 'Mmmm, lovely.'

She dragged him, screaming hysterically, towards the cellar door and yanked it open. An airless dank musty smell immediately emanated from it and the pitch black well below loomed frighteningly. She abruptly halted him at the top of the stairs and, with her hand on the back of his head, forced him to look down.

'They're waiting for you,' she sang sweetly.

He let out a piercing scream and grabbed hold of the door frame, clutching it tightly.

Mildred gave a low cackle. 'That won't save you, boy.'

She began to prise his fingers from the wood, slowly and deliberately prolonging his agony.

'Please, Auntie, please,' he begged. 'Nobody gave me it, I stole it, honest I did.'

'Liar,' she hissed.

Successfully prising one hand free, which she hooked tightly under her own armpit, she began on the other. Desperate, Eustace kicked out with his foot and caught her hard on her bony shin. Startled by his attack and the resulting pain, she let go of him, stepping backwards.

'You little . . .'

The dull thud as she fell down the stairs echoed around the house and lingered long after she had reached the bottom.

Eustace, wide-eyed in horror, his jaw gaping, stared blindly down into the inky blackness below.

'Have you heard the news?'

Tilda turned her head and looked absently at Molly. 'Pardon?'

'I said, have you . . .' Molly tutted loudly. 'You ain't hearing a word I'm saying, a' you? You're thinking about that garden o' yours.'

Tilda smiled sheepishly. In truth she had been thinking of Ben McCraven and how surprising it was that he was still working for Taffy Jones. She would have gambled precious money on either Ben's having disappeared weeks ago, along with Taffy's belongings, or else being caught with his hands full of something they shouldn't and being carted off to jail. Still, she supposed, there was time. Then inwardly she scolded herself. Why she should be thinking of a man she didn't like or trust was beyond her reasoning when she had better things to occupy her mind. As Molly had said, her garden for one.

'Sorry, Molly, you're right, I was thinking of my garden,' she fibbed. 'I can't wait for it to warm up a bit more and then start sowing some seed.'

'Got you fair excited has that garden. I've got to say, Tilda, I do admire you.'

Her eyebrows rose in surprise. 'You do?'

'Why, yes.' Molly's attention was taken by a customer. 'Wadda yer mean, it ain't worth two bob? Good quality wool that skirt is. Came from a good home, I can assure you.' She snatched the skirt off the customer and plonked it back with all the other items she had for sale. 'I'll thank you not to manhandle goods you've no intention of buying.' The customer scowled and indignantly marched off and Molly turned her attention back to Tilda. 'Bloody cheek. Some folks want stuff for nothing. Now what was I saying. I can't ruddy remember. Oh, I know what I was going to tell you. My Eric – yer know, my eldest lad – well, he's landed some work at a farm and I've asked him to see if he can scrounge some seed potatoes for you, and anything else he can put his hands on.'

Tilda's eyes lit up, delighted. 'Oh, Molly, thank you.'

'Well, don't get yer hopes up, just in case. But Eric'll do his best. Now there was something else . . .' She grimaced in thought. 'Oh, yes.' Her face lit up in excitement. 'Have you heard the news about Mildred Bilson? She fell down the cellar steps and broke her neck.'

Tilda gasped, horrified. 'What! Are you sure?'

''Course I'm bloody sure!' Molly replied, offended, then

grinned wickedly. 'Pardon me for speaking ill of the dead but personally I can't think of a better person for it to happen to. Too full of herself for her own good, that one, and as nasty as they come. I never heard her say a nice word to anyone. 'Course, you know, she never forgave her sister for running off to wed and leaving her to look after the mother. The old gel lived 'til she wa' seventy and a right crotchety old cow she was an' all. Her and Mildred made a fine pair. The sister's husband got killed in the war and then the sister died herself . . . they said it was consumption, but I think it were more like a broken heart. She loved that man to bits. Well suited they were. Shame, innit? But then, that's life for yer. That left Mildred with the boy 'cos there weren't no other relatives. She didn't like that one bit. Had her eye on the new Reverend, see.'

Molly laughed scornfully. 'Well, he weren't interested, but Mildred thought he was. But let's be honest, who in their right mind would have took on an old sour puss like her, even without the lad in tow?' Molly stopped abruptly and stared at Tilda. 'You ain't listening to me, are you?'

'What? Oh, yes. Yes, of course I am, Molly.'

'What was I saying then?'

'Er . . .'

'Thought so.' Molly eyed her curiously. 'What's on your mind?'

'When did all this happen?' Tilda asked anxiously. 'Mildred's death, I mean?'

'Night afore last, so they say. One of her do-gooding cronies raised the alarm yesterday morning. It's reckoned she'd been lying there all night.'

'Yesterday morning!'

'That's right. What you so concerned for? I didn't realise you knew her?'

'I don't. It's Eustace I'm worried for.'

'Eustace? Oh, the boy. What about him?'

'What happened to him, that's what.'

Molly shrugged her shoulders. 'Dunno. 'Spect he's been carted off to the children's home, poor little tyke. Though if you want my opinion, he'll be better off there than he was living with Mildred. Treated him rotten, she did. Everyone knew that.' She eyed Tilda sharply. 'Why, you've gone all white, girl. Feeling ill?'

Tilda's mind whirled frantically, pain for Eustace overwhelming her. The little lad, whom she loved so deeply, had been terrified of his Aunt Mildred, but when all was said and done she was his only kin. Now he had no one. The thought of him being dragged off to the children's home to face God knows what was unbearable, as was the thought that she might never see him again. But more importantly, she knew Eustace would be needing some love and comfort and she was the only one who could give it to him. Her arms ached with longing.

Eyes filling with tears, she grabbed Molly's arm and gripped it tightly. 'Where can I find out where they've taken him to? I must find out, I really must.'

'Eh, calm down,' the older woman ordered. 'You'll give yourself a heart attack, carrying on like that.' She eyed the agitated girl, puzzled. 'What's with you and the boy?'

Tilda took a deep breath. 'He's my friend, Molly,' she said softly. 'I love him.'

'Oh, I see. I'm surprised the beady-eyed Mildred knew nothing of this.'

'If she had've done, she'd have put a stop to it.'

'I've no doubt of that!' Molly said scathingly, then smiled warmly at Tilda. 'Thank God that lad has you as a friend, Tilda, 'cos by Christ he doesn't have much else.' She paused thoughtfully. 'The police'll know.'

'The police!'

'Yeah, they'll know where he's been taken to. Probably organised it in the circumstances. Couldn't leave a little lad of his age to fend for himself. Poor little love.' She looked across the green. 'There's Constable Whatjamacallit now. Go and ask him. No need, he's coming this way.'

Tilda waited anxiously as the constable wandered over.

'Leave this to me,' Molly instructed, and attracted his attention. 'Oy, Constable. Have you got a minute.' she bellowed.

Constable Willets nodded and joined them. 'Morning, ladies. What's the problem?'

'There ain't no problem, Constable. It's information we're after.'

'What sort of information?'

'About Mildred Bilson.'

Constable Willets frowned. 'What about her? Do you know something we don't?'

'Like what?'

He frowned severely. 'So far as the Coroner and we are concerned she fell down the stairs and broke her neck but if you know different . . .'

'No, no, we don't,' Molly interrupted, agitated. 'That's as much as we know. It's the boy we're worried for. What's happened to him?'

Constable Willets pursed his lips. 'We don't know either. He's disappeared. More than likely ran off.' He eyed them both sharply. 'Does either of you know where he is?'

'If we did, Constable, we wouldn't be asking you, now would we?' Molly said sarcastically.

Constable Willets eyed her, annoyed.

'What will happen to him when he's found, Constable?' Tilda asked softly.

He turned to her and rubbed his chin. 'He'll be sent to an orphanage. No other kin that we know of, so there isn't any other option.'

Tilda's heart sank.

A disturbance further down alerted the constable's attention. 'Excuse me, ladies.' He strode off, then stopped and turned back. 'If you do see the lad or hear of his whereabouts, you will inform us?'

'Of course,' Molly assured him, then turned to Tilda and took the girl's arm. 'Well, you got your answer.'

Tilda clasped her hands tightly, her face lined with pain. 'Poor Eustace. He's all on his own. He'll be frightened to death.' She looked questioningly at the older woman. 'Molly, do you think . . .'

'I know what you're going to say,' she interjected. 'Will the authorities let you have him? I don't think so, Tilda lovey. And whether they will or not, one thing's for certain – from what I know of that father of yours, he wouldn't even consider it. So you'd better stop thinking along those lines.'

Tilda swallowed hard and took a deep breath. 'There must be something I can do. The thought of him going into an orphanage . . . Oh, Molly, I can't bear it.'

She patted Tilda's arm affectionately, her face filled with commiseration. 'You've done more than most, Tilda, you've been his friend. Besides, before anyone can do anything he has to be found. And by my reckoning, knowing kids as I do, it won't be long afore he finds his way to you.'

Tilda's eyes widened hopefully. 'Do you think so, Molly?'

'I know so, lovey. You're his friend.' She frowned sternly. 'But be warned. As much as you love that boy, you've got to prepare him for what he's facing, and you have to inform the authorities else you'll be in trouble. A' you listening to me? You're in no position to care for him whether you want to or not.

113

You can hardly feed yourself. Wouldn't be so bad if your father was different, but he ain't, and he ain't likely to change neither.'

Tilda sighed heavily. 'I know you're right, Molly, I also know that wanting to keep him wouldn't be fair on him. My father wouldn't give him a minute's peace. But I can't hand him over to the authorities. I just can't do it.' She raised her head defiantly. 'I can't think straight at the moment. I'm worried to death about him. Maybe once I know he's all right an answer will come.'

Molly smiled wanly. Tilda was fooling herself. There was no alternative. When the lad did turn up, and she had no doubt he would, he would have to be handed over.

Tilda gathered her basket. 'I'm going home, Molly, just in case.'

She nodded in understanding. 'Leave the rest of your stuff with me. I'll see if I can sell it. Give you the money tomorrow.'

Tilda smiled gratefully. 'Thanks, I do appreciate it.'

'Just get off home. Eh, and remember what I said.'

'I will. Ta, Molly.'

Tilda prowled the floor unable to rest. It was growing dark and she was worried to death. In her search for Eustace she had looked in every conceivable place she could think of but had uncovered no sign of the little boy. As the afternoon had worn away worry for his welfare had deepened; now she was sick with fear. For all she knew he had already spent one night in the open. Would his little undernourished body stand another?

Looking out of the window, she scanned the sky. Thick grey clouds hung low. At least there wouldn't be a frost, but heavy rain was a possibility. Absently she rubbed her withered arm. Oh, Eustace, she thought. Where on earth are you?

Across the room her father grunted loudly and turned over on his shakedown. Her head jerked and she stared over at him. As her eyes scanned the length of him, huddled in his bed, his mess of wild matted hair sticking out of the top of the holey blanket that covered him, an overwhelming feeling of hatred filled her and for a moment she wished him dead. The alien feeling shocked her and she shuddered at its intensity.

Over the years this man had said and done some terrible things to her but never before had she felt such loathing towards him. She knew it was because of Eustace. If her father had been a more approachable man the little lad would have headed straight for her comforting arms. As things stood, knowing how he would be received, coming to the cottage was probably the last thing he would do.

Suddenly Eli's hand moved aside the mass of hair, eyes opening rapidly, and he stared across at her unblinkingly. 'What yous staring at, you ugly bitch?' he hissed.

She jumped. 'Nothing, nothing.' She dived towards the fireplace, leaned over the home-made clothes horse full of things she had washed that morning before going to market, haphazardly threw on some logs and swung across the pan, then went across to the table and uncovered the bread. Grabbing up the bread knife, she made to cut several slices for him to have with his soup. For a moment she stared at it, knowing for certain that when she had left that morning for the market over half a loaf had been there; now there was hardly any. Her father must have risen in the day and eaten it and there was no time to make any more.

Behind her she heard the commotion as he rose and began muttering profanities. As she sliced the remains of the bread she screwed up her eyes tightly. Dear God, she prayed, please don't let my father be in one of his dreadful black moods tonight. I don't think I can take it.

He arrived at the table, roughly pulled out a stool and sat himself down. Picking up his spoon, he raised it ready. Hurriedly she filled a bowl and put it in front of him. Without a word he scooped up a spoonful. No sooner had it touched his lips than it was spat out. Angrily his arm swept across the table, sending the bowl and plate of bread flying across the room. The crockery crashed against the wall, the soup splattering.

'It's fucking cold!' he shouted furiously.

Eyes wide in fright, Tilda gasped. 'Oh Dad, I'm sorry, I'm sorry.' She flew towards the fire. 'I'll heat the rest up properly.' Stirring what was left of the soup, she turned to see him rising from the table, unbuckling his worn heavy leather belt. She was in for a beating. Backing away, she eyed him pleadingly. 'No, Dad, no. It was an accident, honest. Please sit down, this won't take a minute.'

He just stared at her, eyes filled with malice.

Suddenly there was a pounding on the door and they both looked across at it.

'Yous expecting someone?' he snarled.

'No, Dad,' she uttered.

The knock came again, louder, more urgent.

Eli grimaced hard and fingered the belt wrapped round his hand. 'Get rid of them,' he hissed. 'And hurry up about it.'

Eyes fixed on her father, Tilda inched her way round the table. On reaching the door, she stood before it and took a deep breath. Slowly she lifted the latch and pulled it open. On seeing who was there her mouth dropped in surprise. She had thought the caller to be a tramp or a traveller looking for directions. Not for an instant had she envisaged it would be Ben McCraven.

She could sense her father's eyes burning into her back, feel his anger at the nerve of someone for daring to knock their door. Of all the times to come calling, Ben McCraven had picked the worst.

'What do you want?' she asked curtly.

At her tone his eyes narrowed. 'I came to give you, this,' he replied gruffly, handing her the horseshoe.

She stared at it, bewildered, unsure what to say.

'I thought it might bring yous luck, but to be honest I wish I never bothered.'

Her face filled with shame. 'I'm sorry. I'm grateful, really I am.' She forced a smile. 'I'll hang it over the fire.'

He turned from her and it was then she noticed he was carrying a bundle and was dressed for the road. 'Are you leaving?'

He turned back and nodded.

'Oh, I see. Well, all the best and thank you for this.'

He smiled. 'I hope it works.'

As he strode down the path she suddenly envied Ben his freedom and wished wholeheartedly she could just turn her back on everything and walk away as he was doing. She would have given anything not to have to go back inside, but choices were not hers for the making. Clutching the horseshoe, she backed into the cottage and closed the door. Slowly she turned to face her father. He was standing as she had left him. Eyes fixed rigidly upon her, he was rubbing his hand up and down the belt.

'Yous should have asked him in.'

His icy tone made her shudder and she flattened herself against the door, waiting for the onslaught to erupt.

'So it's a fancy man yous have now is it? What is he, blind or something? And bringing yous presents. Payment for favours, I take it?'

Her face fell, horrified. 'No, Dad, it's not. It's just an old horseshoe he thought might bring me luck. How could you think that?'

'How could I?' He spat disgustedly. 'Easy. Look at yous, girl.

No man in their right mind is gonna give yous something for nothing.' He threw back his head. 'I've bred a whore,' he bellowed. 'Go on, admit it, you trollop.' Before she could move he had lunged across to her and grabbed her by the hair, forcing her head backwards. 'Yous telling me that bloke came all the way oot here just to give yous that. Now tell me the truth. Who is he? If yers not giving out favours, what did he want?'

Her terrified eyes looked up into his. 'He wanted nothing. He's just ... just a man I met in the village. He's not even a friend. Honestly, Dad, it's the truth I'm telling.'

His eyes grew suspicious as realisation suddenly dawned. He'd seen that man before. He couldn't remember where but just knew that he had. He pulled her hair even harder and she yelped out in pain. 'He has been here. I've seen him, I know I have.' He let go of her and knocked her to the floor. Raising his hand, he brought the belt down heavily upon her back. She screamed out in agony. 'How many more men yous had here?' He kicked out his wooden stump, catching her hard near her ribs. 'I asked a question. Answer me, damn it.'

Writhing on the floor, Tilda gasped for breath. 'None. Believe me, Dad. No one comes here.'

As she tried to rise a movement across the room caught her eye. The door at the back was opening and in the widening space a small figure appeared. It was Eustace. She froze, mixed emotions racing through her. Elation that Eustace was safe, but terror of her father discovering he was there. In the mood he was in there was no telling what he would do. Before she could gesture a warning to the little boy he had run towards the fireplace, picked up a log from the stack at the side and was heading for Eli, murder in his eyes.

Tilda screamed out: 'No, Eustace. NOOOO!'

Eli spun round and instinctively his arm shot out. The blow caught Eustace under his chin, lifting him bodily. He crashed against the far wall and slithered down, unconscious.

Tilda gave an agonised wail. Before she could move she felt the weight of Eli's stump pinning her down.

'No one comes here, eh,' he spat at her, incensed. 'So who the fuck's that?' Removing his wooden stump, he bent down, grabbed her by the shoulders and hauled her up. He stuck the hand with the belt wrapped round it under her chin, forcing her head back. 'So who the hell is he?'

'Eustace.' she uttered, terrified. 'Eustace Sprocket.'

'What's he doing here?'

'He's upset. His . . . his auntie's just died. He's just come to see me, that's all.'

Eli grinned mockingly. 'Oh, what a shame.' He shook her hard, eyes darkening in fury. 'No one comes here,' he shrieked. 'No one, are yous listening? And that includes yer men friends.'

She nodded vigorously. 'Yes, Dad, yes. But I've told you, Ben was only . . .'

'Oh, Ben now, is it.' He grabbed hold of her chin and squeezed it tightly. 'I thought yous didn't know him?'

She yelped in agony. 'I don't. Not like you're thinking.' Her mind raced frantically. She needed to get to Eustace and see how hurt he was. She needed to get her father out of the cottage before any more damage was done. 'Ben came here by chance. He was looking for work and I told him to try the blacksmith. The horseshoe was by way of thanks, that's all.'

'Liar.'

'It's the truth, Dad. If you don't believe me go and ask Mr Jones if Ben McCraven . . .'

She got no further. The look of horror that filled his eyes froze her rigid.

'McCraven?' he rasped, jaw gaping. 'Did you say . . . McCraven?'

119

Bewildered, she nodded.

Face draining of colour alarmingly, he released his grip and thrust her from him, a wail of terror issued forth. Tilda watched, confused, as he backed away from her, arm out-stretched, wagging an accusatory finger. 'Yous . . . yous . . .' He came upon the table, turned abruptly, and with one furious heave upended it. The table landed on the stone floor and disintegrated. Arms flailing wildly, he caught the edge of the clothes horse which tipped towards the fire. The items upon it ignited immediately.

Tilda screamed in terror as flames soared outwards and upwards and old timber from the shattered table caught light. Black smoke billowed forth and through the smoke advanced her father. He was holding a blazing log he had scooped up from the fire and waving it wildly. 'You bitch, you bitch!' he screamed hysterically, seemingly oblivious of the fire raging round him.

All Tilda could think of was Eustace. She had to get to him. Mustering all her strength, she dropped to her knees and skirted the walls. Smoke filled her lungs and she started to choke.

Blinded, she groped along until thankfully she came upon him. 'Eustace,' she whispered urgently, patting his face. 'Eustace, Eustace.'

He gave no response and for a terrified moment she thought he was dead, then he groaned.

'Oh, thank God,' she uttered.

The heat from the flames was intensifying now and all she could think of was getting out before they all perished. There was a loud crash from somewhere near the door. Part of the ceiling had come down. The way forward was blocked. Suddenly she remembered the room at the back and its tiny window. Hooking her arm around Eustace, inch by inch she dragged him towards it, conscious that time was of the essence. Not only was the cottage going up like dry paper, her father was getting closer by the second. Above the noise of the fire she could hear his stump slamming against the slabs in his search for her. Both things terrified her to near insensibility.

On reaching the window, she laid Eustace carefully on the floor and tried to ease the frame up. Blind panic filled her. It was stuck. Her eyes darted round as she tried to remember what was in this room that she could use to force it open. Suddenly the smoke parted for an instant and in the doorway loomed Eli. Behind him flames licked furiously. He spotted her at that second and their eyes locked. The hatred in his made her shudder.

He thrust the burning log in her direction. 'There yous are, you bitch. I'm gonna kill yous.'

Wafting smoke closed the gap and in fear for her life Tilda spun back to face the window. She screamed out in fright at the sight of a grotesque face pressed against it. Then it was gone to be replaced by a hand waving a warning for her to move aside. Without further thought she did so. As the window smashed, a rush of air hit her and she gasped for breath. Through a cloud of billowing black smoke a head popped through the aperture.

Tilda stared in astonishment. 'Ben...'

'Hey, there's no time for pleasantries. Give me your hands and I'll pull yous through. Just watch for the glass.'

She shook her head. 'Eustace first.'

Disappearing from view, she bent down and heaved up the unconscious little boy.

Ben stared at him, shocked. 'Who the hell... That's the boy they're all looking for. Oh, God!' Leaning through the window, he hooked his arms under Eustace's armpits. 'Lift his legs so we can ease him through. If I drag him he'll be cut to pieces.'

Coughing and spluttering, Tilda hurriedly obeyed. Safely outside, Ben ran and placed the boy at a safe distance then returned for Tilda. She was already half out of the window, deep gouges on both leg and arm bleeding profusely where she had caught some jagged glass.

'Come on, come on,' he cried urgently, grabbing her waist. 'The whole place is going to go up in a minute.

'I'm doing my best,' she shouted, wrenching at her skirt which had caught on a nail. Ben leaned through, ripped it free and yanked her out. They both landed heavily on the ground. Jumping up, he grabbed the stunned girl's arm and half dragged, half carried her a safe distance away. As they collapsed, panting for breath, a loud crash resounded as the cottage disintegrated, flames spiralling upwards.

She struggled to rise. 'My father,' she gasped. 'My father's inside.'

Ben's face fell, horrified. It was too late for any one to escape. 'He might have got out the other way . . .'

'But he was behind me, he couldn't have.' She scrambled her way upright, voice rising hysterically. 'He's still in there. I've got to get him!'

Jumping up, he grabbed her, restraining her forcibly. 'It's too late. Go back and you'll be killed yoursel'.' As she struggled against him to break free, he slapped her face hard. 'It's too late, I tell yous.'

Stunned, she slowly turned and looked across at the blazing cottage. Legs buckling, she slumped to the ground, sobbing hysterically.

He stared down at her helplessly.

Just then sounds reached their ears.

'It'll be the villagers,' he announced.

She froze then eyed him frantically. 'Eustace. Oh my God, please don't let them find Eustace. They'll send him away.

'Tilda . . .'

She grabbed hold of his arm, gripping it tightly. 'Please, Ben please. Help me hide him while I think what to do.'

The shouts were getting closer. Without further ado he scooped the unconscious child and ran off into the woods.

Tilda's eyes jerked open and for a moment she stared around, alarmed, wondering where she was. Dawn was just breaking. The air was sharp and cold and she shuddered. Suddenly memories of a few hours before flooded back and her whole body sagged.

The villagers had done what they could but nothing could be salvaged and as soon as was possible the remains of her father had been taken away and the problem of his burial lifted from her shoulders. It was known she had no money to bury him so the Parish would do the honours. Nobody seemed surprised by the fire; even Constable Willets when he had finally arrived took it for granted Eli Penny had started the blaze in one of his drunken rages, and consequently Tilda was hardly questioned on the matter. Offers of shelter for the rest of the night were pressed upon herself and Ben but politely declined. Tilda was relieved that if anyone thought it odd, they didn't bother to question this.

Slowly she raised her head and looked over to what remained of her home. Smoke still spiralled up from smouldering timbers. Piles of debris lay scattered. Black ashes wafted silently upwards. She stared at it all, numbed. Her past and her future lay ruined before her. The only things she had left were the threadbare clothes on her back.

Casting down her eyes, she stared at the grass. Something caught her eye and she leaned over and picked it up. It was the horseshoe Ben had given her. The intensity of the heat had caused it to buckle out of shape. Distractedly she rubbed the charred surface over the damp grass then stared at it forlornly. Some luck it had brought her. Without thinking, she pushed it into her skirt pocket.

She felt a hand on her shoulder and jumped.

'How's the lad?'

Her eyes went to Eustace, nestling in her lap. 'He's still sleeping.'

'Best thing for him. Just thank God he never came to whilst the villagers were here or yous would've had a lot of explaining to do.' He squatted down on his haunches beside her. 'Have yous made up your mind what you're going to do with him yet?'

She shut her eyes tightly and shook her head. 'I'll die before they take him from me.'

He stared at her thoughtfully then turned and studied the ruins. 'I can't see how yous can care for him, Tilda.' He bent down and picked up a brown paper bag. 'I walked down to the village and got yous some bread and milk.'

She looked at the bags then up at him gratefully. 'You did that for me? Thank you,' she uttered.

'Well, I thought the lad would be hungry.' He ran his fingers through his dishevelled hair. 'Look, I have to be going. I've a few miles I want to cover today.'

'Oh, yes, of course,' she said hurriedly. 'You must get going.'

'You'll be all right?'

She forced a smile. 'Yes. We'll be fine. Thank you again for what you've done.'

He shrugged his shoulders. 'I only did what anyone would do. Though I'm not sure I did right in hiding Eustace ... But, well, I'm sure you'll do what's best for the lad.'

'I will,' she said with conviction.

He picked up his bundle. 'Best of luck.'

She nodded. 'And you.'

She watched as he walked down the path, rounded a bend and disappeared from view. Then suddenly the silence of the woods and the hopelessness of her situation crowded in on her. She looked down at Eustace and a tear rolled down her cheek. Oh, God what am I to do? she thought. At this moment in time she had no answers.

Eustace stirred and opened his eyes. He looked up at her, confused.

'It's all right, sweetheart,' she whispered, tenderly stroking his face. 'I'm here.' The bruise on his chin where her father had hit him was blackening rapidly. 'Does anything hurt?'

He grimaced. 'Only me face. And me leg a bit.' He looked at her. 'What happened?' Suddenly his face clouded over and he struggled from her hold, jumping up. 'I killed her! Oh, Tilda, I killed me auntie.'

Her face paled alarmingly. Struggling to her knees, she pulled him protectively towards her. 'No, you didn't, Eustace, you didn't. She fell down the steps.'

Eyes streaming with tears, he pulled back from her. 'I did, I tell you, I did! I kicked her and she fell. It's my fault she's dead.'

Grabbing his arms, she gripped him tightly. 'Why did you kick her, Eustace? Why?'

He stared at her blankly.

'Answer me? Why did you kick her? What was she doing to you?'

He shuddered, choking back sobs. 'I'd been bad. She was punishing me.'

'How was she punishing you?'

'She . . . she was . . . going to lock me in the cellar. She knows I hate the dark, Tilda. She knows how much it scares me. She said the demons would eat my gizzard. I didn't want to go. I said I'd be good but she wouldn't listen. She was 'urting me, Tilda.'

He fell against her, sobbing hysterically. Cradling him tightly, a wave of sadness flooded through her and not for the first time she asked herself how Mildred could have treated her nephew so badly.

'You didn't kill her, Eustace,' she whispered. 'When you kicked her you were protecting yourself. She should not have tried to lock you in the cellar. She knew you hated the dark. And it wasn't your fault she fell. A kick from a little boy like you wouldn't be enough to make her fall.'

He shuddered against her. 'Wouldn't ... wouldn't it?'

'Sweetheart, no. She must have slipped just after you kicked her.'

He pulled back from her. 'Do yer think so?'

She smiled warmly. 'I know so,' she lied.

In fact she knew, but would never tell Eustace, that the shock of his retaliation must have caught Mildred unawares and resulted in her death. Surely she couldn't have expected the boy to take so harsh a punishment willingly? If she had, she'd been a fool.

'I was ever so worried about you,' said Tilda.

'Were yer?'

'I was wondering where you were.'

'I hid in your back room. It was so cold. I wanted to tell you I was there, but I daren't in case your dad catched me.' His face fell guiltily. 'I ate your bread. I was 'ungry.'

'Oh, it was you, was it? I'm glad.'

His face lit up in surprise. 'You are? But I didn't ask.'

'Eustace you didn't need to. Whatever I've got is yours, you know that.' She hugged him tightly then held him at arm's length, her face filled with concern. 'Do you remember what happened last night?'

He stared at her thoughtfully then shook his head. 'No. But I did dream that yer dad was hitting yer. I tried to save you ... but I don't remember anythin' else.'

'Oh, Eustace. My knight in shining armour, eh?'

She smiled at him tenderly, grateful she hadn't to explain in detail the dreadful events of last night. She just told him as briefly as she could of the accident with the clothes horse, the resulting inferno and how Ben had rescued them. At this stage she did not mention her father and thankfully Eustace didn't ask about him.

Without a word he rose, walked towards the ruins and stared at them for several long moments. Finally he walked back to her and sat down.

'The cottage burned down while I was sleeping?'

She nodded.

'Oh, Tilda,' he whispered, distressed. 'That was your 'ome. What are you going ter do?'

She breathed deeply. 'I don't know yet.'

They sat in silence for several moments.

'Tilda?'

She turned to face him. 'Yes.'

'Will I have to go in an orphanage?'

She caught hold of his hand and squeezed it tightly, unable to answer. What other alternative had she to offer? Love did not put food in his mouth, clothes on his back or a roof over his head, as much as she desperately wished it would. She had nothing on which to build. She'd be lucky if she herself even ate tonight. Finding somewhere to rent with no money would be impossible. She lowered her head, absently plucking several blades of grass and rolling them between her fingers. Molly was right. She had no choice but to hand Eustace over to the authorities. But the thought of his being inside one of those cheerless places chilled her to the bone. Fear for his plight overrode everything else.

Her eyes fell on the brown paper bag which held the remains

of their breakfast. It was a nice gesture, she thought, for Ben to do that. For a moment she wondered where he was heading and how far he'd got.

Suddenly an idea began to take shape. She pondered on it for several moments. And then she knew exactly what they were going to do. After all, what had she to lose? There was nothing here for her now.

She turned and grabbed his arms. 'Eustace, how do you fancy going on a journey?'

He stared at her quizzically. 'Where to?'

'I don't know. Anywhere the road leads us.'

'You and me?'

'Yes, you and me.'

'Oh, Tilda,' he said excitedly. 'And I . . . and I wouldn't have to go to a home.'

She shook her head.

He threw his arms around her neck and hugged her tightly. 'I love you, Tilda.'

'And I love you too.'

Chapter Nine

'Which way shall we go then, Eustace?'

Hand in hand they stood in front of the signpost at a deserted country crossroads and stared up at it. To any onlooker they would have seemed a ragged and dirty pair. Evidence of the fire and their night in the open was still apparent even though Tilda had done her best to tidy them both up before setting off.

According to the signpost they had four choices. All, give or take a few miles, were in Tilda's estimation several days' walk, possibly more considering Eustace's little legs. There were villages in between, but a town was where Tilda felt they should ultimately be heading. The chance of finding work was bound to be greater there.

'Tell me again what it says?' asked Eustace.

'Nottingham that way.' She pointed east. 'Birmingham that way.' To the west. 'Leicester.' South. 'And Derby.' North.

He frowned thoughtfully. 'I dunno. What do you think?'

'Well, never having been to any of them, I suspect one's as good as another. But Derby is back in the direction we came from. So I think that narrows things down.'

'Yes, I do as well,' he agreed, puffing out his chest importantly. He liked Tilda asking his opinion, it made him feel grown up.

'Tell you what,' she said, squeezing his hand, 'let's sit on the grass verge over there and finish the bread and milk Ben bought us. We can decide while we're eating.'

He looked up at her adoringly. 'All right.'

Seated, Tilda stretched out her legs gratefully. She would have given anything to curl up, close her eyes, and for a few hours forget the nightmare of the fire and its resulting problems. But she couldn't, she had Eustace's welfare to think of and they must press on.

She reckoned they had covered about four or five miles but would feel happier with more distance between them and the village. There was still the fact that a search was on for Eustace and it wouldn't take much for an intelligent person to spot them and put two and two together. She gnawed her lip anxiously, hoping that what she had done could not be classed as kidnapping.

Suddenly the enormity of her own actions dawned on her. With Eustace in tow, she had skirted the village like a thief on the run, not even daring to inform Molly of what she was doing. That in itself makes me seem guilty, she thought. Molly at least had deserved some sort of explanation for her sudden disappearance. But if she had heard Tilda's plan she would no doubt have tried to talk her out of it. For Eustace's sake, her decision had been correct. She would write to Molly and explain all when she felt it was safe to do so.

Her only regret was that Molly might have taken a few pennies for her from the basket of kindling she had left. Those few coins would have been gratefully received, but the collecting of them would not have been worth the possible consequences. A few miles further down the road she would begin in earnest to look for some kind of work; anything, she didn't mind what. She had gone without food herself many times before. So long as she earned enough at first to feed Eustace, that was all that was important.

Hurriedly packing away a crust of bread and the remainder of the milk, she jumped up and grabbed his hand.

'Come on, let's make our decision and be on our way. I tell you what. You shut your eyes and hold out your arm. I'll spin you round, whatever direction you're pointing in, that's where we'll go. All right?'

He giggled delightedly. 'All right.'

The road leading to Birmingham seemed to wind on endlessly. The night was now drawing in, and apart from the odd rest and a diversion across a field to catch a rabbit for their supper, the bedraggled pair had journeyed nonstop.

Tilda glanced down at Eustace in concern. 'You tired?' she asked.

He shook his head vigorously. 'No, Tilda, I'm fine.'

She smiled. She knew he was lying. Her own legs felt as though they didn't belong to her any more; she had long ago reached the stage when she had to concentrate hard just to put one foot in front of the other. Eustace, she knew, was about dead on his feet. Not one word of complaint had she received from him, though.

'Just a bit further then we'll find somewhere to stop.'

The night promised to be cold and spending it out in the open did not appeal. But while the rabbit was cooking over the fire she would build, they'd gather plenty of soft leaves and branches to make themselves as comfortable as possible. Tomorrow . . . well, who knew what tomorrow would bring? The main thing was that they were together, and in Tilda's eyes that was more important than anything.

On rounding a bend, she surveyed the road ahead for a place to spend the night. Suddenly she halted, abruptly gripping Eustace's hand tightly. In the distance, sitting on a milestone, was a man with his head in his hands. Suddenly Tilda felt very vulnerable. But unless she wanted to turn back, the only way was to brazen it out.

Eustace looked up at her enquiringly. 'What's up, Tilda?'

Not wanting to alarm him, she planted a smile on her weary face. 'Nothing. Just . . . er . . . when we walk past that man down there, put your head down and don't say a word.'

Eustace studied him for a moment. 'Why? Is he a robber?'

Tilda pursed her lips. 'I don't know what he is.' She laughed wryly. 'But it'll be a waste of time if he is, 'cos we ain't got nothing to rob, have we? Only the rabbit, so yer'd better hide it.'

'No, only the rabbit,' Eustace chuckled, stuffing it inside his jacket. 'And if he nicks that we can get another.'

Pressed tightly together, keeping as close to the other side of the dried dirt road as they could, they resumed their journey. As they passed him Tilda took a quick sideways glance. All she caught sight of was the top of his bright red head, his face being covered by his hands. But whoever he was, he was certainly upset about something. Her worry concerning the stranger had been an unnecessary precaution. So preoccupied was he, he didn't move a muscle as they passed by.

As they crested the brow of a hill she suddenly stopped. Red hair! She was acquainted with a man who had hair exactly that colour: Ben McCraven. But he was the last person she'd ever expected to see again. It couldn't possibly be him, could it?

Dropping Eustace's hand, she turned and hurriedly retraced her steps. Eustace ran after her. As she neared the man, she took a good look at him to satisfy herself. If it wasn't Ben, then he had a twin brother.

She crossed over to him and gently tapped his shoulder. 'Ben, what's the matter?'

At the sound of his name, his hands came down and his head jerked in surprise. 'How . . . ? Oh, it's you.' He sighed loudly and rubbed the stubble on his chin. 'You're a bit far from the village to be out on a stroll.' He caught sight of Eustace and frowned deeply. 'Kidnapping, is it?'

'I had no choice,' snapped Tilda.

'I doubt a judge 'ud believe you.'

'I don't care what you think. Anyway I asked you a question. What's the matter?'

He rose abruptly, stared around, then fixed his eyes on her. 'If yous must know, I've been robbed. Of everything. Two of them came from nowhere. They even took the blanket I sleep in.' His face blackened thunderously. 'Just let me ever catch up with the louses who did it. I'll...' He stopped abruptly, remembering the presence of Eustace, and smiled wryly. 'Well, let's just say they'll regret being born.'

'Oh, Ben, I am sorry,' Tilda said sincerely. 'They really took everything?'

'I said so, didn't I?' he snapped. 'I don't care about the other stuff, but the money I am mad about. I worked hard for six weeks to earn it. Over five pounds, I had, counting the bonus Taffy paid me, and they didn't even have the decency to leave me a shilling.'

Tilda gasped. Five pounds was a fortune to her.

Eustace, who had been listening intently, suddenly yelped. 'Ben! Is this the man who saved me life?' Without waiting for an answer, he grabbed Ben's hand, shaking it vigorously. 'Oh, ta, mister, ta. And I thought you were a robber!'

Tilda lowered her head. To her way of thinking, Eustace had characterised Ben perfectly.

He ruffled the boy's hair. 'Did yous, son?' He flashed a quick glance at Tilda and smiled ironically. 'I know people who would probably agree with yous there. That right, Tilda?'

She looked at him haughtily. There was no need for her to answer. Ben knew exactly what she thought of him and that was enough for her.

She grabbed Eustace's hand. 'We'd better be going.'

'See yous then.' Ben ruffled Eustace's hair again. 'Best of luck, laddie.' He looked hard at Tilda. 'Hope it all works out.'

'So do I,' she replied sharply, before launching forward, dragging Eustace behind her.

He pulled her back. 'But, Tilda, Ben saved me life and he's bin robbed. Shouldn't we ask him to share our rabbit? He'll starve else, won't he? He seems really nice. I like him, don't you?'

Tilda stared down at him, then back towards Ben who had returned to his seat on the milestone, and sighed resignedly. Eustace was right. It was the least she could do. 'Go and ask him then.'

So as not to hurt the little boy's feelings, Ben reluctantly agreed.

An hour or so later, in a clearing near a copse only yards from a bubbling stream, Tilda was busy gathering what she could to make up some bedding. Eustace had been given the job of tending the fire and carefully turning the rabbit on a precariously constructed wooden spit. His mind was filled with thoughts of Ben who was now his hero. He lifted his head, searching for Ben, and when he could not see him, looked at Tilda in concern.

'Where's Ben gone?' he shouted.

Without raising her head from the bedding she was arranging, she shrugged her shoulders. 'Don't know. How's the rabbit coming along?'

'Fine?' he replied, sniffing the tantalising aroma. He wished it would hurry up and cook.

Ben suddenly appeared, carrying a handful of potatoes. Tilda, standing to stretch her aching back, eyed them suspiciously as he passed.

'Where did you get those from?' she asked.

'Where d'yous think.'

'You stole them!' she accused

He stopped abruptly and faced her. 'Tilda I don't know about you but I'm starving hungry and so is Eustace. There's a field full of early spuds over there so I helped mysel'. You might call that stealing, I call it surviving. If you don't want any, then go without.'

Speechless, she watched as he marched off to join Eustace and the laughing pair put the potatoes in the fire to roast.

A while later, all huddled close to the flames to eat their supper. Afterwards Ben turned to her and grinned. 'Enjoy that?'

She tightened her lips. 'I did, thank you.'

He grinned more broadly. 'See, they didn't choke you.'

Tilda ignored his taunt. The meal had been delicious. When the time had come to eat, she had been so hungry she could have eaten her own boots.

She stiffly rose to check on Eustace, sleeping peacefully, sheltered under a bush on the makeshift bedding.

'He seems happy enough,' Ben said, yawning as she returned to join him.

Yes, she thought, happier than he has been for a long long time now he hasn't the spite and callousness of his aunt to contend with. 'Yes, he does,' she replied.

She squatted down near him and stared into the fire, conscious of the rustling trees and vast dark expanse of countryside surrounding her. Suddenly it felt comforting to have this man's company. For a moment she forgot her mistrust and dislike of him.

As if reading her thoughts, he suddenly piped up: 'The lad's been good company tonight. This is all an adventure to him. But you do realise it's not a wise thing you've done?'

'I know that,' she said sharply. 'Don't you think if I had had any other choice I'd have taken it? But I couldn't send Eustace to an orphanage. He deserves more than that.'

He turned his head and looked hard at her. 'And being on the road is better?'

'Yes,' she said with conviction. 'It's only 'til we get to Birmingham and I find work and lodgings.'

He shook his head. 'It won't be easy, Tilda. Yous ain't the only one looking for work. I was lucky with Taffy, that's why I grabbed my chance. It might be better to go back. It isn't too late. I'd think seriously about it, if I were you.' He rose and stretched himself. 'I want to be off sharpish in the morning. If I've gone when yous wake, say goodbye to Eustace for me.'

She eyed him for a moment, shocked by his announcement although she had been expecting it. 'I will,' she murmured.

Long after Ben had retired she sat staring into the remains of the fire. He was right, blast the man. On making her decision to leave with Eustace, she hadn't given proper thought to the perils they could face. She had always had to struggle for survival so that had not been an issue, but the fact that someone as tough as Ben had been robbed was frightening. She turned her head and looked at him. Slowly a solution to her immediate problem occurred to her. She didn't want to resort to it but she had Eustace to consider.

On all fours she crept over, knelt beside Ben and shook him. 'Ben,' she whispered urgently. 'Wake up, Ben. Wake up.'

His eyes opened. 'What the blazes . . .' He sat bolt upright. 'What's happened? What's the matter?'

'Nothing. I just wanted to speak to you.'

He groaned loudly. 'Good God, woman, what on earth do yous want to speak to me about now? I was fast asleep, damn it.'

'There's no need for blasphemy,' she hissed. 'Eustace might hear you.'

136

Sighing, he looked across at the boy. 'A thunderclap wouldn't wake him. And I've no doubt he's heard worse.' He turned back to Tilda, eyes narrowed in annoyance. 'What do yous want?'

She took a deep breath. 'Take us with you, please, Ben?'

'What!'

'Only as far as Birmingham. We'd be no trouble. I'm not asking for me, but for Eustace. Please?'

He stared at her, stunned. He travelled alone. Liked travelling alone. He was trying to find an elusive man and avenge his father's death. He needed to be flexible, afford himself the freedom to follow even the smallest of leads. Besides, the last person he would want to saddle himself with was Tilda, even if it was only for a week or so. He wasn't all that struck on her, and she definitely didn't like him.

'It wouldn't work, Tilda.'

'But it would,' she pleaded. 'Look, I know we're not exactly fond of each other but ... well, I could be useful.'

'How?'

'Er ... cook your meals,' she offered hopefully.

'I can do that mesel'.'

'All right then, other things. I dunno.' Her eyes narrowed, annoyed. 'Don't make me beg.'

'That's not my intention. The answer's no, Tilda. Now leave me alone.'

'But...'

'NO. Goodnight, Tilda.'

She stared at him angrily as he turned his back on her and closed his eyes. Several choice words her father had taught her came to mind. Jumping up, she strode across to her own bedding and threw herself down. Blast the man, she fumed inwardly.

She awoke just as dawn was breaking, sat up and rubbed her

eyes. Eustace was still fast asleep. She would leave him for a few more minutes, he needed his strength, they had many miles to cover today. Her eyes travelled to where Ben had lain. The bedding was empty, no sign of him. So he had kept to his word and gone without them. She took a deep breath and tried to quell a niggle of worry that fluttered around in her stomach. Suddenly there was a rustling in the bushes nearby and she jumped. Someone was approaching. As she jumped up the horseshoe fell from her pocket. She snatched it up and held it out menacingly, her eyes riveted to the undergrowth.

Through a parting in the vegetation a man appeared. It was Ben.

'Oh!' Tilda exclaimed, greatly relieved. 'It's you.' She eyed him quizzically. 'But I thought you'd gone.'

'I had.' He eyed the horseshoe, somewhat surprised that she had it. 'Oh, for goodness' sake, put that away. It wouldn't protect yous from a tame dog. And if yous coming, hurry up, I ain't got all day.'

I just hope I don't live to regret this, he thought to himself.

Chapter Ten

'You're not well, Eustace,' Tilda announced withdrawing her hand from his hot forehead.

'I'm fine, honestly,' he lied.

In truth he felt dreadful, sweaty and nauseous. All he wanted to do was curl up and sleep on the dirty pile of sacks in a corner of the ramshackle shed where they had taken shelter out of a raging storm. But he couldn't let her know that. He didn't want to be any trouble, hold them up in any way. He was just grateful to be here.

'Where's Ben?' he asked.

'I don't know, sweetheart. He's probably taken shelter somewhere,' she replied lightly, although she herself was concerned. He'd been gone ages but when he had left she hadn't felt it her place to ask where he was going. She was beginning to wonder if he was ever coming back.

Just then the door burst open and Ben strode through, bringing with him a blast of cold March wind and enough rain to fill several buckets.

'Shut the door,' she said sharply, relieved to see him, but more worried about Eustace.

'It is shut,' he snapped back, shaking himself down. He peeled off his wet jacket, walked over to her and stared down at Eustace. 'What's up with the lad? He's not ill, is he?'

Misinterpreting his tone as annoyance, she eyed him sharply. 'It's just a cold. He'll be fine.'

He shook his head. 'I did warn yous . . .'

'He'll be fine, I said. I'll keep my eye on him.'

'If that's the way you want it, Tilda.' He took her arm and pulled her aside. 'I've got us some work.'

Her eyes lit up. 'You have? Where? Doing what?'

'On a farm, just over the field. You're to help the missus, me the farmer.'

'Oh, that's great.'

He smiled cheekily. 'Must be my Scot's charm, eh? Anyway it's only for a few days. They're behind with the planting and she needs some help in the dairy.'

'What are they like?'

He shrugged his shoulders. 'All right, I suppose, for farmers. I didn't take too much notice.' He held out his hands and studied them. He didn't want to tell her he had found them a strange couple. Work was work and at the moment they were in no position to be choosy. 'There's er . . . just one thing. Well, two really.'

'Oh?'

'They . . . er . . .'

'They what, Ben?' she interrupted impatiently.

'They think we're married.'

She stared at him. 'What! Ben, did you tell them that?'

'Well, I had to. I doubt they'd have taken us on otherwise.'

'Wouldn't it have been better to be honest? It's not as though we're doing anything wrong. They'll soon twig we're not.'

'Tilda, stop going on. And they won't twig. If yous are that worried about it, call me "dear" now and again. That should do the trick.'

She sighed. 'Do married couples call each other "dear"?'

'How should I know? It sounds all right to me. Just do it, Tilda. For God's sake, it's only for a few days.'

'Well, so long as I don't have to call you "darling",' she said sarcastically.

He raised his eyebrows in annoyance. 'Tilda, we've been on the road for three days, this is the first work we've managed to get and we're still a good way from Birmingham. If yous have to call me "darling" to keep the job, then I suggest yous do.'

She pursed her lips. 'And I suppose you're blaming Eustace and me for the fact you haven't got any work? Couldn't be this dreadful weather having anything to do with it, could it? Or that maybe no one needs anybody at the moment.'

'I never blamed yous or the boy, did I?'

'No, but you implied it.' She inhaled sharply. 'All right, I suppose we could manage to get along for a few days, but you'll have to make an effort as well. What's the other thing?'

'What?'

'You said there were two things.'

'Oh, yes, I did.' He scratched his head. 'Eustace.'

'What about him?' Her mouth suddenly dropped open in shock. 'You never told them about him, did you? Ben!'

'Well, farmers are wary of kids. Some of them wreak havoc, especially amongst the animals. So I thought it best not to mention him.'

'You thought it best, did you! And what do you propose I do? Abandon him? Well, I won't. Where I go, Eustace goes.'

'I'm not saying yous should abandon him. He could stay here.'

'What? On his own? That's cruel. Anyway, I won't do it.'

'Suit yersel'. But that lad needs some good food down him. Yous could get that at the farm, and yous need the money you'll earn. Think about it before yous shoot your mouth off.'

'It's all right, Tilda, I don't mind staying on me own.'

She gasped. She hadn't realised they'd been talking so loudly. She rushed over to Eustace, knelt down and gathered him in her arms. 'Are you sure? You wouldn't be frightened?'

'No, 'course not. This place ain't so bad as the cellar.'

She smiled at him tenderly. 'Oh, Eustace. I'll come and see you every chance I get, and bring you food. A couple of days will soon pass, you'll see.'

The little boy smiled. Truthfully he didn't like the thought of staying in this shed by himself. But for Tilda, and now his hero Ben, he'd do anything. He felt he owed them both a debt of gratitude.

'When do we start?' she asked Ben.

'Now. I said you were sheltering from the rain and they told me to fetch you.'

'Now? But it's late. Must be gone seven.'

'Tilda, do yous want this job or not?'

She had no choice. 'All right. Just give me a minute with Eustace.'

Fanny Brindle, a big woman, square and solid, with a large mole on her cheek which sprouted whiskers, scrutinised Tilda sharply through small shrewd grey eyes as soon as Ben shoved her through the farmhouse door.

'Done farmwork before,' she asked bluntly.

Intimidated, Tilda shook her head. 'Not exactly. But I'm quick to learn,' she added hurriedly.

'Mmmm.' Fanny frowned deeply. 'Strange. Your husband seemed to think you have. Still, never mind. It don't need much of a brain to tackle what I need yer to do.' She eyed Tilda's withered arm for several moments. 'Needs muscles, though. Think you'll manage?'

Tilda instinctively pulled down her damp cardigan sleeve.

'I can manage whatever it is. My arm doesn't stop me doing anything.'

'I didn't say it did. I just asked if you thought you could. You say you can, that's fair enough by me. Come this way.'

She led Tilda across the yard and into the dairy. After she had briefly explained what the girl had to do, she folded flabby arms under her huge bosom. 'Well, still think yer can manage?'

'Yes,' she replied, with more conviction than she actually felt. 'Seems straightforward enough to me.'

'Good.'

Fanny turned and strode out of the door. Tilda hovered for a moment, unsure whether to follow.

'Come on,' Fanny ordered.

Tilda shot after her.

The room, partitioned off from the hayloft over the barn, was surprisingly cosy. In the doorway Tilda gazed in horror at the big ancient wooden bed dominating its centre.

'This do yer?' Fanny asked.

She gulped. 'Er . . . yes, yes. Thank you very much.'

Fanny eyed her quizzically. 'Is there anything wrong?'

'No, no, not at all. I've never seen such a big bed before, that's all.'

'Was me Great-auntie Nelly's, so mind you look after it. There's fresh sheets in the chest of drawers.' She eyed Tilda sharply. 'Now, is there anything yer want ter tell me?'

Her question was most unexpected. 'Pardon?' Tilda exclaimed. 'Er . . . no, no, I don't think so.'

Fanny slowly nodded. 'Well, I'll leave yer to it then. I'll expect you in the morning, just after the cows have been led out ter pasture.'

About half an hour later, Ben walked in carrying a tray. He looked at the bed, and at Tilda sitting on the edge of it somewhat forlornly, and grinned. 'Enough room for six, eh.'

She scowled at him. The thought of sharing it with him was bad enough without him making stupid jokes. She eyed the tray. 'What's that?'

'Food. Mrs Brindle thought we'd be peckish, so she did us a snack. There's enough here for six.'

'Like the bed, eh?'

Ignoring her remark, he put the tray beside her. She stared at the contents, amazed. She'd never seen so much food all in one go. Snack indeed! She picked up several sandwiches and placed them together, then made to grab a piece of pork pie.

'Yous must be hungry?'

'It's for Eustace,' she said icily.

'Oh, yeah, 'course.'

'Have you forgotten about him already?'

'No, I haven't.'

He couldn't be bothered to tell her he had already piled a plate for the lad, that having been his first concern. It was the one she was now taking the sandwiches off.

Wrapping them and the pie inside a napkin from the tray, she rose and headed for the door.

'Where are yous going?'

'To see Eustace.'

'What about your supper?'

'I'll have it when I come back. If there's any left, that is,' she added flatly, noticing the way he was ramming food into his mouth.

'Don't let anyone see yous.'

'I won't. Besides it's dark. I'll have a job finding the way myself.' She stood for a moment, waiting for an offer to accompany her. None came.

'Don't wake me up when you come back.'

'I wouldn't dream of it,' she said coldly.

Concentrating on quietly creeping across the yard, she

did not see Fanny Brindle watching her movements from a darkened upstairs window of the farmhouse.

Eustace was fine, or so he said. Tilda did not like the clammy feeling of his forehead but still he insisted he was all right and just wanted to sleep. He would eat the food later. She sat with him for a couple of hours, for most of which he slept. Do him good, she thought. Sleep was the best cure for most ailments. Before she left she lit the candle with the matches she had found in their bedroom, glad that at least he wouldn't be in the dark and reassured him that at the first opportunity in the morning she would come across, bringing with her whatever she could sneak out. She wanted to stay with him, hated the thought of leaving him on his own, but they desperately needed the money from this job so she had no choice.

Riddled with guilt, she secured the shed door behind her and made her way back.

Crouching in the shadows, she skirted the yard, still unaware that Fanny was watching her from an upstairs window.

Ben was fast asleep. Quietly, in the darkness, Tilda undressed as far as her patched cotton petticoat and washed in the ice cold water in the basin on top of the chest of drawers. She stood shivering by the bed, staring at it, indignant that Ben had had the nerve to tell the Brindles they were married. But there was nothing else for it, if she was to get any sleep, which she was desperate for, she would have to climb inside. There was nowhere else except the bare floorboards.

Taking a deep breath, she drew back the covers and gingerly slid under. Lying on the very edge of the bed, she closed her eyes, very aware of the man sleeping next to her. Several times he rolled over, throwing an arm or leg across her which she gently removed so as not to wake him. Gradually the need for sleep overtook her and she began to relax. This was the first time she had ever slept in a proper bed. As she dozed she found herself comforted by Ben's rhythmical breathing, the warmth of his body, the feeling of security his presence brought. It must be nice, she thought, to sleep beside someone you loved in a wonderful comfy bed such as this.

She woke with a start. She was being manhandled and nearly screamed out, but thankfully just managed in time to remember where she was and the circumstances.

'Move over, Tilda. You're lying on top of me. I can hardly breathe.'

Acutely embarrassed, she rolled across the bed, stammering apologies.

Ben grinned in the darkness as he settled himself. 'Sorry, "dear" but you're not my type.'

She held her breath, controlling her anger. 'Thank goodness for that because you're definitely not mine! And I can't be responsible for what I do when I'm sleeping. I have apologised.'

'Yous sure yous were sleeping?'

'Positive,' she hissed.

As she turned over her ears pricked. She was sure he was chuckling. Pulling the covers over her head, she shut her eyes.

When she awoke he had already risen and departed, for which she was thankful.

Fanny was obviously not very communicative in the morning. She only nodded a greeting at Tilda when she arrived in the kitchen just as the last of the herd was being led out of the farm gate. After downing a large mug of tea, she made her way to the dairy and began her work, her mind filled with thoughts of how quickly she could sneak away and check on Eustace.

Just after eight Fanny called her for breakfast. Inside the large warm kitchen she pointed to the table.

'Sit down,' she ordered, placing before Tilda a large plate

filled with bacon, eggs, fried bread and tomatoes. 'If you want any more, just 'oller.'

Tilda stared at the plate. She had never had such a breakfast before. It looked delicious. Again she thought of Eustace.

'Mrs Brindle, would you mind if I made a sandwich and took it to the dairy to eat later.'

Fanny turned round and looked hard at her. 'Yes, I would. Food's to be eaten at the table. What you don't want, the pigs'll be glad of.'

Tilda's heart sank. How was she going to sneak any of this out for Eustace with Fanny Brindle's beady eyes on her? The pigs might be glad, but Eustace would have been ecstatic to have such fare put before him. She hoped Ben had managed to do something although she doubted he'd think of it.

The farmer's wife sat down opposite with a large mug of tea. 'Eat up. It's a long time 'til dinner.'

There was nothing else for it. Resigned, Tilda picked up her knife and fork and tucked in.

'Been married long?'

'Pardon? Oh, er . . . a year.'

'Really? Husband said six months.'

'Did he?' Tilda replied, startled. 'Oh, well, you know what men are like,' she said, her tone implying she did.

'Yes, I should do. I've bin married to one long enough. But I'll say one thing for him, he remembers the day we got married. Sleep well, did you?'

'Oh, yes,' she said uneasily. 'Very well, thank you.'

'Mmmm,' Fanny murmured, stroking her chin. 'Bed to your liking then?'

Tilda looked guiltily at her through her lashes. 'Yes, thank you.'

'More tea?'

'Er . . . no, I've not quite finished this.'

'So where did you say you came from?'

I can't remember saying I did, Tilda thought. 'Derby.'

'Really? Husband said Carlisle. Though I could have sworn his accent is Scottish.'

Carlisle? She'd never heard of the place. 'Scottish? Yes, Ben is Scottish. We met in Carlisle originally, then we moved for a while to Derby. For the work you see. We move around a lot. Derby's where we've just come from in fact.' Oh, hell, these lies are getting worse, she thought, wishing Mrs Brindle would stop asking questions. She scraped back her chair. 'I'd better get back to work. Don't want you sacking me for slacking.'

Fanny rose also and lumbered across to the sink. 'No fear of that. You've done good this morning.'

Tilda carried across her empty plate and handed it to Fanny. 'Would you like a hand with the washing up?'

'No. You get back to what you were doing. I'll see to these. When you've finished, take a break for an hour. Go for a walk or something.'

Tilda looked at her astonished. This was the last thing she had expected. What she had anticipated was being worked to death. 'Oh, thank you, I will. But if you do need me to do anything, just let me know.'

As she trotted across the yard she hummed a tune. She could go and see Eustace. She felt dreadfully guilty because she hadn't managed to save him anything from her breakfast but come next mealtime she would definitely manage, by hell or high water, to secure something from her plate.

Tilda caught up with Ben in the yard around mid-morning. Thankfully the rain had stopped but it was still cold. She shivered as he approached her.

'How yous getting on?' he asked.

'All right, I think. Work's hard, but it's easy enough. What about you?'

'Same here. He seems a fair man. What's the missus like?'

Tilda looked at him thoughtfully. To be truthful she didn't know what to think. Fanny Brindle was a very hard woman to fathom. 'She seems all right, but . . .'

'But what?'

'I dunno. I can't make up my mind whether she's horrible or nice. She's very blunt anyway. And asks a lot of questions. I get the feeling she doesn't trust us.'

'You're just imagining it.'

'Am I? I don't think so, Ben. I get the feeling she can see straight through us. Oh, I wish you'd just told her the truth about us.'

'Yeah, and doing that would have lost us the job.'

She shrugged her shoulders. 'I suppose you're right. But, you know, you really landed me in it.'

'Did I? How?'

'You told her we'd been married six months and I said a year. And that we came from Carlisle when I've never even heard of the place. You could have warned me, Ben.'

'I forgot,' he said, shrugging his shoulders. 'I don't know why you're making such an issue of it.'

'I'm not,' she said indignantly.

'Yes, yous are. So while we're at it, let's get things straight. How long would yous like us to have been married? Two years, three? And we come from . . . I know, Auchtermuchty. And before yous ask, that's a village in Scotland. Shall we throw in a couple of kids we've left with their granny?'

'Oh, shut up,' she snapped angrily.

'Tilda,' he said, a frown on his face, 'that's no way to speak to your husband. Women should respect their menfolk.'

'Respect?' she hissed. 'How could I be expected to ever respect a lying, conniving thief like you, eh?' As soon as the words were out of her mouth she felt guilty for saying them.

Despite all that had happened she still couldn't quite convince herself she hadn't caught him about to steal her savings.

He scowled deeply at her. 'I never realised yous thought so highly of me, "dear". I shall have to watch out for you in bed tonight.' He laughed loudly, made to walk away, then stopped, pulling something out of his pocket which he thrust towards her. 'This is for Eustace.' He turned, stomped across the yard and disappeared inside the barn.

She looked down at her hand. Wrapped inside a piece of brown paper was a bacon sandwich. She raised her head and looked across at the barn door. Damn that man, she thought with irritation. No sooner had she thought she had him worked out than he would go and surprise her. He must have gone without most of his breakfast to save Eustace this. She put the package deep inside her shirt pocket, trotted across the yard and popped her head around the kitchen door.

'I thought I'd take my break then, Mrs Brindle, unless you have something you want me to do?'

Fanny was standing at the table chopping vegetables. 'Not at the minute but I will in a bit. Dairy all done and dusted?' She said all this without lifting her head.

'Yes, just like you showed me. And I've fed the pigs.'

'Have yer now?'

'Well . . . I saw the buckets lined up outside so I thought I'd do it to save you a job. Did I do wrong?'

'No.'

'Oh.' Tilda frowned apprehensively. Fanny's tone had implied that she had. Or had it? 'Well, I'm . . . just going for a walk.'

'To calm you down?'

'Pardon?'

'After that set to with yer husband.'

Tilda's eyes widened. Fanny must have been watching them

from the window. Was she like this with everyone who worked for her, or just them? 'We never had a set to. No, definitely not. Just talking, we were.'

Fanny slowly raised her head and looked across at her. 'Really! Mmm. Well, if you're going for that walk, you'd better go. Soon be dinnertime.' Her attention returned to her chopping. 'Though personally I feel it's far too cold for a stroll. Still, each to their own.'

Taking her time crossing the yard, Tilda slipped through the gate and then ran swiftly across the wet field towards the shed. Unlatching the door, she stepped inside. She was horrified at the sight that met her. Eustace lay huddled on the sacking, his clothing soaked with sweat. He was mumbling incoherently. The food she had left him last night remained untouched. She dropped down beside him, slipped her hand under his neck and cradled him to her.

'Oh, Eustace,' she uttered remorsefully, fat tears filling her eyes. 'I should never have left you. Oh, God, please forgive me.' Her mind raced frantically. What on earth was she to do? Eustace needed a doctor.

'Put this around him.'

At the sound of the voice Tilda screamed in fright, her head swivelling round.

'No time for hysterics, girl. Do as I say.'

She froze in horror. Filling the doorway, almost blocking the light, stood Fanny Brindle. She was holding out a blanket.

Speechless with shock, Tilda gently laid Eustace back down on the sacking, leaned over him and took the blanket. Tenderly she wrapped it round him, then rose to face Fanny. She opened her mouth but Fanny raised a hand to stop her.

'We can talk later. The boy needs attention.'

Moving past Tilda, she bent down, picked up Eustace and cradled him in her huge arms, his small body looking lost

151

inside them. Without a word Fanny left the shed and strode across the fields towards the farm, a distraught Tilda hurrying behind.

A mug of strong tea was placed before Tilda who stared blindly down at it. On numerous occasions in the past, when she had sat alone at the makeshift table in the cottage she had dreamed of mugs of strong sweet tea. Now at the thought of drinking this one she felt she would choke.

Fanny sat down opposite, folded her big arms and leaned on the table. 'Right, now's the time for talk and I'm listenin'.'

Tilda slowly raised her head. 'He's mine.'

Fanny slammed her flattened hand down hard on the table which shook. 'No twaddle, girl. The truth. He's no more yours than he's mine. You're not even married, let alone had a child.'

Tilda gulped. 'How'd you know?'

Fanny shook her head. 'How do I know? Child, it sticks out a mile. You should have seen your face when you saw the bed. It was a picture.'

Tilda squirmed in her seat, too embarrassed to say anything.

'You're not married, are you?' challenged Fanny.

'No,' Tilda whispered. 'We're just together through circumstances, that's all.'

'Oh I see. So what's yer tale?'

'It's not what you think,' Tilda said defensively.

'Listen, girl, at this moment there's all sorts I'm thinking. See, I know people. Studying them's bin me lifetime hobby. So just tell me straight. And drink yer tea up afore it gets cold.'

Tilda picked up her mug and slowly sipped on the hot dark liquid. What was she to do? If she told the truth about Eustace, would Fanny Brindle run straight to the police? Then what would happen to him? Oh, damn Ben! Where was he? He'd got them into this mess, he should be here to help get them out. But at least Eustace was going to be all right. Just a bad cold which a day or so in bed and some good food down him would cure, so Fanny had assured her.

There was nothing else for it. The truth would have to be told. Hopefully this woman would understand and not turn them in.

She shifted uncomfortably in her chair. 'Eustace . . .'

'No.' Fanny stopped her. 'We'll get to the boy in a minute. I want to know about you.'

Tilda stared stunned. Nobody before had asked her about herself. She frowned bewildered. 'Why? Why should someone like me be of interest to you?'

Fanny leaned her arms heavily on the table. 'You're right, you deserve an explanation.' She took a deep breath. 'I took to you the moment you walked through my door. You've seen sorrow, child, and carry burdens far too great for a girl of your age. You're asking yourself how I know, and I'll tell you. It's because, my dear, the likes of you and me are from similar moulds. I recognised that fact straight away.'

'I don't understand what you're talking about.'

'No, I don't expect you do. I suspect I'm the very first person who's ever talked properly to you. Wanted to know about you as a person. Looked past that withered arm and plain face of yours. I'm right, aren't I?'

Tilda stared, dumbfounded, then slowly nodded.

'Now I'll show you why I'm interested.' Fanny swung her hefty body around on her chair and pulled up her long skirt. One of her legs was strong and muscly, the other thin, the foot at the end encased in a large black boot, the sole of which was over four inches deep. 'I had polio as a child and my penniless parents abandoned me. It was thought I would die. But no, I was too strong, see.

'Big hefty Fanny with a face like cracked cobblestones wasn't going to be done down by polio. When I recovered sufficiently I was thrown in an orphanage and it was dreadful, like hell on earth. Then at fourteen I was out on the street. I've lost count of the times I slept in the gutter. People shunned me. People don't like ugliness, do they, Tilda? Though you're far from ugly in the face. But affliction frightens 'em, you know that. Not many can handle it. Times I felt like topping myself but couldn't quite bring myself to do it. Always kept telling meself I'd been put on this earth for some good reason, though at that time I couldn't think what it was.

'Then, just by chance, I met my Harry and it was like the sun had finally come out. He didn't see my ugliness or affliction, his eyes saw deeper than that. He saw what was underneath. The beautiful side of me. And I am beautiful, Tilda. Inside, where it matters. It took my Harry to make me see it.' She laughed, a deep throaty chuckle. 'Although I didn't make it easy for him. I thought, you see, for quite a while that he couldn't be right in the brain. But finally he convinced me. He got me a built up boot, bought me some decent clothes, and married me. We've been happy ever since. He's never regretted it once and neither have I.' She smiled proudly. 'Raised three kids together who are now happily married themselves. I've friends, plenty of them, all decent people who respect and like me for myself.'

She sat back in her chair and eyed Tilda sharply. 'So that's why I can read you. I see in you the burdens I had to carry, the cruelties you've suffered at others' hands, the same as I did. You have to learn like I did that other people's ignorance is *their* problem. You have a lot to give, girl, and some day there will be someone there for you to give it to.'

Tilda smiled wryly. She doubted that very much but nevertheless was speechless at what Fanny had told her. But comforted too. Fanny Brindle had triumphed against the odds. Her story had given Tilda renewed hope that maybe so could she.

Fanny smiled warmly 'Now come on, it's your turn. Tell me what brought you here, right from the start.'

Tilda had no hesitation. She began with her earliest memories. When she had finished Fanny pulled absently on the whiskers sprouting from her mole. 'You've had it hard, child, a lot harder than most, but you've come through it all right. You'll maybe hate me for saying this but to my mind the best thing your father ever did for you was to get himself killed. I know it wasn't a good way to die, but then your father doesn't sound like a very good man. And you stuck by him, which is more than most would have done in the circumstances.'

'I did try my best,' said Tilda softly.

'Then you've nothing to reproach yourself with. Put it all behind you now, Tilda. Think of your future. And you do have one, you know, even though it looks bleak at the moment. No one knows what's around the corner. Look at me. I never thought I'd meet anyone like my Harry.'

Tilda sighed heavily. 'No, I suppose not.'

Fanny smiled kindly. 'What you did for Eustace was a grand thing, my dear.'

The girl eyed hesitantly. 'Are you going to turn him over to the authorities?'

Fanny took a deep breath. 'We have to consider what's best for the child. I will need to think on it. But be assured, I won't do anything without discussing it with you first. And don't look so worried. I might look like an ogre but I can assure you, I'm not one.' Fanny picked up her mug and took a deep gulp then looked at Tilda with a twinkle in her eyes. 'Are you sure there's nothing going on between you and Ben?'

Tilda's eyes flashed. 'Yes, I'm sure.'

155

Fanny grinned. 'If you say so, my dear. I suppose you didn't meet in the best of circumstances. Despite what's happened between you both, you're still unsure of him, aren't you?'

Tilda smiled wryly. She hadn't realised she was so transparent. 'To be honest, I don't know what to make of him.'

'Well, if you want the truth, neither do I. But regardless, I happen to like him and my instincts have never let me down yet. Eh, look at the time!' she exclaimed scraping back her chair. 'The men will be coming in soon with empty bellies.' She looked hard at Tilda. 'I bet you've never had such good food, or as much before?'

'I haven't.'

'Well, you can have some more if you'll give me a hand.'

'It'll be my pleasure.'

'I'm glad you said that. But before I ask you to set the table, just check on the lad, see he's all right.'

'What do yous mean, she knows everything?' Ben stared at Tilda, dumbfounded. 'Was that wise?'

'Don't shout at me, Ben McCraven, I had no choice. It's your fault.'

'Mine?'

'Yes. She saw through your lies.'

'I didn't exactly lie, Tilda, I just exaggerated a bit.'

'Just a bit! Ben, you told her we were married. Oh, it's not important now anyway. Fanny knows the truth.'

She felt the need to tell Ben she thought Fanny a truly astonishing woman with a rare insight into people. Since her talk with Fanny, despite the fact Eustace's future was held in the balance, she felt uplifted somehow, more positive about herself, more able to face what life had in store. But, Ben she felt, would not understand any of this even if she was to explain.

'What if she informs the authorities about Eustace?'

She gnawed her bottom lip. 'She said she would discuss any decision with me first and I have to trust her.'

Tilda was about to turn in when she decided to say her goodnights to the Brindles. As she crossed the yard she passed by the kitchen window and the sight that met her eyes froze her rigid. Sitting in a large rocking chair by the fire was Fanny; opposite her in a comfy armchair her husband, puffing on his pipe and reading the newspaper. Curled in Fanny's ample lap was Eustace, his head buried in her huge bosom. He was fast asleep. Fanny stroked the top of his head, then bent and tenderly kissed it. The look on her face was of utter contentment, the sort only seen on a motherly type of woman cuddling a child.

Tilda caught her breath, suddenly feeling like an intruder before such a tender family scene. Fighting back tears, she turned and made her way to the hayloft.

'Well now, I've thought over our little problem and I'm ready to suggest a solution.'

A worried Tilda eyed Fanny. 'Oh?'

Their time at the farm was just about over. Tilda had finished the last of her chores and had accepted the offer of tea with Fanny while Ben was just finishing a last job for Mr Brindle. Fanny had not mentioned the subject of Eustace's future after their long conversation and Tilda had been hoping the farmer's wife had forgotten all about it and they could just leave as unobtrusively as they had arrived.

She was mistaken on all counts. Fanny had thought long and hard about the matter, but until she had given it her full consideration and explored all the possibilities, she had said nothing. It was the way she normally went about things.

Now she folded her arms and leaned heavily on the table. 'Let the lad stay with me. I'll raise him.'

Tilda stared at her. She hadn't expected this. She had thought Fanny might urge her to hand him over to the authorities, not suggest that she herself might keep him. But witnessing the tender scene through window, and on other occasions when Fanny had cared for Eustace during his illness, should have forewarned her. Maybe she hadn't wanted to think about the inevitable, had shut it out.

Tilda sighed heavily and lowered her head, studying the plate of ham and potatoes in front of her. She had been ravenous when she first sat down. Now she felt sick. The decision she had to make pained her more than any suffering she had endured in the past.

Fanny would make Eustace a wonderful mother, give him a home, all the stability he needed and deserved. Tilda knew what it was like to grow up without a mother and she felt it wasn't fair to put Eustace through the torment she had endured. Mr Brindle, she knew, was a kind man, devoted to his wife, and would be a good father figure to Eustace, of that she had no doubts. Against all that, what had she to offer? Nothing but her love. If she refused, was she being fair, dragging Eustace miles in the hope she might find work and a roof? She wrestled with her conscience. What she wanted to do was grab him and run, keep him with her forever. It took all her will-power not to jump up from her chair and do just that.

Fanny smiled sympathetically. 'Thought my suggestion might tek the wind from yer sails. Listen, my dear, I know how much you love that boy and he you. You might not know it but Eustace and I have talked at length and that boy idolises you, as he does Ben. But you, my dear, he would die for. It's highly commendable. Pity his aunt never loved him as much. If she had she might not be lying six feet under. Still, in my book she

158

deserved all she got. I'm not religious but I do believe the Lord shows his hand in his own way. Now, I've raised three healthy girls. Got families of their own, bless 'em. But I've still room in me heart and me life for a lad such as Eustace. I'll look after him proper, that I can assure yer.'

'I know you would, Mrs Brindle,' Tilda said softly. 'I'm not worried about that.'

'Call me Fanny, dear. All me friends do.'

Tilda managed to smile at her.

'Any time you want to come and see him, you just turn up. You'll be welcome. When you're settled, we can come and see you. He could even have holidays with you. I'm not suggesting for a minute you lose touch.' She shifted position on her chair. 'Now I'm not going to the authorities. Doing that would not be in Eustace's interests. I know he'd be better even staying with you on the road than being in one of them 'omes.' She shook her head sadly. 'It grieves me when I think of all those poor little mites stuck inside such places. I wish I could tek 'em all, but I can't.' She took another deep gulp of her tea. 'So, the decision you have ter make is whether you take him with you or accept my offer. Now I know you and Ben are leaving at first light so I'll let you sleep on it. And I know it ain't an easy decision for you. I don't envy yer.'

Just then the back door burst open and Eustace charged through. Tilda looked hard at him. Four days ago she had thought him at death's door. To see him now, she'd never have known he'd even been ill. Fanny had been right. A comfortable warm bed and good food had mended him. Would the outcome have been the same if he had had to stay in the damp shed?

He darted over to her and threw his arms round her neck. 'I love it 'ere, Tilda. Can we stay? I've bin in the fields and helped to plant the spuds. When they grow they have all little spuds on 'em. Later I'm gonna help milk the cows.'

She pulled him from her embrace and held him at arm's length, fighting the distressing flow of tears that threatened. 'Would you really like to stay, Eustace? Would you like to grow up here and help on the farm and go to school with all the other children?'

He nodded vigorously. 'Can we? Can we really?'

Tilda pulled him close and buried her head in his neck. She swallowed hard and pulled away from him. 'Go and get yourself washed. Mrs Brindle has your tea ready.'

Eustace's eyes darted to the table laden with food. 'Oh, good, I'm starving.'

As he rushed by Fanny to the sink he stopped and impulsively kissed the large woman on her cheek. In turn she patted him affectionately on his bottom before he continued on his way.

Tilda's sad eyes looked across at her. 'I think you have your answer,' she said haltingly. 'I ask only one thing.'

'Whatever, my dear.'

Tilda's voice lowered to a hoarse whisper. 'After me and Ben have gone in the morning, will you explain to Eustace? Tell him I love him and feel this is best.'

Fanny sniffed back tears of her own. ''Course I will. You leave it ter me.'

Chapter Eleven

Dawn was just breaking and it promised to be a fine day. At long last spring appeared to have arrived. But despite the warming weather, the trees and shrubs bursting into bud, lambs frolicking in fields and a general feeling of well-being stirring in people fed up with the long winter months, it was a heavy-hearted Tilda who dragged her feet along the muddy dirt path, each step taking her further away from the little boy she loved so deeply.

She knew her decision to leave him with the Brindles had been correct; she had never even questioned it as she had tossed and turned all night in one of the bedrooms Fanny had turned over to her once the truth of her 'marriage' to Ben had been revealed.

When she had explained to him what had transpired he had announced that the decision was hers alone, but he thought Fanny's suggestion a good one. The road was no place for a young boy, especially now such a wonderful opportunity had so unexpectedly presented itself.

'You'd be selfish, Tilda, if yous denied him this chance of a good home.'

She'd been too distressed to answer him.

Now he turned to her, hitching the bundle he carried more comfortably on his shoulder. 'Yous all right?'

It was a stupid question but he didn't know what else to ask her. They had walked at least ten miles in silence. For Ben's part he was delighted to have covered such a good distance in such a short time, but with each step they had taken he had become more aware of the torment Tilda was suffering. She hadn't said a word during the whole journey and looked about ready to drop.

As they rounded a corner a crossroads loomed. Erected in the middle was a signpost. Standing before it, Ben frowned quizzically. 'That's strange,' he murmured.

Tilda lifted her eyes and stared at the sign blankly. 'What is?'

He turned and looked at her. At least she had spoken.

'The sign,' he said. 'It points to Birmingham that way, forty-four miles. According to this we're travelling in the wrong direction. To my reckoning we should only be aboot twenty or so miles away. We must have gone wrong somehow but for the life of me I cannot think where.'

'Oh,' was all she replied.

He scratched his head, bewildered. 'Look, I tell yous what, let's sit down and eat some of that food Fanny packed up for us.'

She sighed heavily. 'I'm not hungry but I'd welcome a sit down.'

'You have to eat, Tilda. Moping won't do yous any good.'

'And what would you know?' she replied sharply. 'I can't just turn my feelings off because Eustace is no longer with me. I can't stop loving him just like that.'

Ben narrowed his eyes. That was just it, he *did* know how Tilda was feeling. The pain of his mother's early death still cut deep, and the loss of the father he'd hardly known. A picture of his mother sprang to mind, hands red raw, back bent double, struggling with a basketload of other people's washing – and when that lot was done another was always ready. He saw the endless floors she had scrubbed and all the other demeaning

162

work she had grabbed at in order to keep a roof over their heads and the most basic of food on the table. He pictured himself running barefoot through the streets, backside hanging out of his short trousers, a life of petty crime enforced on him so he could aid his mother in the task of survival.

He tightened his lips angrily. At least Tilda knew Eustace was alive and well and had the promise of a good long life stretching before him. His mother and father had had theirs cut short in one way or another through the murderous action of a selfish man. Well, that man had better watch out, because one day, and he didn't care if his search took years, Ben McCraven was going to come face to face with Duggie Smilie.

'You're right, Tilda. What would I know?' he said coldly. Turning from her, he marched towards a stile, climbed over and headed off across a sloping field towards a small group of trees. 'If yous ain't hungry that's your problem. I am,' he shouted back to her.

A short while later she sat nearby him, nibbling on one of Fanny's delicious ham sandwiches. To Tilda, though, the food might as well have been cardboard for all she was tasting it. The small wooded area where they sat was on the side of a hill at the bottom of which ran a fast-flowing river. She stared down at it, sighing heavily, wishing wholeheartedly she could raise her spirits, but nothing she thought of did the trick. All she could picture was Eustace, and memories of times they had spent together danced before her eyes. Her arms ached with longing for him but despite her own heartbreak she hoped vehemently that his sadness at her departure would soon pass; that with the Brindles' help he would understand why she had left without a word, put the suffering he had endured since his mother's death to the back of his mind, and get on with living his new life. Take full advantage of it.

She drew a deep breath. That was what she had to do as well. Get on with living. She had many hurdles to cross. Problems to deal with. As Ben had pointed out, nothing in life came easy. But she already knew that. For someone like herself, everything she had ever done, and would do in the future, had to be striven for.

Tilting her head, she glanced across at Ben. She wasn't being fair to the man. Her sombre mood was causing her to be surly to the point of rudeness towards him. It was wrong of her, she felt, to be like this when she should be extremely grateful he was still allowing her to accompany him.

She turned her gaze back towards the swollen river. Maybe now was the time for them to part. Ben would get on a lot better without her trailing behind and she could cope without him. Now Eustace wasn't with her she wasn't afraid of travelling alone. That wasn't entirely true, she had grown used to the protection a man afforded, and if she was really truthful with herself a tiny part of her was even beginning to like Ben. No, she chided herself, that wasn't true. She couldn't stand him. She was mistaking gratitude for liking. She had spent the majority of her life looking out for herself and had managed well enough. She was right, now was the time to part company.

Tilda smiled wryly. Ben would welcome her decision, she knew that without even asking him. Despite their being thrown together this last week or so, their attitudes had not changed. Besides, the sooner she got a job and somewhere to live, the sooner Eustace could come and visit her.

Before she could change her mind she stood up, brushed herself down and walked towards Ben.

'I've been thinking,' she said.

He raised his head, mouth full of pork pie. 'Oh, what aboot?'

'That maybe it's time we parted company.'

He looked at her, surprised, then nodded. 'If that's what yous think best.'

'I do.'

Ben put the last of the pie into his mouth and stood up. 'That's fine by me then. Have yous changed yer mind aboot going to Birmingham?'

She shrugged her shoulders. In truth she hadn't given it much thought. 'I thought I'd try a farm or something. I quite enjoyed the work with the Brindles.'

Ben grimaced. 'Just a word of warning, Tilda. Not all farm folk are like them.'

'I'll take my chances. If I don't like it, I can always leave.'

'Well, yous seem to have it all worked out. It just remains to split the rest of the food and wish yous all the best.'

She gave a nervous smile. 'Yes.' She shuffled her feet uncomfortably. 'I just want to say thanks for all you've done. You didn't have to let us tag along. I am grateful.'

He shrugged his shoulders. If it wasn't for Tilda and Eustace, he doubted he'd have eaten such good food and slept in a warm bed for the last few nights. Tilda's presence had gone a long way towards securing that job. Plus he would not be carrying the bundle of Mr Brindle's old clothing and other odds and ends Fanny had pressed on him once she had found out he had been robbed of all his belongings.

'Think nothing of it,' he said matter-of-factly.

Back on the main track Ben hitched his bundle over his shoulder, as did Tilda. Fanny had been generous to her also.

'Well, cheerio then. I hope everything works out.'

'Same here. 'Bye, Ben.'

As they turned away from each other, Tilda stopped, her ears pricking. 'What was that?'

Ben turned back. 'What was what?'

'That noise. It sounded like a baby.'

'Och, you're hearing things.'

'No, listen. It's very faint but it's definitely a baby crying – and it's very upset by the sound of it.'

'So what?' Ben was beginning to grow cross. He wanted to be on his way. If he hadn't known better he would have thought Tilda was trying to stall him. 'I cannae hear anything.'

'Are you deaf or something?' she said crossly. 'If you can't hear that baby then you must be.'

Ignoring her remark, he tilted his head then nodded. 'Aye, there is a child crying. So what?'

'It may have escaped your notice but we happen to be in the middle of nowhere. We haven't seen a soul for ages.'

'Oh, so you're trying to tell me we're the only people in England now, are yous?'

'Don't be stupid,' she snapped.

'Well, what are yous trying to say?'

'Oh, nothing, Ben. Just forget it. The cries have stopped now. They seemed to be coming from the direction I'm heading so I'll check as I'm passing. Probably a family of travellers or something.'

'Probably,' he said. 'If it is, just be careful.'

'I can take care of myself.'

'I've no doubt, Tilda. But don't forget, I was robbed.' He breathed in sharply. 'Well, can I go now or is there anything else?'

She eyed him coldly. 'Goodbye Ben.'

''Bye, Tilda.'

Head held high, the brave smile on her face not revealing the apprehension that was now building inside her, Tilda headed off down a narrow track. Somewhere en route it had to cross the river and hopefully on the other side would be a farm where she could start her enquiries about work. For a moment her apprehension was replaced by annoyance. They had passed several farms as they had journeyed and she hoped she hadn't missed any opportunities.

As she rounded a bend the landscape briefly opened out and she had a clear view down to the river several hundred feet away. She was right, there was an ancient three-arched pack bridge spanning angry waters continuously being fed from the surrounding hills after the recent heavy rains. The river had burst its bank in places and infiltrated nearby fields. She smiled. From this distance it looked a picturesque sight. As she studied the view her eyes were drawn towards an object to one side of the bridge and her smile froze. 'Oh, my God!' she gasped.

Dropping her bundle, she turned and raced back up the hill towards the crossroads. Once there she screamed at the top of her voice: 'Ben, BEN!' Her mind raced frantically. Where was he? How far could he have travelled in such a short space of time? Drawing in her breath, she screamed again: 'BEN! BEN!'

A few seconds passed during which she became more agitated, wondering whether she should go after Ben or if she should try to seek help somewhere else. Then, thankfully, she saw his lanky frame come running round a bend in the track.

'Oh, Ben!' she cried frantically, running towards him. 'There's been an accident.'

'Accident? What kind of accident?' he asked breathlessly.

'An empty cart. It's on a bridge. And there's something on the bank below. It looks like a man. Come quick!'

Without further explanation she turned and bolted back down the track, Ben following behind. As he overtook Tilda by the place she had dropped her bundle, he dropped his also. Arriving at the scene, he quickly sized up the situation. The wagon must have somehow hit the side of the bridge and thrown the occupant out. The side of the vehicle was smashed. The horse, bridle still in place, was happily munching away on some grass. Several feet away an the bank an unconscious man lay sprawled across a boulder, water lapping over his boots. He was covered in caked blood.

Ben rushed towards him, knelt down and felt for his pulse. 'He's still alive!' he cried. 'Barely, but still alive.'

Getting the injured man into the wagon was not easy. He was no lightweight. As they struggled to lift him up the bank, Tilda worried they were causing him more harm than he had already suffered. But to leave him and search for help was out of the question. He needed medical help quickly.

The task finally completed, Ben collapsed, exhausted. 'Well, I didnae think we'd do it, but thank God we have. Now all we have to do is find the nearest hospital. But God knows where that is, or the nearest village for a doctor.'

Tilda clambered inside the wagon and from her vantage point gazed around. As far as she could see stretched open country-side. The track over the bridge rose sharply to disappear over a tree-lined hill.

'We'll just have to hope this track leads somewhere. It's no good going back where we came from. We didn't pass through anything remotely large enough to warrant a doctor.'

Tilda looked out across the countryside, wondering how far the nearest town was. She had no idea where they were.

'He needs hospital treatment,' Ben replied in concern, and bent over to feel through the man's pockets.

'We'd better get going,' Tilda said, turning her attention back towards Ben. She gasped, horrified. 'What on earth do you think you're doing?'

Pulling a wallet out of the man's inside pocket, he looked up at her, his face grim. 'What do yous think I'm doing, Tilda? Stealing his belongings, is that it?'

'Well...' she flustered, stunned at his blunt accusation, which was in fact exactly what she had thought.

He scowled at her angrily. 'What do yous take me for, Tilda Penny? Think I'd stoop low enough to rob a dying man, do yous?' He narrowed his eyes, lips tightening. 'For your information, I'm looking for identification.'

Guilt welled up in her. 'I'm sorry,' she stuttered.

'I should bloody think so,' he growled.

The wallet held over forty pounds. A small fortune to Ben. He hurriedly shoved it back. 'We're wasting time,' he said icily. 'Yous stay in the back with him whilst I drive – and be careful of the hole in the side. Let's just hope the wheels weren't damaged in the accident.'

'Have you driven a cart before?' she asked anxiously.

'Whether I have or not is immaterial, unless you want to do it?'

She stared at him then shook her head silently.

As Ben was about to gee up the horse a loud groan escaped the man's lips and his eyes flickered open. Ben spun round in his seat and watched as Tilda bent over him and gently touched his cheek with her fingertips.

'It's all right,' she soothed. 'You've had an accident. We're going to get help.'

The man stared at her through pain-filled eyes. His mouth opened and he strained to speak.

'He's trying to say something, Ben.'

'What?'

'I don't know. I can't make it out.'

The man took several painful breaths. 'Me wife?' he uttered, barely audibly. Painfully lifting his hand, he sought Tilda's arm and gripped it. 'Me wife?' he pleaded. His grip slackened, his eyes flickered shut, and he lapsed back into unconsciousness again.

169

Ben and Tilda's eyes met. 'Wife?' they both said in unison.

'Ben, you don't think his wife is here somewhere, do you?'

He grimaced thoughtfully. 'No,' he said, shaking his head. 'He was just trying to tell us he had one. Get in touch with her, that's all.'

'I don't agree,' she said, leaning back on her haunches. 'I think he was trying to tell us she's here.'

'Tilda, we're wasting time. We've got to get going.'

'No, Ben, she's here. You didn't see the look in his eyes. He was trying to tell us, I know he was,' she cried, crawling to the back of the wagon. 'The least we can do is look to make sure.' Poised to jump out, realisation struck her. Face filling with horror, she swung round. 'The child I heard crying. Oh, Ben, what if his wife and child were travelling with him and the impact threw them out too?'

Without waiting for a response she jumped down from the tailboard and ran to the side of the bridge. Ben, not knowing quite what to think, joined her and they both stared around them.

He took control. 'We'll start a search by the river bank. I'll go this side of the bridge and you that. Shout if you see anything. And hurry up aboot it. We haven't got all day.'

Tilda negotiated the short sharp incline down to the overgrown edge of the river bank, eyes peeled for anything amiss as she hurried along. Several times she stopped to call out before moving off again. About five hundred yards on she had to give up, having reached an area where the river had burst its bank. Reluctantly she turned back, hoping Ben had come across something. She knew the woman was here somewhere, her every instinct told her. And possibly a child.

Rounding a bend, the bridge came back into view and her eyes caught a glimpse of something blue swirling about in the water by the side of the pillar supporting the middle arch. She stared hard but whatever it was had gone. Then she caught sight of it again, only momentarily but it was there. Something was caught in the current.

Again her instincts took over and she ran as quickly as she could to the bridge, several times narrowly avoiding tripping over low-growing roots or slipping in mud. Arriving at the bridge, she stared fearfully across. The void beneath the first arch was several feet wide and there was no telling how deep the water ran. But there was no time to think of her own safety. If the woman was trapped, for whatever reason, her life was at stake.

She whipped off her skirt, tugged off her boots, lifted her petticoat and, shutting her eyes, made to step into the icy cold waters.

'TILDA!'

She jumped in fright and looked up.

Ben was leaning over the side of the bridge, looking down at her. 'What the hell are yous doing?' he demanded.

'She's here, Ben. She's round the other side of the pillar.'

'How do yous know?'

'I . . . I saw something.'

'Saw what, for Christ's sake?'

'I dunno. Something. It's her, Ben, I know it is.'

He shook his head in disbelief as he watched her step into the water. 'Hold on, I'll see if I can see anything from up here.'

'Well, hurry up then.'

He ran to the middle of the bridge and leaned over as far as he could. Tilda was right, there was something blue, which looked like material, swirling intermittently in the current. It was either caught or attached to something. But he could not be certain as his view was restricted.

He ran back and leaned towards her. 'You're right. There is

something. But it's not necessarily her. Tilda, you'd be mad to risk going in there. You'd be drowned for sure.'

'It's her, Ben. I just know it is. I'm going in.'

'Tilda, don't be foolish. We'll get help.'

'There isn't time.'

'Oh, for God's sake. Stay there,' he ordered sharply. 'I'm coming down.'

He joined her in moments, grabbed her arm and pulled her back on the bank. 'You stupid woman!' he shouted, incensed. 'There's no telling how strong that current is. Get oot the way,' he hissed, pushing her backwards. 'I just hope for your sake you're right. I'd hate to think I'd drowned for nothing.' He started stripping off his own top clothes.

'Can you swim?' she asked.

He momentarily ignored her question. He was terrified of water. Had never got wet above his knee caps before – and that was only paddling in a millpond as a lad. But his conscience wouldn't allow him to stand by and let a woman do this deed. As he pulled off his boots he vehemently rued the night he'd accidentally come across the derelict cottage in the woods. That simple event had resulted in meeting this woman who was rapidly turning into the bane of his life. Together they had begun the journey that had led him to this dangerous situation. If only, he thought, I'd taken another road that night, this wouldn't be happening!

He exhaled sharply as he stood poised on the bank, foaming muddy water lapping inches from his feet. 'Don't ask daft questions, Tilda. No one could swim in that. I'll be lucky I don't end up in the sea, judging by that current.'

She stared at him fearfully and caught his arm. 'Maybe we should try to get help?'

He turned and eyed her scathingly. 'There's no time, remember.'

172

Shrugging his arm free, he took several steps into the icy water then stopped and shook his head. 'This is deeper than I thought. I might just manage to get across but I doubt I'll make it back with a woman in tow.' He stepped out of the water and stared around.

'What are you looking for?' she asked anxiously.

'An old tree trunk or something that I can swing across and anchor somehow. I can pull myself along it and it should stop the current sweeping me downstream. But there's nothing long enough lying around.'

'There's a ladder in the back of the wagon, but I don't think it's long enough either. A rope! There's a rope. Will that do? You could tie one end to this tree.' She pointed to a birch growing at the side of the bridge. 'The other round your waist. If the current does get you, I can pull you back. Once you're across it won't be so bad 'cos you can cling to the ledge and work your way round. Shall I get the rope?'

Ben stared at her, surprised. 'Yeah, get it. Let's hope it does the trick.'

Several minutes later, the rope secured around Ben's waist and the tree, Tilda holding the middle slack, he inched his way into the water. Sharp slimy stones and tangles of weed hampered his progress and as he went deeper the iciness of the water forced the breath from his body. He was filled with concern, and not only for his own safety. He knew that if the injured man's wife was trapped under the arch, she would have breathed her last long ago. But after risking his life this far he might as well see it through, just to make sure.

Several times he was forced off course and had to fight hard to regain his position. It was a great relief, for Ben and for Tilda, when he reached the pillar.

'Are yous still holding the rope?' he shouted.

'Yes, 'course I am,' she replied sharply.

Clinging for grim death to the ledge on which the pillar stood he began to inch his way round and for several long seconds disappeared out of Tilda's sight.

She held her breath and anxiously waited.

The inside of the wide arch spanning the middle was dank and dark, covered in foul green slime. The roar from the torrent of water flowing through bounced off the grey stone walls, echoing eerily.

Ben saw her immediately, thrashing up and down in the water. One hand was gripping the ledge, her other arm pressed against something on top of it which looked to Ben, desperately fighting to keep his position against the current, like a bundle. Then he gasped, horrified. The bundle was a baby. Neither woman nor child showed any sign of life.

'She's here, Tilda,' he shouted.

'What? I can't hear you.'

He took several deep breaths and shouted as loud as he could: 'The wife. I've found her. And there's a baby.'

Tilda shivered, an icy dread filling her. 'Are they alive?' No reply came. 'Ben, are they alive?'

He could not answer her. He did not know.

It took several long minutes to reach them. Thankfully the woman was breathing but only just. The baby . . . it was difficult for him to tell. The woman's arm was shielding it, securing her offspring on the ledge.

If lives were to be saved, Ben knew there was no time to risk two trips. Besides, his own strength was ebbing fast.

The unconscious woman's arm was stiff with cold and it took several precious moments for him to prise it free. Grabbing the baby, he placed it gently across his shoulder, tucking its feet well under his own armpit, then he forced his other arm around the woman's chest, grabbing for a secure grip on her sodden clothing. Then, stealing himself to take her weight, he wrenched her hand off the ledge, at the same time taking several deep breaths. It was now or never.

Bending his knees, he planted his feet flat against the wall and screamed out as loud as he could: 'PULL, TILDA, PULL!'

As he pushed against the wall the current caught hold of them and swung them right out into the middle of the river.

Tilda cried out in terror as the weight at the end of the rope yanked her forward and she fell flat on her face. Behind her she heard the groaning of the birch. Rapidly gathering her wits, she scrambled upright and grabbed again at the rope, heaving on it with all her might, but the weakness in her withered arm proved a problem. Try as she might, there was hardly any strength in her grip. Suddenly the rope slackened and she fell backwards, landing heavily on the ground. The end of the rope flew out of the water to land with a hard slap at her feet. She was stunned for a second then bolted upright, staring stupefied towards the river.

Ben and his human cargo had disappeared.

'Oh, God, no! NO!' she screamed hysterically, a sick horror filling her.

Her body froze rigid, stunned motionless by this shocking turn of events. It had all happened so suddenly. One moment they were there, the next they had gone. Do something! her mind screamed. For God's sake, Tilda, do something!

Jumping up, she belted down the bank, diving around and jumping over obstacles, screaming Ben's name at the top of her voice, eyes darting everywhere for a sign. But there was nothing. No sign whatsoever of anyone, alive or dead.

Finally, she drew to a halt and collapsed in a sodden heap in a pool of mud, a torrent of tears flooding down her cheeks.

'Dear God,' she sobbed, rocking backwards and forwards.

All three lives had been taken so senselessly, but most of all she grieved for Ben. She hadn't liked the man or what she thought he stood for, at times he had annoyed her intensely, their whole relationship in fact had been built on animosity. Nevertheless she would miss him and the realisation shook her. In a funny way, one she would find difficult to explain, she had grown attached to him.

Wiping her face on her wet petticoat, she raised her eyes skywards. The weather was changing again. Grey clouds were gathering, a deluge threatened, but she did not notice; all she saw was Ben's face, the scathing look he had given her before he had waded into the water. He had not wanted to take the risk, she had known that at the time, but she had been too intent on saving the woman – who in reality could have been already dead – to consider Ben. His death was her fault. How would she ever be able to forgive herself for making him do something he hadn't wanted to? Tears of distress flowed again.

Suddenly cutting through her grief she remembered the wagon and the injured man who lay inside. She gasped, horrified. She had forgotten all about him.

Scrambling up, blinded by tears, she attempted to make her way back to the bridge, her mind filled now with thoughts of getting the man the medical attention he so desperately needed. She suddenly felt the pain he would suffer when he learned his wife and child had perished. So preoccupied was she, she did not see the large obstacle blocking her route and fell headlong over it. She lay sprawled for a moment, dazed, then lifting her head, looked over her shoulder to see what had caused her fall. Her mouth dropped open in shock. 'Ben!' she shrieked. 'Ben, oh, Ben! You're not dead! Oh, thank God,' she cried, scrambling to her knees, twisting herself round and throwing herself across him, immensely relieved.

An exhausted, sodden, half-drowned Ben spluttered: 'Get off me, Tilda. I can't breathe.'

'Oh, I'm sorry, I'm sorry,' she cried, forcing herself upright. 'I'm just that glad to see you.'

He coughed long and hard and spat out a mouthful of water. 'Not half so glad as I am to see me!'

If the situation hadn't been so dire Tilda would have laughed at his remark. As it was she stared at him with concern.

'Are you all right?'

He gave an agonised groan. 'Sometimes, woman, you do ask daft questions. Do I look all right? I think I swallowed half the river.'

Wincing painfully, with a great effort he rolled himself over and tried to sit up.

Tilda gasped. In the crook of his arm was a bundle.

She stared at it for a moment then threw herself forward, scooping it up into her arms and cradling it tightly. 'The baby! Ben, you saved the baby.'

He raised sad eyes. 'I don't know if it's alive. I dearly hope so.' He turned his head and stared at the river. He shuddered violently. 'I couldn't save the mother.' His head drooped as a great wash of tears rolled down his face. 'I couldn't hold her, Tilda,' he sobbed. 'God help me, I tried, I just couldn't hold her.'

Chapter Twelve

'Miss.'

The homely middle-aged nurse shook Tilda's arm gently. She hadn't wanted to wake her. The plain, bedraggled girl looked so peaceful huddled on the wooden bench in the corridor. The nurse sighed heavily. This girl had been almost dead on her feet when the wagon had careered to a halt outside the cottage hospital late the previous evening, the injured man lying in the back barely clinging on to life. His injuries were appalling. Both legs were broken and his pelvis, an arm in two places, several ribs, and the doctor was still unsure what else. As it was things didn't look all that bright, but only time would tell.

'Miss,' she said again, shaking her. 'Wake up.'

'Eh, eh? Oh.' Tilda struggled upright and rubbed her gritty eyes. She had trouble adjusting to her surroundings. Her dream had been so vivid. She was back in the cottage, only it wasn't the cottage as it had been. The cottage in her dream had been warm and cheerful with good quality furniture and pictures on the walls. Around the solid oak table had sat her father, Ben and Eustace, and a woman whom she had no doubt was her mother. Not the wicked deserter her father had talked about, but a kind and loving mother whom she had always wished for. They had all been chatting happily whilst she had dished up their dinner. She could even smell the aroma from the piece of roast beef steaming on the plate in the centre of the table. The dream had seemed so real, her innermost desires coming to fruition, and as she tried to wake herself up, part of her wanted to return, to feel again the pleasure, happiness and sense of security it had momentarily afforded her.

She raised blank eyes to the nurse and smiled apologetically. 'I'm sorry,' she said, 'I didn't mean to fall asleep.'

Freda Hooper smiled reassuringly. 'It's understandable. You were exhausted. But you might as well go home. There's nothing you can do here.'

Tilda stared at her. Home? She hadn't got a home. Hers had burned down, everything inside it lost. But the nurse would not know that. Last night everything had happened so quickly. Hospital staff had whisked away the man as soon as they had arrived. The baby too. Ben, on the point of collapse after his horrendous ordeal and then managing to drive the wagon aimlessly for miles down rutted tracks until they came across the hospital by accident, had been put straight to bed. Tilda herself had been left alone in the dimly lit corridor to worry and wait for news, and the last thing she remembered was sitting down on the bench in exhaustion.

'How are they all?' she tentatively asked.

Freda pursed her lips. 'Well, it's too soon to tell about Mr Wragg. He's conscious, though with the pain he's in it'd be better for him if he wasn't. Can't remember nothing about what happened after he left home with his wife and child.' She shook her head. 'It doesn't look good for him I'm afraid.'

Tilda frowned hard. 'What d'you mean, it doesn't look good? If he's conscious . . . ?'

'In this case that means nothing, my dear,' the nurse said kindly. 'It's not his brain that's the problem, it's the extent of his other injuries. His legs are badly smashed and . . .'

'And what?'

'It's not for me to make diagnoses, that's the doctor's job. But the baby's fine,' she added chirpily. 'A bit of a cold coming, but considering what's it's been through, that's nothing short of a miracle. Your...' She faltered. She had been going to say 'boyfriend' but wasn't entirely sure what the situation was between this rather plain girl with the withered arm and the charming Scotsman. Ben McCraven wasn't exactly handsome, not what she herself would call so anyway, but there was definitely something about him. All the young nurses had been fussing over him since he had woken. She decided to be charitable. 'There's nothing wrong with your boyfriend that a good night's sleep didn't cure. Must have the constitution of an ox.'

Tilda sighed with relief remembering how she had felt when she had thought him dead. She rose stiffly, every bone in her body aching. She made to turn down the corridor then paused.

'Do you think I could see the baby, please, before I go?' she asked hopefully, though quite where she was going was a problem she decided not to think about for the moment. She didn't even know where the hospital was. She could be in Timbuktu for all she knew.

Freda hesitated. 'Er ... Oh, I don't see why not. After all, you did help save its life. Come with me.'

As they walked down a corridor Tilda just happened to glance inside an open door. She stopped abruptly. Propped up in bed, looking no worse for his ordeal, sat Ben, eyes glued to a pretty nurse fussing over him. Tilda made to greet him but quickly changed her mind, thinking that in the circumstances he might not welcome her interruption. She would say her goodbyes after she had seen the baby. She scurried after the nurse.

Arriving at the nursery, Tilda looked down into the cot and momentarily her weariness left her. She couldn't help but smile at the sight that met her. A pair of innocent deep blue eyes instantly locked on hers, then a broad smile split the chubby face, showing a row of bare gums. Tilda's heart melted. With not a thought for hospital rules, she leaned over and scooped up the child, cradling it protectively inside her arms.

The nurse didn't chastise her, just ran her hand gently over the baby's head. 'She's a beauty and that's a fact. Break a few hearts she will when she gets older.'

'How old do you think she is?'

'About six months. Poor little lamb. It's a sad shame about her mother. You only have to look at this baby to see she's been well looked after. Wish I could say the same for some of the poor little waifs who come through these doors.'

Tilda sadly shook her head. 'What will happen to her whilst her father recovers?'

Freda shook her head. 'As far as we can gather there are no other relatives. She'll go in a home, I expect. I don't see any alternative for the time being at least. The baby can't stay here so Matron's making the arrangements. Everything hangs in the balance, you see, until the extent of Mr Wragg's injuries is known. But you shouldn't be worried about that. It's not your concern. Just be glad you happened past when you did or she wouldn't be here at all to be worrying over.'

But I am worried, Tilda thought. In a way she felt responsible for the baby. If only they could have saved the mother! Tears of remorse pricked her eyes and she cuddled the baby tighter. This innocent young child could not possibly know what dramatic changes had taken place which would drastically alter her life. How could she? She had probably already cried for her mother and not understood why she wasn't there.

This child needed someone to love and take care of it. It wouldn't get that in the austere confines of a home, with all the poor mites demanding attention they would never receive. Her old fear for Eustace surfaced and she felt so relieved that at least he had managed to escape that fate. But this baby? What was to become of her? Especially whilst her father recovered, and there was no telling how long that would take.

'Well, I have patients to see to, so you'd better put the baby down.'

'Oh, yes.'

Just then another nurse popped her head round the door. 'There you are,' she said addressing Tilda. 'I thought you'd gone home. Mr Wragg is asking for you.'

'Me?'

The nurse nodded. 'The lady who saved his life, he said. The poor man's in dreadful pain so you're not to stay long.' She looked at Freda and lowered her voice to a whisper. 'I wouldn't be surprised if he doesn't make it.'

Tilda's jaw dropped in shock. She knew he was in a bad way but it hadn't sunk in just how dire his situation was. Her eyes darted to each nurse in turn. 'Can I take the baby to see him? It might help.'

The second nurse looked her up and down dubiously.

'Please,' Tilda pleaded.

'Oh, go on, Nancy,' Freda addressed her. 'You never know, it might do some good.'

Nancy sighed. 'All right. But don't let Matron see us or she'll have a dicky fit. Come on, quick.'

Smiling a thank you at Freda, Tilda followed Nancy down several corridors. The nurse paused before a door. 'Now just remember he's in a lot of pain and is not to be tired. Just stay a few minutes, all right? I've a few things to do and I'll be back shortly.'

Tilda silently nodded. Nancy opened the door and she passed through.

Ted Wragg turned his head painfully when she entered the room.

Tilda stared, shocked. She had expected to see a sick man but

Ted Wragg looked as though his life's blood had all but drained from him. Pewter-coloured skin seemed to be stretched across his bones. Pain had done that, she thought, coupled with the devastating news of his wife's demise.

His eyes settled on Tilda and he stared at her for several moments. His words, when they finally came, were in painful low rasps and barely audible. Tilda had to strain to hear them.

'She's taken to you. She usually cries with strangers.'

Tilda stared quizzically at him, then, understanding what he had said, smiled down at the baby. 'She's lovely,' she said, bringing her eyes back to rest on him.

'Just like her mother.' A lone tear rolled down the side of his face. 'We waited years for 'er. Never thought we'd 'ave any. Then along came Daisy and we felt truly blessed.'

Pain filled his face and Tilda knew it wasn't from his injuries.

He took several short breaths and his eyes momentarily closed. She thought he had lapsed into unconsciousness but they opened again and settled on her.

'Thank you for what you did.'

Tilda absently stroked the baby's head. She felt his gratitude unwarranted. If they had managed to save his wife then she might have felt differently.

'I'm sorry about your wife,' she said softly, raising her head to look at him.

'So am I.'

Tilda swallowed hard to rid herself of the lump constricting her throat. She wanted to comfort him but didn't know quite where to start. This man's whole world had crashed around him and the outcome was still held in the balance. Whatever she said she felt would be meaningless.

Just then the door opened and Ben, ready for the road, crept in. Tilda noticed his clothes were clean. The nurses had looked after him well. No one had offered to do anything like that for her. Not that she'd expected it but it would have been nice to have been offered the use of soap and water. For a moment she was extremely conscious of her dirty dishevelled appearance and it was with a sudden pang she remembered both the bundles of clothes Fanny had given them, hurriedly dropped on the track. Anyone finding them would think it their lucky day. For the second time she realised that all she owned in the world was what she was wearing.

Ben smiled half-heartedly at Tilda then looked across at Ted Wragg.

'How yous feeling?' he asked.

Tilda nudged him hard. 'You tell me off for asking stupid questions. How do you *think* he's feeling?' she whispered, annoyed.

Ben smiled sheepishly. 'Well, what am I supposed to say?' he whispered back.

She glared at him. 'Shush, he'll hear you.'

'Sorry.' He grimaced and walked across to the bed. 'Hello, Mr Wragg. I'm Ben McCraven. I'm . . . er . . .' He hung his head. 'Well, I'm sorry.'

Ted tried to smile. 'Don't be sorry, lad. For what you both did, you deserve a medal. I'm just glad you 'appened to be passing.' His eyes grew distant. 'Do yer know, at the moment I can't even remember anything about it. We'd gone to collect some money from a job I'd done. Made a day out of it. Maud was fussing over Daisy getting cold.'

'The money's all there, Mr Wragg,' said Ben. 'It's still in your wallet.'

'I know, lad. The nurse told me. They've put it away safe.'

'We think the cart hit a stone in the road and went out of control hitting the side of the bridge. The impact must have thrown you and your wife out.' Tilda lowered her head. 'Well, that's what we think.'

Ted shut his eyes tightly. 'Oh God, I should never have let Maud persuade me to take her with me. I've not had much experience of driving a wagon. But I could never refuse her anything and she was so looking forward to the day out.' Tears filled his eyes and he took several moments to compose himself. 'I'd . . . I'd like to give you something for your trouble . . .'

Ben's face darkened. 'I won't hear of such a thing,' he erupted.

Ted Wragg tried to smile. 'You have my sincere thanks. I 'ope all this hasn't 'eld you up?'

'No, no. Not at all,' Ben replied brightly. 'Don't you worry on that score. One town's as good as another.'

Ted eyed him quizzically. 'Oh, I see. You're travellers, is that it?'

'Travellers! Definitely not,' Ben replied indignantly. 'I'm . . .' He nearly forgot himself and divulged his real reason for being on the road. 'Searching for work,' he hurriedly added.

A look of horror crossed Ted's already pained face.

'What's the matter?' a worried Tilda asked. 'Shall I get the nurse?'

'No, no. They can't give me anything else for the pain. Not just yet. It was the mention of work. It's my business, you see. If I'm not there to oversee it I could lose me livelihood, and then what will 'appen to Daisy. Oh, God, what am I to do? It's enough coping with the loss of Maud . . .'

'Mr Wragg, you have to concentrate on getting better. Upsetting yourself will only make matters worse,' Tilda said anxiously.

'Business?' asked Ben. 'What sort of business?'

Tilda glared at him. 'Ben!'

'Oh, shut up, Tilda, I was only asking.'

The room fell silent as another wave of pain crossed Ted's face. They both stared at him anxiously.

'We'd better go, Ben.'

'No, no. Please stay,' Ted uttered. 'Bring Daisy closer, please.'

Tilda moved towards the bed and sat down on the chair at the side. Ted settled eyes filled with tenderness on his daughter. 'I owe her life to you both. How can I ever repay you?' He looked at them both helplessly.

'Your recovery will be payment enough.' Tilda said sincerely. 'And as for your business, surely someone will keep an eye on it for you? Is there anyone we could contact for you?'

'No one I could trust,' he replied. 'I've got a small yard. Building, odd jobbing, that sort of thing. I'm not the only one in the area. There's plenty waiting to step in and take what would have been mine.'

'Oh, that's interesting,' Ben piped up. Builder, he thought. He'd never met a builder before. But more important to him was the mention of odd jobbing. A few odd jobs would have suited him fine. But then he remembered the man's predicament. Pity he was out of action or Ben would have asked after the possibility of some work.

Ted misconstrued his reply. 'You're a builder yourself, then?'

Ben stared in astonishment. 'Builder! Me? Well, as a matter of fact I...'

Tilda's eyes were fixed on him, her jaw dropping. Was Ben really about to tell Ted he too was a builder? Before she could question his sudden dubious skills the door opened and the Matron appeared, accompanied by a harassed-looking woman.

Matron glared across at Tilda, her mouth set tight. 'You, young lady, have breached hospital rules. Who gave you permission to bring that baby in here? We didn't know what to think when we found the cot empty.'

Tilda gulped. 'I'm sorry...'

'It was me,' rasped Ted. 'I asked her to bring the baby to see me.'

Tilda looked at him gratefully.

Matron advanced to the bed, clasping her hands across her large stomach. 'Now, Mr Wragg,' she said sternly. 'You're a very sick man. Peace and quiet is what the doctor ordered.' She turned to Tilda and Ben. 'You two had better go. Give the baby to Miss Stringfellow on your way out.'

'Yes, I really must get off,' Miss Stringfellow twittered.

Tilda, rising, frowned deeply. 'Off?' she asked, clutching the baby protectively as Miss Stringfellow advanced, arms outstretched. 'Where are you taking Daisy?'

Matron's eyebrows rose indignantly. 'Well, really, that is not a question *you* should be asking!'

'I'm asking,' Ben interjected.

'Just hand the baby over,' Matron snapped. 'I've no time for this nonsense. It may have escaped your notice but this is a hospital, full of sick people.'

'I'm asking,' uttered Ted. 'Where are you taking my Daisy?'

Matron's eyes settled on him kindly. 'Now, Mr Wragg, your daughter needs caring for. We can't do it here.'

His eyes grew troubled as the truth dawned. 'A home! You're putting my Daisy in a home? But you can't!'

'We have no choice, Mr Wragg. As you have no relatives, Daisy's welfare has to be considered and you could be here for a long time.'

Tilda, eyes filled with horror, backed away towards the windows clutching Daisy tightly. 'But you can't!'

Noticing the look in her eyes, Ben followed her and took her arm. 'Now listen,' he whispered urgently. 'The Matron's right. The baby's got to be cared for. I hope you're not thinking what I think you're thinking? How on earth are yous going to look after Daisy when you've nowhere to go yersel', Tilda?'

Daisy woke and started to cry. Tilda rocked her gently.

Miss Stringfellow joined them and tried to take hold of the child. Tilda stepped sideways. Miss Stringfellow looked across at Matron, expecting her to intervene.

Just then the door opened and a young doctor came through. On seeing the gathering in the room and hearing the growing rumpus, he frowned disapprovingly.

'What's going on?' he asked, and glared at Matron.

'This young woman won't hand over the child.'

Dr Smethwick, who had never got on with the bossy Matron, who in turn thought the young doctor far too inexperienced for his job, looked across at Tilda. 'Won't you? And why not?'

'Because they're going to put her in a home.'

'Have you a better suggestion?' he asked.

'I really must get off,' Miss Stringfellow twittered again.

Ben, who was getting fed up with the situation, and like Miss Stringfellow wanted to get off, glared at Tilda. 'Answer the doctor.'

She bit her lip anxiously. Ben knew very well she hadn't.

'I have.'

All eyes fell an Ted who they had momentarily forgotten.

He took several painful breaths. 'You say you're looking for work?' he asked Tilda.

Frowning quizzically, she nodded.

'Then look after Daisy for me. You can live in my house and I'll pay you.'

Tilda was amazed. This was the last thing she had expected.

'Well, really, Mr Wragg. You're seriously going to hand over your child to this young woman?' Matron erupted, eyeing the dishevelled Tilda disapprovingly. 'Why, you don't even know her!'

'She and this young man saved my life. Mr McCraven nearly

lost his own trying to save my wife. There was money in my wallet. It's still there, Matron. That's good enough for me. And you, Ben, I can't believe me luck that you're a builder too. Keep my business ticking over 'til I get out. Please. You'd be doing me a great service. I'll see you well rewarded.'

Ben's jaw dropped in horror. 'But I . . .'

Matron nearly had a convulsion. 'Mr Wragg, really! I should think very carefully about this.'

'Matron,' Dr Smethwick ordered, 'Mr Wragg's bones are broken, but his brain is functioning perfectly. He's quite capable of expressing his wishes regarding his child and his livelihood. If his mind's at rest on that score, it can only aid his recovery.' Although at this moment he gravely doubted the man would recover.

The sick man eyed him gratefully. 'Will you do it for me?' he pleaded, looking at Ben and Tilda.

'We can't possibly say no, Ben. Mr Wragg is desperate,' Tilda urged.

Ben, sensing all eyes on him, felt totally cornered. But before he even had time to express his own wishes Tilda had turned from him and was nodding her head vigorously.

'We'll be happy to do it, Mr Wragg.'

He sighed with relief.

Dr Smethwick addressed Miss Stringfellow. 'Seems we won't be needing your services after all. Would you like to show the good lady out Matron?'

Face purple with rage, she grabbed hold of Miss Stringfellow's arm and yanked her towards the door. She turned and stared over at the doctor 'I'd like to see you in my office, Dr Smethwick. When it's convenient of course,' she added sarcastically.

'Delighted, Matron. About eleven. I take two sugars in my tea.'

Against hospital rules, the door was banged shut behind them.

Dr Smethwick turned towards the young couple. 'Well, hurry, and sort things out. I need to examine my patient. And you,' he addressed Mr Wragg, 'need to concentrate your efforts on getting better.'

Chapter Thirteen

Tilda, nursing Daisy, sat in the back of the wagon wedged tightly between a pile of sacks, the ladder and some pieces of wood. She hadn't wanted to sit up front with Ben. She wouldn't have felt safe, especially not the way he drove. She supposed she wasn't being very fair to him – after all, the journey to the hospital could never have been classed as a Sunday afternoon jaunt considering the dire circumstances. But regardless she preferred to sit in the back, her excuse being Daisy.

She grimaced, turned her head and watched Ben tightening the reins on a restive horse which had spent the duration in the hospital stables. Ever since they had agreed to help out and made the sketchy arrangements, Ben had been unusually quiet. His quietness concerned her. Not a man to shy away from saying his piece, he had said not one word to her since they had been ushered out of Ted's room.

Sighing, she turned her head and looked across the well-tended hospital grounds. She observed several beds that had been winter dug and were now ready for spring planting. With flowers grown and the sweeping lawns tended this would make the ideal tranquil environment to aid the recovery of the sick residents and she hoped it wouldn't be long before Ted himself was well enough to make a visit.

The sight of the earth brought a lump to her throat as a

vision of the cottage sprang to mind and she remembered all the hard work she and Eustace had done to expand the garden, the hopes she had had of improving their living standards. Suddenly the enormity of her situation flooded through her and she sighed heavily.

Less than two weeks ago she had been living with her father, a day-to-day, hand-to-mouth existence. It had been a hard life, most of the time not very pleasant, but an existence she was used to nevertheless. That life had been taken from her and what had transpired in the intervening days had resulted in more experiences than most people encountered in a lifetime. And it still was not over.

The thought of the undertaking she had just accepted suddenly frightened her. She knew practically nothing about the care of a baby and yet she had agreed to raise and protect one until its father could take over. But what if the nurse had been right and Ted Wragg did not recover?

She shuddered. Whether Mr Wragg made a full recovery and took over the care of his daughter was not her only problem. She had also enthusiastically said she would do whatever she could to aid Ben in his task. But what did she know about running a business?

She took several deep breaths. Well, it was too late for her to be questioning her actions or motives. What was done was done. She would just have to get on with it and hope for the best.

She felt the wagon rock as Ben climbed aboard.

Seated, he turned to face her, eyes full of anger. 'Well, I hope you're happy, Tilda.'

She flinched at his tone. 'Pardon?'

'Yous heard. I said, I hope you're happy.'

'I don't understand?'

'Don't yous?' he snapped. 'You've committed me, Tilda. Got me in a right mess, and you say yous don't understand? I was heading for Birmingham. I have things to do. I didn't want to be tied like this. And besides, I know nothing about building – and through your big mouth, you've got me running the show.'

She stared at him. 'That's not my fault! You told Mr Wragg you were a builder.'

His face darkened. 'Did I? When?'

'Well . . . er . . .' Her lips tightened. 'You led him on by what you said.'

'And what did I say, Tilda?'

'Well . . .' She gnawed her bottom lip anxiously. Ben was right. He had never actually said he was anything of the sort. 'It's what you didn't say,' she said frostily.

Ben narrowed his eyes. 'Yous should make up your mind, Tilda. For your information I was going to say I was good at odd jobbing. And I am. I can tackle most things. But builder I'm not. Even a thick Glaswegian like me,' he poked himself in the chest mockingly, 'knows that it's a trade which takes years to master.'

'Well, why didn't you say something when he asked you to help him out? Why didn't you refuse?'

'It isn't easy, refusing a very sick man. Besides, Tilda, I never got the chance. Yous did all the answering for both of us.'

'Oh!' she exclaimed, shocked.

'Yes, yous can say "Oh". You'll be mouthing a lot of that when things get on top of you in the future.'

She frowned quizzically. 'What do you mean?'

'I mean, Tilda, that when I say I'm heading for Birmingham, that's exactly where I'm headed. I'll take yous to Wragg's door and that's where I leave yous.'

Her face fell in horror. 'But you can't! Ben, you can't do this.'

'Can't I? Watch me.'

He spun round in his seat and whipped up the horse.

* * *

Wharf Street, a densely populated district of interconnecting streets and cul-de-sacs, ran a half mile or so across the boundaries of the city, linking the nearby canal, foundries and gas works. Cramped and defective back-to-back terraces, some built as early as the 1820s, mingled with newer terraced housing of slightly better quality. Rows of assorted shops, the rooms above used either for lodgings or for storage, public houses, snooker halls, a cinema, factories and other small businesses were scattered intermittently along this busy thoroughfare. Families, many atrociously poor, lived alongside shop assistants, schoolteachers, and professional people who worked in the area.

As she bumped up and down in the back of the wagon, its wooden wheels clattering loudly against the cobblestones, Tilda gazed around her in awe. Only used to village life and the solitude of the woods, this busy street filled with people going about their business frightened her witless, and on top of her other problems she worried how she was ever going to get used to the noise and general daily bustle.

Ted had told them they would find his premises easily, but considering they were strangers to this town Tilda thought his assumption optimistic. From what she had observed of the part of Leicester they had travelled through, it appeared to her to be made up of warrens of identical streets leading off in all directions. Their destination could be anywhere amongst them.

A bad-tempered Ben had to stop and ask guidance from several locals before they finally came across their destination, purely by accident, having again driven aimlessly after getting the instructions muddled. Ben's Scottish accent and the local Leicester dialect hadn't agreed. Tilda had thought it best to keep her mouth shut. According to Ben, she had said and done enough already.

Ben finally pulled the wagon to a halt and studied the premises. Wragg's Builder's and General Contractor's consisted of a larger than average terraced house adjoining what was a fair-sized yard, entered via two patched up arched wooden doors. The yard itself was on a corner, surrounded by a high red brick wall topped with blue coping. Running the length of the coping was a line of thick sharp barbed wire, its job obviously to deter intruders.

Ben turned to face Tilda. 'Well, this is it.' He jumped down and held Daisy whilst she climbed out of the wagon. Handing the baby back to her, he held out the bunch of keys Ted had given him. 'You'd better take these.'

She stared at them hesitantly and lifted her eyes to his. 'Please, Ben, won't you change your mind?'

He shook his head. 'No.'

Daisy started to grizzle.

'I'd get the wean inside if I were yous. I think she's hungry.'

Tilda flinched at his abrupt tone. 'There's no need for us to part company like this, Ben. We've been through a lot together. I admit I was wrong when I agreed to all this, but I thought you'd be pleased, that you needed work as much as I did.' She put Daisy across her shoulder and patted her back. 'I'm sorry, truly I am, but all I could think of was Daisy and the worry that poor Mr Wragg must have been feeling. And to be honest, although I'm so sorry for what happened to him, this offer was like a gift from God to me and I thought you'd feel the same way. Shush, Daisy,' she soothed. 'I'll get you some dinner in a minute.'

Ben stared down at her, a mite ashamed of himself. He could truthfully appreciate all of Tilda's feelings and the motives behind her actions. And how was she to know of his quest, of his need to keep moving? He'd never told her.

'Why don't you stay the night, Ben?' she continued. 'It's

getting late and we've had a long day. You'll feel better after a good night's rest.'

'If these are delaying tactics then you're wasting your time. Now or tomorrow, it makes no difference. I'm not staying.'

Tilda's face reddened in embarrassment. She hadn't been trying to delay him, just been concerned for his welfare. But she wasn't about to tell him that fact. Daisy's grizzling suddenly erupted into a wail and passers-by began to look in their direction in earnest. Tilda snatched the keys from Ben's hand and strode towards the door. Unlocking it, she pushed it open and stepped across the threshold. As she turned to shut the door she glanced across at him.

'I'd offer you something to eat but I don't want to be accused of keeping you any longer than necessary.'

At the mention of food, Ben's stomach growled in hunger and he suddenly remembered he hadn't eaten for hours. And he was tired. A short rest and nourishment before he began his journey was just what he needed. If he didn't dally too long, he could still make the outskirts of town before it grew too dark to find a place to sleep. He tilted his head and grinned at her.

'How long will it take yous to throw a sandwich together?'

Her mouth dropped open at the audacity of him. 'I don't know,' she snapped sharply. 'Depends what's in the larder.'

His grin grew wider. 'I suppose I can spare the time it'll take yous to find out.' His gaze fell on Daisy. 'But in fairness you'd better see to the bairn first.'

That's mighty big of you, she wanted to say. Instead she turned on her heel and marched down the passage.

Inside the house Daisy's protests momentarily subsided and, grateful for the interlude, Tilda headed straight for the kitchen with the baby on her hip. Once there she stood and stared around in awe. Under the window by the back door was a large pot sink at the side of which stood a black water pump. She walked across to it and stroked the pump in wonder. Grabbing the handle, she pumped it up and down several times. Cold water spurted into the sink and Tilda gasped in delight.

'Would you look at that!' she cried, addressing Daisy who was now studying her new guardian through large unblinking blue eyes. Mesmerised, Tilda turned and rested her back against the sink, staring around at the rest of the kitchen. Nailed to the back wall above a small pine table were several shelves crammed with every utensil, pot and pan the most professional cook would ever require to produce a meal. In the space where she had expected a fireplace to be was an iron contraption painted green and cream. She walked across to it and stared at it in bewilderment wondering what on earth it was used for.

'Have yous never seen a gas cooker before?' Ben piped up from the doorway. Unbeknown to Tilda he had been watching her for several moments, fascinated by her response to her discoveries.

Eyes fixed on the cooker, she shook her head. 'Is that what it is?' She turned to face him. 'You mean it cooks meals?'

He walked across to her. In truth he himself had only ever seen one of its kind before, and that was in Taffy Williams's kitchen. It had been Mrs Taff's pride and joy. His own mother had cooked all their hot food over an open fire, just like Tilda had done. 'Move out the way, I'll show yous how it works,' he ordered knowledgeably.

Tilda did as she was asked and jumped back in fright as the gas popped loudly when Ben lit it with a match. She felt the heat from the jet on her face.

'Why, it's marvellous,' she whispered. 'Fancy just having to turn a knob and light a match.' She frowned hard. 'Are you sure it's safe? It smells a bit funny.'

''Course it's safe,' Ben chided. 'Only don't turn the gas on and not light it, 'cos that will kill yous. It's poisonous, see.'

199

'Is it?' she said, horrified. 'I don't think I'll bother with it then.'

'Don't be silly, Tilda. Use it properly and it's as safe as houses. Besides, there isn't anything else to cook on so you'll have to use it.'

She stared at it in concern. Then pushing her worries about the cooker to the back of her mind, she turned her head and smiled at Daisy. 'Come on, young madam. Let's get you some supper.'

Feeding Daisy proved an arduous task. She wanted her mother. Although sympathising with the child, nevertheless after twenty minutes of trying to get a spoon in a mouth that was emitting ear-splitting screams, and dodging chubby little arms that were flailing wildly, the usually patient Tilda was nearly at her wit's end as to what to do to coax her to eat.

Ben, who whilst the operation was in progress had miraculously vanished, suddenly reappeared. 'For God's sake, Tilda, stop forcing the child. She'll eat when she's hungry.'

Tilda spun round to face him. 'If she's not hungry, why is she screaming? She's hungry, I tell you.'

'Did the child say she was?'

'Oh, don't be stupid.' In desperation she thrust the spoon in his direction. 'If you're so clever, you have a go.'

Without further ado Ben grabbed the spoon and bowl of food, whipped the screaming baby from her arms and sat in the chair opposite, settling Daisy on his knee. Laden spoon raised, he looked across at Tilda. 'Haven't yous something to be doing?'

Indignantly she rose and strode into the kitchen, and for several moments stood staring out of the window, waiting for her annoyance to subside. Ben McCraven really was an infuriating man.

She felt a weight in her pocket, put her hand inside and pulled out the blackened horseshoe. She found herself smiling, remembering him giving it to her. Spotting a nail protruding from the wall by the side of the door, she hung the shoe on it. 'Now, let's see if you bring any luck.'

She turned and her gaze settled on the table. It was set for two. It also held a cold chicken and ham pie, a lump of cheese, a loaf of bread and slab of butter, and a pot of tea. One of the plates had been used. Ben had obviously eaten his fill whilst she had been trying to feed Daisy. Shutting out the noise from the other room, she sat down suddenly, realising she was ravenous. She smiled. It was surprisingly thoughtful of Ben to include her when he had put the meal together.

She cut a piece of pie and spread a slice of bread. As she raised the laden fork to her lips her stomach lurched and she stared at the pie as though it was poisoned. Maud Wragg had obviously made it ready for when they came back from their trip. The poor woman would never have envisaged not returning to share it with her husband. Tilda sighed and pushed away the plate. Her hunger had left her.

For a while she stared blankly at the whitewashed wall as she pictured Ted, Maud and Daisy all living here happily. She suddenly felt like an intruder in the dead woman's home. What right did she have to be here, using the woman's possessions, eating her food? She pressed her fingers to her temples and shut her eyes.

She sat for an age, just herself and her thoughts, until finally she shuddered, realising she was cold. It had grown dark and the house was silent. Frowning deeply, she rose from the table and poked her head round the door to the back room. She couldn't help but smile at the scene that met her. In the large comfortable brown leather armchair by the side of the fireplace, sat Ben fast asleep. Cuddled protectively in his arms was Daisy. She also was sleeping, the remains of her dinner apparent on her chubby cheeks and staining the front of her clothes.

It was a shame, thought Tilda, to disturb the little one. She looked so comfortable, and so for that matter did Ben. She decided to leave them and made her way back to the kitchen.

Some time later she woke with a start. Ben was leaning over her.

'What is it? What's wrong?' she uttered.

He hurriedly laid his hand on her shoulder. 'Nothing, Tilda. Yous just fell asleep. I was just checking yous were all right, that's all.'

'Oh, I see.' She ran her hand over her dishevelled hair and rubbed sleep from her eyes. 'What time is it?'

'Just gone twelve.'

'Is it!' she exclaimed. 'Oh, I . . .'

'Tilda,' he cut in, 'just sit there for a moment and gather your wits. Do you fancy a cuppa?'

She looked at him, surprised. 'Er . . . yes. I'd love one, thank you.'

He lit the gas and she jumped as it popped. 'I don't think I'll ever get used to that.'

He smiled. 'Yous will, Tilda. Once you've stopped being scared of it.'

She nodded reluctantly. 'I suppose.' She yawned loudly then suddenly eyed him anxiously. 'Where's Daisy?'

'Don't panic. She's fine. She woke. In fact, she woke us both. So I changed her and gave her some warm milk and put her to bed. She went oot like a light.'

She stared at him wide-eyed. 'You did?'

'Don't look so surprised. I'm not helpless, yous know.' He grinned. 'I doubt her nappy'll stay on, but I did my best.' He spooned tea in the pot, poured in boiling water and collected two mugs, then sat down opposite her. 'Yous can be mother,' he said, pushing the teapot towards her.

They sat in silence for a moment whilst she poured the tea.

Ben cradled the mug between his hands and slowly sipped. 'Would yous not be better off in bed? You're done in.'

'I can't,' she answered abruptly.

'Can't? Whyever not?'

She raised her eyes. 'You wouldn't understand, Ben.'

'Try me.'

'I don't feel it's right,' she said softly.

'What isn't?'

Her eyes flashed. 'See, I told you you wouldn't understand.'

'How can I?' he snapped. 'When yous haven't explained yersel'.'

She sighed heavily. 'I'm sorry. No, I haven't, have I? It's just that I feel an intruder, that I shouldn't be here. It's such a lovely home, isn't it.'

'Oh, I get it.'

'Get what?'

'That yous don't think you're good enough.' He shook his head. 'Oh, Tilda Penny, if you're not worthy then naebody is.'

She was taken aback. 'Do you mean that?'

'I wouldn't say it if I didn't. Seems to me that father of yours had a lot to answer for. I doubt he gave yous much credit for anything. You're as good as anyone, but if yous don't start believing it then yous might as well slit your own throat.' His eyes twinkled. 'Shall I get yous a knife?'

She suppressed a smile. 'Not right at this minute.' She sipped her own tea thoughtfully. Ben's words had shocked her. She'd never expected anything like that to come from his mouth, especially since he didn't much care for her. But all the same, she wanted to hug him, he had made her feel so much better. Suddenly a picture of Fanny came to mind. She had told Tilda exactly the same thing. They were right, both of them. It was about time she realised that she had a lot to offer in

203

the right circumstances. And now the circumstances couldn't be more right.

Daisy needed the love and care Tilda could give her until matters sorted themselves out one way or another. Ted had obviously thought so. It couldn't be more apparent how much his child meant to him, and he had put his trust in Tilda, stranger or not. That act had said it all, hadn't it? There were people about who thought she was worthy.

She smiled to herself and suddenly her turmoil lifted and a sense of tranquillity flooded through her. It was as though Maud Wragg herself was giving Tilda her blessing. She raised her eyes. 'I'll do my best, Maud, that I promise you,' she said aloud.

'What did yous say?' asked Ben.

'What? Oh . . . er . . . nothing. Just mumbling to myself, that's all.' She took a deep breath. 'I want to thank you.'

'Me? For what?'

'For what you said. I know you don't think much of me, but I appreciate your words.'

'The feeling's mutual, Tilda. Besides, what I said was the truth. You're no beauty, it's no good saying yous are, but your heart's in the right place.'

Tilda's back stiffened. Now he had spoilt it. Did he really have to go and say that? 'Excuse me, but you're no handsome knight in shining armour yourself!'

Ben cocked an eyebrow. 'Yous might not think so, but others do. I've never been short of female admirers.'

He rose abruptly.

'Where are you going?'

'I'd better get off. I've a long way to go.'

'Don't be daft. It's late. You might as well sleep here 'til morning. Never know who you might meet on the road at this time of night. You don't want to get robbed again, do you?'

'I've not much left to steal, Tilda, and what I've got's not worth the trouble. But I suppose you're right. A few more hours won't make any difference.' He sat back down. 'Any more tea in the pot?'

She poured him a mug then looked at him thoughtfully. 'Ben, I know it's none of my business but why are you refusing this job? I can't understand it. A chance like this doesn't come along often. And why Birmingham anyway? You told Ted Wragg one town was as good as another.' She gnawed her lip anxiously. 'Is your decision anything to do with me?'

He shook his head. 'Nothing whatsoever, Tilda. What makes yous think that?'

'Oh, Ben, come on. You can't get away from me quick enough.'

'Tilda, let me assure yous, it's got nothing to do with yous. And I don't want to discuss my reasons. As yous quite rightly said, it's none of your business.'

She flinched at his tone.

He grinned disarmingly. 'Be honest, Tilda, apart from anything else, can yous really see us two working and living together in harmony?'

She grinned also. 'No, not really. But then, who knows until we give it a try? We managed at the Brindles'.'

He scowled. 'Don't corner me, Tilda. You're good at doing that.'

'And you didn't me with the Brindles?'

'Yes, fair dues, I did put yous on the spot. But these circumstances are different. That was only for days, this could be for ... well, who knows how long it'll take before Wragg's on his feet. If he ever is,' he added.

Tilda frowned. 'You don't think he'll die, do you?'

'I hope not, for the bairn's sake.'

'So do I. But, regardless, Mr Wragg thinks you'll be taking care of his business for him. Do you think it's fair leaving him in the lurch like this?' Leaving me in the lurch, she wanted to add. 'It's not as though I can be any help there.'

'Stop it, Tilda. You're putting me an the spot again and I don't like it, I tell yous. You'll soon get someone else. Someone more qualified. Good God, there must be hundreds of men who'd jump at the chance. I don't want to be tied. I need to be free until . . .' He stopped abruptly, just managing to stop himself from saying until he had found his father's murderer and justice had been served.

She frowned, confused. 'Until what?'

'Nothing,' he snapped. He pushed back his chair and stood up. 'We're both tired. We need to sleep. I'm going to kip on the sofa. I'll probably have gone when yous rise in the morning so I'll say my goodbyes now.' He smiled at her. 'I do wish yous the best. I hope it all works out. I'm sure it will.'

'I wish I had your faith.' She forced a smile. 'We always seem to be saying goodbye. It's becoming a habit.'

He laughed wryly. 'Yes, we do. But this time it's final, Tilda.'

'Yes, I know.' She felt sadness overcome her and wondered why for an instant. She managed a weary smile. 'I wish you the best also.'

They looked at each other for a moment.

'Well,' Ben said, 'goodnight then.'

'Goodnight. Sleep well.'

Chapter Fourteen

Ben woke just as dawn was breaking. Wishing wholeheartedly he could turn over and go back to sleep, he stiffly climbed off the sofa, straightened his crumpled clothes and headed for the window where he pulled aside the curtain slightly. From what he could tell it looked a promising day. The cloud cover seemed light and there hadn't been a frost. He yawned long and loudly. It was fair weather for travelling in, he thought as he let the curtain fall back. He trod lightly towards the kitchen and put together a hasty breakfast of a piece of bread and noggin of cheese.

He was surprised Tilda wasn't up and about. He knew she had had a lifetime of early rising and it was difficult, even if you wanted to, to break a habit. He thought about taking her up a cup of tea, then decided not to. She would need all the sleep she could get considering what was facing her. And besides, waking her would only mean another round of goodbyes and he wanted to avoid that.

He deliberated for a moment whether to make himself some sandwiches to eat later. Why not? he thought, and cut four thick slices of bread and filled them with cheese. He found a brown paper bag to wrap them in, then stuffed them in his pocket.

It was time to go. He was halfway down the dark passageway when he froze in his tracks. The horse and cart. They had been left out in the street all night. He rushed to the front door, opened it as quietly as possible and peered out. His jaw dropped. There was no sign of either.

Think, man, think, he said to himself, frowning hard and thinking that although he couldn't remember doing so, he must have put them in the yard.

Standing inside it, he looked around. Even in the early morning darkness he could tell it was far larger than it had appeared from the outside, but despite that fact it was filled with too many building materials and other items ever to house a horse and cart.

He clamped his hand to his head. He was going mad. They had driven home in the horse and cart. They must be somewhere. Or, the worst possibility, they had been stolen. 'Oh, God,' he groaned.

Just then a noise startled him, coming from over by the two large wooden doors. A smaller door cut inside one of them was opening and a figure stepping through.

'Who's there?' Ben called, moving forward.

The figure froze and stared across at him. 'For the love of God, yers gave me a fright. I wasn't expecting anyone ter be here. Who's yerself?'

'I asked first,' Ben insisted.

There was silence for a moment then a voice replied, ''Tis me – Paddy.'

'Paddy?'

'Yes. Patrick O'Malley.'

'And what are yous doing here at this time in the morning?'

'And why shouldn't I be here? I have every right.'

'Oh, yous do? How come?'

''Cos ... 'cos I work here, that's why.'

'Work here? What – for Mr Wragg? He never mentioned you.'

'And why would he be mentioning me to you?' Paddy, a

solidly built man of about forty had at least two days' stubble on his weatherbeaten face. His clothes looked disreputable: a grubby striped shirt, the pocket of which was ripped and hanging by the last of its stitches and brown corduroy trousers, which had seen better days, held up by a thick piece of string pulled tightly round his middle. He stepped over several obstacles blocking his path and approached Ben. 'Has he took you on? And himself was only telling me the other day he hadn't much work.' He narrowed his eyes and eyed Ben scathingly. 'So yers might as well scarper, there's nothing here for yers.' He frowned hard as a thought struck suddenly. 'Now just one minute. How come he's taking on when himself is in the hospital with just about every bone in his body broke?'

'Yous know about that?'

'It's all over the street. News travels fast. And I thought to myself: Well, Patrick, 'tis up to you to keep the business going until Ted comes home.' He shook his head sadly. ' 'Tis a shame about Maud. Lovely woman she was. Made a grand meat pie. I'll miss her pies, so I will.' He sniffed loudly and wiped a gnarled hand under his nose, surveying Ben closely through beady grey eyes. 'You're Scottish,' he said accusingly.

'I am,' Ben confirmed proudly.

Patrick cleared his throat and spat the phlegm on the ground, just missing Ben's boot. ' 'Tis as I thought, another bloody foreigner trying ter take our jobs. If any more of yers comes to Leicester, Scotland'll be empty.'

'Excuse me,' Ben hissed, anger erupting, 'but if I'm not mistaken you're Irish.'

'And so I am.'

'Well, that makes you a foreigner too.'

'That I'm not,' he cried indignantly. 'I was born in Belfast. I'm British.'

Ben stared at him in disbelief. 'And what d'yous think I am?'

'Scottish, that's what you are. And I'll not work with a Scotsman. Load of wasters, the lot of yers. Wouldn't know a pick from a shovel. But you'd know what a bloody teapot was.'

'Oh, is that right?' snarled Ben, pulling himself up to his full six foot. 'Well, it might interest yous to know that yous have no choice about working with me,' he said, in his anger momentarily forgetting his decision to leave.

'Oh, and how d'yers make that out.'

'Because I'm in charge, that's how.'

Patrick's jaw dropped in shock, then his face turned thunderous. 'In charge? You? Sez who?'

'Mr Wragg, that's who. And I have it in writing.'

'Liar,' spat Patrick. 'Ted Wragg would never do such a thing. You must have forged his hand. If anyone is to be in charge it would be me. Why, I've worked for the man for the last . . .' he searched his mind for a plausible timespan '. . . a good many years.' He sized Ben up and down. 'Yers don't look like a brickie ter me. And yers don't look old enough to be put in charge. How long you been out of yer apprenticeship?'

'Long enough,' Ben replied cagily.

Patrick shook his head. 'It all seems fishy to me and himself on his death bed.' He tilted his head as another thought struck. 'Would you be the one who rescued him now?'

'So what if I am?'

Patrick's lip curled. 'Then it all makes sense.'

Ben grimaced. 'Just what a' yous implying?'

Patrick scowled. 'Implying! What does that mean? Talk English man, if that's possible for a heathen.'

Ben, who had always had a soft spot for his Irish Celtic cousins, feeling akin to them because as he saw it they had suffered as much at the hands of the English as the Scots in the past, now saw red and angrily stabbed a finger in Patrick's direction. 'Who a' yous calling a heathen? If any breed are heathens it's you Irish. The only sense you understand is the bottle.'

'Calling us drunks now, are yers? And you a nation known for it.'

'No more than the Irish.' Ben's eyes narrowed menacingly. 'Now, listen, I think you've said enough. You'd better go.'

'Go?' Patrick spat, stepping over a pile of bricks. 'If anyone's to be leaving it'll be yourself. He also wagged a finger. You ain't no builder, so it's no good telling me yers are. Been in the trade all me life and I knows builders, see.' He eyed Ben mockingly. 'Your hands are like lily pads. They ain't never handled bricks. And by my reckoning yers wouldn't know a Arris from a Bullnose.' He grinned wickedly, eyes alight with malice. 'I've got your measure, laddie. Did it yerself, didn't yer? Done Wragg over for his money, but somehow it didn't work and then you pretended to save him. Oh!' he laughed, showing a row of yellowing teeth. ''Tis very clever, so it is. Might have fooled some, but not Patrick O'Malley. And I'll soon put the authorities right, yers can rest assured on that. Now, as I've already said, if there's anyone ter be leaving, it'll be yerself.'

Ben's fury mounted. This grubby little man before him did not know how right he was in respect of Ben's building knowledge but his mistake had been in accusing him of attacking Ted Wragg with intent to rob. In two strides of his long legs he was in front of the man and before Patrick had the sense to move, Ben had grabbed him by the scruff of his neck and was dragging him across towards the entrance doors. Once there he held Patrick up against the wall and thrust his own face next to his.

'Ted Wragg has put me in charge of his business until further notice. Have yous got that? And as for yous not working with a

Scotsman, I wouldn't breathe the same air as the likes of yersel', let alone share a shovel. And if yous ever dare insinuate again I was responsible for what happened to Mr Wragg you'll not be able to sup from a pint of porter for many a long month. Got that?'

Eyes wide, Patrick nodded.

'Good. Now get oot – and I don't want ter see your ugly face round here again.'

He peeled Patrick off the wall and thrust him towards the door.

Halfway through he turned back to face Ben. 'I'm owed money for wages,' he lied. 'Ten . . . no, fifteen bob, and I want it now.'

'Yous can want as much as you like, you'll get nothing from me unless I have it in writing from Mr Wragg. I'm sure yous know where to find him, being's yous know so much.'

Paddy's face turned thunderous. The scheme which he'd thought would be so easily executed, wasn't even a possibility, thanks to this man's presence. He clenched his fist and stuck it in the air, waving it menacingly. 'I'd watch your back if I was you. One way or another, I'll get yer for this. Be warned. Nobody muscles in on Patrick O'Malley. Nobody, d'yer hear? You Scottish bastard!'

Before Ben could retaliate he had disappeared.

Ben stood for a moment, still fuming from the confrontation. So deep in thought was he that he didn't see another figure enter through the door. Several moments went by before he realised a tall gangly youth was hovering before him, eyeing him curiously.

Raking his fingers through his hair in exasperation, Ben glared at the youth. 'What do you want? Mr Wragg's not here.'

The young man jumped and whipped off his cap which he twisted nervously between his fingers.

'Oh, for God's sake, spit it oot. I havenae got all day.'
Immediately he said it, Ben regretted his abrupt tone.

The youth stepped towards him hesitantly, staring at him.
'I'm reporting for work. Well, I think I am.'

'Pardon?' Ben said disbelievingly. 'Did you say work?'

'I ... I ... I did.'

'Oh, Christ,' he groaned. 'How many actually work here?'

'How ... how many?' The youth looked at him quizzically.
'Just me. And Mr Wragg, of course.'

Ben frowned. 'And what about Patrick O'Malley?'

'Eh? Oh, Paddy. No, he doesn't work here. Mr Wragg don't
like him. Won't touch him with a barge pole. Have ter watch out
for him, you do. He ain't a nice man. So Mr Wragg sez,' he
added hurriedly.

Ben nodded. 'Well, I'll be damned. So that was his game.'

'Game,' the youth queried.

'Oh, it doesn't matter. What's your name?'

'Walter Skuttle, but everyone calls me Wally. I live a few
doors down.'

'And what do yous do, Wully?'

'Wally, sir,' he corrected.

'That's what I said, Wully, well, what do yous do?'

'I'm the apprentice, sir. Well, for the next five months, then
I'm finished,' he added proudly. 'Mr Wragg's promised ter
keep me on. Sez in all the years he's been in business I'm the
best apprentice he's ever had. And me wages'll go up. Me
mam's ever so chuffed. She's a widow, see, so extra money
won't half make a difference.'

'Oh, I see.'

Wally eyed him worriedly. 'I never slept last night after I
heard about Mrs Wragg. She were a lovely woman. I'll miss
her, I will. Mam sez she'll look after Daisy. Sez it's the least she
can do.'

'There's no need.'

'Ain't there? Why?'

''Cos Tilda's looking after her. She's all right, is Tilda. You'll like her. She's going to be staying in the house for the time being with Daisy. Mr Wragg himself asked her to do it.'

'Oh, I see.' Wally grimaced. 'Mam won't like that.' He looked thoughtful. 'How's Mr Wragg? Do yer know?'

Ben nodded gravely. 'Yes, I know. It's very serious.'

'Oh, poor Mr Wragg. I hope he get's better. Me mam told me the gist of what'd happened but I didn't think it were that serious. It was me mam who told me to come today. Said Mr Wragg 'ud expect me to keep things going in the meantime. But I thought it'd only be for a couple of days.'

'It'll be for more than that.'

'Oh,' said Wally, alarmed. 'I'll do me best then but I hope I can manage. We've a few jobs Mr Wragg lined up but it'll be hard an me own.' He scratched his head thoughtfully. 'Excuse me fer asking, sir, but who are you?'

'Me?' Ben stared at him. The lad was right to ask but would he like the reply. Ted Wragg had unwittingly put a man in charge of his business who wasn't qualified to run it. Wally himself would do a better job, but couldn't because he wasn't fully qualified either.

Ben sighed heavily not relishing the fact that he was about to reveal that as matters stood, Wally's finishing his apprenticeship was in grave doubt and a wage rise even less likely. It was a shame he was about to shatter the future of this amiable young man. Even a layman like Ben knew that without the completion of the required full five years and the appropriate signed papers stating the fact, he would never be classed as a proper tradesman, never achieve the status in life and the remuneration that went with it, even though he had worked hard towards it for a pittance for the last few years.

He looked at the lad from the corner of his eye, suddenly envying him his skills. Ben himself had no such claim and at twenty-four was too old now ever to acquire them in the proper way, like Wally had. For a moment he felt totally inadequate. But at least, he thought, the likes of Wally had been afforded the chance. Where he came from apprenticeships had to be secured by bribes which his mother couldn't have afforded.

He raised his head and looked heavenwards. The sky was growing steadily lighter. Over the wall he could hear the trampling of hob-nailed boots on the cobbles. Men were going to work. Soon the whole street would be buzzing with activity. He had meant to be well on his way by now.

He suddenly thought of Tilda and visualised her trying to fulfil her promise to Ted Wragg. And she would. From what he had learned of Tilda in the short time he'd known her, he knew without a doubt she would strive to do her best, whatever the circumstances. He became aware of Wally shifting uneasily on his feet, mulling over what to do.

Ben sighed. The burden of this whole situation weighed heavily and he couldn't entirely blame Tilda for it. He had a tongue in his head; he should, as she had quite rightly pointed out last night, have spoken up at the time. He suddenly felt very guilty but nevertheless had the urge to step through the door, stride off down the street and not look back, leave the whole sorry mess for someone else to sort out.

He opened his mouth, intent on putting Wally fully in the picture, when something Patrick O'Malley had said sprang to mind.

'Wully, do a lot of Scots live in Leicester?'

'Eh? Scots?' he asked quizzically.

'Yes. People who speak like me.'

Wally nodded. 'A fair few, I'd say. And Irish. There's loads of them. And Italians. There's an Italian bloke called Tonio – got

215

an ice cream cart, comes round on a Sunday. Me mam and me always have a twopenny cornet as a treat when we can afford it.'

'I'm not interested in the Irish or Italians. What about the Scots? Whereabouts do they live?'

Wally shrugged his shoulders. 'Dunno where all of them live or how many there are,' he said apologetically. 'But there's Maggie. She's one of you. Her son drinks in the Talbot. Big bloke is Andy Ferguson. Works on the railway repairing the tracks. They live near Kendal's, the rag and bone place. I expect Maggie or Andy'll know some others. Well, more 'an likely. Races stick together, don't they.' He gulped hard. 'No disrespect meant.'

Ben grinned. 'None taken.'

'Is it relatives yers looking for?'

Ben eyed him sharply. 'Yes,' he lied. 'A relative. One I lost touch with eighteen years ago.'

'Oh. Bet you can't wait to see him again?'

Ben grinned wryly. 'I can't and that's a fact.'

He turned from Wally and resting one leg on top of a stack of bricks, leant his elbow on his knee, chin in his hand, and stared thoughtfully into space. His active mind was working overtime as a plan, a very feasible one at that, was forming. And with Wally on his side it just might work. If it did, all concerned would be happy, including himself. Ben smiled. As he'd said to Ted, one town was as good as another. Unwittingly Patrick O'Malley had reinforced that idea.

He straightened up and motioned to Wally. 'Come and sit down a minute, laddie, we need to talk.'

Seated somewhat uncomfortably on top of the bricks, Ben turned to Wally. 'You're a trustworthy lad, I take it?'

'Oh, yes, sir. Yes, indeed. Mr Wragg always trusted me. Left me on me own many a time to do a job.'

Ben smiled. 'Good. Now just listen to what I've got to say,

'cos I'm going to trust yous too, lad.' He took a deep breath. 'Mr Wragg's put me in charge of his business 'til such times . . . well, 'til such times. Only trouble is, I know nothing about building.'

'You don't? No'te at all?'

'Not that I know of. But you do. You could teach me. I would be your apprentice so to speak. And I'll make sure you get paid extra.'

'You will?'

'Goes without saying. In my book a man gets paid for what he does. Only this'll all be between you and me. To all intents and purposes I'll be in charge. And you never know, I might be able to teach you a thing or two. I've tackled a few things in my time.'

'Have yer?'

'Yeah. Last decent job I had was for a blacksmith. I quite enjoyed that. Anyway, this way we'll hopefully be able to keep Mr Wragg's business ticking over and ensure you finish your apprenticeship, and of course keep your mother happy with your wage still coming in.'

And in the meantime, he thought, there were Scots living in the area who needed investigating. It would be ironic to find Duggie Smilie hiding in Leicester when he himself was about to have headed off for Birmingham. Patrick O'Malley could have done him a favour, and whilst he was looking he would be helping Ted Wragg, have a roof over his head and be earning some money. He eyed Wally. 'So what do yous think?'

Wally grinned. 'Sounds good to me, Mr . . . er . . . sir . . . er . . .'

'Me name's Ben McCraven.'

'Right, Mr McCraven. Yeah, sounds good ter me,' Wally enthused.

Ben smiled. 'Good, then that's a deal. Only please just call me Ben.'

'I will, thank you, Ben.'

Ben stood up and stretched himself. 'Now, before we get down to it, there's the small matter of a missing horse and cart.'

'Horse and cart?' Wally piped up. 'I took it back last night.'

'Took it back?'

'Yeah, to the farrier's down the road where Mr Wragg hired it from. I thought the police had brought it back. Did I do wrong?'

A relieved Ben slapped him on the back and laughed loudly. 'No, you did right, laddie. Now what's on the list for today?'

Wally pulled a notebook from his pocket. 'Bath Lane down by the canal. There's a wall needs repairing. We'll have to load the hand cart first.'

'Right, lead the way.'

Ben followed Wally across the yard. 'Just one thing,' he asked as they loaded the cart. 'What the hell are Arrises and Bullnoses?'

'Bricks.'

'Bricks?'

'Yeah. An Arris is a good quality housebrick and a Bullnose has rounded edges. There's a few others but I'll show you them and teach you the names as we go along. And about the tools we use. And we need to check the lime pit. Can't let that get too low or we'll not be able to make cement.'

'Oh, right.' Ben exhaled sharply, suddenly wondering if he'd taken on more than he bargained for.

It was approaching eight o'clock when Tilda finally awoke and it took her several moments to remember where she was. She was stiff, her body aching, having slept on the floor of the nursery in case the child woke during the night and needed attention. The truth of the matter was that Tilda could not bring herself to sleep in Ted and Maud's bed, feeling it was not right. A hard floor was nothing she hadn't coped with before and she would continue to sleep on it until an alternative solution was thought of.

The first thing she did was check on Daisy. The child was just stirring and as Tilda peered into the cot, she opened her eyes and gave her guardian a broad smile as she lifted one chubby leg and fingered her toes. Tilda's heart melted and for a moment she felt sad for the whole situation that had brought her here.

Her sadness was rapidly replaced by fear as it suddenly struck her that she was on her own, left to face God knows what. Ben would be miles away by now and she felt so vulnerable without him. For a moment she wondered how he was. She sincerely hoped that he fared well and life treated him kindly.

As for herself, she prayed that no one would come to the door with work to be done, not until she had explored the possibility of taking somebody on. That person would need to be reliable and trustworthy and good at their job, and finding someone with all those qualities was not going to be easy, she thought, especially when she herself was a stranger to these parts.

Daisy chuckled, cutting through Tilda's thoughts, and she smiled down at the baby. 'Yes, I know you're hungry. Well, you just lie there like a good girl for a moment while I get dressed, then I'm all yours.'

Putting her fears aside, she hurriedly pulled on her clothes, scooped up Daisy and made her way down the stairs.

A fire was already set in the grate and for an instant Tilda thought Ben had laid it before he had departed. A rush of gratitude welled up and rapidly vanished as it struck her that the fire had more than likely been laid not by Ben but by Ted, ready for their return from the trip. She put a match to it and held up a piece of newspaper to keep out the draughts whilst it caught, all the time chatting away to Daisy. Putting several toys on the tray of her high chair to keep her occupied, Tilda affectionately patted the child's head, telling her she wouldn't be a moment, and made for the kitchen.

On seeing the mess that Ben had left after making his breakfast she fumed inwardly. It was a good job he wasn't here or she would have given him a piece of her mind. Typical of a man, she thought. Help themselves to what they want then leave the women to clear up after them. She supposed she was lucky he hadn't woken her up and asked her to make his breakfast.

It wasn't until Daisy was fed, changed and playing happily, and the kitchen was tidied, that she spotted the zinc bath hanging on a nail by the mangle in the outhouse just by the side of the back door. Curiosity had led her inside the shed after a visit to the adjoining privy. She had stared in wonder at the mangle first and then the copper washer next to it. Wash days, she thought, were going to be a pleasure with such implements to aid her. Then the bath had caught her eye and she had stared at it. To a person only used to the basic necessities this house was filled with luxuries but the bath, to Tilda's mind, had to be the most splendid.

She had already had a scrub down in the sink but suddenly the thought of a bath in front of the fire was something she couldn't resist, despite the fact it was early morning.

It took her the best part of an hour to heat enough water to fill it, then, making sure all the curtains were drawn, she sighed in ecstasy as she lowered her naked body into the hot water and stretched herself out.

Daisy chuckled at her.

'You can laugh,' Tilda scolded the child playfully. 'It's you tonight, my girl.'

Oh, this is heaven, she thought as she picked up a flannel, wetted it and rubbed it liberally with a lavender-perfumed soap she had found under the sink.

* * *

'She was lying there as bold as brass.'

'God, love us and save us, she never was!'

'In Maud Wragg's bath naked as the day she was born.'

'Maud's bath! Well, I never, and Maud herself hardly cold in her grave. Shame on the hussy! What did she do when she seen you?'

'Screamed blue murder, that's what she done.'

The two women sitting at the table looked at each other and burst out laughing.

Rose Skuttle wiped away tears of mirth with the back of her hand. 'After I heard the news I thought I'd pop round and check on things. You know, like good neighbours do.'

More like have a good nose round, thought her friend Mary O'Malley.

'I got the bloody shock of me life. Well, yer would, wouldn't yer? Yer don't expect to find a naked hussy bathing in a dead woman's house in the middle of the morning.' Rose sniffed disdainfully. 'I'm annoyed, though.'

'Oh, why's that?'

'Because I shot out so quick, I never got the chance to ask her any questions. But I will. I'm going round later.'

'I'll come with yer, if yer like?' Mary offered keenly.

'Oh, I'm sure you've plenty ter do without bothering yerself with that, Mary. Besides, I think it best I go round meself and welcome the gel, me being a close neighbour an' all. Don't want to frighten her off do we, by half the street parading in?'

'Me and you hardly constitutes half the street, Rose. Anyway I ain't convinced yer intention ain't to frighten her to death and make her leave.'

Hostility filled Rose's pale blue eyes. 'And just what do yer mean by that remark?'

Mary tightened her lips. 'I don't need to explain meself. You know exactly what I meant. Anyway, what's she like then, this girl?'

Rose grimaced. 'As plain as a pike staff and as thin as a clothes prop. And she's something wrong with her arm.'

'Something wrong?'

'Yeah,' Rose shrugged her shoulders. 'From what I saw it looked withered.'

'Oh.' Mary nodded thoughtfully. 'She's no threat then,' she muttered under her breath.

'What did you say?'

'Nothing,' Mary replied innocently, then frowned thoughtfully. 'I can't understand it meself, though.'

'Understand what?'

'Well, I know that the bobby said that her and the young fellow saved Ted and Daisy's life, and Ted's in a really bad way, but it still don't mek sense ter me why he should put her in charge. The man must be off his head.'

'Yer right there, Mary. It don't mek sense. There's a lot of devious people about.'

'Oh, d'yer think she's devious then?'

'Got ter be ain't she? However you look at it she's landed on her feet.'

'Hmm,' Mary mused. 'I wouldn't mind living in that house. It's a little palace.'

My sentiments exactly, thought Rose. And if I get my way that's exactly where I will be living. ''Nother cuppa,' she asked, picking up the teapot.

'Don't mind if I do.' Mary passed her mug over and watched as her friend filled it up. 'And could I have two sugars, d'yer think, this time, Rosie? The last one was a bit sour.'

'Sour! Bloody cheek. Sugar costs money, so bring your own next time. I'm a widow, remember.'

'But not for much longer if you have your way, eh, Rosie?'

Rose scowled across at Mary. 'Just what a' you trying ter say?'

Mary slowly and deliberately took a sup of her tea, then placed the mug down on the table. 'You know exactly what I mean, Rose Skuttle. You've had a twinkle in your eye for Edward Wragg since your Norman passed away over ten years ago.'

Rose's lips tightened indignantly. 'Well, that's where you're wrong, Mary O'Malley. I've had a twinkle in my eye for Edward Wragg since the first day I saw him.' Instantly the words were out of her mouth she regretted saying them, but Mary had annoyed her.

'Well, at long last you've admitted it,' she said triumphantly, puffing out her skinny chest. 'I think I've just called the wrong woman a hussy.'

Rose wagged a warning finger. 'You watch yer mouth. Eh, and don't let me ever hear you repeat that in public!'

'As if I would. Have we not been friends for longer than I care to remember? Never have I repeated anything that's been said in this room.'

Rose smiled. 'No, I'll say that for you, Mary. I couldn't wish for a better friend than you. Been through thick and thin, we have, together.'

Mary raised her mug and toasted Rose. 'More thin than thick if you ask me, but who knows what the future holds?'

'No, indeed,' Rose agreed, smiling.

Mary folded her thin arms and leaned across the table. 'So, come on, Rose, what's yer plan?' she asked eagerly.

'Plan?'

'Well, yer must have one. Don't tell me that you're gonna let a chance like this pass yer by. Don't get me wrong, it's awful what happened to Maud but she's dead and life goes on. So what yer gonna do?'

'I ain't gonna do anything,' Rose said indignantly.

How come I don't believe you? thought Mary, eyeing her friend knowingly.

Rose averted her gaze, pretending to check the fire. Plan? Yes, she did have a plan. She had lain in bed all night concocting it but wasn't about to tell Mary. Mary did not care much for Ted Wragg because he wouldn't give work to her husband. So far as Rose was concerned, Ted was right. Patrick O'Malley was a lazy, good-for-nothing liar, who beat his wife and children when the mood took him. But, regardless, Mary could not see past her husband, she loved him, poor soul, and consequently Rose felt she had better be careful. Best friend was one thing. Husband and wife was another. She wasn't going to take any chances of her plan being ruined.

The first time she had been introduced to Ted Wragg, she had taken a shine to him. He was everything her husband wasn't. Handsome, had his own business, and didn't begrudge his wife a thing. From the outside, the Wraggs' house adjoining the yard looked just like all the other rundown terraces in the area, but the inside was a different matter. The furniture was good quality, some of it had been bought brand new, and Maud did not cook over an open fire like Rose had to. Oh, no, she had had one of those new gas contraptions. Ted also ensured his wife's housekeeping was enough to allow her to buy decent cuts of meat, and she even washed herself in perfumed soap, not the bright yellow hard kind that was the only sort Rose could afford to use.

When her own husband had met his untimely death – his neck broken by stubbornly trying to manoeuvre a wardrobe up the stairs single-handed – she had set her sights on landing herself another husband of the Wragg variety. There was no reason why she shouldn't. She was still a good-looking woman for her age, still had quite a decent figure, but the several men she had tried to ensnare had refused to succumb, she herself never fathoming the reason. Well, now she did not have to settle for a substitute; she could, if she played her hand right, have the genuine article.

She was a free woman, and Ted, when he had got over his grieving, was a free man. Rose would make damned sure he never looked in another female's direction but her own.

Her plan had already been put into motion and the first step had been to make sure her son Wally took care of the business in Ted's absence. He'd be eternally grateful for that. She herself had been going to offer to care for Daisy. Not that she had wanted an infant on her hands, but it would have let Ted see what a caring person she was, a doting substitute mother. Catching a grieving widower off guard was as good a way to catch a man as any she knew of. She would make him believe he couldn't manage without her and then he would marry her as a consequence. She had no doubt it would work, confident of her own abilities. All she had to do was get rid of the girl, and that should be easy enough.

She eyed Mary scathingly. 'How can you ask if I have a plan when the man has just lost his wife? Have you no soul?'

More than you have, Mary wanted to say. She knew Rose better than her friend gave her credit for, but didn't want to get into an argument. Mary was hiding a secret of her own from her friend which a display of temper might just bring forth.

Mary knew that Rose would be pushing her son Wally forward. Well, Rose ought to watch her back because Mary's husband Paddy was intent on furthering his own interests. He'd gone round to the yard at the crack of dawn this very morning to have a nose round, and his plan must be working because she hadn't seen hide nor hair of him since. She smiled inwardly. Her Paddy was a wily old devil and she had faith he would succeed. He'd promised to buy her a mangle on the proceeds, so he'd better. Serve Ted Wragg right, she thought, if Paddy did manage to steal all his business in his absence. It'd teach him a lesson for not giving Paddy work when they so desperately needed it.

She plastered an ashamed look over her face. 'I'm sorry. I wasn't thinking.'

'I should bloody say you weren't!' Rose stood up and began to clear the table. 'You'd best be off. I've got to prepare me lodger's dinner.' Bloody lodger, she thought. She hated letting out her back bedroom but it paid the rent and a bit left over. Still, with a bit of luck she might not have to do it for much longer.

Chapter Fifteen

'Come on, Daisy, just a little, please, there's a good girl.'

Tilda knew her plea was useless. Daisy flatly refused even to sample the bread and milk she had prepared for her. The child was screaming hysterically, and after trying everything to appease her, Tilda was just about at her wit's end.

Maybe it was the food she didn't like. Tilda looked down at it. She had to admit it did look rather bland, even with the bit of brown sugar she had sprinkled over it, but the pantry didn't hold anything else suitable for a child of Daisy's tender age. There was nothing else for it. She would have to venture out to go shopping.

Normally an exercise such as that would not have bothered her in the least, but the thought of pushing her way through the busy streets while she was unused to crowds did not appeal. Even more upsetting was the humiliation of that woman's coming in unannounced and catching her in such an undignified situation. She was so unnerved by it she felt all eyes would be turned on her in laughter as soon as she poked her head out of the front door. Her discomfiture wasn't due solely to the woman's unexpected appearance; it was how she had scrutinised Tilda, then the look of scorn which had filled her face before she had hurriedly departed.

'All right, Daisy, you win,' said Tilda resignedly, putting the bowl on the table. She scooped the still screaming child into her arms and cuddled her. 'There, there, now,' she soothed, kissing her damp forehead. 'I wish you could tell me what you want.'

She sighed despairingly, eyes straying to the chimney breast where they remained for several long moments. Ted had told her and Ben that behind a loose brick he kept a certain amount of money for emergencies and a bit extra. Tilda was to help herself to whatever she needed for household expenses. Ben the same regarding the business.

Although she had been given the authority to do so, Tilda didn't think it right she should help herself and for a moment wondered how she was going to get round this situation. She would have much preferred to have been allotted a set amount each week to make do with. She wondered if Ted had realised that he had unwittingly given her licence to do as she pleased with his money.

She pondered on the problem for several moments, then a simple solution struck her and she smiled as she tenderly wiped Daisy's tear-streaked face and kissed her affectionately on one cheek. 'Yes, that's what I'll do, Daisy. Then we'll be all straight.'

She would keep a record of what money she spent. That way Ted would know she was being honest and above board. Tilda felt much happier now. Solving this problem made her address the incident of earlier this morning with a more positive attitude. During her lifetime she'd lost count of the number of times she had been humiliated, ridiculed, made to feel worthless, so why should this one be any different? This hurt she would treat exactly the same as she had done before by pushing it to the back of her mind. She couldn't lock herself away in the house forever or Daisy and she would starve, and Ted's business would go bankrupt if she didn't begin to do something towards finding someone to help run it.

She decided a bit of fresh air might be good for Daisy and she herself could take advice from an obliging shopkeeper about something appetizing to buy to coax her to eat.

She had just got the child dressed and seated comfortably in the large maroon Silver Cross perambulator, and was about to take out the loose brick and explore behind, when there was a pounding on the front door.

Tilda froze as the noise sounded again and Daisy, whom she had managed to calm down, started to scream again.

She opened the door just as the caller was about to pound on it again. A pair of shrewd hazel eyes looked her up and down.

'I was beginning ter think no one was in, and I'm desperate.'

Tilda stared at the old lady addressing her. She was dressed from head to toe in black. The lines of her face reminded Tilda of deep furrows in newly turned ground. It was anyone's guess how old she was.

'Desperate?' Tilda queried.

'Desperately desperate. I'd 'ave bin 'ere earlier only I couldn't find me coat.'

'Couldn't you?'

'No.' The woman gave a cackle of mirth. 'I'd put it in the pantry and hung up the bag of spuds on the coat peg.'

'An easy mistake. I've done the same myself,' Tilda fibbed.

''Tis when yer my age. I'm eighty-four. Look well on it, don't I?'

Tilda nodded. 'You do.' Daisy's screams were growing louder and she tried not to appear agitated. 'Look, I don't mean to hurry you, but I was just going out. What is it I can do for you?'

'Eh?'

'You called for something didn't you?'

'Did I?' The old lady looked puzzled then her eyes brightened. 'Come ter think of it, I did.' She leaned over and gripped Tilda's arm. 'It's me waterworks, me duck,' she whispered.

'Waterworks?' Tilda repeated quizzically.

The old lady nodded. 'It's really getting me down. I was up all night. I couldn't stop it though. Wet a clean pair of bloomers right through and I wa' going ter wear 'em today. 'Ad ter put last week's on instead.'

Tilda's eyebrows rose. 'Oh, I see. Er . . .' She leaned over and whispered to the old lady: 'I think you've knocked on the wrong door. This is Wragg's the builder's.'

The old lady pulled back and eyed her sharply. 'I know that. Always seen ter me has Wragg, and I'm too old ter change now.'

Tilda looked bemused. 'But I don't think this is quite in our line. Are you sure it's not a doctor you need to see?'

'A doctor! But Mr Wragg sorted it out all the other times. Sent the young lad ter see me. Nice lad too. Couldn't 'ave bin more helpful. Said ter me, "Don't worry, Ma, it won't 'urt a bit." And it never. When he'd finished I gave him a cuppa tea and a slice of me fruit cake.'

Tilda's eyes widened at the vision the old lady was conjuring up. 'And what exactly did he do, this young lad?'

The old lady frowned thoughtfully. 'Plugged it, I think, me duck, with a bit of black rubber wi' an 'ole in it. Yes, that's right.'

'Hello, Mrs Duncan. All right?'

Tilda's head jerked round to see the woman who had caught her in the bath earlier coming towards them. She'd a covered plate in her hand. Tilda groaned inwardly. This was all she needed.

Purposely completely ignoring Tilda, Rose smiled condescendingly at the old woman. 'Waterworks again, Mrs Duncan. Needs fixing, does it?'

'It does. Dripping like hell it is.'

'Well, don't you worry, I'll get Wally to come and sort you out. That all right?'

'Just a moment,' said Tilda, worried that Wragg's business was being poached under her own nose. 'Who is this Wally?'

Rose looked at her as though she was stupid. 'My son,' she replied sharply. 'He's Ted's apprentice. Well, not an apprentice fer much longer 'cos he'll be qualified soon. Though that won't mek no difference. He's always done a better job than a fully qualified bloke. That right, Mrs Duncan?'

'I'll say.'

'Didn't you see him this morning?' Rose asked Tilda.

She shook her head. 'No, I didn't.'

'Well, that shows yer then. Conscientious to the last. Was out working before you were even up. My Wally'll be running the business like it was his own whilst Ted's laid up, and there'll be no complaints, mark my words. That right, Mrs Duncan?'

'I'll say.'

'Now Wally might not manage today,' the busybody continued, 'I ain't sure what he's got on, but he'll get ter yer as soon as he can. Now you go home like a good gel in case your son pops in ter see yer. Don't wanna be out when he calls, do yer?'

'No, I don't,' the old lady agreed. 'Always brings me summat does our Jack. He's a good lad to his mother.'

'I should think so with all the money he's got,' Rose muttered under her breath.

They both stood and watched the old lady shuffle away then Rose turned to Tilda. 'Comes at least twice a week, does Mrs Duncan. It's her tap, see.'

'Tap?'

'Yes, one of those new fangled things you have instead of a pump. Turn it and water pours out. I don't know what she does to it, but it's always leaking and keeping her awake at night. She can't climb the stairs any more so she sleeps in the back room. Her son paid for the tap to be put in, same as he's paid for all the other new fangled gadgets the poor old sod's got in her home.

Anything, you see, to stop her having ter live with him and his stuck up missus. The old duck doesn't use none of 'em. Waste of good money if yer ask me. She still prefers the old ways of doing things but at least it keeps his conscience clear. Anyway, my Wally will sort her out.'

Rose planted a broad smile on her face. 'Now I've come to apologise for what happened this morning and ter bring you these.' She thrust the plate at Tilda. 'Jam tarts. I've just made 'em.' She looked past Tilda down the passageway. 'Is that Daisy crying? What's up with the little duck? Nobody there to fuss over her, I expect. We'd better go and see to 'er. Come on.'

Taking Tilda's arm, she propelled her down the passage. Once inside the back room Rose let go of her arm and rushed towards Daisy.

'Now, now, wassa matter wi' you?' she said in babyish tones, tickling Daisy under her chin. 'Are you playing this nice lady up?' She turned to Tilda 'She's overtired. You put the kettle on and I'll settle her down.'

Tilda took a deep breath. 'I don't want to be rude but I was just going out. I need to get some food for Daisy and some other bits.'

'Oh, yer've plenty o' time. Shops open all day.'

'But Daisy . . .'

'She had her milk?'

'Er . . . yes. I found a can of fresh on the back doorstep this morning.'

Rose's eyebrows rose sharply. 'Did yer indeed? Ernest never does that for anyone else. Go out and get it or go wi'out. I wonder what he's playing at? Anyway, if she's had her milk then there's nothing coming over her. No child starves voluntarily.' Dismissing Tilda she turned back to Daisy and forced her to lie down. 'It's a nap for you, madam. Yer mammy coddled you far too much. You ain't gonna get your own way now.'

Daisy's screams were raised a decibel higher and Tilda shot over to the perambulator. She pulled Daisy out and hugged her protectively, eying Rose in annoyance.

'Please don't force her like that.'

Rose pursed her lips. 'You'll make a rod fer yer own back, running after her like that. She's only six months old, she don't know what's going on.'

'I'm sure she does. Babies do sense things.'

'Oh, and you're an authority, are you?'

Tilda stared at her. 'Not exactly an authority. But I know when a baby's playing up and when it's upset, and Daisy is upset. I thought taking her out would do her some good.'

Rose sniffed haughtily. 'You'll end up like Maud, you will. Running round like a blue-arsed fly pandering to all madam's needs. You need ter show her who's boss.' She eyed Tilda sharply. 'You are the boss, I take it?'

Tilda was angered by her tone but as the woman was older and obviously a neighbour, decided not to show it. She took a deep breath. 'I am,' she said.

'Oh! Oh, I see. Yer must a' known Ted a long time for him to put his trust in you regarding Daisy. I happen ter know you ain't a relative. Neither Maud nor Ted had one between 'em. So who are yer?'

Tilda took a breath. 'A friend.'

Rose's eyes narrowed. 'A friend, I'd have known about yer if you were a friend. Maud told me everything, see. Like that we were,' she said, holding up two crossed fingers. 'And you ain't got a Leicester accent. Where do yer come from?'

Daisy started to whimper again. 'Look, Mrs ... er ...'

'Skuttle. Rose Skuttle.'

'Mrs Skuttle, I really do need to go out.'

'Oh, yer've time fer a cuppa. Look, I'll put the kettle on and you settle Daisy. And you don't need to show me where anything is. Know this house like the back of my hand, I do, me having been such a close friend of Maud's, God rest her soul.'

She strode off into the kitchen.

Tilda sighed heavily, knowing she wasn't going to get rid of this woman very easily.

Daisy decided she wasn't going back in the perambulator so Tilda settled her on her knee on a chair at the table, giving her a spoon to play with which she banged on the table top. The noise was a little irritating but at least she had stopped crying.

Rose eyed both of them sharply when she returned with two mugs of tea and the sugar basin. 'Little madam's got your measure already. You'll learn. Sugar?'

'Please,' Tilda replied evenly.

Rose settled herself. 'So you're a friend, you say?' She helped herself to one of her own jam tarts. 'How long have yer known the Wraggs then?'

'Not long. I . . .' Tilda hesitated then decided she would have to tell Rose how she had met Ted or she'd never get rid of her. 'Ben and I . . . he's a friend of mine . . . came across Mr Wragg after his accident. We were the ones who tried to save his wife. Mr Wragg knew we were looking for work and asked us to take care of things for him until he's fit enough to take over.'

'Oh,' Rose exclaimed. 'That explains things. Ted obviously didn't realise what he was doing, him not being himself, or he'd have asked me.'

'According to the hospital he won't be himself for a long time, Mrs Skuttle. And I'd like to point out that Mr Wragg knew exactly what he was doing when he took on me and Ben. The doctor said it was his bones that were broken not his brain.'

Rose's lips clamped tightly as it struck her that this young girl wasn't going to be manipulated as easily as she had first thought. She scanned Tilda scornfully, noticing the shabbiness of her clothes and her deformed arm, bringing her eyes to rest finally on Tilda's plain face, the hair framing it scraped back and tied unbecomingly with a piece of string. 'That's a matter of opinion. I mean, a man who's just lost his wife and is suffering a lot of pain can't know his own mind, can he?' She leaned over and patted Tilda's arm patronisingly. 'Don't worry, me dear, I shall be going to see Ted meself on Saturday and putting it to him that I can take care of Daisy. Housework and baby care ain't fer a young girl like you. You need to be in a factory or summat, mixing wi' gels yer own age.'

Tilda's hackles rose. For whatever reason Rose Skuttle was obviously hell bent on relieving Tilda of her duties and if she herself didn't put a stop to her, would take over completely in no time. Tilda had no intention of letting her. If Mr Wragg had wanted Mrs Skuttle to look after Daisy he wouldn't have asked Tilda to do it. Besides, from what she had observed in the short space of time she had been acquainted with the Wraggs' neighbour, that wouldn't be in Daisy's best interests. 'I appreciate your sentiment, Mrs Skuttle, but I'm quite happy, thank you, and I'll tell Mr Wragg that when I see him myself. I had thought about going on Thursday.'

'You're going ter see him?'

'Well, yes, of course. It'll do him good to see his daughter. And I'll need to keep him informed about his business.'

Rose stared at her, not able to hide the anger glinting in her small eyes. 'I've told yer, my Wally will take care of that side of things. You've no need ter . . .' Rose had been going to say 'poke your nose in' but quickly corrected herself '. . . bother about that. You've enough on yer plate as it is. Little 'un 'ere 'ull take up all yer time.' Then she couldn't help but add: 'But I hope that if yer are going ter the hospital, you've got something better ter wear than them old things. Ted won't want showing up yer know.'

Humiliation was quickly replaced by anger, and how she stopped herself from showing it Tilda would never know. Glancing down at herself, she raised her eyes and smiled sweetly. 'Oh, dear, I must look a sight. These are my old cleaning clothes. I was just about to change when Mrs Duncan knocked on the door.' The lie slipped easily off her tongue and she wasn't completely happy about telling it but at least she had managed to keep her pride, feeling this woman had damaged it enough for one day. 'I'm so relieved to hear about your son. I shall need to talk to him then I can make some decisions on what I'm going to do regarding the business. Wally will probably need help in some form. It wouldn't be fair to expect him to run things on his own, him still being an apprentice.'

The news that at least someone was doing some work on Ted's behalf had pleased her when she had learned of it, but she sincerely hoped the son was not like the mother.

Tilda scraped back her chair and stood up. 'I really must be going, Mrs Skuttle. I have such a lot to do. Thank you for the tarts, they're much appreciated. I'll make sure you get the plate back.'

Rose's mouth fell open in shock. She was being dismissed and she wasn't happy about it. 'I can get it any time,' she replied, tight-lipped. Her mind was working rapidly. She needed this girl to think her a friend. If she walked out leaving things as they were it would take a lot of work to get back in on the social level she wanted to be on. Taking a deep breath, she looked at Tilda shame-faced. 'I've upset you, me duck, and I'm sorry.' The apology was difficult but once out the rest flowed easier. 'It's all this news about Maud, and poor Ted lying in that hospital in so much pain. I just feel so helpless.' Her eyes filled with genuine tears. Thoughts of Ted brought those on without her even trying. 'I'm just hurt that he never asked me to help out, that's all. I thought I was such a good friend.'

Tilda's face filled with concern. She suddenly felt very guilty for the way she had spoken to this woman. Common sense should have told her Rose was upset and that was causing her rudeness. In the circumstances Tilda could fully appreciate how put out she must feel. She sat back down and settled Daisy again on her knee.

'Look, Mrs Skuttle . . .'

'Rose. Please call me Rose.'

'Rose. Mr Wragg hadn't much time to consider matters. They were going to put Daisy in a home.'

Best place for her, thought Rose. Might teach her not to be so demanding. 'Never,' she said, sounding shocked. 'How could they even contemplate doing such a thing? Maud'd never rest in peace if they'd done that.'

'I think at the time the hospital staff thought there was no other option. You see, Mr Wragg is very sick.'

An expression crossed Rose's face that Tilda couldn't quite fathom.

'He's going ter be all right, though, isn't he?' the woman exclaimed.

Tilda stared at her for a moment. Something was not quite right somewhere. This woman was showing a bit too much concern for a mere neighbour. Still, she had said that she and Mrs Wragg had been really close. Tilda felt sorry for her and for what she must be going through, and eyed her sympathetically. 'We'll probably know more when we visit. Er . . . if you can manage Thursday we could go together?' She hadn't really wanted to suggest that, but felt obliged to.

Rose stalled an answer by dabbing her eyes. She desperately wanted to see Ted by herself but if she turned this offer down she might undo the good she had just achieved in ingratiating herself with this young woman.

She raised watery eyes. 'That's very kind of you, me dear. I'd like that. We'd be company for each other and I can help you with Daisy as it's a long ride on the omnibus. Cartwright's do a service out that way if I'm not mistaken. We can board in Applegate Street.'

'That's a date, then, for Thursday,' Tilda said, trying to sound pleased. 'Mr Wragg will be glad to see us, I'm sure.'

Worry filled Rose for a moment. She hadn't the fare. But regardless she would get it. 'Yes, he will,' she agreed. She rose and made her way towards the door. 'I'll be seeing you then.' She eyed Tilda cautiously. 'Er . . . would yer like some company ter the shops?'

Oh, no, thought Tilda. She'd had enough of this woman for one day. 'That's a very kind offer but you must have plenty to do and I'd feel guilty keeping you. Besides, I need to find my way around and get my bearings because I can't expect you to accompany me all the time, can I? I've no idea for how long I'll be in the neighbourhood.'

Not so long as you think you will, thought Rose, and smiled sweetly. 'You're right, I've plenty to do and you can't really get lost, not if yer keep to Wharf Street. What did you say you needed to get?'

'Just some food,' Tilda replied. And something to wear, she thought, after telling Rose she had on her old cleaning clothes. She hoped Wharf Street had a cheap second-hand shop. She would have to use some of her wage before she had even earned it. She wasn't happy about that and wondered how much to take, never having discussed an amount nor having earned a proper wage before to help her judge.

'I'll leave yer to it then,' Rose said reluctantly. 'I'll . . . er . . . pop in termorrow to see how yer getting on.'

'I'll look forward to it.'

Showing Rose out, Tilda watched her walk down the street towards her home. She frowned as she hitched Daisy more comfortably in her arms. She wasn't sure if she liked Rose Skuttle.

Rose had hardly shut her front door when the back door banged and Mary came in.

'Well, did yers see her? What's she like? How long's she staying?'

Rose folded her arms under her shapely bosom and eyed Mary, annoyed. 'Bloody Nora, can a woman not have two minutes' peace in her own home wi'out the likes of you badgering her? 'Sides, I ain't got a damned clue.'

'Ain't yer? Oh! Well, you must a' talked about something. You were gone long enough.'

'Time me, did yer?'

'No,' Mary said sheepishly. 'It's just I came round ter see yers and yers weren't in. So I sorta guessed where you were.'

'Well, you sorta guessed wrong. I popped in ter see Betty Makepeace. She's not well again,' lied Rose. 'I suppose you wanna cuppa?'

A disappointed Mary nodded. 'Didn't you see her at all?' she asked hopefully.

Having tested the kettle for water, Rose swung it across the fire. She straightened up and without looking at her friend made her way across to the table where she busied herself putting milk and sugar in two mugs. 'As it happens I did, but just for a few minutes.'

'And?' Mary said eagerly.

Rose stopped what she was doing and eyed her in a superior fashion. 'It's my opinion she ain't fit ter care for Daisy. She can't be aged more than eighteen – and her clothes. Well, Piggot's and Kendal's have better stuff they've collected on their rag and bone carts. She reckons she's in charge of the business. I shall speak ter Ted when I see him on Thursday.' The last was said before Rose could stop herself. 'Well, I might go on Thursday, I ain't made up me mind yet.'

'I'll come with yers . . .'

'Don't be stupid, Mary,' Rose erupted. 'How's a sick man going ter cope with half of Wharf Street turning up to visit?'

Mary's eyes narrowed. She knew Rose's little game. She wanted to visit Ted on her own, and it wouldn't surprise Mary in the least if she had had more than a few minutes' chat with the young girl, knew more than she was letting on.

'Don't call me stupid,' she scolded angrily, 'I've enough of me old man accusing me of that. And yer've no right ter say I can't come with yer on Thursday. You don't own the hospital, Rose Skuttle. Ted'd more than likely be glad of a visit from me.'

Rose grimaced. 'Do you really think so?'

Mary scowled. 'And what'd yer mean by that?'

'Nothing.'

'Yes you did. You implied that he wouldn't. That's unkind, Rose Skuttle. Unkind and thoughtless.'

Rose realised she had gone too far. 'I'm sorry, Mary,' she said meekly, doing her best to look ashamed. 'I'm het up, that's all, with what's gone on. I don't know what I'm saying half the time.' She eyed Mary pleadingly. 'Am I forgiven?'

'I suppose,' she replied grudgingly. 'So I take it I can come on Thursday and you ain't gonna cause a fuss?'

'As you said, Mary, I can't stop you. But I was only thinking of Ted when I said it. Anyway, what about the fare?'

'Fare?'

'Omnibus fare. It ain't cheap, yer know. I reckon it'll cost about two bob give or take. It's a fair distance.'

'Two bob, That's a bit steep. But I'll manage.'

'How? You never had no money yesterday.'

Mary eyed her friend, alarmed. 'Er . . . well, I've none today neither but my Paddy has expectations.'

'Expectations?'

'Yes, great expectations,' Mary said proudly.

'That's a book, ain't it?' Rose said knowledgeably. 'By Dick Charles.' She knew this for a fact because Wally had a dog-eared copy in his bedroom which she had dusted several times. 'Anyway what "great expectations" is your Paddy about ter get, may I ask. Apart from a good thump from someone he's swindled. Has someone died and left him a fortune?'

Mary stared at her, stunned. Her and her big mouth. Paddy was right when he said that one day she would open it too wide and fall right in. She quickly tried to think of a plausible story. She couldn't tell Rose about Paddy's plans regarding Wragg's yard which must be working because she hadn't seen sight of him all day.

'He's got 'imself a job.'

'A job! Your Paddy? That'll be the day. What illegal activity is 'e up to this time?' Rose's brain suddenly clicked into action. Her eyes flashed a warning as she leaned over the table. 'Eh, and it'd better have nothing ter do with Wragg's yard or he'll be sorry.'

'Wragg's yard? Whatever makes you think that?' Mary said defensively. 'He's a job, I tell you, which pays very well and is all above board. And that's all I know.'

'If he's a job then you can pay me back the five shillings I lent yer.'

'Five shillings? What five shillings? I don't recall.'

'Oh, Mary, you've a short memory when yer choose. I lent it ter yer eight years ago last Christmas. You couldn't pay the rent, remember.'

'Oh, yes. Come ter think of it now I do. You'll be paid in full, Rose, you have my word.'

'Ah, but when, though?' Rose muttered under her breath. Mary was getting on her nerves and Rose decided it was time that she left. She wanted to be on her own to think. She grabbed her pinafore from the back of the chair and tied it round herself. 'Right, you best get off. I've me lodger's dinner ter see to.'

'But me tea,' Mary wailed. 'I'm parched.'

Rose's head reared back. 'If my lodger leaves me 'cos his dinner ain't ready then I'll expect you ter pay his dues until I find someone else. But then, you won't have much trouble doing that, will yer, Mary? Not with your Paddy having such great expectations.'

Mary eyed her friend scathingly before she turned and headed out of the door. As she reached the entry she felt positive she could hear Rose laughing.

Chapter Sixteen

'That's a good girl,' Tilda praised Daisy with a broad smile. 'One more spoonful and that's it all finished.' But Daisy didn't want another spoonful and Tilda, sooner than push her luck, decided that the child knew when she was full. At least she had eaten something, and whilst she had been eating she hadn't been screaming.

Half an hour later Tilda sank back in an armchair, exhausted. In front of her Daisy was happily lying on the peg rug by the fire, her chubby legs thrashing the air, nappy left off for a while to air her bottom. Her guardian watched her for a moment as she played with her toes, then stuck a foot in her mouth and sucked on it. Peace was bliss.

The child had been a handful all day. Tilda hadn't realised a small human being could scream so much and not be in mortal pain. Still, she mused, little Daisy had a right and enough excuses to voice her opinions in such a way. Had she not lost all that was familiar, had her routine disrupted, and the woman who was caring for her not even clued up enough to know what a six month old liked to eat? Hopefully in a few days that would all change as she and Daisy got used to each other.

Tilda's eyes strayed to the clock on the mantle. It was approaching six-thirty and the night was rapidly drawing in. She frowned. Surely the as yet unseen Wally would come back to the yard to deposit his tools after he had finished for the day?

She wanted to introduce herself and have a talk to him. If they did need to take help on, she hoped that Wally, being in the trade, would know of somebody who would fit the bill.

Her eyes strayed back to Daisy, lying there looking so angelic, and she smiled. An onlooker would have trouble believing the chaos she had caused during her afternoon outing. For Tilda, just negotiating the large perambulator down the crowded cobbled streets, constantly aware of the possibility of causing harm to unsuspecting shoppers and other pedestrians, and crossing the road while avoiding delivery carts and bicycles, had been bad enough. Attempting actually to make her purchases could be classed a nightmare. Daisy made such a noise, Tilda had been sure people felt the child was being mistreated. If it hadn't been for several kindly souls doing their best to keep Daisy occupied, Tilda would have come home empty handed. As it was, so hurriedly had she had to do her buying that until she had reached the house she hadn't been quite sure just what she had bought.

Tilda's smile grew broader. Maybe, though, Daisy's disruptiveness had been a blessing in disguise. On coming across the second-hand shop she hadn't time to think about whether or not she should go inside. Before she knew it she had purchased two serviceable skirts, two high-necked blouses, two sets of underwear, a thick cotton nightdress that needed a slight repair, and a pair of boots. The whole lot had come to seven shillings and threepence-halfpenny. She would have to explain to Ted just what she had done and tell him that the money could be deducted from her wage.

A warm glow spread through her. Never in her life before had she actually bought herself clothing. Everything she had ever owned had been given to her in various ways. It felt so good to have chosen her clothes herself, even though they could hardly be classed the height of fashion. Regardless, they were hers. The decision of what to do with her old clothes, whether to keep them or not, had not come easy. Tilda had never had anything to throw away before. So she wasn't going to. Although not fit to do anything with, they would be washed and kept, just in case.

Thoughts of her newly acquired clothing brought to mind the blue dress that Molly had given her and for a moment she mourned its loss. She had felt so special in that dress. If only she still had it to put on on a Sunday before taking Daisy for a walk in the park.

Thinking of the dress brought to mind Eustace – not that he was ever far from her thoughts despite all that had happened to occupy her since she had seen him last. Oh, Eustace, she thought sadly. How terribly she missed him. She would have to write to him soon and tell him her news, and hoped that the Brindles would somehow manage to bring him for a visit.

She gasped suddenly. Her father! All this thinking of things past had reminded her of him, but with a sense of shock she realised that, unlike Eustace, she didn't miss him, had hardly given him a thought during the last few days. She took a deep breath and exhaled slowly. What would his reaction be, she thought, if he could see her sitting in this lovely home, having been entrusted by a parent with the care of his child? Eli's own daughter, the one he had taken such delight in treating harshly, forever telling her she was unworthy – what would he say to her now? Whatever it was, Tilda knew his words would not be kind.

She was filled with guilt for not being present at his burial, but at the time she'd had such a difficult decision to make and Eustace's plight seemed more pressing. Despite her feeling of guilt, she still felt she had done the right thing.

Thinking of her father had depressed her and despite the presence of Daisy a great feeling of loneliness settled upon her. After years of making do with her own company, since the night of the fire she had spent barely a moment on her own. What she would give at this moment for someone to walk through the door and help lift this mood!

As if on cue she heard a noise in the yard, then moments after the sound of approaching footsteps. She looked down at Daisy. 'Now you be a good girl whilst I talk to Wally, then you can have a drink of milk and I'll put you to bed.'

Daisy gurgled in response and Tilda leaned over and tickled her under her chin. Then, hurriedly rising, she smoothed down her skirt and poked a stray strand of hair behind her ear, wishing she had had the foresight to change into her more presentable clothes and find something better than a piece of string with which to tie back her hair.

The knock was loud. Although expecting it, nevertheless Tilda jumped and a startled Daisy puckered up her face and started to cry.

'Oh, no,' Tilda groaned. 'Shush now, there's a good girl.'

But Daisy wouldn't be quietened. Her cries quickly erupted into a wail. Tilda was torn between answering the door and Daisy's need of her. Daisy won. As she bent to pick her up she heard the sound of the back door opening and before she had time to straighten up properly a tall gangly youth had appeared in the room.

He whipped off his cap and they both stared at each other.

'You ... er ... must be Wally,' Tilda said loudly above the commotion Daisy was making. 'Have you just finished work, only it's getting late? I thought you'd have packed up long ago?'

'Er ... normally we knock off at six but we decided to finish the job. Save us going back termorrow. We didn't even stop for lunch.' He eyed her worriedly. ''Ave I done something wrong?'

'Oh, no, no. It's just that I've been wanting to meet you and I was beginning to think you'd gone straight home. There's such a lot I need to talk to you about.'

Wally's face grew even more worried. 'Do yer?' He gulped. 'What?'

Tilda suddenly remembered her manners. 'Please sit down. You must be parched, would you like a cuppa? Daisy, quiet, there's a good girl. What about something to eat? I've nothing prepared but I could soon rustle something up.'

'No, that's all right, ta very much. Me mam'll have me dinner waiting in the oven.'

'Oh, yes, I see. Well, I'll try not to keep you too long. You'll have a cuppa, though?'

Wally nodded. 'Er ... that'd be nice, thank you. I'll put the kettle on, if you like?' He looked at the baby. 'You've kinda got your hands full.'

Tilda smiled. She had taken an instant liking to this young man. He didn't seem a bit like his mother, thank goodness. 'Do you mind? Then I can give Daisy her bottle, it might help settle her.'

Wally disappeared through into the kitchen and, picking up Daisy's bottle, Tilda sat down by the table and tried to feed her. Daisy was having none of it. As Tilda tried to coax the teat between her lips, the extremely agitated child spat it out. Suddenly something Wally had said registered with Tilda.

'Wally,' she called. 'You said "we". Did you have some help today?'

'Just a minute,' he shouted back. 'I can't hear yer.' He appeared in the doorway, holding the kettle in his hand. 'I can't light the gas,' he said apologetically.

Tilda laughed. 'Don't worry, I have trouble too. You have to turn the white knob towards the door and when you hear the gas hissing, you stick a lighted match to it. Then jump back quick in case it explodes.'

Wally grimaced. 'I'll ... er ... have another go.' He made to turn, then stopped. 'I'm sorry, what did yer ask me?'

Resigned to defeat, Tilda put the bottle of milk on the floor, stood up and rocked Daisy in her arms to try to soothe her. 'I asked if you had help today? Only you said "we".'

Wally frowned at her, confused. 'Well, yes. Ben.'

Tilda couldn't understand why Wally had spoken as though she should know this. 'Ben?' she repeated in amazement.

'Is somebody speaking aboot me? I heard my name mentioned.'

With the noise Daisy was making neither Wally nor Tilda had heard Ben come in. Tilda stared at him stupefied, mixed emotions racing through her as, rubbing his hands together, he pushed past Wally and headed for the fire. He turned his back to it for warmth.

'My, it's getting cold out there. Wouldn't be surprised if we have a frost the nicht.' He looked at Wally. 'I take it you've introduced yersel' to Tilda then? See, I told yous she wouldn't bite. Now, I've put all the tools away ready for tomorrow but I couldn't check the lime pit 'cos it's getting too dark to see properly. We could do that first thing.' He turned to Tilda. 'What's for dinner? I'm starving.' Then to Wally: 'Are yous going to stand all night with that kettle in your hand? It won't make itsel', yous know.'

Wally looked at the kettle, grinned across at Ben and disappeared back into the kitchen.

'Yous found the milk I asked to be left?' he asked Tilda. 'Only I thought by the time yous got up you'd have missed him and you'd need some urgent for the bairn's breakfast?' He grimaced. 'What's wrong with her? She's making an awful racket.'

Still stunned from his appearance, Tilda looked at Daisy. 'There's nothing wrong with the baby, she's just fretting for her parents. We're all strangers to her, remember. Wouldn't you be upset in the circumstances?'

'Yes, I suppose, but can't yous quieten her doon a bit? I can't hear mesel' speak.'

'Quieten her down! What do you think I've been trying to do?' She was so annoyed by his comment she headed towards him and held out Daisy. 'Here, if you think you can do better, you have a go. And be careful, she's fragile.'

Ben had no option but to take hold of the child, and as soon as he did so Daisy stopped her crying and gazed up at him adoringly. Ben looked at Tilda smugly. 'See, there's nothing to it.' Hopefully he eyed the empty table. 'Dinner in the oven, is it?'

'Dinner?' she mouthed, and her eyes flashed crossly. 'Ben McCraven, you really are the limit. The last time we spoke it was to say our goodbyes. You were on your way to Birmingham. Now here you are, as large as life, asking me what's for dinner!'

Ben grinned. 'I take it you're pleased to see me then? Look, Tilda, yous wanted me to stay, and now I have, you're mad.'

She shook her head in disbelief. 'I'm not mad, I'm just . . . just . . .'

'Mad.'

Her temper erupted. 'Yes, I am, and I've every right to be. I hardly slept a wink last night worrying how I was going to manage all this on my own, and when I got up all I found was the mess you'd left making your breakfast. Then I've worried all day about meeting Wally and . . . and . . . what with Daisy playing up and Rose Skuttle catching me in the bath . . . and . . . and . . .'

Tears filled her eyes and she started to cry.

'Och, don't do that, Tilda,' Ben pleaded in embarrassment.

'I can't help it,' she snivelled. And she couldn't. She didn't know why she was crying. She raised tear-filled eyes. 'How long are you stopping for this time?'

He shrugged his shoulders. 'Yous women are never happy, are yous? We men can never do right. Look, I'm here ain't I? And I'm going to be staying for the time being at least. When I decide to leave, I'll give plenty of warning, Now, for God's sake, dry your eyes.'

Having nothing else handy, she wiped her eyes on her sleeve. 'Will you be running the business then?' she asked hesitantly.

'I don't know whether "running it" is quite how I'd put it, but with Wully's help I'm going to try, yes. He's a good laddie is Wully. We got on like a house on fire today. He's promised to show me the ropes as best he can.'

Tilda looked at him quizzically. 'These ropes ... what have they got to do with building? I thought you used bricks?'

'What!' Ben roared with laughter. 'Oh, Tilda, that's just a figure of speech.'

Just then Wally popped his head around the doorway. 'The tea looks a bit ropey, I've never been any good at mashing a brew. Do yer both take sugar?'

He couldn't understand why they looked at each other and started to laugh.

Tilda's laughter suddenly stopped and she stared at Ben in amazement.

'What?' he asked, puzzled. 'What are yous looking at me like that for?'

'It's Daisy, Ben.'

'What about her?'

'She's fast asleep.'

He gazed down at her fondly as she nestled in his arms. 'I've obviously got the knack. Maybe yous should learn the ropes with Wully and I should stay at home with the little 'un?'

An hour later Ben sat back and patted his stomach. 'That was good, Tilda, thanks. Did you enjoy yours, Wully?'

He looked at Tilda appreciatively. 'I did, ta, Miss Penny.'

'My pleasure,' she replied. 'I just hope your mother doesn't mind. And, Wally, please call me Tilda.

'Right then,' she said, pushing away her empty plate. 'If you're both finished, I'd like to discuss how we're going to handle this business.'

Ben scraped back his chair. 'I can't, not now. It'll have to wait 'til tomorrow.'

Confused, she stared at him. 'What do you mean, you can't? I need to talk, Ben. I need to know what you and Wally have sorted out.'

His eyes flashed in annoyance. 'Tomorrow, Tilda. I'm off out. I've people I want to see.'

'People? What people?'

'Tilda,' he said gravely, 'you're sounding like a wife. Now I'm off upstairs for a wash and change.'

'Change? You've nothing to change into,' she challenged.

He sighed with exasperation. 'I'm going to borrow something of Ted's until I can get mesel' sorted out. I'd say we're roughly the same height although he's much wider round the middle, but a belt will sort that out. I'm not in the position to be fussy, am I? Now I'll wish you goodnight.' He winked at her cheekily. 'Don't wait up, I could be late.' He nodded at Wally. 'I'll meet you in the yard at seven.'

Wally grinned and flicked his forelock.

Dumbstruck, Tilda watched as Ben walked out of the door, heard his footsteps on the stairs and across the landing. She turned to Wally and folded her arms. 'Seems it's down to you then to put me right.'

Later that night Tilda lay in the single bed in the small bedroom off the one occupied by Daisy. The mattress was hard and lumpy but regardless there was no comparison between this and the straw shakedown she had slept on for years in the cottage. She hadn't realised the room even existed until she had spotted the door whilst checking on Daisy and gone to investigate. Although clean and dusted, Tilda sensed it had never been used as a regular bedroom, the bed and tallboy having been installed to alleviate its bareness. But it would do her just fine. Her newly acquired clothes were folded up neatly in a drawer inside the tallboy, and she had put a towel and some soap by the bowl and jug of water, ready for her wash in the morning.

Folding her arms behind her head, she stared up at the ceiling and listened for a while to the noises of the night. Now and again she would hear raised voices coming from nearby houses; the clatter of hob-nailed boots on the cobbles as someone came home after a late shift in a nearby factory; the giggles of courting couples leaning against the yard wall. A warm glow spread through her. She had never felt so contented. The noises, instead of being a distraction, were a comfort. There were other people out there. Many times in the cottage she had been so lonely that there had been days when she'd felt like the only person in the world. And now that she had survived her first day in this alien world, things could only get easier.

The residents seemed to be nice enough, helping out with Daisy as they had, smiling shopkeepers readily giving her advice on different foodstuffs to buy, but it had quickly become apparent to her that poverty was just as bad in this town as it was in the village she had come from. If she was honest, she would say it was even worse.

She would have had to be blind not to have noticed the awful conditions many large families had to live in, the children quite ragged and obviously undernourished. She had even witnessed a family being forcibly evicted, their rickety furniture thrown out on the street. She had felt really sorry for them and it had taken all her will-power not to invite them all back to the Wraggs' residence until they found somewhere else. The village hadn't been quite that bad, which was why her own situation had been so noticeable. Maybe now she wouldn't be classed as such an oddity. Apart from the incident with Rose Skuttle today, which she felt she had ultimately handled quite well, life here might be a lot more pleasant and equip her for when the time came to move on.

She smiled to herself. Ben should be home soon. It was disconcerting to find herself feeling comforted by this knowledge. Their association had been forced upon them not by choice on either side, and would have been over long ago if fate had not taken a hand. Although she tried, she still couldn't completely trust him, still saw him standing in the cottage with her precious savings in his hand. Unable to shake this memory she decided that, just like the housekeeping money, she was going to keep a record for Ted of all dealings to do with the business. That way he would know exactly what was going on and his mind would be at peace.

With these thoughts drifting through her head she hadn't realised she had fallen asleep until a commotion from somewhere downstairs woke her. With a start she sat up and listened. She could hear muffled voices and a noise like a chair falling over. She shot out of bed, her immediate concern for Daisy. As she pulled on her old cardigan that had been discarded in a pile with the rest of her clothes to be washed and stored, it suddenly struck her that they could be in the process of being burgled.

Without a thought for her own safety she flew down the stairs and came to an abrupt halt in the doorway at the bottom. She stared at the sight that met her. Several men were gathered around the table engrossed in a game of cards. In the middle of the table stood beer bottles. Empty ones had been discarded on the floor. A man had passed out on the couch. The room was filled with cigarette smoke and smelt of unwashed bodies and stale beer. Sprawled on the floor, having tipped backwards off his chair, was Ben. After the initial shock of her sudden appearance, he hiccuped loudly and grinned.

'Oh, it's only yous, Tilda. Give us a hand up. I can't seem to manage on me own.'

The one thing that frightened her above all else was a man with drink inside him. She had been on the receiving end of the wrath it could cause on so many occasions it was impossible to count them, and still had the scars, mental and physical. Faced with a roomful, old fears surfaced and she glared at Ben angrily. 'Ben McCraven, you're drunk! And how dare you bring this rabble here? Now get up off the floor and tell this lot leave before you wake the baby.'

All eyes were on her. Andy Ferguson, a huge Scotsman, having downed so many beers he could hardly make out the cards he was holding, caught sight of Tilda through his drunken haze as she turned and bolted back up the stairs. What he saw made him stare: a tall woman whose thinness was enhanced by the shapeless shift she wore under the threadbare cardigan. Lank hair, dishevelled by sleep, surrounded a face whose plainness had been accentuated by its mask of fear and anger. And to top it all, in the gloom of the stairwell, the skin covering her withered arm had had the appearance of dried tree bark.

Eyes filled with sympathy he turned to Ben. 'How the hell did yous land yersel' with that? Yous must have bin some bad boy. Did her dad force yous up the aisle?'

Outrage at the man's unwarranted callousness had Ben on his feet before the last words had left his mouth. He grabbed Andy by his collar and thrust his face forward. 'Don't yous dare speak about Tilda like that. Now you apologise.'

'Yeah, Andy,' Maurice Winbourne joined in. 'That were uncalled for. Yer own wife ain't no oil painting.'

Loud mumbles of agreement were expressed from the rest of the group.

Andy grunted and filled his broad chest with air. 'My wife might not be a looker but at least I don't frighten mesel' ter death each time I look at her' He wrenched Ben's hand from his collar and pushed him away. Thrusting back his chair, he staggered to his feet. 'Want to make something of this?' he challenged.

'Leave it be, Andy,' Maurice said, rising also. He caught hold of his arm. 'Come on, man, you've had too much to drink. It's only a friendly game of cards we're having.'

But Andy wouldn't let it rest. His consumption of beer and its effects wouldn't let him back down. 'Speak as I find, I do, and I say you're ter be pitied, man. Now if yous want ter make something of this, I'm ready for yous.'

He landed the first punch which caught Ben squarely on his chin, sending him reeling backwards to fall into the armchair. He was on his feet in seconds, but before he could retaliate all the men round the table had jumped up. Two held him back while the other three restrained Andy.

'Let me at the bugger!' Ben cried, fighting savagely to free himself. 'He'd no business speaking of Tilda like that.'

'Come on then, come on!' Andy bellowed, face red with anger.

'Let it be, Ben,' urged Maurice. 'Andy ain't worth it. He's just an animal when he's had a drink. Any excuse for a fight. The whole family's the same.' He turned to address the other men. 'Tek him home, lads,' he ordered.

Struggling wildly, Andy was unceremoniously dragged outside and once he was safely away a still furious Ben was released.

'You should a' let me have him!' He spat.

'I told yer, he ain't worth it,' Maurice responded. 'I know you Scots all stick together but the likes of Andy and his relatives are a breed apart. Now take a warning. The likes of him yer best ter make friends with. Makes a good friend when he's sober, does Andy, but as an enemy . . . I wouldn't wish him on anyone.'

'Maurice is right,' Sid Blackmore piped up.

'I ain't afraid of him,' Ben hissed. 'I came across worse than him where I grew up.'

'Nobody's saying yer afraid, mate,' Maurice said. 'Let's call it being sensible, eh? Now I must get off, I've to be up in the morning. Come on, Sid, I'll need a hand getting Frankie home.' He grinned, looking over towards the unconscious man prostrate across the couch. 'Don't look like he'll make it ter work in the morning.'

Hooking their arms under Frankie's, Maurice and Sid dragged him off the couch and tried to stand him upright. Frankie's eyes opened and he stared at the two men, bewildered.

'Wass going on?' he slurred.

'It's time to go home, Frankie. Come on, mate, find yer cap and put it on. It's time to face the missus.'

Staggering around, Frankie found his cap and slapped it on crookedly as he lumbered towards the door. Maurice and Sid followed.

'We're in the Talbot most nights after work if yer fancy a drink,' Maurice addressed Ben. 'And don't worry about Andy, he won't remember a thing come morning.'

Rubbing his smarting chin, Ben cocked an eyebrow. 'The likes of him don't worry me. Big men always fall hardest. I might see yous sometime in the pub though.'

'See yer then.'

'Yeah, see yous.'

Meanwhile Tilda was listening upstairs. After the rumpus of a few minutes earlier, which had greatly worried her, she heard the men leave and the place fall silent. Pulling her cardigan around her, she made her way slowly down the stairs. She found Ben sitting in the armchair nursing his chin. The room that she had spent time cleaning and polishing earlier in the day was in chaos.

She picked up a fallen chair and pushed it back under the table. She turned to face Ben but before she could say anything he raised his hand to stop her.

'Don't bother, Tilda. You've said enough for one night. You'd no business ordering my friends oot like that. It was just a game of cards we were having.'

'No right?' she retaliated sharply. '*You'd* no right to bring them back here in the first place. This is not your house, Ben McCraven, and in case you've forgotten, this is a place of mourning.'

He lifted his eyes to hers. He had temporarily forgotten the terrible tragedy that had brought him to Leicester, so intent had he been on becoming acquainted with people who might possibly lead him to the elusive Duggie Smilie. He had suggested the game of cards without thinking. He felt dreadfully ashamed of his thoughtless actions, but pride and his anger at her would not let him acknowledge that to Tilda.

Without a word, he averted his gaze and continued to rub his chin.

His lack of response heightened her own anger. 'Just look at the mess those troublemakers caused. This is no way to treat someone else's property.'

Ben grimaced as he ran his hand through his tousled red hair. 'A few empty beer bottles and some full ashtrays. Take two minutes to clear up. And there wasn't any trouble 'til you came down and started throwing your weight around. You really showed me up.'

Tilda felt remorseful. 'I'm sorry,' she spluttered. 'I didn't mean to do that.'

'Well, you did.' He stood up awkwardly. 'I'm going to bed before I say something I might regret. And for your information I'll be using the main bedroom as there's nowhere else. I'll square it with Ted when I see him.'

Biting her lip anxiously, she watched him stagger past her.

'What's wrong with your chin?' she asked tentatively.

He stopped and spun round to face her. 'I was thumped, Tilda. Satisfied?'

His abrupt tone reawakened her anger. 'Over some woman, I expect,' she said before she could stop herself.

'Yeah,' he said, eyes narrowing. 'Over some woman – and I'm wondering at this moment if she was worth getting a thumping for.'

Before Tilda could ask what he meant, he had gone.

Turning back, she sighed heavily as she surveyed the mess. Ben was wrong. It would take longer than two minutes to clear this lot up.

For what was left of the night Tilda slept fitfully as she struggled with her conscience. She still felt strongly that Ben had had no right to bring those men back to the house, he could hardly know much about them, but then he's right in accusing her of showing him up. She must have looked a sight in her nightclothes, demanding they should leave. She did wonder for a while though who the woman was over whom they had been fighting . . . After deliberating for quite a while on how to tackle her problem, she decided that making Ben breakfast before he went to work might go some way towards making amends, act as a kind of apology.

For practically the first time in her life it was a pleasure to dress. How good it felt to wear clothes that fitted her, with no holes or frayed edges. Wondering what to do with her hair, and not wanting to spoil the effect of her new clothes by tying it with the usual piece of string, she gathered it at the base of her neck, wound it into a knot and secured it with a couple of pins. As she came down the stairs she caught sight of her reflection in the hall-stand mirror. She stopped, hardly recognising the person looking back.

The high-necked blouse, the front of which was decorated with rows of tiny pleats, was tucked neatly into her skirt and bloused out to give the illusion of a shapely bosom. The long sleeves ended just past her wrists, cuffs secured with four tiny white pearl buttons. All that was showing of her withered arm was her slightly misshapen hand. The skirt, ending just below her calves, revealed to her own surprise a shapely pair of ankles, a feature she hadn't noticed before. It was a pity that she had to put on her boots and hide them. Her loosely knotted hair, tendrils of which were framing her face, was far more becoming than her usual severely scraped back bun.

She smiled. She would never be a beauty, no matter what she wore or what hairstyle she sported, but today's effort was such an improvement she felt a warm glow spread through her body.

Just before the break of dawn she was bustling around the kitchen frying bread, humming happily to herself. On hearing movement from upstairs, she broke three eggs into the pan.

There was a knock on the door and she opened it to find Wally grinning at her.

'Mornin', Tilda. Didn't know you'd be up this early.' He sniffed the air appreciatively. 'That smells good.' Then he stared at her, stunned. 'You look nice!'

Flushing crimson with embarrassment, she ushered him through, and shut the door behind him. 'Would you like some?' she offered.

He looked at her hesitantly, unsure whether to accept her generosity again. He was ravenous. His mother had given the last of the bread to Mr Maddock the lodger, and as Ernest the milkman didn't bring his cart around until well after seven, Wally's breakfast had consisted of a mug of milkless tea.

'Sit down,' she ordered, smiling as she sensed his dilemma. 'Pour yourself a cuppa whilst I dish this up. I think Ben will be several minutes yet. He came home the worse for wear last night.'

'Oh, did he have some luck then?'

'Luck?' Tilda asked, putting a filled plate before him. She returned to the stove and put some more bread in the pan to fry.

'In finding Maggie.'

Maggie? she thought. Would that be the women he was fighting over?

'Maggie and her sons usually drink down the Talbot. If he was drunk he was probably with that lot. Drank the place dry they have before now. So I've been told,' he added hurriedly, not wanting Tilda to think he himself drank excessively when two halves of bitter twice a week was usually his limit and all his money allowed. He stabbed his knife into an egg yolk and dipped a piece of fried bread into it, then popped it in his mouth. 'This is grand,' he said gratefully.

For Tilda it was a new experience to be praised for something she had cooked. 'To your liking, is it, sir?' she asked, giving a slight curtsey.

'Yer can say that again. Can I come every morning?' he responded, grinning cheekily.'

'Be glad you've got that,' she bantered back. 'Any more meals in this house and I'll be charging you board.'

Breaking the last three eggs into the pan she sat down at the small kitchen table opposite Wally and looked at him thoughtfully. 'Why did . . . er . . . Ben want to find this Maggie?' she casually asked.

'Eh? Oh, 'cos she's one of them Scots, yer know. I thought it might help him in his search if he went to see Maggie.'

'Search?' she said, frowning. 'For what?'

Wally raised his head and eyed her, puzzled. 'For the relative he's looking for. Didn't you know?'

Tilda shook her head. 'No, actually, I didn't.'

It suddenly struck her how little she knew about Ben. She had been acquainted with him now for five, nearly six weeks, shared several dramatic incidents with him, might in fact not even be alive, or Eustace for that matter, if he hadn't been at hand to help them escape the fire. And there was a strong possibility that neither Ted nor Daisy would still be here had it not been for Ben's bravery. But during all the time she had known him he had never talked of his past. They hardly talked of personal matters at all, come to that. He knew more about her than she did him. Still, Wally's telling her this made one thing that had been puzzling her click into place, and that was Ben's need to keep moving from town to town and his deep interest in any Scots who were living in the area.

'No,' she repeated. 'I didn't even know he had any relatives.' She smiled at Wally. 'Ben kinda keeps himself to himself. Another cuppa tea?'

'Oh, please,' came the enthusiastic reply.

Ben hardly said a word when he did come down. He stared at her for a moment, though as she had her back towards him at the stove she did not notice, before he sat down at the table. What little conversation he did make was directed at Wally. Nor did he eat much of his breakfast, much to Tilda's dismay. The atmosphere in the kitchen could have been cut with a knife. She was glad when he left for work.

About half an hour later, just as she was about to check on Daisy, a knock came at the door. She opened it to find a man standing there, who, judging by his clothes, was obviously on his way to work. He was carrying a battered billy can and across his shoulder was slung a haversack.

She smiled a greeting which faded when she realised he was staring at her, shocked. She hurriedly glanced down at herself, alarmed for an instant.

'Is there something the matter?' she asked in confusion.

'Oh, no, no,' Maurice Winbourne stuttered apologetically, his eyes once again travelling over her. This surely couldn't be the woman he had caught a glimpse of the previous evening, standing at the bottom of the stairs? He knew he had had a few too many drinks but his mind did not usually play such tricks. Nevertheless, to his way of thinking Andy Ferguson had done her a grave injustice when he had spoken out so unkindly and his drunken state was no excuse.

Not a man the ladies would call handsome, Maurice Winbourne had always been extremely shy when it came to dealing with the female species and in all his forty-three years had never had a proper girlfriend, someone to call his own, someone who could care for an easygoing man with simple needs.

Maurice had never had any delusions about himself, his mother had seen to that. 'Maurice,' she would often state, her mountainous body wedged firmly in an armchair, 'it's no good yer ever getting fanciful ideas. You ain't no looker, son, and that's a fact. You're far too skinny for a woman ever to want to take to her bed. Stay with yer mother, son, then yer won't get hurt.' And he had. He'd stayed with her until three years ago when she had passed away and it had taken six strong men to haul out her coffin.

He missed her, it would have been hard not to, and it had taken him a while to adjust to not having her around to do things for. His lack of female companionship was not all down to her, though. Maurice had just never met a woman who had taken his fancy. Until now that was. For the first time in his life he was experiencing love. And would it not be just his luck to fall for someone else's wife?

'Are you sure there's nothing wrong?' Tilda asked again anxiously. The man did not look at all well. He was staring at her in some kind of stupor. 'Would you like to come in and sit down for a minute?'

How he managed to look her in the eyes he would never know. Oh, but she had such lovely eyes: kindly, full of wordly wisdom for one of such tender years, and she looked a picture in her smart skirt and blouse, long dark brown hair pulled back and tied into a knot at the nape of her neck.

Tilda was beginning to grow unnerved, not quite knowing what to make of this stranger standing tongue tied at the door, and instinctively she rubbed her deformed arm. 'Is it some building work you wanted doing?' she asked, taking a stab in the dark.

'What? Oh, er ... no.' He took a deep breath to still his jangling nerves. He lowered his head and studied his booted feet. 'Actually, I called to see if yer husband was all right after last night? You know, with Andy getting a bit out of hand, like. But then, we shouldn't really have come in the first place, not with the house being in mourning.'

'No, you shouldn't have. But what's done is done.' Tilda took a deep breath. She really ought to put this man straight on her and Ben's marital status or before long the whole street would have the wrong impression and she doubted Ben would welcome that. 'By the way, he's not my husband. We're just employed by Mr Wragg until he gets better.'

Maurice's head jerked up and his heart soared. She wasn't married! He couldn't believe his ears. He suddenly felt so happy he wanted to shout out with joy.

The smile that split his face caused Tilda to raise her eyebrows. 'Are you sure there's nothing wrong?'

'Wrong? Oh, my goodness, no.' Maurice could hardly keep the excitement from his voice. Then he suddenly realised this woman must think him an idiot. He was making a fool of himself. He was old enough to be her father. 'I'd better go, I'll be late for work. Goodbye,' he said abruptly.

'Shall I tell Ben you called?' she shouted after him, bemused by his attitude.

He turned and looked across at her, nodding vigorously. 'Yes, please do.'

She watched him skirt obstacles in the yard and disappear out of the gate. She re-entered the house and shut the door. How could she tell Ben he had called when she didn't even know his name? Shaking her head, she put the whole incident at the back of her mind and began to prepare Daisy's breakfast.

Chapter Seventeen

A week had seemingly done nothing to change Ted's condition. When Tilda entered his hospital room, she had to hide her disappointment at the lack of obvious improvement. Bruises he'd sustained during the fall were still black and purple with yellowing edges, and beneath the covers his damaged body was still rigidly encased in bandages and plaster casts. She could tell by his eyes though that he was beside himself with joy to see Daisy when she walked into the room holding the child in her arms.

'Oh, it's good to see yer!' he said with difficulty. 'I didn't expect you, being's it's such a journey.'

'Daisy loved it on the bus. Didn't you, Daisy?' Tilda addressed the child. 'She had all the passengers fussing over her. The journey's not so bad and it's more comfortable than a cart.' She smiled cheerfully, sitting down in the chair next to the bed. Settling the child comfortably on her knee, she eyed Ted searchingly. 'So how are you, Mr Wragg?'

He took several deep breaths. 'Well, the pain's not so bad, gel, and that's a relief.' He averted his gaze from her and stared up at the ceiling. 'They think I might have broken me back, but they ain't sure yet.'

Tilda gasped. 'Oh, Mr Wragg, I'm so sorry.'

He turned his face to her and tried to smile. 'Could be worse, gel. They thought I was going to die. But I proved 'em wrong and I intend to prove 'em wrong over this. Them doctors don't know everything. That's why they say "I think"' or "you could have".'

Tilda didn't know what to say in reply. 'Is there anything you need?'

'You brought what I needed and that's Daisy. She looks well, gel. You're obviously doing a grand job.'

'I hope so. I'm doing my best at any rate.'

He eyed his daughter lovingly. 'Has she screamed much, Daisy loves a good scream. Thinks it gets her her own way. Me, I'm a sucker for it, but Maud had her measure. Didn't she, Daisy? Your mam knew you inside out.' Tears filled his eyes. Slowly, with great difficulty, he lifted his hand and wiped them away. 'Sorry about that. It's still raw. You don't know how much I wish we'd never gone out that day.'

Tilda's heart went out to him. 'If you feel like crying, then do it. Nobody expects you to get over your wife's death just like that.'

'I don't think I ever shall but I've been told the pain gets easier to live with, just like the pain in me body. If I'm truthful it's still as bad but I'm getting used to it. But one thing I ain't getting used to and that's lying here all day, staring up at the ceiling. It's driving me mad. I didn't realise how much I could miss Wharf Street and all my cronies. How are things going? Settling in all right, are you? And the business? Has Mrs Duncan been to see you yet about her waterworks?'

Tilda laughed. 'Yes, she has, and I had a job understanding what she was going on about. Now about money and things . . .' Balancing Daisy on one knee, she delved into her pocket and pulled out a wad of papers. 'I've marked everything down in detail for you and I really need to discuss wages. I don't know how much to take, you see, and . . .'

'Tilda, Tilda,' Ted interrupted her. 'Listen ter me.' He eyed her sharply. 'Are you listening?'

Quizzically, she nodded.

'Good. I trust you both. I've always had faith in my instincts and they've never let me down yet. And you honestly don't think I would have handed my daughter over to you if I didn't trust you, do you? Now stop fretting.'

Tilda stared at him, speechless.

'As for wages, pay yourself what you think you're worth.'

'Oh, but, Mr Wragg . . .'

'Ted. Please call me Ted, all my friends do.'

'Mr Ted . . . Ted,' a flustered Tilda corrected herself, 'I've never had a paying job before,' she said, blushing. 'So I've no idea.'

'Haven't you,' he said, surprised. 'I'd have thought someone like you would have been clambered after. Well, there's a simple answer to that. Find out the highest rate for the job, and the lowest, and then pay yourself somewhere in the middle. Now that's settled. So how's your young man getting on? Keeping my customers happy, I hope?'

'Oh, yes, yes,' Tilda said enthusiastically. 'And him and Wally are getting on famously.'

'Glad to hear it. He's a grand lad is Wally.'

Tilda sighed heavily. 'Mr Wragg – Ted, there is something you should know, though.'

'Oh, what's that then?' he asked, frowning.

'Well, it's me and Ben. We're not a couple, not married. Just friends really.' If you can call our relationship friendly, she thought, staring at Ted anxiously.

'Oh, I see.' His eyes twinkled. 'That'll give the neighbours something to gossip about then, won't it?'

Tilda felt relieved. 'You don't mind then?'

'It's not really an issue as far as I can see. As long as you're

267

taking care of Daisy, which you obviously are, and Ben's looking after me business, that's all I'm concerned about.'

Tilda smiled happily, thinking what a nice man Ted was and how fortunate she was to be working for him. It was just a pity about the circumstances, she thought sadly.

Daisy began to get agitated and started to grizzle.

'Thought it wouldn't last long.' Ted smiled. 'Go on then, Daisy, have a good scream.'

Daisy did.

'I'd better take her outside, see if I can quieten her down a bit.'

'You're not going just yet, are you? I'll see you again before you do.'

'Oh, yes,' she said reassuringly, and suddenly clamped her hand to her mouth. 'Oh, I nearly forgot. Mrs Skuttle's outside, waiting to see you.'

He eyed her in alarm. 'Rose Skuttle? Here?'

'Yes, she travelled with us on the omnibus.'

Ted groaned. 'Oh, Lord, spare me!' He looked worried. 'Please tell her I'm sleeping. I can't face her at the moment. Don't get me wrong, she's not a bad sort, but . . .'

'Cooee, Ted, are yer decent?'

His eyes snapped shut and Tilda turned to face the door. 'Shush,' she mouthed at Rose, 'he's sleeping.'

'Sleeping?' Rose repeated advancing into the room. 'Wadda yer mean, he's sleepin'? Did you tell him I'm here? And how can he be sleeping with the racket that baby's makin'?'

Gathering Daisy to her, Tilda hurriedly stood and headed for the door, ushering Rose outside. 'Let him rest for a while, Mrs Skuttle. Let's see how he is when we've had a cuppa tea or something, eh?'

Rose fought to control her anger. Finding out about the existence of Ben had infuriated her. Now she was even more desperate to see Ted and give him her views on the error of his ways. And she wanted to see the man she planned to marry, a thought that had kept her awake, tossing and turning, for the last four nights. She had dressed especially carefully and taken time over her hair just for the occasion, *and* she'd lashed out precious money on some fruit. 'I suppose,' she said, annoyed. 'But I'll say one thing – I ain't come all this way for nothing. The nurse was wrong to say you should go in first. I've known him years and I could easily have taken Daisy in.'

Ignoring her remark, Tilda stopped a passing nurse and asked directions to the canteen.

Rose did not get her wish. They returned to Ted's room to find the police had arrived. Maud's body had been discovered several miles downriver, trapped under the water by tangled weed. It was a nurse who imparted this news to them. Tilda wanted to stay around to offer him her condolences, but doing so would have meant missing the bus back to Leicester.

Although upset about the news, an extremely disappointed Rose spent the whole return journey desperately trying to fathom a way to raise the fare back so she could visit Ted again.

Rose Skuttle was not a happy woman. She had spent the last three months cutting back on her outgoings in order to finance trips to see Ted, much to the dismay of her son and the lodger. Mr Maddock especially was not pleased with the lowered quality of the food he was presented with. Rose had managed to visit the man she was pinning all her future hopes on three times so far, and would have gone more if she could have scraped up the fare, but regardless of how many times she visited, she never quite managed to have a good long chat with Ted on her own. Either Tilda was around or else nurses would interrupt.

But Rose would not give up. Come hell or high water she

would have her talk, somehow convince Ted of the error of his ways, and install herself in charge of the household and Wally over the yard.

If she was truthful, which she had no intention of being, she had to admit that the young people seemed to be making an excellent job of things. The house was always spotless whenever she called around – mostly uninvited – Daisy was thriving and, surprisingly, not screaming so much, and the business hadn't suffered too badly from Ted's absence, according to her son. But Rose would continue to chip away regardless. She was determined to have her way over this matter.

One thing that did make her happy was that Ted was slowly getting better; even the surprised doctor was delighted with his progress. He was still lying flat on his back, parts of him still encased in plaster, but he was steadily improving though no one was sure if he would ever stand upright again. That was a daunting thought, having an invalid on her hands. But regardless, it was the life of comfort an alliance with him would bring that was uppermost in her mind.

According to Tilda there had been a mention the last time she'd visited – without Rose, to her fury – of the possibility of his being moved to a convalescent home much nearer Leicester. The thought of his becoming more accessible pleased Rose beyond belief.

These thoughts were all running through her mind as she plonked the mug of weak tea in front of Mary and sat down opposite her.

'What's this, Rose Skuttle?' demanded her friend, peering disapprovingly into her mug. 'Washing up water?'

Rose frowned hard. 'If yer don't wannit, leave it.' She folded her arms under her bosom. 'So what's new wi' you?' she asked casually. Knowing Mary so well, she knew the woman had something on her mind which she was desperate to divulge but wouldn't until Rose dragged it from her, which Rose had no intention of giving her the satisfaction of doing.

'Nothing much,' replied Mary, grimacing as she sipped on the tea. 'Any more sugar?' she asked hopefully.

'No, there ain't. But there's plenty in the corner shop should you want any bad enough.'

'You're getting a right tight arse, Rose Skuttle, and it's all in aid of those trips to see Ted. You want to watch it or your lodger'll be leaving. Can't expect him to pay good money for digs and be dished up pig swill.'

'Whose food a' you calling pig swill, Mary O'Malley? Not mine, I hope?'

'No, no,' She backed down hurriedly. 'It's just that you have ter be particular when you've a paying guest.'

Rose narrowed her eyes. 'And what would you know about "paying guests", may I ask?'

Mary inwardly groaned. Her and her big mouth. She had planned to milk her news for all it was worth, build up to divulging it, Rose meantime growing wild with impatience. There was no point now.

''Cos I'm thinking of getting one,' she replied frostily.

Rose glared surprised. 'What! You get a lodger? It'd have ter be somebody who ain't very particular then, wouldn't it?'

'And just what do you mean by that?'

Rose tutted in disgust. If she really said what was on her mind then she would lose Mary's friendship for good. Despite her desire to retaliate for those remarks about pig swill, Rose knew that there were only so many scathing remarks a best friend would stand. Mary wouldn't take kindly to being told openly her house was a hovel already filled to bursting with seven children aged five to thirteen, and a husband who regardless of his 'great expectations' was neither use nor ornament so far as Rose was concerned. And he was handy with his fists when the mood took him and not particular whom he beat, Mary or the kids. Still, with a lodger present, he wouldn't be able to lash out so often, she supposed.

'Particular wasn't the word I meant to use,' she said grudgingly. 'What I meant was, well, yer overcrowded as it is.' She eyed Mary quizzically. 'What happened to his "great expectations", then?'

Mary scratched her neck nervously. 'I don't think they was as great as he was expecting.' Her eyes lit up. 'I got me mangle, though. It ain't new. Well, it's quite rusty really. But much better than the one I had. And the kids got a few bits. Paddy's rigged himself out too. Oh, Rose, he looks ever so handsome in his new togs.' The look her friend gave her made her bristle defensively. 'Well, he had to, Rose. As he said, he couldn't go searching for a decent job looking like a rag bag. Well, he couldn't, could he?'

'Mary!' Rose erupted. 'Nobody in their right mind is gonna give your Paddy a decent job, new togs or old. When are you gonna learn, eh? He can't be trusted. Gets a few quid in his pocket and he squanders it. And don't look at me like that. I'm speaking the truth and you know it. Where did the money come from anyway?'

Mary shrugged her shoulders. 'I don't know. I never asked. I was just glad to be getting some.'

'Well, I suppose you've got ter be grateful that he handed over summat and didn't keep it all to himself. This lodger, though. Where the hell will you put him?'

'In our room. Paddy's got a bed for next to nothing from one of his friends and put it in the recess in the kitchen. We can use that.'

Rose sighed heavily. 'But yer never mentioned ter me you were looking?'

'I wasn't. It's Paddy's idea.'

Rose grunted disdainfully. Now why didn't that fact surprise her? 'Huh, well, a lodger won't affect his lifestyle, will it? You do realise, don't yer, Mary, that you won't see hardly a penny. If yer didn't you're more of a fool than I thought yer were.'

Face contorted in anger, Mary scraped back her chair and stood up. 'That's it, Rose Skuttle. I'm off,' she cried, snatching up her handbag.

Rose stared up at her, alarmed. 'Eh? You ain't really going, are yer?'

'I bloody well am. I'm fed up with your callous remarks. That's my husband you're talking about. I know he's got faults, but I happen to love him all the same.'

'Oh, sit down, Mary. I didn't mean it and you know it. You're me best friend, for God's sake.'

'Am I?' Mary hissed. 'Sometimes, Rose Skuttle, I wonder. I'll sit down on one condition.'

'Oh, and what's that?'

'That you make a decent pot of tea and go and get some sugar.'

Chapter Eighteen

Tilda lifted her head as the back door burst open and Ben came in. She could tell by his face he was pleased about something.

'Well, I've done it,' he announced proudly, walking across to Daisy who was propped in her high chair playing with a wooden spoon which she kept dropping on the floor. He picked up the spoon, put it in her hand and tickled her under her chin.

'Done what?' asked Tilda.

'Repaired my first wall, and if I say it myself I've done a good job. Is Wully around?'

'He came back an hour or so ago. He's in the yard checking the materials. You must have passed him.'

Ben shrugged his shoulders. 'I didn't see him. He must be in the shed or something.' Taking off his jacket, he hung it on the hook on the back door, went over to the sink and pumped water into the enamel basin in the sink. Picking up the bar of soap, he began to wash his hands. 'I wonder what's taking him so long? I cannae wait to tell him my news. He was worried aboot me going oot on my own. Proved him wrong though, didn't I? Just about fully fledged, I am now. Nothing to this building lark.'

On getting no reply he turned his head and looked searchingly across at her. She was engrossed in re-reading a letter she had received by the second post.

'That from Fanny?' he asked.

'Pardon? Oh, yes,' she replied in a distracted voice.

'Eustace all right?'

'Yes, he seems fine.'

'Yous still miss him, don't yous?'

She nodded. 'Yes, I do, very much. Getting a letter is nice but not the same as seeing him.'

'Well, why don't yous visit him then?'

'How can I? It's such a long way and I can't drive a cart.'

'I could take yous.'

She stared at him, shocked. 'I appreciate your offer. And I would like that, Ben, thank you. As soon as I can manage to wangle things here and your work allows. That's if you're still around, of course.'

He raised his eyebrows. 'Is there something yous know that I don't?'

'Like what?'

'Like the fact that I'm leaving.'

'Well, you never did intend staying around. I'm surprised you've lasted this long.'

So was Ben for that matter. What amazed him the most was how much he was enjoying himself. This set up quite suited him. He worked hard for his money, felt he was now aiding Wally in his own right towards keeping the business afloat, and was also managing to fit in enough of a social life to keep a young man of his age happy. But the most important thing was that he had free time to follow new leads in his search for Duggie Smilie. The man had to be hiding somewhere. Ben's desire to catch him was so strong, sometimes he felt he could smell him.

Making a friend of Andy Ferguson had paid off. Every Scot Andy and his family knew of was on the look out for, as they all believed, Ben's longlost relative. Several of the leads had at first appeared promising and Ben had grown quite excited, but nothing had come of them. Even he had been surprised to learn of the large number of fellow countrymen who resided hereabouts, having moved their families lock, stock and barrel in the hope of better things. A conniving murderer such as the one he sought would have no difficulty in keeping a low profile, and as his promising new leads came to nothing Ben realised only too well the enormity of his task.

Still, wherever Duggie Smilie was hiding, he would be sniffed out eventually. Until that day came Ben had no intention of ever giving up. When the Leicester area had been exhausted it would be time for him to move on.

'When I decide it's time to go, I'll give yous plenty of warning, Tilda.'

'Will you? Have I your word you won't leave us in the lurch?'

'Tilda, I've said so, haven't I? Now what on earth's keeping Wully?'

Just then the man himself knocked on the door and entered.

'Ben,' he queried, 'that pile of bricks we had delivered . . .'

Ben turned to face him. 'What aboot them?'

'Well, they're just about gone.'

'Yes, that's right. I used the last of them repairing the wall and it took more than we thought. Talking of walls, aren't yous going to ask how I got on?'

Wally grinned. 'I don't need ter ask I can see by your face. Went all right then, I take it?'

Ben puffed out his chest proudly. 'Wully, you're looking at a master builder. I can tackle anything now. Who says you need to be learning this trade for five years.'

The experts that's who, thought Wally, and having gone through nearly all the required five years of grounding he knew they were right. Repairing a boundary wall was child's play, requiring the minimum of builder's skills. But Wally was too kind-hearted to dampen Ben's high spirits by saying anything.

He had still a long way to go and Wally was aware that Ben knew this, but was happy to let him bask in his glory for now.

'Well, we've got a roof to do tomorrow. Manage on yer own, can yer, whilst I go out and price a couple of jobs?'

Ben's face fell. 'Roof? Er . . . I ain't that keen on heights.'

'What, a master builder scared of heights? Never!' Wally said, hiding a smile. 'You'll never get your papers, lad, if you can't climb a ladder.'

Ben playfully punched him on the arm. 'Yous cheeky beggar! Who a' yous calling a lad? Not me, I hope?'

'As if I'd dare.'

Tilda rose from the table. 'Sit down, you two, I'll put your dinner out.'

'You've done me some as well?' Wally asked in delight, and sat down quickly in case she changed her mind. As she put the hot plate in front of him he smiled up at her appreciatively. 'Ta, Tilda.'

She just smiled. She knew Wally wasn't fed all that well for a still growing man who needed sustenance. Rose had cut back drastically on the quality of food that she gave him. Keeping all the best for her lodger. The money the woman saved was spent on fares to the hospital and things to take in for Ted, Tilda knew, and she accommodated Wally now by giving him most of her own share of the meat, making do with more vegetables, which did not bother her in the slightest considering that until recently vegetables had been her staple diet.

'Aren't you eating, Tilda?' Ben asked.

Still upset by the letter, she wasn't hungry. 'I'm having mine later, after I've put Daisy to bed.'

Tilda looked across at the child, suddenly realising all had gone quiet. Daisy had nodded off. Easing her out of the chair, Tilda sat back at the table and cradled her gently in her arms whilst she finished a mug of tea.

Wally suddenly remembered the unfinished conversation of earlier. 'Ben, about those bricks.'

'Oh, not now, Wully. Can't we forget aboot work until tomorrow?'

The look on Wally's face gave Ben his answer. 'Oh, go on then, what aboot these ruddy bricks?'

'Well, I think there's something funny going on.'

'Something funny, Wally? What do you mean?' asked Tilda.

Wally pushed away his empty plate. 'We had five thousand delivered, do you remember, about three weeks ago?'

'Yes, that's right,' Tilda replied. 'I signed the docket for the man who delivered them. He piled them up in the corner of the yard.'

'Did you see him do it?'

Tilda shook her head. 'No, I just gave the docket to Ben when he came home.'

'Yes, and I put it on the clipboard with the rest to be paid when the invoice came in. So what's the problem, Wully?' he asked.

'Well, I'm not quite sure. I've been over it several times and I keep coming to the same conclusion. It ain't just the bricks either. It's other stuff we've had delivered. The lime blocks, the ton of sand, the wood we need for the roof tomorrow...'

'Get to the point, Wully. I ain't got all night.'

'Going out again?' Tilda asked.

'Only for an hour. I've someone to see.'

Tilda tutted. Ben and his people to see. Another lead, she guessed, in his quest for his longlost relative. But she didn't say anything. Ben didn't know she knew anything about it, and as he had never mentioned it, she left it that way.

'I think it's being stolen,' blurted Wally.

Two pairs of eyes were fixed on him. 'What?' Tilda and Ben said in unison.

'How can the stuff be stolen?' Ben questioned. 'Tilda's here most of the day, and I can't exactly see it being heaved over the top of the wall in the night. Not with that barbed wire there, I can't. Cut a man to shreds, it would.'

'Well, it must be somehow 'cos although we've been fairly busy, we ain't used it.'

Ben sighed heavily.

'Has someone a key to the gates?' Tilda asked.

'No. We've only one set we carry around and they've never been mislaid to my knowledge. There is a spare, though. I know Mr Wragg had two cut when he had the locks changed just before his accident.'

Tilda knew where the spare was. It was behind the brick at the side of the chimney where the money was kept. But she couldn't say anything for fear Ted didn't want anyone but herself and Ben to know. Not that she thought Ted didn't trust Wally, but the fewer who knew about the hidey hole, the safer things would be.

'Why did he have the lock changed,' she asked.

'Because someone tried to break in,' Wally replied. 'We knew it was Paddy O'Malley but we had no proof.'

Ben took a thoughtful breath. 'Are yous sure we just haven't used the stuff, Wully?'

'We can't have used half the order for tomorrow's job 'cos we got it in special.'

Ben nodded thoughtfully. 'Yes, we did. So we're going to have to buy more?'

'Yes, if we're going to complete the jobs.'

Ben noticed Tilda was staring at him. 'What are yous looking at me like that for?'

She frowned. 'Like what?'

'Accusingly, that's what.'

'I wasn't,' she snapped. Which wasn't entirely true. Fleetingly it had crossed her mind to wonder if Ben could be behind this, but somehow she knew he wouldn't do such a thing. If Ben was the thief she had at first thought, then there had been ample opportunity recently for him to do something – and something a lot simpler than stealing materials and selling them off. 'I was just thinking, that's all.'

'Thinking? What aboot?'

'What we're going to do, that's what? 'Cos if we don't do something, all the profits will be gone buying more stuff to replace the missing materials.'

The room fell silent as they sat and thought.

Daisy stirred in Tilda's arms and she looked down fondly. 'I ought to put this little one to bed.'

'No, stay put, Tilda,' Ben said. 'We need to sort this problem oot.'

They sat in silence again.

It was Tilda who spoke first. 'Ben, you're only learning. Is it possible that . . .'

'Eh,' he eyed her sharply. 'I know what you're getting at. But, Tilda, we're talking aboot two and a half thousand bricks. Even I'd find it hard to break and waste that many. I'll admit to a few, yes. And how do yous account for the blocks of lime if that's the case?'

'Oh,' she said, ashamed. 'Well, as I see it, if you've definitely not used the stuff, and it's not been stolen, then there's only one answer.'

They both stared at her.

'We never had it all delivered in the first place. Well, we can't have, can we?'

'But Mr Wragg's been using the same suppliers for years. I can't see them double crossing him,' said Wally, frowning hard.

'Ted's not around, though, is he?' Ben replied. 'Maybe these suppliers all put their heads together and came up with a plan to make some extra money. Maybe thought while Ted's oot the way we were that stupid we wouldn't notice.'

'And they were right, up 'til now.'

Ben glared at Tilda. 'Yous signed the docket for the bricks. So that makes yous responsible for those.'

'Oh, that's right, blame me . . .'

'Eh,' Wally piped up, 'that's enough, you two. Arguing won't get this matter sorted.'

They both looked at him, shamefaced.

'When are you placing another order?' Tilda asked.

'Well, tomorrow. We'll need some more roofing timber and definitely bricks to finish the jobs we've lined up. There's enough lime blocks to manage with at the moment by my reckoning.' Wally eyed Tilda in concern. 'You are remembering to keep well away from the lime pit, ain't yer, Tilda? Fall in there and yer a gonna for sure. That lime would tek the skin off yer bones quicker than 'ote.'

'Yes, don't worry. I don't often go in the yard, not past the washhouse and privy.'

'That's all right then,' he said, relieved. 'Now about these orders. Do we place them or what?'

'We've no choice, otherwise the business will grind to a halt. Tilda will just have to check each one when it comes in.'

Her mind whirled at the thought of counting five thousand bricks and numerous lengths of wood, whilst trying to run the house and care for Daisy, plus keeping meticulous accounts for Ted. But she would do it.

'And what do I do if I find it's short?'

Ben narrowed his eyes. 'You just check, Tilda. If it's short, I'll deal with it personally. If it's not, then it's back to square one.'

She took a deep breath. 'While we're talking business, there's another problem we should discuss.'

Ben groaned loudly.

Undeterred she carried on: 'It's about payment for the jobs we've done. We're still owed for work we did weeks ago. Who's doing anything about collecting it?'

Ben and Wally looked at each other and both shrugged their shoulders.

'It's always bin a problem, Tilda. Mr Wragg was constantly pulling his hair out over it. But it's like everything else: people say they'll pay up when they've got it.'

'Well, it's not good enough. People shouldn't expect to get work done and not have the money to settle up. We have to live as well remember.' Tilda's keen brain had learned a lot since she had struggled to keep the records for Ted and it had been worrying her for a while that unpaid debts were slowly piling up. The money in question wasn't vast amounts but in the long term could become quite serious.

Ben was looking at her in surprise.

'Don't look at me like that,' she said indignantly. 'I have got a brain in my head. I worked out for myself what's going on.'

'If you're that clever, it's a pity yous didna notice what was happening with the deliveries.'

Wally, sensing another row brewing, quickly changed the subject.

'I could visit these people after work,' he offered.

Ben tutted loudly. 'We work a ten- or twelve-hour day most times as it is, Wully. We have to have a couple of hours to ourselves.'

'Well, someone has to do it or we'll never get paid, and we haven't the authority to employ someone else. I'll have to do it,' Tilda declared.

'Yous,' Ben exclaimed, shocked.

'And why not?' she demanded angrily. 'I am capable, you know.'

'I never said yous weren't. All right,' he said, glad that at least that problem was sorted. 'We'll leave that to yous then, and don't come crying to me when someone swears at yous or punches yous in the eye.'

I've had a lifetime of that sort of thing, thought Tilda ruefully. Dealing with potential non-payers and their wrath would be nothing in comparison to what her father had dished out.

Secretly Ben thought it was admirable of Tilda to offer to chase the debts but wouldn't voice that to her face. He pushed back his chair and rose. 'I'm off for a wash and change.'

Just then a loud clatter sounded from the yard. Ben shot to the back door and yanked it open. Sprawled inside the wheelbarrow he had hurriedly discarded by the washhouse that morning after loading the cart was a scruffy lad aged about ten.

'You shouldn't'ta left this 'ere, mister, it's dangerous. Nearly broke me bloody neck.'

Ben advanced towards him; Wally and Tilda, carrying Daisy, following closely behind. Grabbing him by the arm, Ben pulled the lad out. 'I'll give yous dangerous,' he shouted. 'Yous shouldn't be here. How did yous get in?'

The boy pointed towards the yard gates. 'Through the little door.'

'You were the last in, Ben. You must have left it unlocked,' Tilda accused.

Ben turned and scowled at her angrily, then swung to the boy. 'What the hell are yous doing here anyway? Thieving?'

'No, I ain't,' the boy retaliated indignantly. 'Me dad sent me.'

'What for?'

'To tell yer the bloody wall's fell down.'

'The wall? What wall?' Ben questioned.

'The one yer sorted today. And me dad sez if yers don't fix it sharpish he'll get someone else – and don't expect ter be paid if he does!'

Gulping guiltily, Ben let go of the boy who nimbly picked his way across the yard. He stopped halfway through the door and shouted across to Ben.

'Eh, me sister says don't dare forget yer date wi' 'er tomorrow night, and don't be late 'cos she'll be waiting.'

He disappeared through the door.

Ben turned to Tilda and Wally. 'Don't yous two dare say a word aboot the wall or anything else. I'm warning yous!'

Silently they both watched as he strode back into the house.

Wally realised he really should go home, but suddenly the thought didn't appeal to him one little bit. His mother hadn't been in the best of moods for several days now and her wrath, for whatever reason this time, would only be taken out on himself. Oh, she was politeness herself when Mr Maddock was around, but when he wasn't Wally was treated like an imbecile, and if he dared speak his mind, banished to his bedroom like a naughty boy of six. His mother seemed conveniently to forget he would soon be twenty years of age and was already helping to run a business which, taking everything into consideration was not doing too badly.

The thought of a couple of hours nattering to Tilda seemed a very pleasant idea and he did have something on his mind he wanted to discuss with her – his girlfriend. Elsie Battle was the first girl he had ever dared ask for a date. Well, in truth it was Elsie who had done the asking. He was taking her to the Hippodrome cinema on Saturday night and wanted to discuss with Tilda several things that were preying on his mind. She was the only woman he knew of who would not ridicule him or make him feel silly.

He grinned at her cheekily. 'Er ... you weren't thinking of making a cake tonight, were yer, Tilda?'

Making a cake was the last thing she felt like doing. For the first time since the night of the fire she felt a need for solitude.

'I wasn't . . .' Her words were cut short by the disappointment that clouded his face and her better nature took over. 'But you said you had stomach ache the last time I made one,' she playfully chided.

'Oh, I was only joking, Tilda. You know I didn't mean it.'

Wally hadn't the heart to tell her that in truth her cakes were awful. Tilda's dinners were delicious. Her pastry, which she had painstakingly mastered the art of making over the last few months, melted in the mouth, but her cakes were like lead weights and were not improving despite her efforts. But if being a guinea pig for her cakes meant spending a couple of pleasant hours nattering to her in the kitchen, then he would accept punishment gladly.

These cake-tasting sessions had begun one night after he'd stayed late to replenish the lime pit. He had forgotten to ask Ben for his help, realising too late he would have to tackle the job by himself as Ben had already gone out. He hadn't relished the thought much either. It was a thankless, nasty job if ever there was one: manoeuvring the heavy solid blocks of lime into the wooden barrels, then filling them with water, making sure that the long wooden chutes leading over to the deep pit were positioned correctly so that none of the liquefied lime spilled out. The lime then had to sit for several weeks whilst it solidified enough to be used in the cement that bound the bricks together.

Tilda, on realising what Wally was doing, had offered her help. He'd been grateful but had turned her down. Filling the lime pit was a dangerous job, and in Wally's opinion not one to be tackled by a woman.

But since that night any uncertainty he had felt about her had vanished. A fondness for her began to develop, and the more time he spent with her, the more it grew.

When he had first met Tilda he hadn't known what to make of her, the rags she was dressed in hardly fostered a favourable opinion, but very quickly he understood why Mr Wragg had shown such faith in her. He wondered if Tilda realised how at ease he felt in her company, how good she was at listening, how she never forced her own opinions on him. Now he looked forward to these visits which happened once or twice a week, and found that any troubles he was worrying over were eased after sharing them with her.

'A' you there, our Wally?' a voice shouted.

'Oh, God, it's me mam,' he groaned. 'Yes, I'm here.'

'I bloody thought so,' Rose grumbled to herself as she climbed through the doorway in the gate, more than ready to give her son a piece of her mind. She was carrying a plate in her hand filled with his dinner of soggy boiled potatoes, overboiled cabbage and a dried up faggot. As she was about to open her mouth, she suddenly realised Tilda was present and tried unsuccessfully to hide the plate behind her back. 'Oh, 'ello, me duck,' she addressed Tilda sweetly. 'All right, are yer? Only yer weren't in when I called earlier.'

'I'd probably popped out,' Tilda called back. 'I'm fine, thank you, Mrs Skuttle.'

'Right, well, I'll probably see yer termorrer then. Are yer coming for yer dinner, Wally? Only if yer much longer it'll be all dried up.'

The thought of tackling the dinner his mother had prepared on top of the delicious meal he'd just eaten did not appeal at all but unless he wanted to cause a scene he had no choice. 'I'd better go, Tilda,' he said reluctantly. 'I'll see yer tomorrow.'

'Yes, night, Wally.'

She had just settled herself down with another mug of tea when a loud knock sounded on the front door. Gathering Daisy up, she went to answer it to find a nervous Maurice hovering on the doorstep. Despite her mood, she smiled warmly at him. She liked Maurice. 'Hello. You've just missed Ben.'

He already knew Ben had left. He had stood in an entry opposite and watched Wally following his mother then Ben striding off down the street. It was Tilda he had come to see, just as he had all the other times he had done this. He knew he was being stupid, but couldn't help himself. Just two minutes spent in her company was enough to brighten his day.

Tilda herself had no idea, of course. He'd been very careful about that, not wanting to frighten her off. He'd sooner have her friendship than nothing at all. If he gave her time, a feeling for him, something more than friendship, might grow in her. He could only wait and hope, and didn't care how long it took. He'd waited a lifetime for someone like Tilda.

He took off his cap, allowing his face to fall. 'Oh, damn, I haven't, have I?'

'You could try the pub?'

'Er . . . no. I'm not in the mood for a drink tonight.' Maurice shuffled uneasily thinking of an excuse to keep her talking.

'Is anything the matter, Maurice?' she asked.

'Er . . . no. Nothing. I just fancied a natter if Ben was at home, that's all.'

Tilda's heart went out to this man. He always called just after Ben left. She wondered sometimes if Ben knew he was going to come round and planned it this way. Even though Maurice had plenty of friends she knew he was lonely. What he needed, she thought, was to find a loving woman to share his life with, and that shouldn't be too hard for a kind man like himself. She pictured Rose. They were about the same age and both on their own. Then dismissed the idea. Rose was not the type for Maurice, she would nag him to death. Besides, Tilda had begun to have grave suspicions that Rose had her eye fixed firmly elsewhere, and wondered if the man in question realised.

She thought of her need for solitude, then of her dinner drying up in the oven, of the fact that she still wasn't hungry and of how much she hated the thought of waste, then pictured Maurice returning to an empty house. Her own need for solitude was pushed aside.

'Have you eaten?' she asked him. 'If not, so long as you don't mind that it's a bit dried up, I've a plate of dinner going spare.'

Her question was answered by the delight that flooded his face and she stood aside to let him enter. 'Put the kettle on and help yourself to the plate in the oven. I must see to Daisy. I won't be long.'

Two days later Ben strode into the kitchen, followed by Wally.

'Did the order come?' he called to Tilda who was standing at the stove stirring a pan of soup.

She turned to him. 'Yes, and don't shout, Ben, I'm not deaf.'

'I didn't shout.'

'You did.'

'Er . . . and was it all there?' Wally intervened.

Tilda turned her attention to him and smiled a greeting. 'Hello, Wally. Go all right today, did it?'

He smiled back. 'Yeah, ta, Tilda. We got the job finished and it's all paid up.'

She sighed, relieved. 'Oh, good, because I intend to go out some time this week and visit the debtors.' In truth it was a prospect she wasn't relishing. But regardless of that fact, the news she had to give them was far more worrying. 'Sit down, Wally, you must be hungry.' She eyed him. 'Unless, of course, you ought to go home?'

Wally thought of the dinner that would be waiting for him and the delicious smell coming from what Tilda was offering and his decision came quick, 'I'll sit down, ta.'

'Tilda!' Ben erupted. 'What aboot the order?'

Ladling soup into two bowls, she put them on the table then

eyed Ben sharply. 'I asked you not to shout at me. Raise your voice any louder and you'll not only upset Daisy, the neighbours will be able to answer your question.'

On hearing her name mentioned, Daisy, propped in her high chair by the side of the kitchen table, started to chuckle. Ben smiled at her response then turned his attention back to Tilda.

'Yeah, she looks upset,' he said sarcastically.

Ignoring him Tilda filled her own bowl, sat down and began to eat. Ben stared at her then motioned to Wally to sit down.

He picked up his spoon. 'Tilda, what aboot the order?' he asked, his voice even. 'Did yous check it and was it all there?'

She lifted her eyes to him. 'I didn't need to check it, and no, it wasn't all there.'

Ben and Wally stared at her, dumbfounded.

She drew a deep breath and rested her spoon on the plate under her bowl. 'When the delivery cart drew up with the bricks I was outside waiting, and when I asked if the order was all there the man looked at me as though I was stupid. He said of course it wasn't. Half had been delivered as instructed to the old tobacco warehouse by the canal.'

'As instructed?' Ben said, bewildered. 'By whom?'

'Mr Wragg.'

'What,' Ben turned to Wally. 'Did yous know aboot this?'

Wally shook his head, as confused as Ben. 'No. Anyway, why would Mr Wragg instruct such a thing? It don't make sense.'

'No, it doesn't,' agreed Tilda. 'So I asked how long this had been going on and the man said it was nothing to do with him, he was just delivering the bricks. So I went to see the supplier himself.'

Ben's eyes widened in surprise. 'Yous did?'

'Yes, Ben, I did,' she retorted indignantly. 'Mr Gimson was very helpful. Said he'd received a note from Mr Wragg explaining that the yard wasn't big enough now to hold all our materials and until further notice would they be kind enough to deliver half of everything we order to the warehouse by the canal. He said he'd been supplying Mr Wragg for years and was only too happy to oblige.'

'Did he show yous this note?'

'It was pinned on his office wall. Just a scribbled note, Ben, but good enough for Mr Gimson.' She folded her arms and leaned on the table. 'But what's more worrying is the fact that this note was received several days after Mr Wragg's accident. So he couldn't have written it, could he. Anyway...'

'Well, he could have, I suppose,' Ben interrupted. 'He just aboot managed to write that letter of authority for us to run the business, but why should he do it? That's what's puzzling. Unless, of course ... No, that's ludicrous.'

'What, Ben? What's ludicrous?' asked Wally.

'Well, I was just thinking that maybe he's running a business on the side, selling stuff on, but that's pointless when people could just go straight to the supplier themselves. Would he just be storing the stuff in the warehouse, do yous reckon?'

'No, he's not.'

Ben's attention returned to Tilda. 'How do yous know that?'

'Because I went down there to check.'

'Yous did?' he said, impressed. 'And what did yous find? And why didn't yous say so before?'

'Because you were too busy coming up with your own conclusions to listen to what else I had to say.'

'Well, we're all ears now.'

An apology is obviously out of the question, thought Tilda, annoyed. 'The place was locked up but there was a man pushing a cart down the street loaded with bricks and he had some wood as well. So I rushed after him and asked where he got it. He was very cagey, asked me why I wanted to know. So I said I was interested in getting some bricks cheap.'

'Yous did?' Ben said, even more impressed.

'Yes, and he said he'd just bought the last load so I was outta luck.'

'Who did he buy them off, Tilda? Who?' demanded Ben.

'Well, I'm sorry but I never got the chance to ask because Daisy started to gripe. She was hungry, bless her. We'd been out all morning and the man went off before I could ask him anything else.'

'Oh, blast!' Ben fumed. 'You should have ignored Daisy, Tilda, and gone after him.' He blew out his cheeks. 'Well, not to worry, we'll make another order and me and yous Wally, will visit this warehouse and see who takes delivery. Then we've got the bastard.'

'Ah . . .' Tilda said, biting her lip anxiously. 'That'll be pointless.'

Ben eyed her quizzically. 'Why will it?'

'Because I've been to see all our suppliers, who as it happens had all received the same instructions, and told them that things have changed and they're to go back to delivering all the stuff to the yard. Well, I thought I was doing right, Ben. We've lost God knows how much money already. Surely you'll agree we can't risk any more?'

'She's right, Ben,' Wally confirmed.

'Yeah, I suppose. But now we're never going to find out who was doing it.' He banged his fist angrily on the table, making Tilda and Wally jump and Daisy start to cry. 'Damn!' he fumed. 'I'd like to know who was behind this. I'd bloody well knock their head off!'

'Don't shout,' Tilda scolded, jumping up and retrieving Daisy from the high chair. 'You've upset Daisy.'

'Upset Daisy, *I'm* upset, Tilda. I want to know who's behind it.'

'You're not the only one, Ben. But I did what I thought best.'

'This sounds like the kind of stunt Paddy would pull,' Wally said thoughtfully.

Two pairs of eyes turned to him.

'Paddy? Paddy O'Malley?' Ben queried. 'The Irish chap I met the first day I was here?'

Wally nodded. 'I'm only saying it's just the kind a thing he would do, not that he did it.'

Ben narrowed his eyes. 'Well, I think I'll pay Paddy a visit.'

'And what are you going to say, Ben?' asked Tilda, sitting down and settling Daisy on her knee. 'You can't accuse him of something you have no evidence of.'

'And whose fault's that?' he hissed.

'I can't win with you, Ben, can I?' she retorted angrily. 'If I'd done nothing you would have shouted at me for maybe losing more money. I did what I thought was best, and if you say one word more I won't do anything else regarding the business in future. You can handle it all yourself.'

'I think yer did great, Tilda,' Wally said sincerely. 'Didn't she, Ben? He's just mad, Tilda. Ain't yer? Just angry about Mr Wragg being cheated.'

Ben scraped back his chair. 'I'm going for a pint.' As he reached the back door he turned to Tilda. 'Just make sure in future that what yous sign for is what we've received.'

With that he disappeared through the door and banged it shut behind himself.

Chapter Nineteen

Ben opened his packup tin and smiled. 'Cheese and piccalilli today. Yous like cheese and piccalilli, don't yous, Wully? Here, help yersel'.'

Wally, sitting alongside Ben on a bare wooden floor in a terraced house off the London Road where they were repairing a ceiling, stared at Ben's pile of sandwiches then at his own limp offerings of fish paste. He didn't need another invitation.

Munching happily, he looked at Ben. 'Why does Tilda pack yer up so many? Does she know yer end up giving half ter me?'

Ben selected another sandwich and took a drink of cold tea from his billy can. 'That's just why she does do it. Not that it's ever been spoken of. But even I know Tilda's not daft enough to think I could eat all she packs up.'

Wally stared at him. 'She does? Really? Oh, Ben, she's lovely, is Tilda. Don't yer reckon?'

He shrugged his shoulders. 'She's all right, I suppose.' He laughed. 'She's not a bad cook now she's mastered that stove.'

Wally eyed him sharply. How could he proclaim Tilda just 'all right'? It upset Wally to think that Ben showed such scant regard for her. 'You don't like her much, do yer, Ben?'

It was Ben's turn to eye him sharply. 'Eh? What do yous mean?'

'I mean, you don't like her much.'

He frowned hard. 'And what makes yous say that?'

Wally shrugged his shoulders. 'You don't treat her very nicely.'

'I don't treat her very nicely! I say thanks for my dinner. What else am I supposed to do?'

Wally took a breath, worried he was going too far. After all, Ben was the boss. He looked longingly at the remaining sandwiches in the tin. 'Can I 'elp meself, Ben? I'm still starvin'.'

Ben thrust the tin at him. 'Finish them off. Yous won't be happy 'til yous do. And you're not going to get out of this by changing the subject. Answer my question.'

'Well, yer could take more of an interest in her.'

'Could I?' Ben was starting to grow annoyed now. 'In what way?'

Wally fidgeted nervously. 'I'm sorry, Ben, I shouldn't be speaking like this.'

'Every man has a right to say what's on his mind, Wully. Now come on.'

'All right. Well, for instance, when she sorted that delivery business, you just shouted at her instead of thanking her for finding out what was going on. We might not have managed to get the culprit but at least she put a stop to it. And you didn't seem all that bothered when she offered to collect the debts. I thought it was really good of her, offering ter do that. But you just told her not ter come crying to you if 'ote went wrong.'

Ben turned and looked at him hard. 'Yeah, and I meant it as well. Yous get some right hard-nosed buggers who'd sell their granny for a packet of fags. They wouldn't think twice aboot landing her one if the mood took them. I was warning her aboot them, that's all.'

'That's not the way it came across.'

'Isn't it? Oh! Well, I tell yous what. When we go home tonight, I'll ask her how she got on. How's that?'

'She's not going to collect the debts today because she's gone with my mother to see Mr Wragg. If you listened to her, Ben, you would've known that. She told us both last night. Anyway, you could ask 'er if she's had a good day. That'd be a start.'

Ben grinned wryly. 'I'll let yous into a little secret, Wully. Tilda doesn't really like me – and don't tell me yous haven't noticed that we don't exactly see eye to eye. We only met by chance, and it's by chance so to speak that we're still having to put up with each other now. I bet if yous asked Tilda she'd tell yous she'll be glad to see the back of me when the time comes.' He eyed Wally searchingly. 'Why all the interest in Tilda? Fancy her yersel', do yous?'

Wally blushed. 'No, not like that. I just like her, that's all. She's me friend.' He grinned broadly. 'But I know someone who does.'

'What? Fancy Tilda? Who?'

'Maurice.'

'Maurice! Maurice Winbourne? What makes you think that?'

'I don't think, I know. And I bet *you* didn't know that he hides over the street until you've gone out, then calls and asks if you're in.'

'No, I didn't. Why, the crafty beggar!' He eyed Wally quizzically. 'Yous notice a lot for a young 'un.'

'I'm not that young. I'm only five years behind you.'

'Yes, that's true.' Ben downed the last of his cold tea and replaced the lid. 'So, when have yous seen all this?'

'When I've been topping up the lime pit or checking on stuff in the yard. All sorts of different times, really. And I spent quite a bit of time with Tilda. I tell me mam I'm going out and pop round for a natter.'

'Do yous? Oh, I see. Seems there's a lot I don't know. But

Maurice. Well ... I never would have thought it. He's old enough to be her father.'

'That don't matter, not if two people like each other.'

'Does Tilda like Maurice then?'

Wally paused thoughtfully. 'Yeah. Yeah, I think she does. I don't know if it's as much as Maurice likes her though.'

Ben frowned, then slapped Wally on his leg. 'Maybe we'll get to go to a wedding soon.'

'You wouldn't mind?'

'Mind? Why would I mind? I'd be glad for her. She's not had it easy, hasn't Tilda, and she deserves to be happy.'

Wally looked at him, worried. 'Yeah, she does, but what would happen if she did marry Maurice? We'd have ter get someone else ter care for Daisy and look after the house and all the rest she does, 'til Mr Wragg comes home. I know I'm being selfish but I don't think I'd like that, Ben. Tilda's good to us, ain't she. She does things for us that someone else might not do and...'

'Excuse me, but who's in charge round here?'

Both heads jerked round towards the door. Stepping over the debris as she advanced towards them was a very smartly dressed middle-aged woman.

They both scrambled to their feet.

'I am,' replied Ben, brushing his hands over his dusty overalls.

The woman eyed him coolly. 'A bit young to be in charge, aren't you?'

'People tell me I don't look my age,' he replied, tongue in cheek. 'But I assure yous I am in charge, madam. So what can I do for yous?'

She glanced around the room, studied the repairs to the ceiling that were in progress, then brought her eyes back to rest on Ben.

298

'Scottish, are you?'

'Yes, I am,' he said proudly, then frowned. 'Is that a problem?'

'No, not that I know of. I need some work doing.'

He eyed her with interest. 'What kind of work?'

'I want a water closet installing.'

Wally stepped forward. 'Oh, we don't...'

'A water closet?' Ben interrupted. 'In your house, I take it?'

'Yes, of course in my house. Where else would I want one putting?'

Ben held his tongue. He did not like this woman's attitude and had to fight a desire to ask her to leave, but work was work. 'I'll need to come and take a look and give you a price.'

'I'm not worried about the cost. I can afford to pay for a job well done. You do a good job, I take it?'

'None better,' he said defensively. 'I can give yous some names of people we've done work for. Yous can check up, if you like?'

'That won't be necessary. I can see for myself that you know what you're doing.'

She must be blind then, thought Wally. That ceiling had been attempted three times and still wasn't quite straight. It was an old house and the walls had started to subside; not much, but enough to cause a problem with the ceiling. Wally had learned some very choice language from Ben whilst they had been tackling the job.

The woman handed Ben a card. 'I'll expect you tomorrow evening around six.'

Without waiting for a reply she turned and made her way out of the room.

Ben looked down at the card. 'Dr and Mrs Jerome Riddington, The Larches, Ratcliffe Road, Leicester.'

'Oh, my God, Ben! That's them huge houses further up off the London Road. You have ter have money to live in them places. We can't go up there.'

'And why not? You saying we're not good enough? I admit I've made some mistakes but we ain't doing too badly now.'

'No, we're not,' Wally agreed. 'I think you're doing really well, considering, but – well, a water closet. Ben, we're builders not plumbers. We don't know the first thing about installing one of those.'

'So we'll have to learn then, won't we? And I know just how we can do that. Anyway, there can't be much to it. It can't be any more difficult than fixing this damn' ceiling. Come on, Wully, this is an opportunity. If we do a good job then she's bound to recommend us to her posh friends.'

'Yeah, I see what yer getting at but . . .'

'But what?'

'What if it goes wrong?'

'It won't. Have faith. Besides, we have to make up for the lost money over the deliveries, which we haven't told Ted about yet. And besides that, think of the bonus he'll pay us.' And that's exactly what Ben was thinking of.

Wally sighed. He'd got to know Ben well enough by now to see that the man wasn't to be budged. 'I suppose it won't hurt to go and take a look.'

'That's more like it.' Ben thrust the card into his top pocket and stared up at the ceiling. 'Right, it's your turn up the ladder.'

Later that night he walked ahead of Wally into the kitchen. Tilda, after hearing them coming into the yard, was just dishing up the dinner.

'Er . . . evening, Tilda,' he said as he sidestepped to the sink and began to wash his hands.

Straightening up, holding two hot plates, she looked across at him, surprised. 'Er . . . evening, Ben.' She smiled at Wally.

'Hello, Wally. I'm afraid you've to go straight home tonight on your mother's instructions. She reminded me several times as we walked home from the tram stop after going to see Ted.'

His face fell. 'Oh.' He sighed heavily. 'Oh, all right.'

Tilda felt sorry for him. She knew he loved their evening get togethers around the table after they came in from work and automatically made enough dinner for three now. But she hadn't tonight after Rose's orders. 'You've time for a cuppa, though.'

His eyes lit up. 'Yeah, I have.'

Having finished washing his hands, Ben sat down at the table and smiled as Tilda put a plate of yesterday's meat pie and potatoes in front of him. 'Leftovers, I'm afraid. I haven't had time to do anything else.'

'That's all right, Tilda,' he said appreciatively. 'Whatever you rustle up is welcome.'

She eyed him closely. 'Are you all right?' she asked.

'Yes, why?'

'Nothing. Nothing at all.'

'How's Mr Wragg, Tilda?' Wally asked, pouring out the tea.

Blowing on a spoonful of food for Daisy who, sitting in the high chair, had her little mouth already open in readiness, Tilda looked across at him. 'Progressing slowly but surely, Wally. He's fed up, though. It must be hell for him, lying in that hospital day after day, not being able to move much. But as always he was delighted to see us. Your mother seemed pleased to see him too.'

'Did she?' he said. Good, he thought, she'll be in a better mood than of late. He too had begun to realise that his mother was taking quite a bit of interest in Mr Wragg, more than just a neighbourly one.

'Yous didn't mention about the delivery business, did yous Tilda?' Ben asked as he tucked in.

'No, I thought it best not to just yet. He's enough worry getting himself better. There's still the threat of never walking again hanging over him.'

'Yes, you're right,' agreed Ben. 'It will also give us a chance to try and make up the money somehow, and then he might never need to know.'

'We'll have to tell him eventually,' she said.

'Why?'

'Because it's Ted's business, that's why, and it's only honest that we do. I felt awful keeping it back when he asked how things were going. And I don't think it would hurt for you to find the time to go and visit him either. You make time for . . .' she was just about to say finding his longlost relative but quickly realised she was supposed to know nothing about it . . . 'all your girlfriends.'

'All?'

'Yes, all. You've had four to my knowledge. Not that it concerns me what you do in your free time, but as I said, you could make time to go and see Ted.'

'Well, I will when I can, but I would've thought keeping the business going was more important to him. I don't get that much free time. It's a day's job visiting the hospital, remember.'

'Yes, it is,' she agreed. 'Still, I have some good news on that score. The doctor told Ted that if nothing untoward happens over the next few weeks, he can definitely be transferred to a nursing home and it'll be one within easy travelling distance for us. You won't have any excuse then, Ben, will you? And we'll be able to see Daddy more often, won't we, Daisy?' she said, slipping a spoon into her mouth and dabbing away food that had dribbled down her chin.

'So . . . er . . . yous had a good day then?' Ben asked quickly, eyeing Wally.

She stared at him, surprised again. 'Yes, I did, thank you for asking.'

Ben pushed away his empty plate. 'I want yous to do something, Tilda.'

Oh, what? she thought. She hardly had time to do everything as it was. 'And what's that?' she asked, frowning.

'I want yous to put on your smartest clothes and go round to that plumbers' merchants on Humberstone Gate and make some enquiries aboot water closets. Ask how they go aboot installing them. Tomorrow. I want yous to do it tomorrow.'

She frowned even harder. 'What for?'

'Oh, Tilda, can't yous do anything withoot asking a load of questions?'

'No, I can't. I have enough to do as it is and I wanted to go out collecting the debts. That's more important, don't you think, than going on a fool's errand.'

'Oh, it's no fool's errand, Tilda, far from it. That right, Wully? If yous manage to find out exactly what I want then this could turn oot to be very lucrative.'

'Why can't you go yourself?'

'Because,' Ben said, fighting annoyance, 'it'd look better coming from a woman. They'd be more willing to answer your questions than they would me or Wully. I want yous to act as though you're interested in having one installed and then ask what work is involved. Yous know the sort of thing.'

'No, I don't know the sort of thing. What are you up to, Ben? I'm not going unless you tell me.'

'Oh, bloody hell, Tilda!' he said, exasperated. 'I ain't the time. I've a date tonight.'

'Well, you'd better make time, because I'm not going otherwise.'

'Just tell her, Ben. She's a right to know. It's no secret anyway, is it?'

'No, it's no secret.' He sighed heavily. 'If yous must know, a woman who lives in a posh house off the London Road has asked us to put in a water closet.'

Tilda tutted loudly. 'Oh, for God's sake, Ben, we're builders not plumbers. And you've hardly mastered the rudiments of *that* yet. And what about Wally?'

Ben looked at him then back at Tilda. 'What aboot him?'

'Well, it'll be him doing most of the work. After all, he's the experienced one, not you.'

'Don't keep throwing that at me, Tilda. I've learned a lot over these last few months. I've picked it up better than most and I pull my weight. That right, Wully?'

'Er . . . yes,' he replied meekly.

'I know what you're getting at, Tilda,' Ben continued angrily. 'That bloody wall! Well, we all make mistakes and I put that one right mysel'. *And* it's still standing 'cos I checked the other day.' He narrowed his eyes and glared at her. 'Pity all my other mistakes couldn't be put right so easily.'

Tilda caught her breath. She knew what he was getting at. His mistake, as he saw it, was the night he had come across the cottage in the woods. He was wishing he could have his time again and would definitely give the woods a wide berth, of that she had no doubt.

'I don't care what you say, Ben. I still think you're wrong even to be considering it. You really ought to go and ask Ted what he thinks.'

'There isn't time. We've an appointment tomorrow night to price it. Now are yous going to do as I ask, or not?'

She shook her head and sighed heavily. 'Oh, I suppose so.'

'Good. I don't know why yous couldn't just have agreed in the first place instead of giving me all this backchat.' He pushed back his chair. 'I'm off to get ready.'

'But, Ben, you haven't finished your dinner. I've made a . . .'

'I dinnae want it,' he snapped abruptly, disappearing through the door.

Tight-lipped, she turned to Wally. 'Now I know why he was so nice to me when he came in. I was stupid not to have realised there was something behind it.' She sighed wearily, rising to lift Daisy out of the high chair. 'You'd better go home, Wally, else your mother will be round here creating merry hell and I don't think I could cope with that tonight.'

'Yeah, I'd better be making tracks. Thanks for the tea.' He lingered hesitantly. 'Don't take to heart what Ben said, Tilda. He's only thinking of building up the business for Ted.'

She hadn't the heart to tell Wally that in her opinion all Ben thought about was himself. She hitched Daisy more comfortably in her arms. 'I won't, Wally, don't worry. I'll see you tomorrow, eh?'

'Yes. Night, Tilda.'

A few minutes later Ben came down ready to go out. Tilda was bathing Daisy in front of the fire in the zinc tub. The child was giggling happily as she splashed her hands in the water. The more she did this, the wetter Tilda was becoming. But she didn't mind. It pleased her to watch the contented child and know that she herself was playing a big part in Daisy's welfare.

Ben stood and watched them for a moment, thinking what a lovely picture it made, and suddenly felt guilty for the way he had treated Tilda earlier. Wally was right, his own attitude on many occasions was uncalled for, but he could give no reason for the way he acted. Maybe it was something in her that brought out this behaviour in him.

From the dark recess of the stairwell he eyed Tilda searchingly. There was something different about her. He frowned thoughtfully. Apart from the better clothes and much more flattering hairstyle, outwardly she still appeared the same. So what was it? He studied her for several moments more and then it struck him. The change came from within. Without the burden of her father, and with the faith shown in her by Ted Wragg, Tilda had blossomed.

She suddenly sensed him there and turned to glance at him. 'Oh, you gave me a scare.' She frowned at him quizzically. 'What are you looking at? Is there something wrong?'

He advanced into the room. 'No, no. I was just thinking, that's all. I've a lot on my mind at the moment.'

'Yes, I expect you have,' she said tritely. Daisy splashed her and Tilda giggled. 'Come on, you,' she said, scooping up the child. 'There's more water on me than in the bath.' As she wrapped a towel around Daisy she raised her eyes to Ben. 'Oh, I nearly forgot. A letter came for you this morning. It's propped on the mantle.'

'Oh, good, I've been waiting for this,' he said, walking over to retrieve it and stuffing it unopened into his pocket.

Intrigued as to who would be writing to him, Tilda had tried to determine from the postmark but it had been smudged. She would have liked to have asked who it was from but was too polite. Besides, she knew Ben's only reaction would be to tell her to mind her own business.

He shuffled his feet uneasily. 'Er . . . Tilda?'

His hesitant tone made her eye him cautiously. 'Yes?'

'I'm . . . er . . . sorry for having a go at yous earlier, and I do appreciate what yous do.'

'Do you?' she uttered. 'I wonder?' She turned her full attention back to Daisy. 'Hadn't you better be going, Ben?' she called over her shoulder. 'You'll be late else. For whoever,' she muttered under her breath.

'Yes, I had.' He headed for the door then stopped and turned. 'Er . . .'

'Ben, if you've something on your mind, just say it.'

Her tone made his hackles rise. 'I just wanted to say that it's all right with me if yous want to get married. That we'd manage, like.'

'Pardon?'

'Well, I don't want yous to think that yous have to turn down a chance of being happy because of your promise to Ted.'

Tilda frowned, confused. 'Ben, what are you talking about?'

'About you and Maurice.'

'Me and Maurice?'

'Look, Tilda,' he said gruffly, 'I know what's going on.'

Her eyebrows rose. She wished she did. 'Oh, you do, do you?'

'Yes. And what I'm trying to say is . . . that, well . . . yous have to grab what happiness yous can.'

She stared at him, shocked. 'Oh, I do, do I? Because I won't get another chance. Is that what you're trying to say, Ben? And not only that, but that I have your permission?'

'No, no, that's not what I meant at all.'

'Yes, it is,' she erupted. 'Because I'm not attractive and have a deformity, you think I should grab the first man who asks me and be grateful. Well, let me tell you something, Ben McCraven, I have had a proposal before, twice in fact, and I turned him down.'

Ben stared. 'Did yous?'

'Yes, I did.' She just managed to stop herself from saying it was because her suitor was far too young to be considering marriage. Nevertheless, she had no doubt that at the time Eustace had meant what he had said. 'I expect you find that surprising, Ben, don't you?'

His lips tightened. 'There's nae need to be like that, Tilda.'

'Isn't there? Well, you listen to me. Maurice only comes round here looking for you. Usually you're not here so I ask him in for a mug of tea.' She took a deep breath, her bottom lip trembling. 'Now how come that constitutes a proposal of marriage in your eyes? And have you ever thought Maurice might not take kindly to your assumptions? He looks on me as someone to have a natter with, Ben. Nothing more, I can assure you.'

She felt tears sting the back of her eyes. Maurice was a nice man but even if he had got designs on her, he was old enough to be her father. Yet Ben was still of the opinion that she should be thankful and grab him before he changed his mind, just to save her being a spinster for the rest of her life. Tears of humiliation threatened to flow and she took several deep breaths to try and quell them. 'You were going out, weren't you?' she said chokingly.

With a sense of shock he realised how much he had hurt her but did not know what to say to try and salvage the situation. So he did the only thing he could: he turned abruptly on his heel and strode out of the door.

For the first time in months Tilda felt the old loneliness steal over her. All the steps forward she had made suddenly disappeared and she was back in the village, being taunted for her plainness and deformity. She knew deep down that Ben had not meant to be so blunt, it was just his way. But nevertheless it had cut her to the quick.

Cuddling Daisy tightly, she sank down into the armchair by the fire and sobbed into the child's shoulder.

'Ben, are you listening ter me? That's the third time I've spoken and you ain't heard a word. I don't like being ignored. What a' yer thinking about?'

Ben turned to Jeanie Claymore and looked at her blankly. For the last twenty minutes he had forgotten she was with him, so preoccupied had he been. 'Eh?'

She tightened her lips in exasperation. 'I asked what yer were thinking about?'

He shrugged his shoulders. How could he tell her he had

been thinking of Tilda and the hurt he'd unintentionally caused her? Previously that would not have mattered to him but for some reason it did now and he knew it must be because of what Wally had pointed out to him. Tilda was always doing things to make their life pleasant, things she didn't have to do, and he repaid her only by his offhand attitude. That wasn't fair.

He felt the urge to go back and apologise, try to explain to her that he did have her best interests at heart despite the way the words had come out of his mouth. But he suspected that, whatever he tried to say, as usual she would misconstrue his intentions and they would end up having a row, so it was probably pointless. He remembered the letter in his pocket and absently smiled. It had said all he had been hoping for. He could now go ahead with his plan, and that thought pleased him.

'Oh, that's it,' Jeanie huffed, rising abruptly and grabbing her bag. 'I don't need to stay here and be insulted. You ain't n'ote special, you know, Ben McCraven.'

He eyed her sharply. 'Well, if that's how yous feel, what are yous doing here with me?'

She stared at him for a moment. At his shock of bright red hair which he had a habit of raking his fingers through when distracted; the face beneath not handsome compared to the likes of Rudolph Valentino but far from ugly. He was on the thinnish side, but then she wasn't fond of muscular men. No, Ben McCraven was not the type to cause women to faint, but regardless there was something about him that kept her awake at night, longing to be with him, and she knew she wasn't the only woman around who felt this way. But Jeanie had enough about her to realise the biggest mistake she could make was to make Ben himself aware she felt like this.

'Precisely what I thought.' Her pretty face was filled with anger. 'You've no idea how ter treat a woman, you ain't. I feel sorry for anyone else that teks you on.'

Ben narrowed his eyes. 'Jeanie, I think you'd better go home.'

She prodded him in his shoulder. 'Don't worry, I'm going. And don't bother coming calling again because I won't be in.'

He watched emotionless as she turned and stalked out of the door.

'Had a row, have yous?'

Ben turned and grinned as Andy Ferguson plonked his huge muscular body down on the bench next to him.

'Good looker, that one. Wouldn't say no mesel'.' Andy slapped Ben on his leg. 'Don't know how you do it. Me, I think yous an ugly bugger.' He turned and looked across at the door. 'She had her temper up. What did yous say to her?'

'Oh, nothing. I'm not in the best of moods tonight and yous know how Jeanie likes to chatter. She'll be back when she's calmed down. Anyway, enough talk of women. I've had them up to here tonight,' said Ben, resting his chin on his hand. 'Got any news for me?' he asked hopefully.

'Nah, bin too busy, Ben, sorry. I take it the bloke I told yous about last week came to nothing then?'

'No. He was a crofter from Orkney, got a wife and ten kids in tow.' Ben sighed. 'I'm beginning to think my cousin ain't in these parts. Maybe it's time I moved on.'

Andy frowned, his black bushy eyebrows meeting in the middle. 'Cousin? I thought yous were looking for your uncle?'

Ben nearly choked. 'Did I say cousin? I'm just tired, Andy. I meant my uncle.' He rose. 'I could do with another drink. How aboot yersel'?' he asked heading for the bar.

'You've known me long enough to know I never say no,' Andy replied, following him.

Ben rested his foot on the brass rail running around the bottom of the bar and leaned across the counter. 'Two halves o' bitter, Barney, when you're ready.'

'Coming up, squire,' Barney replied.

'Halves?' Andy said disgustedly. 'I dinnae drink anything but pints. Halves are for namby-pambies.'

'Halves is all I can afford,' Ben replied flatly, counting out the coppers in his hand.

'I'd have thought you'd have bin flusher, considering you're running Wragg's business?'

'Well, I ain't. I get a wage same as anyone else.'

Andy frowned. 'Seems a rum set up to me.' He eyed Ben for a moment, then moved closer to him. 'A' yous interested in earning some extra?' he whispered.

Ben picked up his glass and took a gulp, senses alert. He knew Andy well enough by now to understand that not all his earnings were from legitimate means. 'Some extra' could mean handling something dodgy and that was the last thing Ben wanted to get himself into. Whenever he had taken anything in the past that hadn't belonged to himself, the act had been one of desperation, because he had had no choice. Regardless, though, he didn't want to cause unnecessary antagonism between Andy and himself so he would have to be careful how he handled the situation.

He placed his glass on the bar and turned to face him. 'Earning extra's always of interest, but to be honest, Andy, I'm up to my eyes at the moment. The better the business does, the more bonus I'll get at the end of the day. That's what was wrong with Jeanie. She wants to see more of me but I cannae find the time. Actually, you've just given me an idea. Yous can't lay your hands on one of those new fangled water closets, now can yous? I'd be interested in one of those. At the right price, of course.'

'Eh?'

Ben grinned. 'What these monied Leicester folks would call a "posh lavvy".'

'Oh!' Andy laughed. 'Oh, I see. Bloody bottom of the yard is good enough for most. Don't see the need for one of them things mesel'. Waste of good money.' He grimaced hard and shook his head. 'Never had call for anything like that before. Don't think I can help yous.'

Ben kept the relief from showing on his face. It would have been just fine had Andy been able to supply him, for himself to fix it in – and then have the police call on Dr Riddington to confiscate it and them all be carted off to jail! 'Oh, no bother. Thought I'd ask anyway.'

Ben leaned heavily on the bar, picked up his glass and sipped thoughtfully.

A couple of Andy's mates came in and he went over to speak to them for several minutes. He came back and slapped Ben on the back. 'We're having a game of cards round Pete's. Fancy coming?'

'Nah,' Ben replied, shaking his head. 'Not tonight, Andy, thanks all the same. I've an early start in the morning. I've not much money anyway.'

'Ah, come on. The stakes won't be high and yous could do with a bit of cheering up. A couple of beers and a few hands of cards should do the trick.'

'No, really, Andy, not tonight.'

'Well, if yous change your mind, we'll be here for a bit.'

Andy sauntered off again for a crack with his mates and Ben resumed his stance at the bar.

It was approaching nine and the place was rapidly filling up. An old regular sat down at the piano and started to play a medley of music hall songs, several other regulars singing along tunelessly. Ben delved into his pocket and pulled out his change which he counted. Just enough for another couple of halves and then he would be off. Probably a good job Jeanie had decided to go home as he hadn't enough cash on him to keep her supplied with gin all night. Still, it was pay day tomorrow.

Across the bar his eye fell on a man trying to catch the

attention of the barman. Ben stared hard. It was Paddy O'Malley. He watched, shocked, as the man peeled a note from a wad in his hand and handed it to the barman. Even Barney looked at it in surprise before he turned and made his way to the cash box.

Legitimate reasons for Paddy having this kind of money raced through Ben's mind, but as hard as he thought, no plausible explanation could he think of. His anger rose. Wally must be right. It must have been Paddy who had been behind the delivery business or how else would he have acquired such a hoard? And the audacity of the man, flaunting his ill-gotten wealth in the local pub! He fought the urge to leap on Paddy and force the truth from him. But it was as Tilda had pointed out. As much as he wanted to, he couldn't go round accusing people without evidence or he himself could be heavily punished.

Thinking rapidly, he ordered his next half of bitter and supped slowly on it all the time secretly observing Paddy. The man seemed to be acting naturally enough, passing the time of day with several people who came to the bar. He didn't appear to be a man who was up to anything underhand. But then, many of the men in this pub would break out in a sweat if the law paid a visit, Andy included, and none of them was acting anything but normal. There was nothing for it, Ben thought. He would have to get into conversation with Paddy and see what he could casually get out of him.

He started to walk, a little unsteadily, around the bar, purposely heading for the part where Paddy was standing. As he passed by he 'accidentally' nudged Paddy and spilt some of his pint.

'Here!' Paddy erupted, spinning round.

'Ah, man, I'm sorry,' Ben said, brushing the spilt liquid from the front of Paddy's suit. It was new, he noticed, not second hand, and neither was the shirt beneath nor the boots on his feet. It took all Ben's self-control not to confront the man there and then. 'Let me buy yous another,' he offered.

Paddy, realising who was addressing him, scowled fiercely. 'Yers did that on purpose.'

Ben innocently raised his eyebrows. 'Do yous think I'd do something so childish, that'd cost me good money? Now do yous want that topping up or not?'

'Aye, I do that. I'll have a pint of best.'

Pint, thought Ben, annoyed, and best at that which cost a halfpenny a pint more. The drop spilt would hardly have measured two sups. He took a breath and leaned over the bar. 'Pint of best, Barney, when you've time.'

'Coming up, squire,' the harassed barman replied.

Ben turned to Paddy, wondering what best to say to lull the man into a false sense of security. He was just about to start by asking how he was keeping when Andy came up and interrupted him.

'Can I change your mind aboot the game, Ben?'

He turned to answer. Paddy grabbed the pint, winked broadly at Ben and sidled off. His chance was gone. He tutted, extremely annoyed. 'All right, Andy. I can see you're not going to give up. Lead the way.'

Chapter Twenty

The knock on the back door was loud and Rose stared crossly. She was in a rush and had no time for callers whoever they were. But she had no chance of ignoring it because the back door banged open and an extremely agitated Mary came in. The assortment of shabby clothes she was wearing had been hurriedly thrown on and her wispy greying hair was standing out wildly. She looked to all intents and purposes like a woman possessed.

'Oh, Rose, there you are!' she erupted hysterically. 'I thought for a minute you weren't in.'

Rose sighed. 'I'm in a hurry. What do yer want?' she demanded.

Mary stopped in her tracks and glared at her friend. 'You are rude sometimes, Rose Skuttle. Can you not see I'm upset?'

This fact hadn't escaped Rose, but upset or not she hadn't time to chatter to Mary. 'Can't this wait?'

'No, it can't.' For a moment the reason for her call left her as Mary eyed Rose critically. 'You look posh. Where you off?'

'Out,' she snapped. 'I don't have ter have your permission, you know.'

'I never said you did. But you don't always look like you're off to visit royalty.'

Rose smoothed her hands over her shapely hips. 'I look nice then, do I?'

Mary pouted. 'You'll do,' she said grudgingly, wondering where Rose had found the money to purchase the pale blue calf-length dress with its Nottingham lace collar. And it must be newly acquired because Mary hadn't clapped eyes on it before. 'I hope you're not going to put your old coat on top?'

Rose flared her nostrils. 'My old coat, as you put it, is better than the one you're wearing, Mary O'Malley.'

Her face darkened in anger. 'I can't help it if me money don't stretch to buying new clothes. So how did yer get yours? Use the rent money, did yer?'

Rose abruptly turned from her and grabbed her handbag. Mary spoke the truth. That was exactly what she had done. It galled her that her dress was second hand, but regardless it was from a classy second-hand shop in the town. 'I've no time for this chatter, Mary.'

The reason for her visit resurfaced. 'Oh, Rose, have yer seen my Paddy?'

Grabbing Mary's arm, Rose ushered her towards the door. 'Now how would I see him when I ain't been out this morning?'

Mary shook herself free, her eyes filled with worry. 'Oh, Rose, when I woke this morning he wasn't beside me.'

'And what's so unusual about that? Your Paddy's bin known ter go missing for days.'

'Yes, I know, but I'm still worried.'

'I don't know why. He'll be plaguing you 'til the day you die. He's probably at home beating hell out the kids.'

'Oh, d'yer think so?'

'There's only one way ter find out, Mary, and that's to go home and see for yerself.'

'Yes, yes, you're right. I'll go now.' She disappeared out of the back door, then a second later popped her head back round. 'Eh, I hope yer remember to curtsey.'

'Curtsey?'

'To this royalty you're visiting. But you must think me a fool, Rose Skuttle. I know exactly where your going. You're off to see Ted Wragg.'

Before Rose could retaliate Mary was gone, but her laughter could be heard echoing down the entry.

Several moments later, after checking the coast was clear, Rose set off down the street, intent on catching the next tram into town. So preoccupied was she as she rounded the corner, she nearly fell over a perambulator.

'I'm so sorry, Mrs Skuttle,' Tilda blurted, jamming on the brake and rushing towards her.

'I should bloody well think so!' Rose spat, righting herself. She suddenly realised the woman facing her was the very one she had been desperate to avoid. 'Oh, er . . . 'ello, me duck. Teking Daisy for a walk, are yer? Nice day for it.' She straightened her hat. 'Well, I must be off. Tarra, me duck.'

'Er . . . tarra, Mrs Skuttle,' Tilda replied, wondering what on earth was wrong with the woman. She bent over the perambulator and tucked the covers securely around Daisy who was babbling away contentedly to herself. 'I wonder what's ado with Wally's mam?' she addressed the child. 'And she was done up nice. Don't you think Wally's mam looked nice?' she said, chucking Daisy affectionately under her chin. 'Now, you're going to be a good girl for me, aren't you, whilst I try and collect the debts? I'm not looking forward to this, I can tell you.' Although, she mused, collecting the debts couldn't be as daunting as her visit to the plumbers' merchants, pretending to be a potential customer. She had managed to come away with all her questions answered but the manager had become highly suspicious of her, especially when she had asked how they found out where the sewer ran so the outlet pipe could be connected up. Ben had been delighted with her efforts and, more surprisingly, had expressed his gratitude.

Releasing the brake, she placed her hands on the handlebar. Just as she prepared to set off the child held out chubby arms towards her. 'Mam,' she said clearly.

Shocked, Tilda stared down at her, her heart melting. But her delight was tinged with sadness. If only Daisy's own mother had been alive to hear her daughter's first proper word.

Rose walked the length of the winding hospital drive, feeling mighty pleased with herself. At long last she had managed it. Managed to get here on her own.

The journey had been long, tedious and very uncomfortable, her backside bouncing up and down on the hard seat as the wooden wheels had travelled at twenty miles an hour down the pitted roads. The roar of the engine filled her ears, the stench of diesel filled her nostrils, but regardless she had spent the time thinking, going over and over her mission, and the conclusion she had reached was that the time was definitely right for her to speak her mind to Ted, and nothing was going to stop her.

Since his wife's death her plan to land him had taken her over. It filled her thoughts when she woke, was the last she had before sleeping. She saw an alliance with Ted as a means to an end. Then she would be set up for life, no longer having to make do and mend, wear second-hand clothes, wash with hard yellow soap, take in bloody lodgers to help pay the rent.

She paused before the entrance doors and straightened her hat, then raised her head proudly and entered the hospital.

Ted was sitting propped up in bed when she entered the room and appeared vastly improved since her last visit.

He turned his head and eyed her in surprise. 'Hello ... er ... Rose. I wasn't expecting anyone today.' He looked expectantly past her at the door. 'Tilda chatting to the nurses, is she?'

Rose unbuttoned her coat to afford Ted a view of her new

dress and sat down on the chair at the side of the bed, crossing her shapely legs. He in turn couldn't help but stare, astounded. He wondered if she realised what a sight she looked. Her face was caked in make-up and the dress she wore was far too young a style for her forty-two years. The hat perched on her head was meant to enhance her outfit but did nothing save make her ridiculous. But he was too much of a gentleman to express these feelings.

Rose mistook his look of astonishment for appreciation and patted her hair. 'Tilda said she couldn't be bothered to make the journey today, Ted, so I'm here on me own.' She did not feel guilty for the lie. Surely Ted would be more receptive to what she had to say if he thought she was the only one who truly cared for him?

He frowned. 'Tilda said that? I find it hard ter believe. I expect she's busy, what with all she has to do.'

'Oh, yes, she's very busy,' Rose agreed, thinking it best. 'And before yer start whittling, little Daisy's fine. Missing her daddy. But it's difficult for youngsters such as Tilda to juggle their time, trying to fit everything in. Inexperience, you see. That's why some things don't get done proper. But you can't blame her, Ted, not really. I expect she's doing her best.'

By the look he gave her Rose knew she had said the wrong thing, was treading on dangerous ground. It was very apparent that he thought more of Tilda than she had envisaged. She quickly decided to change her tactics and smiled at him warmly. 'You look so much better. Yer've got some colour in yer cheeks.'

'I do feel better, and I was helped by the news I received yesterday.'

'Oh, what was that then?'

'That they don't think me back is broken after all.'

'They don't! Oh, Ted, that *is* good news. So you'll soon be up and about then, I take it?'

He sighed heavily. 'That remains to be seen. As you know, the doctor is amazed that I lived through that first night, I was so badly messed up.'

'Yes, yer were.' She leaned over to help him as he tried to ease his body more comfortably against the pillows and witnessed the wave of pain that momentarily clouded his face. She wanted to hold his hand but stopped herself. It was too early for demonstrative actions such as those. For her plan to work she would have to tread carefully. He was, after all, a man in mourning.

'I still can't believe she's gone,' he said softly.

'No, neither can I,' Rose said, faking sincerity.

'I loved her so much. There's times when I feel I can't go on without her.'

'Yes, yes, Ted, that's understandable. You were married to her for such a long time. You get used ter people, don't yer?'

'Used to?' He eyed her sharply. 'Is that how the neighbours saw things between me and Maud?'

'Well, no,' she said hurriedly. 'I didn't mean "used to" exactly. I just meant, well, that you yet used to people's ways. It's like there's nobody's cooking like yer own mam's. It's what yer used to, in't it?'

He sighed again. 'Yes, I suppose yer right.'

'After all,' Rose continued, 'her death was sudden. Nobody expects you to get over her just like that.' She eyed him sympathetically and placed her hand gently on his arm. I know what happened was dreadful but you still have a life ter live. There are people out there who care, Ted.' She eyed him hesitantly. 'I do for one.' She cleared her throat. 'Is there any news of when you'll be 'ome because I want to talk to you about that.'

'I'm beginning to wonder if I'll ever get home, Rose. It seems I'm to be sent to a convalescent place first. The doctor's hoping the staff there will do more for me in the way of getting strength back in my legs, and if I am ever to walk again those'll be the ones to help me do it.'

The door to the room burst open and a cheery-faced woman popped her head through. 'Tea?'

'Yes, that'd be nice,' Rose answered. 'You like yours good and strong, Ted, don't you?'

'Just as it comes, Rose, I ain't fussy.'

'Well, you should be,' she said sharply. 'Just 'cos yer beholden to these people, 'cos your dependent on them at the moment, don't mean ter say you have to put up and shut up.' She turned to the woman in the doorway. 'Two strong cups and plenty of sugar.'

The cheery face disappeared.

'Rose, there was no need to speak to Mrs Marshall in that way. She's a very obliging woman.'

Rose frowned. 'Obliging? In what way?'

'Just obliging, Rose. All the staff are. Bin kindness itself.' He narrowed his eyes. 'What did you think I meant?'

'Oh, nothing,' she blustered, embarrassed. 'I was just worried for a moment that they were taking advantage.'

Mrs Marshall came back carrying a tray holding two cups of tea and a plate of arrowroot biscuits. She winked at Ted as she put the tray on the cabinet at the side of his bed. 'All right are you this afternoon, Mr Wragg? Anything else I can get you?'

Ted smiled warmly at the woman. 'No, thank you, Mrs Marshall, not at the minute.'

'Right then, I'll pop back later after visiting,' she said before disappearing out of the door.

I bet you will, thought Rose, jealousy mounting. Ted must be blind if he didn't see that Mrs Marshall had designs on him. And how many more women in this hospital were there with such intent? Ted was very vulnerable at the moment. Easy prey for unscrupulous women hell bent on landing themselves a husband. He was a good catch. Not only was he a good-looking man, he would be perceived as being well set, having his own business. She was right, there was no time to waste in putting the rest of her plan into action. She sat back in her seat and recrossed her legs. 'I've bin thinking, Ted.'

He eyed her curiously. 'Oh, what about?'

'About when you come home. You'll need someone to look after yer.'

'No, I won't. You heard what I said about the nursing home. They're going to get me on my feet.'

'But what if they don't? What I mean is,' she added hurriedly, 'what if yer not quite on yer feet when they send you home? You'll need someone to help out. And don't forget Daisy. She needs caring for proper.'

'What do you mean, caring for proper? I can see by looking at her she's being cared for proper. She's a picture of health. Tilda's doing a good job, Rose, and I won't have you saying otherwise.'

'Oh, I wasn't, I wasn't. What I meant was, well, this Tilda's young ain't she? She can't have had much experience with raising kids, now can she?'

'What's age got to do with it? Listen, Rose, I know some mothers Tilda would put to shame, for all her young years.'

Rose swallowed hard. 'Yes, I suppose yer right. Daisy does seem happy enough. I still can't help being concerned, though. I would suggest you consider getting someone older in the near future.'

'Rose, I'm more than happy with the way things are.' He faked a yawn. 'I'm tired and I really don't want to be thinking too much about the future just now. I just want to concentrate on getting back the use of me legs. Take one step at a time so to speak.'

'But you have to, Ted.'

'No, I don't. Tilda and Ben are more than taking care of matters for me. I know it's not been easy for them, I know they've had problems. I might be ill, but I ain't stupid. But they've coped well and I'll be eternally grateful for what they've done. I trusted me instincts regarding them and I wasn't wrong.'

Fear erupted inside Rose as she realised that her plan wasn't going to be carried out as easily as she had thought. Then fear turned to anger and she opened her mouth before she could stop herself. 'How do you know that for certain?' she said sharply. 'You're lying in here and Tilda tells you what she wants you to hear. How do you know she's telling the truth? They could be taking you for every penny, for all you know.'

'And are they, Rose?' He scowled at her fiercely. 'Are you trying to tell me that that's what they're doing? Then answer me this. When they found me after the accident, why didn't they just take what was in my wallet and be done with it?'

'I don't know, Ted,' she flustered. 'But when all's said and done, what do you know about these people? It's one thing them saving your life, another letting 'em loose with your child and running yer business.' She took a deep breath, her plan to tread carefully flying out of the window. 'I have to say, Ted, I was shocked the first time I clapped eyes on that girl, and I'm not the only one who thought you'd taken leave of your senses. But I put it down to your injuries and grief over Maud.

'Well, that's all months ago now and it's time you took stock. I personally dread to think where that girl comes from, and as for him, that Ben McCraven, well . . . my Wally has had to carry him. It's my Wally who's kept your business running and it's about time you recognised that fact.'

'Have you finished, Rose?'

'No, I ain't,' she erupted. She was off and nothing was going to stop her. 'I fear for you, Ted. You're stuck in here without a clue of what's going on outside. How do you know that any day they ain't gonna just up and leave? There's nothing holding 'em, Ted. They ain't beholden to you for anything. The way I see it is they were both desperate when they came across you. Your offer of work and a roof was like a miracle. 'Course they were bound to grab it, who wouldn't in their position?'

'Have you finished, Rose?'

'No, I ain't. I was hurt when yer never turned to me for help. I would have thought my years of being a good neighbour would have meant something. I want you to know I care for you. Care a lot. So do the decent thing, Ted. Tell that Tilda and Ben that their help's bin appreciated but their services are no longer required. My Wally's applied for his final papers. He's fully qualified now. That means he's capable of hiring and firing under his own steam, and he can do that until you're able to take over. I'll run your house and care for Daisy and have everything ready like it should be for when you return.' She eyed him beseechingly. 'Maud would have wanted that.'

'Have you finished now?'

'Yes, I've finished,' she snapped.

'I'm glad, because I've never heard such a load of clap-trap in all my life. Care for me indeed! You see me as a meal ticket, Rose Skuttle. You can't wait to get yourself installed in my house and don't care what you do to achieve it. Well, let me tell you, you're wasting your time. And another thing. How the hell do you know what Maud would have wanted? You never liked her. The only reason you were neighbourly, as you call it, was for the things you could wangle out of her. Don't think I don't know about the stuff she gave you. She was too good was my Maud, too kind-hearted, but I didn't chastise her because I knew what she did gave her pleasure. Now *I'd* be obliged if you left.'

Rose's eyes widened in shocked disbelief. 'Pardon!'

'You heard me, and please don't come back.'

Her bottom lip trembled. 'But I don't understand?'

'I'm sure you do. Your little plan has failed, Rose. I've said it before and I'll say it again. My body might be messed up but my brain's as agile as ever. Now, please go.'

The door opened and a nurse entered. 'Everything all right, Mr Wragg?'

Ted eyed her gratefully. 'Yes, thank you, nurse. I'm tired, though, so Mrs Skuttle was just leaving.' He turned his attention back to Rose. 'Thank you for coming,' he said flatly. 'I hope you have a safe journey home.'

She stared at him, stunned. Nothing had gone according to plan. She had thought he would have grabbed at her offer, been eternally grateful for what she was prepared to do. All her dreams of a secure future were crumbling before her but she couldn't leave without having another go. She turned to the nurse. 'You don't need to wait, I can find my own way out.' The nurse nodded and left and Rose turned back to Ted. 'Listen to me, please. What I've said has all come out wrong.'

'Rose, please don't make this any worse.'

'I'm not, I'm not,' she beseeched. 'You just don't understand.'

'What don't I understand? I understand that you're trying to blacken Tilda and Ben, trying to make me get rid of them so you can install yourself in their place.'

'Yes, yes, I admit it sounded like that. But, you see, I only did it because ... because ...'

With horror he suddenly knew what she was going to say and didn't want to hear it. 'Rose, don't say any more.'

'I have to,' she erupted. 'I need yer to know, then you'll understand. It's because I love you,' she blurted. 'There, I've said it.' Tears filled her eyes and she sniffed hard. She was clutching at straws and knew she was, but couldn't give up without a fight. 'Me and you would be good together. I could help yer, Ted. I could take an interest in the business. I could ... I could ... Well, there's all sorts I could do. So what do yer say, Ted? What d'yer say, eh?'

He sighed despairingly. 'Rose, I've asked you to leave and I meant it. I don't want to hear all this. Everything you've said is a lie. You know it and I know it. Now if you don't go, I'll call for the nurse and have you removed.'

She leapt up from the chair as though it was on fire and backed away towards the door, eyes ablaze in fury. 'I know why you're turning me down. I see it all now. It's her, ain't it? It's that Tilda. She's turned you against me.'

'Tilda's never said a word against you.'

'I don't believe yer,' she spat. 'She has turned you against me, I know she has.'

'Rose, you're wrong.'

'No, I ain't. Why else would you be turning down my offer? What's she got, eh? Why, she's ugly, that's what she is. Skinny, ugly and deformed. And she's young enough ter be yer daughter. You should be ashamed of yerself.'

'Rose, stop it.'

'No, I won't,' she shouted, wagging her finger at him. 'Maud would turn in her grave if she could see what's happening.'

The door opened and Matron came through. 'What on earth's going on? I could hear you right down the corridor.'

'Why don't you ask him?' Rose erupted. 'Led me on, he has,' she lied. 'And now he's dumped me for a little tramp young enough to be his daughter.'

Matron grabbed hold of her arm and yanked her through the door. 'I think you'd better go. And if you can't conduct yourself better, I would ask you not to return.'

'Oh, you needn't worry on that score,' cried Rose, pulling

herself free from her grip. 'I wouldn't lower meself to come back here. He can rot in hell for all I care.'

Fighting tears of humiliation, she turned and fled down the corridor.

It took all her self-control not to weep on the journey home. Her life was in ruins. She had pinned all her hopes on landing herself Ted Wragg, now she felt stupid.

Reaching the top of Wharf Street, she paused inside a shop doorway. What was she going to do? She saw her life stretching before her, growing only older and more lonely. She shuddered at the thought. But catching sight of her reflection in the plate glass window, she stiffened and raised her head haughtily. Ted Wragg might not want her, but she was an attractive woman, still capable of turning a male head or two. She'd get someone else, that's what she'd do, and show Ted Wragg what a fool he'd been not to take her on.

She smiled as a thought struck her. Mr Maddock. Now that was a prospect worth exploring. She wasn't particularly fond of the man, but he was better than nothing. He had a reasonably well-paying job for a start. Her smile broadened. What was the saying? The way to a man's heart was through his stomach. She'd cook him a nice dinner. Mr Simpkin would let her have something on tick until Wally got paid, then after dinner she'd invite the lodger to sit in the parlour – the furniture was shabby but with luck he'd be too interested in Rose herself to take notice. With a new sense of purpose growing rapidly within her, she wiped her face, straightened her hat and headed for home.

She arrived to find Wally sitting at the table. He rose as she entered the door.

'What's up with you?' she snapped, pulling off her coat.

'I was worried, Mam.'

'Worried? What about?'

'You.'

'Me? Why?'

'Well, I bumped into Mary earlier and she told me you went out sharpish this morning, dressed up to the nines. I thought summat had happened, being's you weren't back.'

'I've bin out, so what? I don't need your permission.'

'No, I know that, Mam. But I was worried about yer all the same.'

'Well, yer needn't 'ave bin.' She pushed past him and wrenched open the sideboard drawer, removing a table-cloth which she thrust at him. 'I'm surprised yer here, to be honest. Yer usually spend most of yer time up the road these days.'

'Up the road?' Wally questioned, instinctively taking the cloth.

'You know what I mean. With 'er. That Tilda.' She grabbed a handful of cutlery then snatched back the cloth, shook it out and threw it across the table. 'I don't know why you don't just move in there, save us all a lot of bother.'

'Oh, Mam, I only stay to discuss work.'

Banging the cutlery down on the table, she turned to him and placed her hands on her hips. 'Oh, Mam, I only discuss work,' she mimicked sarcastically. 'Well, you're a liar, Walter Skuttle. The truth being that you prefer her dinners to mine.' She shoved past him again and headed for the kitchen. 'Well, I hope yer've eaten tonight 'cos I'm only making for Mr Maddock and meself.'

Wally's face paled. 'Er . . . Mam,' he uttered, hovering in the doorway.

She turned and glared at him. 'What now, can't yer see I'm busy?'

'It's Mr Maddock.'

His tone made her stop what she was doing and turn to face him. 'What about Mr Maddock?'

'He's . . . er . . . left, Mam.'

'Left? Wadda you mean, left?'

'Said he'd found better lodgings.'

Her face fell. 'Better lodgings? Bloody cheek! Did he pay the rent he owed?'

Wally shook his head. 'No, he didn't. Shall I make you a cuppa?' he offered, feeling sorry for her. He knew how much she relied on her lodger's money.

'No, I don't want a ruddy cuppa.' But she knew what she did want. She eyed him sharply and held out her hand. 'What money have yer got?'

'Eh? Er . . . not much, Mam. I don't get paid 'til tomorrow.'

'Well, hand over what yer have got. I need a drink.' After the day she'd had she felt she had never needed a stiff drink so much in all her life.

Reluctantly he handed over the two shillings he had been going to use to take Elsie to the pictures. He'd gone without all week to save that.

She snatched it from him, pushed past him and grabbed her coat. 'Don't wait up,' were her parting words.

She marched all the way down Wharf Street and on towards the town, and with each step she took her temper rose higher so that by the time she reached the Queen's Head on Charles Street she was ready for anything.

Thrusting open the door of the public house, she marched inside and headed for the bar, where she fought with several other thirsty customers for the attention of the barman.

'Oh, yer a hard woman to keep up with, Rose Skuttle. Been trying to catch your attention since yer passed by the Talbot. Let me buy you a drink. What's it ter be?'

Rose turned abruptly and scowled deeply into the face that met hers. 'You buy me a drink?' she spat. 'In all the years I've known yer, Paddy O'Malley, I've never known yer to offer me as much as a cuppa tea.'

'That's unfair, Rose.'

'Is it? Look, just bugger off and leave me alone.'

'Suit yerself. Shame when I had a proposition for yers.'

She narrowed her eyes. 'Proposition? What proposition?'

He grinned. 'Large gin, is it?'

Bemused, she nodded and watched him order the drinks. He handed hers over. 'Seems me and you have a grudge against the same person.'

'Oh, and how'd you make that out?'

'My Mary told me your intentions. Set yer sights on marrying Ted Wragg, didn't yer? You've been ter see him today and by my reckoning he's turned yer down. Am I right, Rose?'

'Your Mary's got a big mouth. She's no right discussing any of this with you. And she's supposed ter be my best friend an' all.'

'Mary's always had a big mouth, you of all people should know that, Rose. Anyway, am I right or not?'

'So what if you are?' she spat.

'Well, I'm thinking that you and me could be useful to each other. How would yer like to get your own back and make some money into the bargain?'

She frowned cautiously at him. 'Money? How much money?'

'Enough to set us both up for life.' He grinned wickedly. 'I knew you were a woman after my own heart, Rose Skuttle. Let's sit down and discuss it.'

She eyed him for a moment. What had she got to lose? As she followed him across the room her eyes sparkled. Maybe, she thought, it wasn't going to turn out such a disastrous day after all.

Chapter Twenty-One

Back at Wragg's yard Tilda was feeling really pleased with herself. Her day had gone much better than she had thought it would. Out of the six debtors she had visited she had managed to collect the money from four, even if it had been a job – she had wondered if the fact that she had Daisy with her had helped to sway their decision to pay. The other two she had told firmly she would call back the following week, and if the money still wasn't forthcoming, then matters would have to be taken further. After the ordeal of knocking on the first few doors, the prospect of collecting all Wragg's outstanding monies didn't seem so daunting now.

She hummed a tune to herself as she turned on the gas and struck a match, then instinctively jumped back just before the gas ignited with its usual explosion. She couldn't wait to see the look on Ben's face when she told him how things had gone. Then she wondered fleetingly why his reaction should mean anything to her. This thought was rapidly overtaken by a sense of well-being as she hurried around the house, tackling the jobs that should have been done during the day.

A while later, sitting contentedly feeding Daisy, her mind began to stray. How far she had come in a few short months – nearly ten to be exact, but a short time compared to the eighteen and a half years she had lived altogether. A year ago she hadn't felt she had much of a future. Now her future could not exactly be predicted, but regardless of what happened, where she ended up next, she felt so much more able to cope.

She suddenly felt so fortunate to be living for the time being in such a lovely home where even tackling the washing was a pleasure. She shuddered as she remembered the arduous chore of washing her near rags in a tub of stream water, many times without even the luxury of soap to aid her. She thought of the gas stove here; of the sweeping brush with all its bristles; of the bath and the wonderful hot soaks she was able to take in front of the fire. Although she was getting used to having these and more at her disposal, never, ever would she take them for granted. She knew too well, remembered too vividly, what it had been like to have survived without them.

Fortunate in her changed status she might feel, but that wasn't a strong enough word for her feelings towards the wonderful people she had encountered, who each in their own way had helped to forge this strength of character within her. There had initially been Eustace – oh, how she still missed him – then Molly. How kind she had keen to have given Tilda that dress. Then there had been Fanny, bless her and her wisdom. If anyone had been the real instigator of her new awareness, taught her to be proud and not afraid or ashamed of who she was, it had been Fanny. Tilda suddenly felt a great longing to see her and thank her profusely for what she had done. Then came Ted Wragg and the unquestioning faith and trust he had shown in her while he himself was going through what must have been his darkest hour. How could she ever repay him? How could she ever repay any of them when all could so easily have dismissed her as many others had done before?

Then the friends she had met since she had arrived in Leicester filled her thoughts, and she smiled. There was Wally and Maurice and Mr Simpkin the helpful grocer; Mrs Cottage the baker's wife; Nellie Dudley and Sadie Hackett, the two old dears who lived on the opposite corner, who always stopped her to ask after Ted and Daisy; and there was . . .

She suddenly froze. One person was missing from her list. How could she have left him off? Yet how could she put him on it when she didn't know just where he fitted? Was he a friend? Well, was he? Just how did you categorise someone when you knew they didn't really like you, were only around because of unforeseen circumstances – just by chance really? If fate had altered the path of life just a little they would probably never have met in the first place. She remembered that first night, how she had found Ben inside the cottage, and a tremor of fear ran through her. What if fate had not stepped in? What if Ben and she had never met? The chances were she wouldn't be sitting here now feeding Daisy.

Tilda took a steadying breath and leaned back in her chair as realisation filled her. Much as she hated to admit it, Ben and she had been destined to meet. Without realising it each in their turn had shaped the other's life over the last ten months, just by being there. Ben, whether she liked it or not, had become an important part of her life, probably more important than anyone else. If it wasn't for him, she and Eustace could well have perished in the fire.

An alien sensation fluttered in her stomach and she felt a rush of heat right through her. She frowned in shock, not under-standing what this feeling was. All she did know was that Ben, for some strange reason, mattered to her. Mattered a great deal. But why?

Daisy suddenly announced her disapproval at being kept waiting for her food.

'Oh, Daisy, Daisy. I'm sorry my darlin'. Here,' Tilda cried apologetically as she put a spoonful into the child's mouth. Just then the front door knocker sounded. 'Oh, no,' groaned

Tilda as she rose. 'Daisy, I won't be a moment. Now you sit there like a good girl.'

She gave Daisy a wooden spoon to play with and hurried to answer the door. She opened it to find an attractive woman of about twenty standing on the doorstep. She eyed Tilda crossly.

'Is Ben in?' she asked.

'Er . . . no,' Tilda replied. 'He's not home from work yet.'

'Why not?' the woman asked. 'It's gone six. He should be home by now, shouldn't he?'

'Is it that late? I hadn't realised. Er . . . yes, he's usually in by now. Something must have held him up.'

'Such as?'

Tilda shrugged her shoulders. 'I really don't know. Could be anything.'

'Oh, well, I don't expect you would know, you being just the housekeeper.'

Tilda's eyebrows rose in shock. Was that how Ben had described her, as just the housekeeper? But then, she supposed that was what she was when all was said and done.

'Bit young for the job, ain't yer?' the woman asked, eyeing her critically.

Tilda chose to ignore her. She was getting cold and was conscious she had left Daisy. 'Would you like me to tell Ben you've called?'

'I'll come in and wait.'

She made to step inside but Tilda stopped her.

'I don't think that's a good idea. He hasn't had his dinner, and after all, I don't know who you are.'

'Who *I* am?' the woman erupted indignantly. 'It's who you think *you* are that's concerning me.'

'Me?' Tilda said lightly. 'Why, as you said, I'm just the housekeeper and I'm doing my job. Now would you like me to tell him you've called or not?'

'Brenda Brownside, what a' you doing here?'

She spun round to face the person who had addressed her. ''Ello Jeanie. I ain't seen you for ages. How a' yer?'

'Cut the bull, Brenda. I asked what yer doing here?'

The two women faced each other.

'I've come ter see Ben,' Brenda said haughtily. 'He's supposed ter be teking me out tonight.'

'You!' Jeanie spat, pushing Brenda hard on her shoulder. 'Ben McCraven's mine, as you bloody well know. Now clear off if yer know what's good for yer, and keep yer eyes off him!'

'Is that a threat?'

'Yeah, it's a threat.'

'Trouble, Tilda?'

Watching the proceedings with bemused interest, she turned to find Maurice at her side and smiled a greeting. 'Hello, Maurice, I didn't see you there. It seems Ben's very popular.'

'Oh, ah, he is,' Maurice agreed. 'Got several on the go, but personally I don't think he's all that bothered about any of 'em.'

Now why, Tilda wondered, did that fact please her?

'As you've probably gathered, Maurice, Ben's not in.'

'Oh, er . . . it's not him I've come ter see,' he said, his voice rising slightly over the row taking place between the two women nearby. He whipped off his cap and eyed her nervously. 'I er . . . wondered if you'd like to come to the music hall tonight? I've two tickets, see,' he babbled.

'Oh, and someone's let you down, have they?' she interrupted.

Maurice eyed her warily. In truth he'd bought the tickets specially, hoping that she would agree to go. 'Will you come then, Tilda? You'd really enjoy it and there's some good turns on tonight.'

She stared at him. She'd never been asked to accompany

anyone before and his request shocked her. 'Are you sure you want me to go with you, Maurice?' she asked softly.

More than anyone else he could think of. 'I'd be delighted if you'd do me the honour.'

She took a deep breath. 'Then I'd love to.' She smiled at him. 'But just in case the person you bought the ticket for changes their mind, I want you to know I'll understand.' She suddenly remembered the baby. 'Look, I'd better go, I'm in the middle of feeding Daisy.' She nodded towards the two arguing women. 'I think those two can manage without me.'

'I'll call for yer about seven-thirty, then?'

'Yes, I'll be ready. And thank you again for thinking of me.'

As she shut the door and made her way back to Daisy she suddenly realised that she hadn't anything suitable to wear for a night at the music hall. People dressed up in their finery to visit such places. But, more importantly, what about Daisy? Who could she ask to care for the child while she was out? Definitely not Rose, and Wally she already knew was hoping to see Elsie.

As she mulled over these problems while she finished attending to the child, the back door opened and Ben came in. He looked excited.

'We got the job!' he shouted to her as he pumped water into the basin to wash his hands.

'The plumbing job!' she queried, lifting Daisy and carrying her through to the kitchen.

He turned to face her as he dried his hands. 'Yes. We start Monday, and that's worked in fine because we finished the ceiling job early this afternoon. And don't look so worried, I wouldn't have taken it on if I didn't think we could handle it. Hello, Daisy,' he said, tickling the child under her chin. 'Been a good girl today?'

She responded by chuckling loudly and pulling his hair.

'It's not that, Ben. I would just feel happier it you'd done plumbing before, that's all. But, as you said, you know what you're doing. And what does my opinion matter? I'm just the housekeeper, aren't I? Oh, that reminds me. Two visitors called. They're out the front now, brawling over you.'

'Pardon?'

'A Jeanie and a Brenda.'

Ben grinned. 'Brawling, yous say?'

'Like fishwives. They both seem to think you're taking them out tonight.'

'Well, they're both out of luck, 'cos I ain't.'

'Oh, in that case you couldn't watch Daisy for me, could you? Maurice has asked me to go to the music hall with him.'

'Has he?'

The way Ben looked at her made Tilda think that for some reason he wasn't happy about that. I must be mistaken, she thought. The two women outside are what he's thinking of.

'No, I'm sorry, Tilda, I can't watch Daisy, I've got to go out.'

'But you said you weren't going out tonight. Daisy wouldn't be any trouble, would you, darlin'?'

'Tilda,' Ben said sharply, 'I'd gladly watch Daisy for yous but I can't.'

'Oh, I see,' she responded sharply. 'Two women aren't enough for you. Do Jeanie and Brenda know you've another on the go?'

'Eh? Oh, Tilda, shut up. Whether I've six or seven is none of your business – or anybody else's come to that. What I do in my spare time is nobody's business but mine.' Angrily he grabbed his cap from the hook on the door and slapped it on his head. 'Have a good time tonight, Tilda.'

'But, Ben, your dinner . . .'

'Oh my God, you're sounding like a wife! Heat it up for me tomorrow – that's what wives do, isn't it?' he said sarcastically, slamming out of the door.

Daisy jumped as it banged shut and Tilda hurriedly soothed her. What was Ben up to? she wondered. It was unlike him not to want his dinner after a long day's work.

There was another knock at the front door and she shook her head in exasperation. Her life had gone from one extreme to another. Days, sometimes weeks, had gone by at the cottage in the woods and no one had passed by except the odd tramp to whom she had done her best to give food. Now it seemed that the whole world came calling on this house for one reason or another.

Carrying Daisy, she went to open the door and found a spruced up Maurice standing nervously on the pavement.

'I'm early,' he said apologetically. 'Oh, yer not ready?'

'Er... no. Look, I'm sorry, Maurice, I haven't been able to get anyone to watch Daisy.'

A look of disappointment appeared on his face. 'Oh, I see.' Then his eyes lit up. 'Well, not ter worry, we'll take her with us.'

'Can you take children to the music hall?'

'I don't know. There's only one way ter find out, isn't there? And if not, we'll go to Wynn's Cafe and have our dinner. Have you ever bin to Wynn's Cafe? They do a grand pie and mash. That's if yer've not eaten a 'course?'

Tilda thought of her dinner in the oven along with Ben's. 'No, I haven't eaten. And what I've prepared can be used tomorrow. That sounds lovely, Maurice.' She stood aside to let him in. What a nice man he was, she thought, and the idea of spending an evening in his company sounded very pleasant. She'd never eaten out before and the prospect seemed quite daunting, she not knowing what to expect, but it was an experience she was willing to undertake with Maurice as her guide. 'If you want to help yourself to a cuppa,' she said, shutting the door behind them, 'I'll just get myself ready.'

* * *

It was well into the early hours of the morning by the time Rose returned home from the Queen's Arms.

''Ello, Wally,' she said, pulling off her coat and slinging it across the back of a dining chair. 'I thought you were seeing that Elsie tonight.'

'I did, Mam. I got back ages ago. I waited up for you. I was worried.'

'Worried? I told you earlier that I'm old enough to stay out as long as I like. But being's yer did stay up, yer can make yerself useful. Put the kettle on, there's a love, I could murder a cuppa.'

Wally stared. His mother had never addressed him as 'love' before and it sounded strange. As he made for the kitchen he scrutinised her as she stood before the fireplace mirror pulling a brush through her hair. There was something different about her. Then it struck him. She was drunk.

He brought the tea things through and put them on the table. 'I'm off to bed then, Mam.'

'Oh, don't, son. Come and sit down. Tell me what yer got up to today.'

He frowned, eyeing his mother cautiously. Drunk or not, it was most unlikely her to take an interest in him. Tentatively he sat down.

'Not much. Oh, except Paddy's back safe and sound.'

'I knew he would be. I told Mary she was making a big fuss for nothing.' Rose folded her arms and leaned on the table. 'So how are things at the yard? Keeping busy?'

His eyebrows raised in surprise. 'So, so,' he replied.

'And what's "so, so" supposed ter mean?'

He shrugged his shoulders. 'Well, we're starting a job on Monday, plumbing in a water closet. It's a new area for us but if we do a good job it could lead to more in that line coming our way.'

'Are yer?' she asked keenly. 'Pay well, does it?'

'I don't know about well but Ben's costed the job to show a good return, so I expect it will.'

'Do you still have problems collecting some of the money? I remember Maud saying once that Ted had trouble sometimes. People were only too glad to get their work done but not willing to pay out after.'

Wally eyed her quizzically. Her sudden interest in Ted Wragg's business was most puzzling. All she usually cared about was the money in his wage packet, not how it got there. 'Er ... yeah, we still have trouble, but Tilda's taken that over and is doing really well. But there's still money outstanding. Quite a bit, I think.'

She rested her elbows on the table and eyed him keenly. 'Who still owes then?'

Her question was so blunt he answered without hesitation and she listened intently to the list he reeled off.

She grimaced when he'd finished. 'Hmm, I see. Must add up to quite a bit,' she said absently.

'Mam, why are you asking all this?'

'Eh? Oh, er ... I've just been thinking, son, that's all. I've not been a very good mother to you, have I? I'm just trying my best to take an interest in what you do, nothing more.' She raised her head haughtily. 'If yer don't want me to, I won't.'

'No, Mam, you can ask all you want. I like you to show an interest.'

She smiled secretively. 'Good, then I shall.'

Chapter Twenty-Two

Tilda woke very early the next morning. It was still pitch dark and she was conscious of the freezing nip in the air and reluctant to rise. Daisy was still sleeping so she decided to stay where she was for a few moments longer. She smiled to herself. Not that it really mattered but she felt as though she was indulging herself by stealing these moments.

As she gathered the covers more closely around her, she sighed contentedly. She had had a lovely evening with Maurice who had been a very pleasant companion. Tilda had not been keen to take Daisy to the music hall even if they had been allowed, which Tilda doubted they would have been, feeling the noise might upset the child. Maurice had readily agreed and dismissed out of hand Tilda's worry about the wasted price of the tickets. He could get a refund, he told her.

Wynn's Cafe was a popular eating place in Leicester and all sorts of people filled its tables. The whole atmosphere buzzed with excitement: the constant chatter, the comings and goings of the waitresses, the clattering of crockery and a wonderful aroma of appetising food filling the air.

Maurice, Tilda thought, must have sensed her apprehension and realised she had never been inside such a place before. He took charge with ease, finding them a table with a special chair for Daisy, then helping Tilda to order. She had tucked into succulent sausages and potatoes covered in a thick onion gravy, and for pudding they had jam suet roll and custard, washed down with a huge pot of tea. The meal had been delicious and Tilda had made a mental note to add thick slices of onion to her gravy the next time she cooked sausages.

The only blight on the whole evening had been the fact that Maurice would not let her pay her share of the bill and she worried that he had paid out his hard-earned money on her. It never occurred to her that that was his choice, that he had wanted to, that he himself had enjoyed every minute of her company – and during the evening and after he had left her at her front door was planning ways in which to spend more time with her. None of this crossed her mind at all.

Daisy began to stir in the adjoining room and Tilda reluctantly rose.

She had lit the fire, fed and dressed Daisy, who was now happily toddling around aided by the furniture, and was preparing breakfast when the back door opened and Wally entered.

'Reporting for work,' he said, smiling broadly.

Tilda eyed him sharply. 'You look happy?'

'I am. It's me mother, Tilda. She's had a personality change. We had a good chat last night, first I can ever remember.' He grinned. 'I reckon she's got herself a new chap.'

Tilda smiled back. 'Well, good for her. Would you like to stay for some breakfast?'

'A' yer sure, Tilda?' he asked, sitting down before she changed her mind.

She just smiled and told him to pour himself a mug of tea. As she turned to see to the frying pan on the stove she thought of the Wally she had first encountered all those months ago. He had been a nervous kind of youth, arms and legs seeming to stretch forever and his thick thatch of corn-coloured hair sticking up however much he tried to plaster it down. These last ten months had changed him and she didn't know whether it was having the responsibility of working with Ben or Mother Nature herself who had brought about the changes. Regardless, a handsome young man was now sitting at the table, one much more sure of himself. His arms and legs rippled with muscle. The thatch of corn-coloured hair still stuck up in places but that was only when he ruffled it with his long fingers while thinking about something. Tilda smiled. She had grown very fond of Wally, cared for him very much. He was like the brother she'd never had and she valued his friendship greatly.

A dull thud sounded in the back room followed by a wail.

Before Tilda could move Wally had jumped up and rushed through. He came back cradling a crying Daisy in his arms. 'Little duck just came a cropper, that's all.'

Tilda looked at them both fondly. 'She's getting into all sorts at the moment. It won't be long before she's walking properly. I don't know what I'll do then. I've already secured everything moveable, and what I can't I've put away so she won't hurt herself.'

'Well, yer can't do more than that, Tilda,' Wally agreed. He eyed her searchingly for a moment then put the now calm Daisy in her high chair and handed her some toys to play with. Sitting back down, he put his elbows on the table and rested his chin in his hands. 'Maud would have liked you, Tilda,' he said most unexpectedly.

She motioned him to move his elbows and placed a plate of bacon, fried bread and eggs in front of him. 'From what I've heard, I know I'd have liked her too.' Tilda looked at Daisy then back at Wally. 'Daisy called me "Mam" the other day.'

'Did she? Ah, bless her. But then, in a kinda way, you are now, ain't yer?'

Tilda sighed and nodded. 'Yes, I suppose I am. But, you know, nothing can replace your own mother. I do feel for her because all kids need their real mothers whilst they're growing up. And after.'

Wally stared thoughtfully at her. Physically, she was almost the same girl he had clapped eyes on that very first evening when they had awkwardly introduced themselves. She was better dressed now, most noticeably having replaced the piece of string she had used to tie back her hair with a piece of brightly coloured ribbon to match her clothes. Her thin frame had a little more shape as her girlish body slowly developed into womanhood, but her plainness and her deformed arm he never noticed now. This fact did not surprise him funnily enough. To him Tilda possessed so many good qualities they outshone all else. And he couldn't help but admire the way she had taken over the care of Daisy and the running of the house, as well as doing more than was required in helping himself and Ben to manage the business.

She was, he knew, a good year or so younger than him but he had always looked upon her as being older and wiser. He didn't understand how, but knew deep down that her coming here and the friendship that had developed between them had made a big difference in his life. Tilda's patience and ability to listen while not overloading him with advice had taught him to think and act for himself, something his mother had never done. Yes, he did have a lot to thank Tilda for, as he did Ben.

He smiled as he thought of Ben. What a character he was! So positive, not afraid to take chances. He was very deep – Wally doubted anyone knew what he was thinking – and was exasperating in the extreme at times. Once Wally had not known what to make of the red-haired man with the thick Scottish brogue which he had had trouble understanding. But after working alongside him, and studying the way he handled situations, that initial reserve had been replaced by admiration and trust.

Take for instance the wall that had fallen down. Ben had returned, learned by his mistakes and put it right when he could so easily have given the task to Wally. And now the plumbing job which at first had frightened the lad to death. Not Ben. He had gone round and sized up the job with the air of an expert, come back and sat down in the kitchen, and with the aid of the information Tilda had come back with, worked out precisely how it could be done and costed it accordingly. A man who could do that with so little knowledge of the trade had to be admired. So, for that matter, had Ted Wragg in seeing this ability in Ben while himself suffering a malign fate.

Wally hid a smile as a picture of both Tilda and Ben rose before him, having one of their heated exchanges. He had grown used to them now, expected them even. But he wondered if Tilda and Ben themselves realised that, from an outsider's point of view, these exchanges of opinion had changed also over the last few months. Wally could see that a real regard and respect had grown up between them. That, whether they knew it or not, underneath they quite liked one another. Neither would admit to this fact, but it was there, whether they acknowledged it or not.

Before they had both arrived, Wally himself had not possessed the insight to recognise something like that. His own development had been aided by these two special people. Yes, all in all he was very glad and honoured to be classed as their friend.

He took a deep breath and smiled warmly at Tilda. 'Is your mam like you – lovely?'

She laughed. 'Oh, Wally, really.'

'No, you are, Tilda. Seriously, you're lovely. So is yer mam like you?'

Tilda abruptly turned and busied herself at the stove so he couldn't see the tears glistening in her eyes. 'I don't know,' she said, fighting to compose herself. 'My mother died when I was very little.' She raised her head and stared blankly at the ceiling. She remembered all the things her father had told her. How her birth had caused such embarrassment to her mother she couldn't stand it any more and had left, the act which had eventually led to her own death. How her mother's parting words had been to call her own baby daughter 'the Devil's own'.

She swallowed hard, fixed a smile on her face and turned to face Wally. 'I like to think she was nice. I'm sure she was.' She eyed his empty plate. 'Finished?'

'Yeah, I have, and it were grand, Tilda, ta.'

'Could you go and give Ben a shout for me then, please? He's usually down by now.'

Wally scraped back his chair. 'Yeah, 'course I will. Lazy bugger's probably having a lie in,' he laughed. 'We've quite a bit to do this morning. We're going to straighten up the yard and refill the lime pit.'

He disappeared through the door to return moments later.

'He ain't there, Tilda.'

Putting a plate of food on the table, she stared across at him quizzically. 'What, you mean he's already gone out?'

'I don't think so. I don't think he was there in the first place. His bed ain't bin slept in.'

Tilda's face fell.

'Now don't go fretting,' said Wally. 'He's probably stayed at one of his friend's.'

She nodded. 'Yes, you're right. More than likely they had a game of cards or something and are still at it.' But this didn't stop her from worrying. What if something had happened? She would have no idea where to start looking. Ben never told her what he did or where he was headed. Mentally she shook herself. She had no business worrying herself over Ben McCraven, he wouldn't thank her for doing so.

'Another cuppa tea, Wally?'

'Don't mind if I do, Tilda, ta.'

The front door knocker sounded.

'I wonder who that is this early?' she said, frowning.

'D'you want me to go?' Wally offered.

'Er ... would you?' she replied. She hoped whoever it was hadn't come bearing bad news.

It seemed to take forever for Wally to reach the front door. She heard it open, then the low mumble of voices, then Wally returned. She couldn't read his expression.

'It's for you.'

'Who is it?' she asked apprehensively.

He avoided her eyes. 'You'd better go, Tilda.'

Her heart raced rapidly. Something was dreadfully wrong, so terrible Wally couldn't tell her. And it must be something to do with Ben. She pushed back her chair and rushed from the room, and as she hurried down the passageway, wondered why Wally had shut the door. With all that was rushing through her mind she still thought it very rude of him to do that.

She halted before the door to gather her wits, then taking a deep breath, prepared herself for the worst and pulled it open.

For all that had gone through her mind she wasn't prepared for what faced her. Her mouth fell open in surprise, eyes widened in shock. She fell to her knees, threw her arms around her visitor and hugged him tightly. 'Eustace! Oh, Eustace!' she cried. 'I can't believe it, really I can't.'

Tears of happiness spurted from her eyes as she pulled away from him and held him at arm's length. A face filled with happiness grinned back at her. This time he threw himself at her and hugged her fiercely.

'Oh, Eustace, you don't know how glad I am to see you! I've dreamed of this moment since the last time I saw you.' She

347

pulled back from him and studied him, eyes drinking him in. 'How long can you stop? Is Fanny with you or Mr Brindle?'

'No, I'm here on me own and I'm stopping 'til tomorrow. I've brought me 'jamas.'

'You're on your own? But how did you get here?'

'In the cart. Oh, Tilda, I was ever so excited when we got the letter.'

'Letter? What letter?'

'From Ben, asking if I could come for a visit. He said you missed me and a visit would do you good. Mammy Fanny said it would too. She's sorry she couldn't come too.'

Tilda straightened up. 'Ben fetched you? It's him who's behind this?'

'Yeah. He came ever so late last night and we left really early this morning. Oh, yes, he told me to tell yer he's got things to do so he won't be back 'til later tonight.' He started to wriggle.

'What's the matter?' she asked, concerned.

'I need the lavvy. I'm bursting.'

She laughed. 'Oh, Eustace, I'm so excited I forgot my manners. Come on in, make yourself at home, the privy's out the back. And don't stray into the yard,' she called after him as he belted down the passage. 'It's dangerous.'

She closed the door, leaned against the wall and shut her eyes. She couldn't believe he was here. A prayer, one she said every night, had been answered. She felt a hand on her arm. It was Wally.

'Are you all right, Tilda?'

She swallowed hard. 'Oh, Wally, I'm fine. I can't tell you how fine I am. Did you know about this?'

'Not a thing. Ben never said a word ter me. He must have really wanted to surprise yer.'

'And he did. Oh, Wally, it's just the best surprise I could ever have wished for.'

'You love that little lad, don't you?'

'Oh, yes. More than I can ever explain to anyone. We went through a lot together, Wally. He was the only friend I had at one time. I'd do anything for him.'

'Ben said that.'

She eyed him, surprised. 'He told you about Eustace?'

'Oh, yes. Not much. Just that you worried about the lad and that you'd never be settled in your mind until you could see for yerself that he was faring well.'

'And he's right. It was a terrible wrench to leave him with Fanny. She and her husband own a farm. Nicer people you couldn't wish to meet. When they offered Eustace a home I knew it was the best thing for him, but I had such a struggle with myself, leaving him behind. But you've only to look at him, haven't you, Wally, to see I did the right thing. He's grown, filled out, and looks so happy. You should have seen him before. He looked like a little lost soul, always with a haunted look in his eyes, and I wanted so much to care for him, protect him, but I couldn't. I hadn't the means to care for myself, let alone a little boy. At the end of the day I could not offer him what the Brindles could.' She suddenly laughed. 'What are we standing in the passage for? Come on, Wally. I need to cook some breakfast for Eustace, 'cos if I know that little lad, he'll be starving.'

'I'll go and make a start on the yard. Leave you with Eustace. Can I pop in later?'

'You're welcome any time, you know that.'

Eustace's visit passed far too quickly. Tilda made sure she filled each moment for him with all the enjoyable things she thought a little boy would like to do. With Daisy in the perambulator, their first destination was to Muggy Measures confectionery shop where he spent fifteen happy minutes choosing sweets to buy with the sixpence Tilda had given him. Then they visited the Abbey Park and had tea and cakes in the pavilion, and walked down to the wharf at the canal on Westbridge and watched the barges being loaded with goods destined for all over the world. She pointed out places of local interest, telling him all she herself had learned about the town where she now resided, the one where she was beginning to feel at home.

In turn she learned such a lot from him. How well he was getting on at school; about all his friends and what they got up to; sat enthralled as he enthused about life on the farm and all Mr Brindle was teaching him; of how he now looked on Fanny as his mother and the rest of her family as his own.

Tilda was speechless when she unpacked the bag that Fanny had sent her. It was filled to bursting with farm produce. Butter, cheese, eggs, a ham big enough to feed an army, several pots of home-made jam and a large fruit cake. 'Just in case Eustace gets hungry', Fanny had written on a note which also stressed that Tilda was welcome to visit any time for as long as she wanted.

When it was time for him to leave for home early on Sunday afternoon Tilda didn't know who was more exhausted, Eustace or herself, but one thing she did know and that was that the wrench of parting from him was still very painful. But this time it was different. This time she was sure that Eustace was happy, being cared for as part of a family, and most importantly loved. These facts made all the difference as she watched him climb up on the seat of the cart after she'd hugged him fiercely and embarrassed him with her many kisses.

Before Ben joined Eustace for the long journey back she pulled him aside and, not for the first time, thanked him profusely for what he had done.

He shrugged his shoulders dismissively. 'It was no bother, Tilda. I had to go out that way anyway.'

She knew he wasn't telling the truth but decided it was best not to embarrass him any further. The most important thing was that Ben knew she was grateful, that was all that mattered.

She couldn't stop the tears from filling her eyes as she waved the cart off and stood there long after it had disappeared down the street.

Chapter Twenty-Three

'Some house, ain't it, Ben?' Wally said in awe as they halted the hand cart outside the latticework iron gates of The Larches.

As apprentice to Ted Wragg, Wally had carried out work in all sorts of different places but Ratcliffe Road, with its imposing gabled houses, all with sweeping back gardens of at least half an acre plus their lawned tennis courts, was the most impressive address he'd ever brought his tools to.

'I've seen bigger on my travels,' Ben replied, unimpressed, leaning over to secure the canvas bag of tools which was balancing precariously on the edge of the cart thanks to the jolting of the wooden wheels over the uneven road. 'I hope Mrs Riddington lets us leave the cart here overnight. I don't fancy pushing this weight morning and night for over a week. Though we'll need it when we bring up the closet.'

'Depends. Sometimes they do, sometimes they don't. She seemed the type that don't ter me,' Wally said knowledgeably. 'I still think it's some house,' he said peering through the gate. 'Must cost a packet ter run it. And they've a car. Look, Ben, what a beauty it is. A Rover if I ain't mistaken. I seen one in a magazine once.'

'Well, her husband's a doctor, or that's what it said on the card, and we all know they earn a fortune. Come on, Wully, stop gawping, let's get started. Quicker we get finished, quicker word gets round aboot us. But, more to the point, quicker we get the money in. A few more jobs like this and with a bit of luck we might be able to cover the losses over that delivery business. I've still not forgotten aboot that. And just woe betide him if ever I put me hands on the bugger behind it.'

Wally thought it best to remain silent on that subject. He took hold of the handles of the cart and with an almighty heave started to push it down the road.

'Where you going?' asked Ben.

'Ter find the way round the back.'

'Eh, if yous think we're going to push this bloody cart another half-mile trying to find the back entrance, you've another think coming,' said Ben, unlatching the gates and opening them wide.

Before Wally had time to question his actions Mrs Riddington, seemed to appear from nowhere, striding down the short gravel drive towards them.

'And where do you think you're going?' she snapped as she reached the gates.

Ben respectfully whipped off his cap. 'Morning, Mrs Riddington. Wragg's the builders reporting for work. Yous hadn't forgotten, had yous?'

'I hadn't forgotten,' she replied brusquely. 'But you seem to have mislaid your manners. Tradesmen's entrance is round the back.'

Ben's hackles rose sharply but he managed by sheer will-power not to let his anger show. 'Tradesmen? Now I've never liked that word mysel'. I consider us to be craftsmen. Skilled at our jobs. Don't you agree, Mrs Riddington?'

Caught off guard by his unexpected remark, she stared at him, shocked. 'Well, er . . . when you put it like that, I suppose I do.'

Ben gave her one of his most charming smiles. 'This back entrance, Mrs Riddington, where would we find it?'

She took an exasperated breath. 'Turn next left, then first left, then straight along. You can't miss it.'

'And how far would yous say that was?'

'Pardon? Oh, not that far.'

'Not far, eh?' he mused. 'Do yous know, Mrs Riddington, when you've pushed a loaded cart three miles already, not far can seem endless. Through the front would be a lot easier for us and it would mean we got started much quicker.'

'I don't care if it's quicker or whether round the back is another three miles, tradesmen do not come through my front!'

Ben exhaled sharply. 'All right, Mrs Riddington. I appreciate yous have rules yous must stick to.'

He strode across to Wally, took hold of the cart handles and began to heave it round.

'What are yer doing?' whispered Wally, confused.

Ben winked, warning him to shut up.

'I said the back entrance is that way,' Margaret Riddington snapped sharply. 'Didn't you hear me?'

'I heard yous quite clearly, Mrs Riddington. We craftsmen ain't deaf, yous know. Neither are we scum to be ordered round the back. Your husband wouldn't be sent round the back when he was summoned on a visit, would he? He'd walk up the front drive and ring the doorbell.'

'That's different,' she replied indignantly.

'Is it? How? When all's said and done, he learned his trade just like we did. Now, Mrs Riddington, yous appointed us to carry out some work but just 'cos you're paying us doesn't mean yous can treat us like dirt.' Ben slapped on his cap and tipped its brim. 'I'll say good day to yous.'

Margaret Riddington stared at him, shocked. 'Where do you think you're going?'

'Off ta start our next job,' he answered innocently.

'Ben,' Wally whispered urgently. 'What d'yer think yer playing at?'

Again he shot Wally a warning glance.

'But what about my closet? I've people coming to stay next week and I've told them about it.' Margaret Riddington's face turned red with anger. How dare this impertinent Scotsman treat her with such disrespect? It was a pity flogging had been abolished. But she knew he was not going to back down and desperately needed her closet installing or she'd look a fool in front of her relatives. She hid a smile. This tradesman might think he was clever but not so clever as she was – which he'd find out to his cost. She took several deep breaths and, without saying a word, stood aside.

Ben smiled at her. 'Thank yous, Mrs Riddington. Your gesture is much appreciated. Come on, Wully.'

As Margaret strode ahead, Wally turned to Ben as they both pushed the hand cart round the side of the house. 'I don't know how you had the nerve to do that.'

'Nerve, Wully? That wasn't nerve, I was mad. Just 'cos these people have money, it doesn't give them the right to treat those less well off like dogs. Round the back indeed! Could you imagine what she'd have said if she'd come to Wragg's front door and I'd sent her round the back?'

Wally nodded in agreement. 'I get yer point.' His admiration for Ben, already high, rose even higher.

The path down the side of the house seemed to Ben to go on forever and he groaned. 'Might have been quicker to go by the road after all.'

As they negotiated the corner of some adjoining outbuildings a middle-aged woman dressed in an old-fashioned maid's outfit, complete with mob cap pulled so far down her head it obscured most of her face, appeared suddenly from out of a doorway. Before Ben and Wally could halt the hand cart a protruding length of sewerage pipe caught the corner of the wicker basket she was carrying, which was loaded with wet washing, and sent it flying from her hands.

'Oh, no!' the maid cried in despair, clasping her hands to her face as both Ben and Wally, having halted the cart, rushed to her aid.

Margaret Riddington spun round and hurriedly sized up the situation. She sprang over to the woman and slapped her hard across the head. 'You dozy good-for-nothing! Just look what you've done!'

'I'm sorry, I'm so sorry,' the distraught maid exclaimed.

'Now hang on, missus,' Ben erupted angrily. 'It wasnae her fault. It was an accident. Nae harm's done.'

'No harm's done?' hissed the mistress of the house. 'That washing is ruined! I wanted that blouse to wear tomorrow,' she said, pointing to a garment lying in a muddy puddle. Tight-lipped, she glared at Ben. 'I would advise you to keep out of this. I could blame you, you know. That pipe looks to have caused it to me.'

Wally instinctively grabbed hold of Ben's arm in warning.

'I can still have it ready for tomorrow, Mrs Riddington,' the maid uttered softly.

'Just get this lot picked up and get out of my sight.'

Bowing her head, the maid hurriedly began to gather the scattered washing.

'Park the cart over there and follow me,' Mrs Riddington ordered Ben and Wally, then turning to the maid: 'You had better have the blouse ready or I'll dock your wages.'

'She's a tartar, she is,' Wally whispered to Ben as they followed Mrs Riddington down a passage to the side of the kitchen.

Ben said nothing, he was too angry.

Arriving at the room intended to house the water closet,

Mrs Riddington stopped and faced them. 'I trust you can be left to get on with it. And a warning: I don't expect to find either of you past this point.' She eyed Ben sharply. 'I will not have tradesmen walking over my carpets in muddy boots. Is that understood?'

'Very clearly, Mrs Riddington,' he replied icily.

She smiled cynically. 'Good.' She made to walk off then turned back. 'Oh, and don't hinder Brown. She wastes enough time as it is.'

When she was safely out of earshot, Ben exhaled with disgust. 'I never took to that woman the first time I met her. You're right, Wully, she is a tartar and a nasty one at that. Let's get this job done as quick as we can and get oot of here. I for one will be glad when we can turn our backs on that woman.'

Several hours later he was loading waste material on to the cart, ready for taking away, when he noticed the maid bringing in the washing. He stood and observed her. Her age was hard to determine as the cap obscured most of her face but he guessed her to be elderly by the stoop of her shoulders. She bent down to pick up the heavy basket and instinctively he rushed towards her.

'I'll do that for yous.'

She jumped back and Ben realised she was frightened of him. No, not just frightened, she was terrified. Her whole body shook.

'Thank you, thank you so much, but I can manage,' she stammered nervously. With a great effort she picked up the basket. 'Please don't let Mrs Riddington see you talking to me, she doesn't allow it.'

'But...'

'Please,' she begged. 'Just let me pass. I'm so sorry. No offence to you.'

With a grim face he stood aside to let her by. He was furious that Mrs Riddington should apply such restrictive rules to her employee. What harm could be caused by a fellow worker aiding another? He took a deep breath as he walked back to the cart and resumed his task then suddenly stopped as something struck him. The maid wasn't elderly at all. From what he had seen of her face he guessed she wasn't much older than forty. The stoop of her shoulders was not from great age, it was a sign of submissiveness.

The whole incident had a profound effect on Ben and for the rest of the day he could not get it out of his mind.

He was unusually quiet all through the evening meal. At first Tilda thought he was not enjoying the faggots and peas she had cooked, and she couldn't blame him, finding she wasn't particularly fond of faggots herself, but as time wore on she realised Ben's quietness had nothing to do with the food. Finally, she could stand the suspense no longer. She decided to approach it diplomatically and broke the silence by first talking of Wally.

'From what he tells me, it seems a miracle has happened to his mother.'

Ben raised his head. 'Miracle? What are yous blethering about, Tilda? A new type of washing soap or something?'

She laughed as she rose to clear the plates and dish up the pudding. 'Oh, Ben, for goodness' sake. I'm taking about Rose Skuttle, Wally's mother. She's . . . well, she's actually talking to him. Haven't you noticed he hasn't stayed for dinner? He said Rose had given him strict instructions to go home as she was cooking him something special.'

'Did she? Oh, that's nice,' he said distractedly.

Tilda sat down and eyed him with concern. 'Ben, what's the matter? The job not going well, is that it?'

'Eh? Oh, no, it's nothing like that.' He exhaled slowly. 'The job's going fine. It's just that I don't like Mrs Riddington, she's a rum piece of work. She has a maid that she treats badly and I dinnae like it.'

'I see,' replied Tilda thoughtfully, thinking that it was obvious Ben had taken a fancy to this maid. 'Why doesn't this maid just leave then if she's treated so badly?'

'How should I know why she doesn't?' he retorted sharply.

'I'm sorry,' she snapped. 'I didn't mean to pry.'

Ben sighed, ashamed of his outburst. 'Oh, you're not prying, Tilda. I'm just annoyed that's all.' He leaned over and retrieved several toys that Daisy had dropped on the floor, putting them on the tray in front of her, then leaned back in his chair and looked hard at Tilda. 'How did yous get on today, collecting the money?'

'I didn't. I had to stay in, remember, and take delivery of that confounded water closet. They didn't turn up 'til gone four and it was too late to go out then.'

'Oh, it's arrived, has it?' he said, scraping back his chair.

'Ben, it's too dark to inspect it now. I had them put it safe. I must say, it's a beauty. All the porcelain is covered in blue roses.'

'Did yous check it?'

'I checked it and it's fine.'

'Good, good,' he said, pulling his chair back up to the table. He raised his spoon and began to eat his rice pudding.

There was a knock on the front door and Tilda went to answer it. It was Maurice. She led him through to the kitchen.

'Take a seat, Maurice. Would you like a cuppa?'

'I'd love one, thanks,' he replied, pulling out a chair.

The two men nodded a greeting to each other.

'How are you, Ben?' Maurice asked.

'Not bad. And yersel'?'

'Same. Played any cards lately?' Maurice asked.

'Ain't had the time. But I might this coming Friday.'

'Well, I'll leave you two to natter,' Tilda said, retrieving Daisy from her high chair. 'I need to put the little 'un to bed.'

Maurice looked across at her hesitantly. 'Er ... actually it was you I came to see, Tilda.'

'Was it?'

'Er, yes.' He looked at Ben. Maurice didn't really want to say what was on his mind in front of him but felt he didn't really have any option. It was a rare occasion to catch Tilda on her own. If Ben wasn't around then it was Wally or some other neighbour.

'Oh, don't mind me,' Ben said gruffly, scraping back his chair. 'I was just off doon the yard anyway.'

'But I thought...' began Tilda.

The look he gave her prevented her from finishing.

When the back door had shut, Maurice looked at her anxiously. 'What's the matter with Ben? It's not anything I've done, is it?'

'Oh, no. He's just got a lot on his mind.' She smiled warmly at him. 'What did you want to see me about?'

'Oh, er, yes. I wondered ... er ... if you'd fancy a walk on Sunday? The Christmas tree's been put up in the Town Hall square. I thought Daisy would like to see it. Then you could come to my house for tea after, if you'd like to? I just thought it'd be a change for yer, that's all.'

Taken aback but pleased, Tilda smiled. 'I'm sure Daisy would love to see the tree and so would I for that matter. If you're sure it's not putting you out?'

'Putting me out? Not at all, Tilda. It'd be my pleasure.' And he doubted she realised just how much of a pleasure it would be.

'Oh, right then, that's settled. Sunday it is. We'll look forward to it, won't we, Daisy?' said Tilda, smiling fondly at the child who was almost asleep in her arms.

Maurice rose. 'I'd best be off then.'

'You don't need to go yet, you haven't drunk your tea.'

'I've things to do and you're busy with Daisy. I'll see you Sunday then?' In truth he wanted to leave just in case Tilda realised she had something else to do, or something happened to change her mind.

'I'll look forward to it.'

She returned from putting Daisy to bed to find Ben back in the kitchen. He was sitting at the table, fingers tracing a knot in the wood. 'You were rude to Maurice,' said Tilda sharply, going over to the sink in order to wash the dishes.

He raised his head. 'What!'

She turned to face him. 'I said, you were rude to Maurice and there was no need for it, Ben. You made him feel uncomfortable.'

He sighed heavily. 'Stop going on, Tilda. If I was then I didn't mean to be. I presumed he called to ask you oot?'

'Yes, he did, as a matter of fact, but not in the way you imply. He asked me if I would like to take Daisy to see the Christmas tree in the Town Hall square on Sunday, then to have tea with him. I thought Daisy would like that.'

Ben leaned back in his chair and eyed her searchingly. 'And what aboot you?'

'Me? What about me?'

He sighed heavily. 'Just forget I asked, Tilda. I don't know why I did anyway. What yous do is your own business.' He rose. 'I'm off to bed.'

'Bed? But it's barely seven-thirty.'

'And what rules say I can't go to bed that early? Goodnight, Tilda.'

'Goodnight,' she replied, frowning.

Tilda rested her arms on the rails of the cot and stared down at Daisy sleeping peacefully below. The child's arms were extended above her head and one of her chubby legs was hanging down between two rungs of the cot's side bars. A sudden rush of love for the little girl filled her. When the time came it was going to be such a struggle to leave her, the same as it had been with Eustace. Tilda sighed deeply. She had not learned her lesson. She had known from the very start that caring for Daisy was only an interim measure, but despite that knowledge and the pain she had experienced when having to part from Eustace, she had not been able to stop herself from loving this child.

She smiled tenderly. The love of a child was so special. A child did not see a person's looks or deformities, they accepted everything at face value and asked for nothing from their guardians but love, warmth and food in their belly. It was a shame, she thought, that children had to grow up. It was the loss of innocence that brought the real problems. Even Eustace, one day in the not too distant future, would see her for what she really was. Not the princess he now saw through innocent eyes, but the plain, deformed woman his peers knew.

She leaned over and gently eased Daisy's leg from between the bars, tucking it beneath the covers. Daisy stirred, her eyes flickered open and focused on Tilda. A smile of utter contentment crossed her face before she fell back to sleep. Tilda's immediate thoughts were of Ted, lying in his hospital bed missing all these special moments in his daughter's life. It wasn't fair, she thought, that after losing his wife so tragically, then having to endure all the pain of his injuries, he should also be denied these simple but so meaningful experiences.

Straightening up, she headed for the window and peered out. Below her spread the yard, filled with building equipment and materials. The outbuildings loomed eerily in the darkness and by the far wall the moonlight caught the lime pit. It looked from where she stood like a pool of white water, the plank of wood spanning it as a bridge. A vision of the view from the cottage fleetingly filled her; the trees swaying in the wind, the winding path leading towards the village. She remembered how loneliness had forever been her lot; how despite having their own problems to contend with, the small community of the village had classed her and her father as oddities, which had only added to her miseries. Tilda shuddered to remember it.

She raised her eyes and studied the moon. It was full and appeared to be smiling down on her. She found herself smiling back. The moon was right. She did have things to smile about now. She sighed thoughtfully. How much her life had changed in so short a time. She never had time to be lonely; hardly ever had time to dwell on the past or worry what others might think of her. The large mixed community she had landed amongst had their own concerns, far too many, to be much concerned for another on their doorstep. For the first time in her life she felt at home, felt part of her surroundings. What the future held for her she would not think about, it would happen without her worrying. Besides, with a bit of luck Ted might just keep her on. Hopefully he would fully recover but surely he would still need someone to take care of Daisy and his home? She could only hope so.

Drawing the curtains, she moved towards the cot and peered inside. Daisy's leg was again dangling between the bars so once more Tilda eased it gently out and covered her up, then let herself quietly out of the room.

In the bedroom down the landing, still fully dressed, Ben sat on the edge of his bed and stared out of the window. Below him he could hear the comings and goings in the street. He visualised the still busy shops that would not close their doors until midnight; the men and women making their way home from work, towards the pub, the picture house, or just congregating on street corners as they waited for friends. He listened to the rattle of cart wheels over cobbles; the clip-clop of the horses' hooves leading them; the angry cries of mothers herding their children inside. He sighed loudly, lay down on the bed and folded his arms under his head. Normally he would be outside, amongst that activity, but tonight he didn't feel like company and knew exactly what was causing his mood.

His ears pricked at the sound of a door closing and the soft padding of footsteps on the linoleum of the landing. They paused momentarily at his bedroom door then continued on and down the stairs. He shut his eyes. Tilda had hesitated before his door because she was concerned about him. He knew he did not warrant her concern. He had been unjustly rude to Maurice and sharp towards her. But then, that was Tilda all over. She was far too concerned for other people's welfare to consider her own.

The reason for his depression filled him again and he narrowed his eyes. The stooped shoulders of Mrs Riddington's maid had reminded him so vividly of his own mother. Her shoulders had been permanently stooped from years of scrubbing floors and leaning over the wash tub, hands red raw and chapped from continually being in hot water; taking, without retaliation, the dismissive attitudes and harsh treatments of those she worked for, for fear of losing her work to the many others only too willing to step into her shoes.

The sole cause had been poverty, the dreadful social disease that split societies. People without money forced to work night and day for less than a pittance were afforded no opportunity to better themselves, but branded for life. That's why he couldn't blame his father entirely for trying to claw his way out of the trap. He had wanted more for his family and took the only possible avenue he saw open to him. The rights and wrongs of his decision were arguable, but regardless he hadn't deserved to die the way he had, leaving his wife without means to support herself and her son.

Guilt suddenly filled him. Guilt because he had as yet failed to avenge his mother's early death and the murder of his father. The very reason that had brought him here in the first place. As soon as he had exhausted any possibility of Duggie Smilie's hiding somewhere in this town, he should have taken to the road again just as he had done previously.

He suddenly thought of Glasgow and of the dismal grey fortress called the Gorbals where he'd grown up. Of the sparse room in the sprawling filthy tenement he had shared with his mother, a woman too tired and dispirited to take much notice of her son. He remembered the scattering of relatives who at first had even vowed vengeance themselves and rallied round and tried to help, but very quickly the anger faded and the help dwindled until it was practically non-existent. He couldn't blame them, they had their own lives to lead; their own worries regarding survival. He sighed heavily. Although he felt a great longing to see Scotland, the thought of eventually returning had somehow lost its appeal. For some inexplicable reason this city had now become his home. He associated with its people, liked the honest work he was doing and having a decent home to come back to, good food on the table, a comfortable bed to sleep in. He didn't want to up and leave it behind. But he knew that he had to or he would be forever visualising his parents, feeling anger about their deaths, never be able truly to settle and live a normal life until his conscience was clear.

It had to be now. To leave it any longer would only make things harder.

Swinging his legs over the side of the bed, he jumped up and hurriedly gathered his belongings. Then he made his way down the stairs. He found Tilda sitting by the fire darning a sock. It was his sock.

She laid down her darning and rose, smiling, pleased to see him. She had been mulling something over in her mind and wanted to ask Ben's opinion. 'Why don't you sit by the fire? I'll make you a cuppa. You look as though you could do with one. And there is something I need to talk to you about.'

He took a breath and shook his head. 'I've no time for tea. Have yous a bag or something?'

She frowned quizzically. 'A bag? What kind of bag?'

'Big enough to hold my clothes. Look, there's no easy way of saying this, but I'm leaving.'

Her face drained of colour. 'I see,' she said softly.

He grimaced, a feeling of unease rising within him. He supposed he really did owe her some kind of explanation. Suddenly he felt the need to explain to her, make her understand his actions, but he couldn't quite bring himself to, despite the fact he had noticed that she appeared to be upset by his news which surprised him. But his decision weighed heavily on him. It had been hard to make. He must stick by it.

'Do yous have a bag big enough or what?'

Her answer took several long moments to come. 'You'll probably find something in the kitchen.'

Having found a hessian sack tucked in the pantry, he retraced his steps. Tilda had resumed her darning. As he reached the door leading to the stairs, she snapped the woollen thread and held out the sock. 'You'll need this, Ben.'

He stopped, eyed her, then walked over to retrieve it.

'Thanks,' he said gruffly.

'There's a few things waiting to be ironed. I'll do them for you while you pack.'

'You don't have to.'

'I know I don't, but I will.'

He rubbed his hand over the back of his neck. 'Aren't yous going to say anything, Tilda? Have a go at me or something?'

She clasped her hands in her lap. 'What's the point, Ben? You've made your mind up. Anything I say won't change your mind. Except...' She raised her head and fixed her eyes upon him. 'Of all the things I had you down for, I never thought you were selfish.'

'Selfish! Is that how yous see me?'

'How else can I? You've volunteered no explanation for your decision. You obviously don't consider me worthy of one. But then you owe me nothing. But what about the people who are relying on you? Ted, Wally – Mrs Riddington even. When you decided to stay you made commitments, Ben, whether you like it or not. And your friends, Andy, Maurice and all the other lads down the pub, not to mention your several girlfriends – don't they even deserve a goodbye? And what about your reason for leaving so suddenly? Whatever it is can't be so urgent it won't wait for a little while, at least until Ted is home safe and sound.'

Ben sighed heavily. 'Trying to make me feel guilty won't change my mind.'

'I didn't intend to make you feel guilty.'

Just then the door opened and Wally walked through. ''Ello, Tilda. I didn't knock too loudly in case I woke Daisy.' He suddenly sensed Ben lurking in the shadows by the door to the stairs. 'Ah, just the man. I've come to see if yer fancy a pint? You seemed not yer usual self today and I thought you might need cheering up. And, well ... I need a drink meself, Ben. I can't cope with this change in me mam. She's being that nice, she's driving me crazy.' He grinned broadly and stuck his hands in his pockets. 'So you on or what?'

Ben eyed Tilda, then Wally, then scratched his chin. He was in turmoil, didn't know which way to turn. Tilda was right. He did have commitments here which in their way were just as important as the one he had imposed on himself. He thought of the winter looming; of haphazardly tramping the roads in freezing weather, sometimes without a bed for the night, many times without any money in his pocket, but more importantly with no familiar faces round him. He didn't relish that at all. The reversal of his decision came quickly and he spoke out before he could change his mind. 'Yeah, I'm on. A pint's just what I need. Several, in fact. I'll just get my coat.'

'Would you still like that ironing doing, Ben?' Tilda asked.

'Er . . . no.' He eyed her meaningfully. 'It can wait for a while. And . . . er yous mentioned yous had something yous wanted to talk to me about?'

'Yes, I did. I wanted to ask you what you thought of us trying to work out a way Ted could come to us for Christmas. I wanted your opinion.'

'Eh up, that's a cracking idea, Tilda,' Wally intervened enthusiastically. 'We could make a real do of it. Might help mek him better quicker. Sorry,' he hurriedly added, 'I'm presuming I'm invited?'

Tilda just smiled at him.

Ben slowly nodded. 'I'll think on it and we'll discuss it tomorrow.'

Her smile broadened.

An hour later, having finished her darning, had a tidy round and checked on Daisy, Tilda sat curled in the armchair by the fire holding a mug of tea. Her thoughts were muddled, her emotions in turmoil, and Ben was the cause. She couldn't understand why.

She had always known he would leave eventually so why had his announcement upset her so deeply and why had his change of heart come as such a relief?

She pondered on her problem for several long minutes and came to the conclusion that her response was only natural. After all, they had been living in the same house, sharing meals and responsibilities, for many months. She had grown used to his ways. Of course, that was it. She was used to him. It was just the thought of the arduous task of having to find someone else that had caused her initial distress.

The door banged loudly and she jumped. Calming herself, she went to answer it and found an agitated Mrs Duncan on her doorstep.

'Hello, Mrs Duncan. Your waterworks again, is it?'

'Waterworks? Oh, no, duck, me waterworks 'ave bin fine since your young Ben sorted it. No, it's me leg. It's fell off. 'Ere.' She thrust an object in Tilda's direction, an action which caused her to jump and shriek out in shock.

Horrified, she turned eyes down to study Mrs Duncan's feet. They were both there, peeking out beneath the long calico nightdress she wore under her black coat. Tilda's head came up. 'I don't understand, Mrs Duncan? What "leg" are you talking about?'

'Eh? Oh.' She giggled girlishly. 'This 'un.' She waved the object in her hand. 'The leg of me bed.'

Tilda erupted into laughter. 'Oh, I see. Oh, Mrs Duncan, I thought . . . I thought . . .'

'Thought what, me duck?'

'That . . . oh, never mind.' She grimaced suddenly. 'But your bed's new, isn't it? Didn't you tell me your son bought you a new one only weeks ago? Paid a lot of money for it, I understand.'

'Oh, I don't sleep in that thing. Those springs make me giddy. Bounce me all over the place and the mattress is far too hard for my old bones. I've a mind to give it to the Churleys several doors up. They ain't got a bed between the ten of 'em, poor souls, and here's me wi' two. But don't you tell my Arnold, he'd have a fit.'

'No, I won't tell him, Mrs Duncan, your secret's safe with

me. Er ... I can't do anything tonight, I'm afraid, Ben and Wally have gone out, but we'll try for tomorrow. Can you manage 'til then?' Although she didn't like leaving the old lady in such a predicament, and for a moment she thought about fetching Ben from the pub, she decided that might not be a good idea. He might change his mind about leaving. Suddenly an idea struck. 'Have you some old books?'

Mrs Duncan frowned. 'Books? Yes, I 'ave, as a matter of fact. Arnold bought me a set of those encyclopseeders. Though God knows what for. What I don't know now ain't worth learning at my age. Fancy a read of 'em, do yer?'

'Reading them is not quite what I had in mind,' Tilda said, smiling. Latching the door behind herself, she took Mrs Duncan's arm. 'Come on, we'll soon have you sorted, but I must hurry because of Daisy.'

Mrs Duncan's problem satisfactorily sorted until Ben or Wally could fix the bed properly, Tilda hurriedly made her way home. Stacking the books under the bed had taken less than ten minutes, but even so, it was ten minutes that she hadn't liked leaving Daisy on her own. As she closed the front door, she stopped as movement across the street caught her attention.

Head bowed, Rose Skuttle was hurrying along the cobbled pavement and as she passed under a gas lamp Tilda could not help but notice the quality of the clothing she was wearing. It looked brand new. She frowned. Rose must have a job, and Tilda wondered what it was that obviously paid so well. Good for her, she thought as she closed the door. Rose couldn't have had it easy as a widow and she deserved some good fortune.

It suddenly struck Tilda that she had not seen Wally's mother for several days which was most unusual. It must be that her job was keeping her really busy. But Tilda had to admit, unkindly or not, the break from Rose's visits, her general nosiness and scathing remarks directed towards the way Tilda looked after Daisy and ran the home, was a welcome relief for however long it lasted.

Chapter Twenty-Four

'Are yous going to do it, Wully, or me?'

'Oh, you, Ben, definitely you. And while you do it, I think I'll stand outside.'

'That yous will not! We'll do it together.'

Wally grimaced. 'If yer sure?'

'Just take hold of the handle and pull when I give the say so. Right?'

'All right.'

Ben spat into his hands and rubbed them together. 'Well, here goes.'

They both took hold of the carved bell-shaped piece of wood hanging from the end of the chain secured to the tank above them. The whole job had taken them just under a week and had gone better even than they had hoped. Fixing in the closet and connecting it to the water supply had been relatively simple, apart from a couple of mishaps which thankfully they had managed to sort. The most laborious task had been the digging of the deep trench to house the drain pipe to take away the waste material to the main sewer that ran down the middle of the road, then the making good afterwards. Mrs Riddington had minutely inspected her whole garden to make sure nothing was amiss. And it wasn't – Ben thought much to their employer's disgust.

They would be glad when they loaded their tools on to the

hand cart and pushed it out of The Larches' wrought-iron gates for the last time. Mrs Riddington appeared to go out of her way to find problems. Several times a day she would pounce and demand to know what they were doing, then proceed to criticise. How Ben had kept his temper Wally would never know. But all credit due to the man, not once had he raised his voice or said anything back to the woman that could have been misconstrued. Although Wally had noticed that before he had answered her, he had taken several deep breaths and gripped his tools tightly.

'Right, pull,' Ben instructed.

Together they both pulled hard and stepped back.

The tank grumbled loudly, shook, then dispersed its contents down the pipe extending from it to the heavily ornate bowl below. The water swirled around and the excess disappeared.

Ben was delighted. 'It works, Wully. It works.'

'Yeah, it does,' he replied just as enthusiastically.

Ben turned to him and frowned. 'Yous didn't doubt it would, did yous?'

He eyed Ben hesitantly. 'Not doubt exactly. Just let's say that whilst we pulled the handle, I had me fingers crossed. And me legs!'

Ben laughed, slapping him on his back. 'Me too, Wully. Me too.' He turned and stared proudly at their work. 'We've done a bloody good job if I say it mysel'. We make a good team, eh?'

'Definitely, Ben, most definitely. Ted'll be pleased.'

Ben smiled. 'Yes, he will, and yous can have the honour of telling him.'

'Can I, Ben?'

'Yes, 'course. This job was a gamble, a big gamble, but I couldn't have pulled if off without the help I got from yous. Thanks, Wully.'

Wally beamed, reddening in embarrassment.

'Well, all that remains is for us to secure that tank a bit more to stop it shaking when the handle's pulled. Yous can tackle that if yous like while I put the odds and ends lying about on the cart. Then we can collect our money and go – and I think I speak for both of us when I say, "thank God".'

'You can thank Him twice for me, Ben. I personally don't know how she keeps anyone working for 'er. She's a mean 'un that's fer sure. I feel sorry for Brown meself. That woman is run ragged and I've yet to hear Mrs Riddington say a thank you.'

'Don't think she knows the word, Wully.'

Having loaded the hand cart with the remains of the materials, Ben made his way back to Wally. As he passed by a door leading to the kitchen he happened to glance inside and what he saw made him gasp. The maid, Brown, was bent double across the table. She appeared to be on the point of collapse. Ben rushed towards her, grabbed her round her waist and guided her towards a chair, sitting her down. He squatted beside her, laying a comforting hand on her arm.

'Yous stay there, I'll get, Mrs Riddington.'

A shaking hand shot out and gripped his arm tightly. 'No, please don't, I'll be fine in a minute.'

Ben tilted his head and looked at the face beneath the cap. 'A minute be damned. Yous ain't well at all.'

'I'll be fine. Honest, I will. I'm just tired.' She raised her head and looked at him pleadingly. 'Please.'

'Well, what aboot me fetching someone else? A relative or something?'

She slowly shook her head. 'There's no one,' she whispered.

'You've no one at all?'

She shook her head and the brief smile that touched her lips took a great effort. 'You had better go. If she found you here . . .'

'She'll dock your wages or sack yous, is that it? Ah, but she wouldn't sack yous, would she? She wouldn't get anybody else to do all yous do.' He sighed heavily. 'All right. Let me get yous a cuppa tea or something. It's the least I can do after all the cups you've slipped me and Wully on the sly.'

She raised weary eyes. 'Please don't let Mrs Riddington know about that.'

'Don't worry, I won't. But thanks, they were much appreciated.'

Her face filled with pain and she groaned loudly and doubled over again. Instinctively Ben's arm shot around her and he felt her whole body slump. 'You need a doctor,' he said worriedly.

'What's going on here?'

Ben's head jerked up. Looming in the doorway was Mrs Riddington.

'When I ask a question, I expect an answer.'

Ben stood up. 'It's . . .' He detested addressing the maid as Brown. 'Mrs Brown. She's ill. Needs a doctor.'

'I'll be the judge of that,' snapped her mistress, advancing to stand before Ben. 'Have you finished your work?'

He glanced worriedly at Brown, still slumped in the chair, then back at Mrs Riddington. 'All but a tidy up.'

'Then I suggest you get back to it.'

'But what aboot . . .'

'I don't need the likes of you to tell me how to deal with my staff.'

Ben fought to stop himself from giving this woman a piece of his mind. Doing so, he knew, would only make matters worse for Brown. Clenching his fists in anger, he strode from the room. Outside the door, he flattened himself against the wall and listened.

'Get up, Brown, and pull yourself together. Lazy, that's what you are, and I'll not have it. I have guests arriving tomorrow and you've nowhere near finished a thorough cleaning of this house. You've still the curtains in the drawing room to take down and beat and the guest rooms are not prepared. And when, may I enquire, are you going to make a start on the food?'

Incensed, Ben peeked around the door to see Brown raise her head defeatedly. 'After I've cleared away the dinner tonight, madam.'

'Huh, well, I suggest you get back to it. Oh, and by the way, I've changed my mind about the blue towels for the male guests. I want the green ones and I want them all freshly washed and aired. Now, after I've seen the tradesmen off the premises, I shall be taking a nap. Wake me up at four with a cup of tea and a biscuit. And have the water ready for my bath. Dr Riddington will be home around six and we'll dine at eight sharp, not two minutes past like last night.'

Ben could listen to no more. He arrived back at the closet room, his face wreathed in anger.

Wally, having completed his task, was just packing away his tools. He eyed Ben sharply. 'What's the matter? Yer look as if yer could murder somebody.'

Ben shook his head. 'Just let's get this place tidied up and we'll be out of here.'

Ten minutes later they were packed and ready to leave and Ben was just about to go in search of Mrs Riddington when the woman herself appeared at the door.

'Finished, have you?'

Ben turned to her and nodded.

'Good.'

She looked slowly all around then settled her eyes on the water closet. 'I shall be envied,' she said, a satisfied smile playing on her lips. She eyed Ben coldly. 'Send me your bill.'

He thrust his hand into his pocket and pulled out a folded piece of paper. 'I have our invoice here.'

She snatched it from him, opened it out and glanced at it. 'Seems a trifle high to me.'

'It's what we agreed on, Mrs Riddington, not a penny more.'

'Huh, well, I will send you a cheque at the end of the month.'

'Oh!' Ben exclaimed, frowning. 'I was expecting to collect payment today.'

'Were you indeed?' Margaret Riddington smiled condescendingly. 'Let me inform you that no self-respecting tradesman would expect payment until the end of the month. That's when I settle all my bills and I make no exceptions.'

Ben breathed deeply. 'I'll call at the end of the month.'

'I will post it,' she said icily. 'Now, if you've got everything, I'll see you out.'

It was a very subdued Ben who helped Wally push the hand cart out of the gates.

They were halfway down Ratcliffe Road before Wally dared speak. 'Are you all right, Ben?' he asked hesitantly.

He stopped and turned to face Wally. 'No, I ain't all right. That woman has fair got my back up.'

'Well, er . . . she is right, Ben. Most of the posh ones do settle up at the end of the month.'

'It's not that, Wully. That's not what's got my temper up.'

'Well, what has then?'

Ben opened his mouth to reply then snapped it shut. How could he begin to explain to Wally what was causing his anger without going into great detail? This wasn't the time, and besides, his conscience would not let him walk away without doing something.

'Just help me swing this cart round.'

'Why?' Wally asked, confused.

'Because we're going back, that's why?'

'Have we forgot summat?'

'Yes, we have.'

Leaving Wally and the cart just before the gates, with a stern warning to stay put, Ben unlatched them and slipped inside, skirted the gravel drive and crept softly down the side of the house. He found the maid unconscious on the kitchen floor. He rushed towards her and knelt down. 'Mrs Brown,' he whispered urgently. 'Mrs Brown, Mrs Brown!'

He was not surprised to receive no response. An imbecile would have had no trouble seeing the woman was exhausted.

He bent down and lifted her up in his arms. He stared down into her unconscious face. 'I'm doing this for you, Mam,' he whispered.

Wally stared as Ben struggled through the gates, and rushed towards him. 'What on earth are yer doing, Ben?' He looked down at the burden in his arms. 'That's Brown, ain't it?'

In no mood for questions, Ben continued towards the cart. 'Move that stuff aside, Wully. Quick!'

He obeyed.

Ben gently laid Brown down and tried to position her as comfortably as he could. He stripped off his jacket and laid it across her as well as a couple of empty sacks.

They were well down London Road before Wally spoke. 'Mrs Riddington's gonna go mad when she finds out.'

'I don't give a damn what Mrs Riddington does. That woman can hang herself for all I care. She ain't fit to employ humans, she ain't.' He turned to Wally and grinned triumphantly. 'Besides, she isn't going to have a clue what's happened. She's having a nap and when she wakes up, after screaming blue murder for a cuppa tea she isn't going to get, all she'll find is her maid gone.'

Wally nodded vigorously. 'Serves her right.'

'It certainly does.'

'So what are yer gonna do with her?'

'First thing is to get her a doctor. After that,' he shrugged his

379

shoulders, a smile spreading across his face, 'Tilda will help us think of something.'

Wally nodded in agreement. 'Yeah, you're right, Ben. Tilda will know what to do.'

Chapter Twenty-Five

Earlier in the day Tilda tapped on a door marked OFFICE, stepped back and waited. Although the weather was surprisingly mild for the beginning of December she would still be glad when she had finished her calls and could get back home. She looked around her. Simpson's, manufacturers of boots and shoes, consisted of a huddle of old, grimy Victorian buildings. Several male workers were loading boxes on to a wagon; one looked over in her direction and gave her a brief nod before he resumed his task.

The air was filled with the pungent smells of leather and rubber and as she waited she tried to visualise what it must be like to be shut inside these factory walls for long stretches at a time, operating machinery that, if you weren't careful, could maim you for life. She did not relish the thought at all but knew it could be possible employment for her in the future.

She realised the office door was opening. An elderly besuited man stood on the threshold. He looked harassed, but smiled kindly at her. 'Yes?'

'Mr Simpson?'

'That's me.'

Tilda smiled warmly. 'My name is Matilda Penny. I'm from Wragg's the builders. We did repairs to the factory wall.'

Mr Simpson nodded. 'Yes, that's right, my dear. Young Wally and ... er ... Ben did it. I was very pleased. It's a good job they've done. I've got another couple of things need doing if you'd like to send one of them round to give me a price.'

'Er . . . yes, I will.' Tilda took a steadying breath. 'I would like to collect the money for the wall first, though.'

'Pardon?' He frowned, perplexed. 'I thought that'd been paid. Step inside a minute and I'll check.'

'I'll stay here if you don't mind, sir. I have the baby with me.'

Mr Simpson popped his head around the door, smiled and gave a little wave to Daisy sitting in the perambulator who was doing her best to dismember her dolly. 'I was sorry to hear about Ted. I keep meaning to try and get to the hospital but, well, it's the time.' He brought his gaze back to her. 'We go back a long way, do me and Ted. I use Wragg's for all my work. How's he progressing?'

'Very well, thank you, Mr Simpson. I'm hoping we might get him home for a couple of days at Christmas.'

'Good. Well, if you do, let me know and I'll pop in and see him.' His eyes twinkled merrily. 'I'll bring a bottle of malt with me. Tell him I was asking after him when you visit him next.'

'I will.'

'Right, just stay here, I won't be a moment,' he said, disappearing back inside the office. He reappeared several moments later. 'Yes, I thought I was right. It was settled up last week.'

'Oh! Er . . . who collected it, Mr Simpson?'

'Just a minute,' he said, studying the signature at the bottom of the page. 'My office clerk, Mr Gilbert, usually deals with all this sort of thing but he's gone to the bank. It's not very clear but it looks like Hilda or something. Just a minute.' From his pocket he took a pair of tiny metal-rimmed spectacles and put them on. 'Ah, that's better. Oh, it's Matilda. Matilda Penny.' He looked at her, surprised. 'You collected it yourself, my dear.'

Tilda gawped. 'Are you sure, Mr Simpson?'

'Most definitely. Here, take a look.'

She stared at the signature at the bottom of the invoice. 'Payment received', it said, and was signed 'Matilda Penny'. It was quite clear.

Her heart thumped painfully. She had not collected this money. So who had?

'I'm sorry to have bothered you, Mr Simpson. I've made a mistake, I do apologise.'

'No problem, my dear. When you're busy things can get overlooked. Don't forget to send Wally or Ben round, will you, to price that work?'

'I won't.'

Mary stared at Rose pleadingly. 'Can you not help me out at all, Rose? Please, I beg yer. It'd only be a loan.'

'No, I can't. And if I did, how do yer propose to pay me back? You still owe me money from years ago.'

'I know I do. But I will pay yer back, honest.' Mary leaned heavily across the table. 'Look, Rose, yer said that new job paid yer well, surely you could manage summat? A few shillin' 'ud do.' Her gaze flew to Rose's new coat lying across the back of the chair; to her new shoes on the floor by the door; to the leather handbag she was clutching in her hand – and she thought of all her things gathering dust inside Leif's the pawnbroker's which she had no hope of ever redeeming. What a fool she had been! She could have done so much with the bit of money Paddy had given her and had wasted it all under the misguided illusion that there was more where that came from. She had really thought that Paddy had a decent job at last.

Rose tossed her head haughtily. 'I see where your thoughts are headed. Well, yer can forget it, Mary O'Malley. I ain't hocking me new stuff just for you.' She fought a great desire to divulge just what she and Mary's own husband were up to, but couldn't give the game away. A time would come soon enough when they would all know exactly what was happening. Rose grinned smugly. She couldn't wait! She narrowed her eyes, a smile twitching the corners of her lips. 'And let me tell you, I've money in me bag, Mary O'Malley, that'd feed, clothe and house your family for months but *you* ain't seeing a penny of it. I worked hard for this money and I'm gonna bloody spend it an' all.' She sniffed loudly and leaned back in her chair. 'Why doesn't that Irish layabout of a man of yours get himself a proper job, or you for that matter, then you wouldn't have to come snivelling ter me?'

Mary lowered her head. 'Paddy's gone.'

Rose hid a smile. She knew that. He was lying low in a derelict building at the bottom of Denman Street whilst they put their plans into operation. She tutted loudly. 'How many times have I heard that?'

'He has, Rose, he's left me and it's fer good this time. Before he went he pawned anything moveable and took every penny I had. He left me nothing, Rose, not a crust. My kids are gonna starve unless I do summat.'

She folded her arms and exhaled loudly. 'Well, what did you expect. You knew what Paddy were like when yer married him. He never had a job then, and if I remember right he borrowed the money off you to buy your wedding ring. You were a fool then, Mary, and yer an even bigger one now.'

Mary stared at her friend, aghast. 'What's happened to yer, Rose? You've gone as hard as nails. Where's yer feelings? Yer pity? I'm yer friend, Rose. The only one yer've bloody got.'

'That you ain't. I've a new friend now. One that's shown me the light. I've a chance of a new life and I'm gonna grab it, and even you can't blame me fer doing that.'

Mary's eyes filled with tears. She wasn't interested in Rose's new friend or her plans for the future. At this moment in time she had no means with which to put food into the mouths of her children tonight and the rent was a week overdue which meant the bailiffs were looming. 'So you'll not help me then, Rose? Not even a few coppers? That's all I'm asking for.'

'You can ask for as much as you like but the answer's still no.' Rose's eyes twinkled maliciously. 'What happened about the lodger you were supposed to be getting?'

Mary lowered her head. 'I couldn't get anyone.'

Rose smiled smugly. Now why did that not surprise her? 'Would yer like another cuppa before you go, Mary? I've plenty of sugar.'

Mary's jaw dropped. She scraped back her chair, stood up and banged her fists heavily on the table. 'You can stuff your bloody tea, Rose Skuttle. I wouldn't touch it if I was dying of thirst.' She wagged one shaking finger. 'You'll come a cropper, you will. Folks don't turn their backs on their friends like you have and get away with it. Now you listen ter me. When whatever it is you're up to falls around your ears, don't come running ter me, 'cos I'll laugh, that's what I'll do.'

'You'll laugh the other side of yer face then, Mary O'Malley. Now if yer don't mind I have a guest coming fer dinner so I've things ter do. Got a nice bit of shin beef, should mek a tasty stew. Wadda you think, Mary? Should I do roast spuds or boiled?'

Mary stared at Rose, utterly defeated, as all fight drained from her. She could not believe that her one and only friend, a woman she had been through thin and thick with, was turning her away. Without a word she turned to the door and slammed it so hard behind herself its hinges barely held it.

Tilda was deep in thought as she negotiated the perambulator over the cobbles and down the busy street towards home. The evening was rapidly drawing in, the mild air of the day turning extremely cold, but she noticed none of it. She couldn't for the life of her fathom who had impersonated herself and collected that money because that's what must have happened. She herself had not collected it, unless she was going mad. Why she hadn't thought to wait and ask the clerk for a description of the woman was beyond her but it had all come as such a shock. And how was she going to explain to Ben and then Ted? They were bound to think her a thief.

Filled with fear that it wasn't an isolated incident she had visited all the debtors on her list and it was a tremendous relief to find the money was still waiting to be collected. Three paid up, one said if she called at the end of the week they could settle then, and she had instilled in the clerk that he was only to pay herself in future and no one else. But the most puzzling thing of all was the fact that the Simpson job had been for the largest amount. Thirty pounds, eighteen shillings and ninepence to be exact, for the repair of the main factory roof, the replacing of perished bricks around the damp course and the bricking up of an old building's windows to make a new store room. She took a deep breath. Why hadn't the trickster gone round and collected all the money outstanding from the other jobs? But even more worrying was the question of how they had known Wragg's business in the first place?

As she paused at the kerb to cross the road running by the side of the yard she raised her eyes and noticed the gas lights flickering inside Ben's bedroom. She stared up for several seconds. How on earth was she going to tell him?

The gates to the yard were secured tightly and so preoccupied was she that she had almost passed by before she noticed the huddled shape, head pressed against knees, whole body shaking wretchedly, in one corner of the archway. She jerked the perambulator to a halt, conscious that she really ought to get

Daisy inside and fed before the child voiced her disapproval but concern for the poor person breaking their heart overrode all else.

As she squatted on her haunches recognition dawned. 'It's Mrs O'Malley, isn't it? What's the matter? Can I help?'

Mary's head flew up. 'Yes, yer can go along ter the Ragged School Mission and ask 'em to mek room for me and me kids, that's what yer can do. 'Cos me husband's left me wi'out a bean ter me name and I don't know what the hell I'm gonna do.'

Tilda's whole being filled with pity. She remembered only too well herself what it was like to be desperate, to go for days with nothing but hot water as nourishment, and that luxury had only been thanks to the endless supply of wood at her disposal. There was no chance of even that in these streets. Plus the fact that she had had no children to worry over and Mrs O'Malley had seven. 'Could Mrs Skuttle not help? She's your friend, isn't she?'

''Er?' she spat. 'She's no friend of mine. I belittled meself to that woman and she laughed at me, she did – laughed! Well, it's the last time she'll do it 'cos I'll never speak to 'er again as long as I live. I hope she rots in hell.'

Tilda shrank back at her savage tone. 'Oh, I see.'

Mary sniffed hard and wiped the back of her hand under her nose. 'No, I don't think you do, me duck. That woman's had 'er 'ead turned. She's living in cuckoo land and she'll come a cropper, mark my words.' Tears filled her eyes again and gushed down her face. 'And I thought we were friends. Oh, God, what am I ter do? Rose was the only one I could turn to.'

Tilda's mind worked frantically. What could she do to help this woman? It wasn't her place to offer her work, even if they had any going, and she knew only too well what Ted thought of her husband. But she had to do something. She suddenly remembered the money she had saved for Christmas presents. It amounted to nearly two pounds, saved very carefully from her wages. It was the first time in her life she had planned to go Christmas shopping and she had been so looking forward to browsing around the shops, taking her time and carefully choosing the gifts she had been going to purchase. The presents the money would buy would have been small when eked out between all, but as a lump sum two pounds would be Mrs O'Malley's salvation if she used it sparingly. Tilda jumped up and grabbed her handbag from inside the perambulator, quickly extracting her savings tucked at the bottom.

She knelt down again, took Mary's hand and placed the money inside.

'Pay the rent, Mrs O'Malley, and buy some food for the children. If you're very careful with the money it should last a while. I'm sorry I cannot offer any work but this will give you a breathing space.'

Mystified, Mary looked down into her hand at the handful of silver coins. She raised her head and stared at Tilda, dumbstruck.

Tilda smiled at her and helped her up.

Daisy then decided to voice her opinion and began to scream loudly.

'You will excuse me, won't you, Mrs O'Malley, but Daisy will have the street out if I don't get her inside sharpish.'

Mary absently nodded then without warning threw herself at Tilda and hugged her tightly. 'I can't thank yer enough. You're an angel from heaven, that's what you are.'

Prising Mary from her, Tilda grabbed the perambulator handle. 'Make a big pot of vegetable stew for the kids, Mrs O'Malley. Keep adding to it and it will last you a week at least. I'll come and see you as soon as I can and check how you're getting on.'

'I will,' Mary replied, smiling. 'I'll do just that. And you're welcome any time. Any time, you hear.'

Chapter Twenty-Six

Ben was waiting for her in the kitchen when she walked through carrying Daisy in her arms.

'You're not usually as late as this, Tilda.'

'No, I ... er ... had a problem,' she said, putting Daisy in her high chair. Daisy didn't want to go in her chair and fought against it but Tilda was insistent. 'I need to speak to you, Ben,' she said, giving Daisy a noggin of bread to gnaw on until her dinner was ready.

'I need to speak to you as well.'

Taking a saucepan from the shelf on the wall, she eyed him sharply. 'I hope it's not to moan because your dinner's not ready?'

His eyebrows lifted. 'Oh, had a bad day, have we? If you'd care to open your eyes you'd see I've already got dinner ready. Sausages and mashed potatoes. The sausages are a bit burnt though. It's in the oven keeping hot.'

Her mouth fell open in shock. 'Why, thank you, Ben.'

He sniffed, embarrassed. 'I've been invited oot, so I won't be having any. Can yous believe that Rose Skuttle has asked me round? It was a shock to me, I can tells yous, but then I couldn't really refuse.' He grimaced. 'I hope her cooking's not as bad as Wully says it is.'

A noise came from above and Tilda's eyes jerked upwards. 'Who's up there?'

'Ah, that's what I wanted to speak to yous about . . .'

Before he could continue loud footsteps pounded down the stairs and a man appeared. He was carrying a black bag which he put on the table.

'How is she, Dr Mason?' Ben asked.

'Doctor? And who's "she"?' Tilda asked Ben.

'I'll explain in a minute,' he replied.

'You are?' Dr Mason addressed Tilda, extending his hand.

'Er, Tilda . . . Matilda Penny,' she replied, holding out her own, then withdrew it, realising it still held the saucepan which she put down on the table next to the bag.

'So, Doctor, how is she?' Ben asked again.

Dr Mason shook his head. 'From what I can tell she's suffering from exhaustion.' He turned and tickled Daisy under the chin. 'She's growing into a very pretty girl.' Daisy giggled and Dr Mason turned to Tilda. 'I delivered this child and you're doing a grand job of looking after her.'

'Thank you, Doctor. I do my best,' she replied, pleased by his words.

Ben shuffled his feet. 'What did yous mean, from what yous can tell, Dr Mason?'

'It's difficult to do a thorough examination as she's sleeping. By the way, who's Mrs Riddledon. She was muttering something like that in her sleep.'

'Mrs Riddington? That's her employer,' Ben said coldly. 'It's that woman's fault she's in this state. Treated her rotten, she did.'

'Well, that's by the by, but this Mrs Riddington certainly didn't feed her very well. She's very weak. Is she a relative of yours?'

Ben shook his head. 'No.'

'So why is she here?'

Ben shrugged his shoulders, sniffed in embarrassment and stuffed his hands into his trouser pockets.

'Well, Ben, answer the doctor,' Tilda said, intrigued to know the answer, probably more than the doctor.

'I just couldn't leave her,' he said gruffly. 'I've seen dogs treated better than she was. I found her collapsed on the floor. That woman was working her to death. She's staying, Tilda, until I can sort something else out. She can have my room. I'll sleep down here. And I'll square it with Ted,' he said defensively.

Tilda stared at him. Ben obviously felt very strongly about this young woman. 'All right, Ben. We only wanted to know.' She turned her attention to the doctor. 'We'll take care of her, Dr Mason, if you'll tell us what to do?'

'I recommend plenty of rest and nourishing food to build up her strength.'

Tilda smiled. 'We'll see she gets it.'

Dr Mason patted her arm and smiled. 'I'm sure you will. I should leave her sleeping for a while then give her some soup or something light. He picked up his bag and eyed Tilda searchingly. 'Does your arm give you much trouble, my dear?'

'My arm? Trouble?' For the first time in months Tilda yanked down the sleeve of her cardigan to cover her deformity. 'Er, not unduly, why do you ask?'

'Just as a doctor, my dear, that's all. I didn't mean to upset you. I shouldn't have mentioned it, only if you're interested I know of some exercises you can do that will help strengthen it. Well, there's no guarantee but they might.'

'I'll bear that in mind, thank you, Doctor,' she said evenly.

'You can always find me at the surgery.'

'How much do I owe you, Doctor?' Ben asked.

Dr Mason retrieved his bag. 'We'll just call it a shilling.'

The doctor paid and seen to the door, Ben returned to find Tilda staring out of the kitchen window.

'Dr Mason didn't mean no harm, Tilda.'

She sighed. 'I know he didn't. It's just that I'd almost forgotten I'd got a withered arm.' She turned to face Ben and he noticed the glistening tears in her eyes. 'I thought you'd been invited out for dinner. You'd better go, hadn't you?'

'But what about Mrs Brown?'

'Mrs Brown?'

'The woman upstairs.'

So, thought Tilda, she was already married? She'd have thought, by the way Ben was acting, that they were at least betrothed themselves. 'Leave her to me, Ben. I'll see to her.'

'Are yous sure? After all, I brought her here so she's my responsibility.'

Tilda was touched by his compassion, a side of him she'd never quite witnessed before. 'I'll take care of your friend for you. Now go before Mrs Skuttle fetches you herself.'

'Thanks, Tilda.'

She smiled. 'Consider it payment for cooking my dinner.'

As soon as he had gone she realised she had forgotten all about her own problem and sighed worriedly. She would have to wait until he came back to tell him. But the sooner she got it off her chest the better she would feel.

Then concern for the woman upstairs took over. After making sure Daisy was safe and suitably occupied for a few moments, she made her way up the stairs, gently opened the door of the room Ben had been using for his bedroom and slipped inside. She tiptoed towards the bed and peered down.

The woman was lying on her side, her face almost hidden by an old-fashioned white mob cap, blankets pulled right up over her chin. All that was visible was the end of her dark lashes and the outline of her nose. What shocked Tilda was the fact that this woman was not as young as she had expected. Several wisps of grey hair escaping from under the cap and age lines round the side of her mouth told Tilda she was at the very least middle-aged. So much for thinking that this was Ben's girlfriend, she thought. Still, it was a very kind gesture on his part.

Deeply puzzled, Tilda looked at her for several long moments, wondering what it was about her that had driven Ben to act so impulsively. Then she sighed softly. All would be revealed soon enough. The main thing at the moment was for her to do all she could to aid her on the road to recovery.

As quietly as possible she let herself out of the room.

Chapter Twenty-Seven

'Have some more, Ben. There's plenty.'

'Ooh, no thanks, Mrs Skuttle, I'm stuffed as it is.'

'Ah, yer not, are yer? Why, yer've hardly eaten anything,' Rose said, dismayed. 'I've made a treacle pudding fer afters with nice thick custard.' She gave Ben a broad smile. 'You'll manage a bit, I'm sure, a strapping lad like yerself.'

He inwardly groaned. The meat in the stew had been as tough as boot leather, the gravy watery, the roast potatoes hard and the greens mushy. No wonder Wally had always jumped at the chance of eating with them. Now Ben knew he hadn't been exaggerating; if anything, he'd been kind about his mother's cooking. This meal had taught Ben something, though, he would never take Tilda's meals for granted again. Compared to Rose she was a master chef. 'Maybe just a little bit,' he offered to be polite.

Satisfied, Rose went through to the kitchen to collect the pudding.

'She's done her best but it's awful, Ben, ain't it?' Wally whispered. 'I did try ter tell yer.'

'Shush, Wully, she'll hear yous. It was nice of her to ask me round.'

'Yeah, I suppose,' Wally replied, unconvinced. 'I'll need a pint after though, Ben, ter wash the taste from me mouth. This has got to be the worst dinner me mam's ever cooked.'

'Some people have the knack, Wully, and some people haven't.'

'And me mam hasn't, has she? Not like, Tilda, eh?'

'No, not like Tilda,' he agreed. 'Not now she's got the hang of that gas stove.'

Just then Rose returned, carrying a plate on which sat a pale-looking lump of something resembling an upturned chimney pot. She proudly set it down on the table. 'A big piece for you, Wally,' she said, taking up a sharp knife and forcing the blade down through the pudding.

Wally grimaced. 'Just a bit like Ben, Mam, please. I'm stuffed an' all.'

She ignored him and cut a huge chunk. She slapped it in a dish then poured on a dollop of thick custard that on contact seemed to glue itself to the lump then slowly slide down its sides. Ben and Wally both stared down at their dishes before reluctantly picking up their spoons.

'Thanks, Mrs Skuttle, this looks delicious,' Ben lied.

'I daren't have any meself,' she said, patting her stomach. 'Have ter watch me figure. I shall content meself with watching you two.' She reached for the teapot and poured herself a mug, then topped up theirs. 'Help yerself ter sugar, I've plenty.' She settled herself comfortably in her chair and fixed her eyes on Ben. 'How d'yer like living in Leicester then? You must miss Scotland, you being Scottish like?'

Ben swallowed hard to rid himself of the lump of hard dough in his mouth. 'Funnily enough I don't miss Glasgow, or not so much as I did when I first left,' he said truthfully. 'As for Leicester, it's nae such a bad place.' He turned his head and grinned at Wally. 'I've made some good mates.'

'So you think you'll stop then?'

Ben raised his eyebrows. 'For the time being.'

'Oh, I took it for granted that someone like you wouldn't

stay round here for long. Well, Wharf Street ain't exactly paradise, now is it?'

'It'll do me for now, Mrs Skuttle, at least 'til Mr Wragg gets back, then we'll see.'

Rose seemed happy with that. 'Wally tells me that the job of putting the water closet in went better than you expected?'

'We had a couple of mishaps, didn't we, Wully? But we managed to sort them out.'

Wally nodded. 'We had a job ter fix the cistern to the wall. Nearly dropped it once, didn't we, Ben? Good job my shoulder was in the way ter stop it landing on the floor. I've a lovely bruise ter show for it, though.'

'All in the line of duty, Wully,' Ben said, tongue in cheek.

'Seems so,' Wally laughed, forcing another spoonful of pudding in his mouth. He pushed his dish away. 'I've had enough, Mam.'

'That's all right, son, I'll heat it up for you tomorrow.'

She missed the look of utter dismay that crossed his face.

'I expect a lot of money can be made putting in them water closets?' She spoke almost to herself. 'Well, not for yerself exactly, but for Ted you could?'

Ben nodded. 'Yes, it could, Mrs Skuttle.'

'So is that the line you intend to take then?'

'That'll be up to Ted, Mrs Skuttle. After all he owns the business and has the last say on everything.'

'It's my understanding he knew nothing about the installing of the water closet. Well, that's what you said, our Wally. Said it'd' be a nice surprise fer Ted when he finds out how much profit yer've made for him.'

Wally eyed Ben sheepishly. 'I did tell me mam that.'

A feeling of annoyance came over Ben who felt that Ted Wragg's financial and business affairs were none of Rose Skuttle's concern, even though her son did work for him. 'Yes, well, it was only a one off so I didn't think it important enough to take a trip all the way oot to the hospital to bother Ted with it.'

'Yes, I thought so,' Rose said.

Ben frowned. 'I'm sorry. Thought what?'

'That you were an enterprising young man. You'll go places, you will. Ted's lucky to have yer.'

'Is he?'

'Most definitely. I hope he's paying yer well?'

Ben remained silent. He didn't like the way this conversation was heading, wasn't sure what Rose's motives were for asking all these questions. He laid his spoon in the half-empty dish. 'That was grand, Mrs Skuttle. Me and Wully'll do the pots for yous.'

Wally took his cue and scraped back his chair. 'D'yer wanna wash or dry, Ben?'

'Stay where you are,' Rose ordered. 'Give yerself time for yer dinner to go down. Another cuppa tea?'

Reluctantly Wally pulled his chair back to the table.

Ben didn't want the stodge to settle in his stomach, he'd never manage to sleep. He needed to move around, thinking his digestive system had to be working at full capacity to cope with what had been thrown at it, but Rose had already grabbed his mug so there would be no escape just yet.

'There, nice and strong,' she said, shoving it back towards him. 'So, d'yer think you'll be doing more of these closets if there's so much money in 'em?'

'I never said there was that much, Mrs Skuttle,' he replied flatly.

'Now that's exactly what I've bin getting at. You've worked yerselves ter the bone fer what? A few shillings' profit. Hardly worth the effort, would yer say?'

'Well, I . . .' Ben began.

'Let me finish,' Rose interrupted. 'What I seen today got me ter thinking.'

'You thinking, Mam?'

'You watch yer mouth. You ain't that big that you can't get a clout from yer mother. I have got a brain, yer know, and I do use it sometimes.'

Wally lowered his head, ashamed. 'Sorry, Mam, you were saying?'

She breathed deeply, folded her arms and leaned back in her chair. 'I seen a row of empty houses. Six houses ter be exact. Down the bottom of Denman Street.'

'What were you doing down there, Mam?' Wally asked quizzically. 'Bit off the beaten track fer you, ain't it?'

'I was teking a walk,' she snapped crossly. 'I do sometimes when I get fed up. I don't have ter have your permission, do I?'

'No, Mam, 'course not.'

'Well then, shut up. Now, as I was saying, these houses ter my mind 'ud be going quite reasonable 'cos they need a fair bit of work doing to 'em. Seems the bloke that owns 'em don't want the responsibility any more.'

'How d'yer know this, Mam?' Wally asked quizzically, which was exactly what Ben himself was thinking.

'I asked, that's how.'

'Oh?' Wally mouthed. 'So what yer telling us for?'

'If you'll let me finish, you'll see what I'm getting at.'

'Sorry, Mam.'

'Well, as I looked at 'em I thought it just seemed a pity that Wragg's couldn't raise the money ter buy 'em.'

Ben frowned. 'And why would Wragg's want to buy them, Mrs Skuttle?'

Rose looked at him hard and pursed her lips. 'Seems I was hasty when I said you were enterprising. Can't yer work it out for yerself what I'm getting at?'

Ben's eyebrows raised. 'You mean Wragg's should buy them to do up?'

Rose smiled. 'See, I knew I wasn't wrong about you. Yes, that's exactly what I meant.' She tossed her head nonchalantly. 'Mind you, it's no business of mine what Wragg's does – only in as much as if the business prospers, my Wally keeps his wage.' She smiled affectionately at her son, then stood up and began to gather the dishes.

She had taken a pile into the kitchen when Ben turned to Wally. 'Your mother has a point.'

'Does she?' he said quizzically.

'Wully, for God's sake, buying those houses could lift Wragg's from run-of-the-mill odd jobbers to something much bigger.'

'Could it? How? I'm sorry, Ben, I don't follow yer.'

'Look, say for argument's sake we had the money to buy those houses. We could do the work much cheaper than someone who isn't in the trade. That means more profit to be made when they are sold.'

Wally stared at him, surprised. 'Fancy my mam realising something like that. She's never took an interest before.'

'Maybe it's as she said. She's only concerned for keeping your wage coming in.'

'Yeah, 'course, that's exactly what it would be. Soon as I get in on a Friday night me mam's got her hand held out.'

Rose returned. 'You two not going for a pint? Well, half for you, Wally. You know what you're like with a drink inside yer.'

'Mam, I'm not like anything.'

'Yes, you are. You go all silly. What about Fred Parish's stag night? You never made it ter bed.' She turned to Ben and grinned. 'Found him in the morning, I did, sprawled halfway up the stairs. He slept the night there. Didn't half give you backache, didn't it, Wally? And a sore head.'

'Mother!' He scraped back his chair. 'A' we going, Ben?'

Hiding his laughter, he nodded and stood up. 'Thanks for the dinner, Mrs Skuttle. I really enjoyed it.'

'My pleasure, and yer must come again.'

Not if I can help it, he thought. 'I'll look forward to it,' he lied.

For a while after they had left Rose sat at the table deep in thought. Her eyes were twinkling wickedly.

As they walked down the street, both with their hands tucked deep in their pockets, shoulders hunched against the icy wind that had risen, Ben looked at Wally. 'Where did your mother say these hooses were?'

'Denman Street, I think. Yes, that's right, it was Denman Street.' Wally eyed him curiously. 'Why? Eh up, Ben, you ain't thinking of . . .'

'I ain't thinking nothing, Wully.' He grinned. 'But it wouldn't hurt to take a look, now would it?'

As Ben gazed at the row of houses he could feel a stirring of excitement within him. 'What do yous think, Wully?'

He pursed his lips. 'It's hard ter tell, Ben. I mean, let's face it, it's bloody near pitch dark. I can't see all that much. But they ain't in as bad shape as I expected 'em ter be. But then, they ain't good either. There's a fair bit of work ter be done.'

'Any structural faults, do yous reckon?'

'It's hard ter say without a proper look, but if they were across in Bow Lane and around about, I'd say yes. Them houses are over a hundred years old and just about falling down. But these were built later and to a bit better standard.'

Ben eyed him, impressed. 'Know your stuff, Wully, don't yous?'

'Ted taught me well.'

Ben stood for several moments weighing up the houses.

He took a deep breath. 'Right then, are we going for that pint or what?'

'Er, yeah, Ben, yeah. Is ... er ... that it then?'

Ben grinned. 'For now.'

Chapter Twenty-Eight

It was dark. Thin strips of moonlight filtered through the cotton sprig curtains, casting long eerie shadows. A pair of terrified eyes stared round the room, ears alert for any sound. The frightened woman in the bed slowly eased herself up taking the covers with her, pulling them up under her chin. She had no idea where she was or how she had got here. The last thing she remembered was being in the kitchen preparing the vegetables for the Riddingtons' supper and worrying over the mountain of work that had to be tackled before she went to bed, if in fact she ever got to bed that night.

She slumped back against the pillows, momentarily shutting her eyes. Every fibre of her being screamed out for rest and she would have done anything to have laid back in this comfortable bed and gone to sleep, but she daren't. Taking a deep breath, she slowly opened her eyes again and stared around. The outline of a tallboy came into view and behind it she could see that the walls were hung with a rose-patterned paper. She sensed it was a pretty room, comfortable and inviting. But how come she was in it?

All her instincts told her she was safe, that danger was not present, but her reasoning could not fathom how she knew this. Then suddenly it came to her. She had died. She was in a waiting room – a halfway place between earth and the beyond. A spiritual being would fetch her shortly and so would begin her journey to the hereafter. An explosion of untold joy burst within her. At long last her suffering, all those years of pain, was over. The joy quickly subsided. If this was true, how come her earthly body still ached so much? Joy was rapidly replaced by bewilderment.

With a great effort she drew back the covers and eased her aching legs over the side of the bed. Gripping the headboard for support, she gingerly raised herself. Thankfully her legs held her fragile weight. She made her way slowly to the door and put her hand on the brass knob. To her surprise it turned freely. Whoever had brought her here, and for whatever reason, she wasn't a prisoner.

She found the stairs and slowly descended step by step, all the time fearful of what she might find at the bottom. The room she entered was dimly lit, a low fire burning in the grate. She caught her breath. In the armchair by the fire was a young girl, sound asleep. The woman frowned. Could this be her abductor? Inching her way past the table, she paused and peered at her. This girl did not look menacing. Curled up in the armchair, she appeared vulnerable. For some inexplicable reason the woman felt drawn to her, wanting to reach out and stroke the top of her head. But she must not do that. Despite what her instincts told her, they could be wrong; she could be in mortal danger. She had to get away.

The icy air hit her full force and she gasped for breath as she stumbled forward. A bank of thick cloud now covered the moon and the yard she had entered was almost pitch black, dark objects looming, blocking her path. Blind panic reared up. Which way did she go to secure her escape?

A noise in the distance startled her and she jumped in fear. Clasping a shaking hand to her mouth, she flattened herself against a wall. She could hear the creaking of a door opening and it seemed to be coming from the boundary wall. Someone was entering the yard.

Ben was having a job controlling his excitement and whistled tunelessly as he fumbled with his key to open the door to the yard. The seeds Rose Skuttle had planted had taken root and, after a scant inspection of the houses, even to a novice like himself the possibilities were glaring. The only obstacle he could see was money. It would be not his own money that he would be taking a gamble with but Ted's.

A part of him was angry with himself for letting this idea develop. Only a day or so ago he had been on the verge of leaving to resume his search for Duggie Smilie; now he was planning a venture that could keep him here for several more weeks, maybe even longer. He was stupid even to be thinking of it.

Relocking the gate behind himself, he stepped forward and fell headlong over a pile of bricks which he had forgotten were there. His cry of surprise filled the air.

Tilda woke with a start and fought to focus her eyes in the dimly lit room. The house was as silent as the grave, but something had woken her. An uneasiness settled over her. 'Ben,' she called, 'is that you?' She frowned on receiving no response. She must have been dreaming, she decided.

Rubbing gritty eyes, she eased her legs from under her, rose awkwardly and made her way to the kitchen where she lit the gas mantle. She shivered. After being by the fire the kitchen struck cold. She reached for the kettle and struck a match for the gas.

As she placed the blackened kettle over the flames her ears pricked. Someone was in the yard. Reaching for the nearest thing handy, which happened to be the sweeping brush, she lunged for the door and yanked it open. 'Who's there?' she demanded, waving the brush menacingly.

'It's me,' Ben responded gruffly from the other side of the yard.

'Oh, Ben,' she said, relieved, leaning the brush against the wall. 'You nearly frightened me to death. I thought we had burglars. What are you doing out there?'

'Taking the air,' he responded sarcastically. 'For goodness' sake, what do yous think? It's too dark for me to see where I'm going. I fell over the bricks.'

'Oh, I see. You're drunk, is that it?'

'Two halves of bitter is not enough to get a man drunk.'

'If you're not drunk then why didn't you come round the front?'

'Because I didn't, that's why.'

'Well, hurry up and come in. I need to talk to you.'

'I need to talk to yous too and I'm doing my best. I've got my jacket caught on a nail and I cannae get it free.'

Tilda groaned. 'Hold on, I'll come and help you.'

'That's a stupid idea. If I can't see where I'm going then neither will yous. Just go back inside and leave the kitchen door open. It'll give me something to head for.'

'Well, keep the noise down or you'll wake Mrs Brown and Daisy. That's if you've not already done so.'

As she turned to go back inside a slight movement at the side of the outbuildings caught Tilda's eye and she stopped and stared over at it. 'Who's there?' she demanded.

'What?' Ben replied.

'Ben, shut up!' she cried, gingerly advancing. 'There's someone here. Someone else besides us.'

'Tilda Penny, you're imagining things.'

A cry of anguish came forth followed by a dull thud.

Tilda gasped. 'Ben, quickly! It's Mrs Brown. She's fainted.'

He yanked his jacket off the nail and sprang over, managing by sheer luck and not judgement to avoid all the obstacles.

'What's she doing oot here, Tilda? I thought yous were supposed to be keeping an eye on her?'

'Ben, just help me get her inside,' she snapped.

Minutes later Tilda was looking worriedly at the older woman, wrapped warmly in blankets and lying on the sofa. 'Do you think we ought to get the doctor again, Ben? I don't like the look of her.'

He shrugged his shoulders. 'Do what yous think best, Tilda. But you're right, she looks awful.'

The woman's eyes flickered open and Tilda knelt down beside her and took hold of her hand for reassurance. 'It's all right, Mrs Brown,' she said soothingly. 'We're going to get the doctor.'

'Doctor! No. No, doctor. I'm all right, honest I am.' She eyed Tilda hesitantly. 'Please tell me where I am?'

'You're at Wragg's yard, Mrs Brown.'

'It was me. I brought yous here,' Ben said, crouching down beside Tilda. 'I couldn't leave you at the Riddingtons', not after the way they were treating yous. If I did wrong, I'm sorry.' He stood up. 'I'll heat some soup, Tilda. We should really try to get something doon her.'

'Tilda!' the older woman gasped. A stricken look filled her face. Her eyes shut then slowly opened again. 'Tell me . . . tell me I'm not dreaming?'

Tilda frowned. 'You're not dreaming.'

'Then I did hear right. You are . . . you really are . . .' she appeared to have great difficulty in saying the words . . . 'Matilda Penny?'

Tilda stared at her fearfully. There was something happening here that she couldn't understand. 'Yes,' she said, confused.

'I'm Matilda Penny.' Her eyebrows drew together. She glanced fleetingly up at Ben then back at the woman on the sofa. 'Do you know me?'

Mrs Brown's whole body sagged, face paling alarmingly. With shaking hands, she reached out and ran her fingertips tenderly down the side of Tilda's face then gently took hold of her withered arm and stroked it. 'It's not so bad as I dreaded it would be.' She raised eyes filled with emotion. 'Oh, my dear,' she said chokingly, 'you don't know how I've longed for this moment. I never thought it would come. I still can't believe it.'

'Believe what?' Tilda asked, greatly confused.

'That I've found you.' Her face filled with happiness, tears of joy overspilling to cascade down her face. 'Tilda. Oh, Tilda, my dear. I'm your mother.'

She reeled back in shock. 'No!' she cried, astounded. Wrenching her hands away, she jumped up and stepped back. 'No, you're not. You're not my mother. My mother's dead.'

Ben rushed across to her and grabbed her shoulders. 'Tilda . . .'

'Don't, Ben, don't!' she shrieked, shaking herself free. 'Did you know about this? Have you planned this between you?'

'Tilda, stop it. Why would we do that? I'm as shocked as yous are. But just listen to her.'

'No, I won't. This woman is lying. Why is she saying this? My mother is dead. And I should know – I killed her.'

Eileen Calister gasped, horrified. 'Did your father tell you that? Did Eli tell you that lie, Tilda?'

She spun round and glared at the sick woman. 'How did you know my father's name? How? Tell me? And you can't be my mother. Your name's Brown.'

'No, it isn't. Brown was just the name Mrs Riddington called me. She thought Calister unsuitable for a maid.'

'Calister!'

Eileen clasped her hands and wrung them, distraught. 'Your father and I weren't married, Tilda. But that made no difference to me. I loved you from the moment you were born and I've never stopped loving you. You've got to believe me.'

Tilda's eyes flashed. 'If you loved me so much then how come you deserted me? And said I was a child of the Devil.'

'A what!' A cry of anguish escaped her lips. 'Oh, my God, *he* told you that. But I didn't, Tilda. I didn't desert you. I would never do such a thing. Why would I, when I love you so much?' Reaching for the mob cap on her head, she wrenched it off and turned her profile to Tilda. 'He did this to me, Tilda. He left me for dead. I didn't desert you, you have to believe me,' she pleaded.

Tilda gasped to see the hideous scar running down the side of the woman's face. She dropped to her knees, tears spurting from her eyes. 'My father did that to you?'

Eileen slowly nodded as she pulled the cap back on, making sure it hid the scar.

Ben stared horrified at her disfigurement. 'The bastard,' he hissed.

'Why?' Tilda whispered. 'What made him?'

Eileen froze. How could she tell her daughter the truth? How could she tell Tilda her father was a murderer and it was the threat of exposure that lay behind his violent act? 'I can't remember,' she said softly. 'I was found in a ditch by the farmer whose land we lived on and taken to the hospital. It was thought I wouldn't live. It was many weeks before I was fit enough to leave and then I did everything I could to find you. But it seemed that you'd both disappeared from the face of the earth.' She took a breath and wiped tears from her eyes. 'I was in a Salvation Army soup kitchen one morning when Mrs Riddington came by. She offered me a job as her maid. Of course I jumped at the chance. I thought I could get some money together which would help me in my search for you. But I was all but held prisoner once she got me to her house.' She eyed Tilda pleadingly. 'Take me to your father, Tilda. If it will make you believe me, I will confront him.'

'You can't,' she uttered. 'He's dead.'

'Dead?' Eileen gasped, reeling in shock. She shut her eyes tightly and bowed her head. 'I'm not sorry. At least he can't harm us any more.'

'Oh, God,' Tilda groaned, doubling over and clutching her stomach. 'I can't bear it. All those lies he told me. All those years he treated me no better than dirt, making me feel worthless and responsible for everything that had happened.' Her face filled with horror as realisation struck and she raised her head and stared at her mother transfixed. 'So that's why we stayed in the cottage in the wood? He thought he had murdered you. He was hiding from the police.'

Eileen lowered her head. Better for Tilda to think just that. What good would come of telling her the real truth? She raised her head and held out her arms. 'Tilda, please come here. Please let me look at you. Let me hold you. I've waited so long to do just that and I never thought this day would come. Come to me, please.'

Tilda stared at her, her mind muddled, still unsure whether this woman was telling her the truth, finding it difficult to comprehend it all. But the urgency in her mother's voice compelled her to obey. Slowly she made her way over.

Eileen reached up and tenderly cupped her face in her hands. 'Oh, my daughter, you've grown into such a lovely young woman. You're beautiful, Tilda. I'm so proud of you.'

Her whole body sagged. She knew then that this was truly her mother. Only the woman who had given birth to her would proclaim her beautiful. She threw her arms around her and pulled her close. 'Oh, Mam,' she sobbed.

* * *

Ben tapped lightly on Tilda's door and entered without waiting for a response. He found her sitting up in bed, her chin resting on her bent knees, staring towards the window. She turned her head as he walked in and smiled faintly.

'I just thought I'd come and see how yous were.'

'That was nice of you,' she said softly.

'Well, I couldn't sleep,' he said, sitting on the edge of the bed. 'Yous obviously can't either.'

She shook her head. 'I still can't take in what's happened. I woke up this morning an orphan. Tonight my mother's asleep downstairs on the sofa. It's like one of those fairy-tales, isn't it? Had you any idea at all who she was, Ben?'

He shook his head.

'Then why did you bring her back here? What made you do it?'

He shrugged his shoulders. 'Just something. I cannae explain, Tilda. Just be glad I did, eh?'

'Oh, yes, yes,' she uttered. 'I just dread to think that if you hadn't taken that job at the Riddingtons' this wouldn't have happened. Then I would never have known she was alive.' Tears filled her eyes and she buried her face in her hands. 'My father was such a terrible man. Ever since I can remember he told me my mother hated me, that the very sight of me disgusted her, and that was why she went away. I believed him, Ben. I believed his lies. What a fool I was! My mother was the only person who ever loved me, and I know she's telling the truth. I feel sure now that he would have got rid of me also if he hadn't needed me to put food on the table and give him money for his gin. I just hope that wherever his spirit is, he's showing some remorse for the dreadful things he did.'

Ben doubted that very much. People like Eli Penny possessed no soul. He laid his hand gently on her arm. 'Forget him, Tilda.

He belongs to the past. You have your mother back now. Just be thankful for that.'

She raised her head, wiping her eyes on the sheet. 'Oh, I am, I am. It's like a miracle. Oh, Ben, there's so much I want to ask her, things I need to know, but she was exhausted so I left her to sleep.' She smiled. 'I daren't go to sleep myself in case I wake up and it's all been a dream.'

'It's no dream, Tilda. Your mother really is downstairs and yous have a lifetime in which to talk to her.'

Her smile spread over her face, lighting it up. 'Yes, I have, haven't I? A whole lifetime. Isn't it wonderful?' Her face grew suddenly troubled again. 'Do you think Ted will mind her stopping here until I can make other arrangements for us?'

'I don't see why he should. You can only ask him.' He rose. 'I'm going to make a cuppa, would yous like one?'

She shook her head. 'No, thanks. I think I'll try and get some sleep now.'

She watched Ben make his way to the door, then gasped as a new thought struck her. 'Oh, Ben, I have something to tell you.'

Her grave tone alerted him. 'What?' he asked, instantly making his way back.

She took a deep breath. 'When I went to Simpson's today to collect the outstanding debt, it had already been collected. And, Ben, it was by someone using my name. They had signed the receipt forging my signature.'

'What!' he erupted. 'Are yous sure?'

'Honestly, Ben. I can't understand it. Who'd do such a thing?'

He frowned, bewildered. 'It was just that debt? None of the others?'

Tilda nodded. 'You do believe me, don't you?'

He exhaled sharply. 'Tilda, if there's one thing I have learned

412

about you it's that you're honest. It's a pity yous can't think the same about me. I wouldn't put it past you to have wondered if I was in some way behind this.' He eyed her searchingly. 'Yous have, haven't you? Go on, admit it, Tilda?'

She eyed him crossly. 'As a matter of fact, I never thought that.'

He stared at her in surprise. 'You didn't? Not at all?'

'No.'

'Oh!' He took a deep breath. 'Regardless, it's got to be someone who knows Wragg's business.'

'Yes, and a woman at that.'

Ben ran his hand through his hair which stuck up wildly. 'It's a lot of money to lose.'

'I know. Over thirty pounds. A small fortune.'

He groaned loudly. 'Oh, God, Tilda. I can't believe this has happened. Not after all our hard work.'

'We'll have to tell Ted, Ben. We can't cover this up. If he sacks us, he sacks us.'

Ben grinned wryly. 'See what I mean about you being honest?' His eyes narrowed. 'What about O'Malley's missus? O'Malley's got a grudge against us and he hates Ted. Maybe this is his way of paying him back?'

'No,' Tilda said. 'Mary O'Malley wouldn't have it in her. Besides, she's enough on her plate. Paddy's done a runner and left her penniless.'

'Oh, has he? Now why doesn't that surprise me? But he could have put someone up to doing it before he went. It could have been that money he left with.'

'Oh, Ben, do you think so? Would he really do such a thing?'

'It makes sense. That's twice, Tilda. Twice someone has done the dirty on us. In clever ways as well. It's got to be someone with a devious mind and someone who's not frightened to take a risk. O'Malley fits the picture. I can't rule him out even if he has left the area.' He sighed heavily. 'Regardless, we have to tighten up. We cannae allow this to happen again.'

'What do you suggest?'

'I don't know. I'll have to sleep on it. But maybe it's time that Ted came back.' He turned and walked towards the door. 'Goodnight, Tilda.'

'Goodnight, Ben. Oh, when you were in the yard you said you had something you wanted to talk to me about. What was it?'

'Eh? Oh, it'll keep.'

As Tilda snuggled beneath the covers a warm glow enveloped her. Her very own mother was downstairs asleep. It was all she could think of. For several moments she tossed and turned, then sat upright. Diving from the bed, she grabbed all the blankets and dragged them downstairs. Her mother was still sleeping peacefully and Tilda looked at her in wonder before she lay down on the floor next to the sofa, gathered the blankets round her and, with a contented smile on her lips, closed her eyes.

Chapter Twenty-Nine

It did not surprise Tilda that they all slept late the following morning. It was Wally's knocking that woke her.

'Shush,' she mouthed, opening the door to him. 'You'll wake my mother.'

'Mother?' he queried, shocked, stamping his wet feet on the mat just inside the kitchen door. 'But you told me she . . .'

'I know, Wally. For all these years I thought she was, but she wasn't. Isn't that wonderful? It was Ben who did it.'

'Ben? What did he do then?'

'Don't you know?' she teased. 'You helped him?'

'Did I?'

A tender smile appeared on her face. 'Wally, you remember the lady you brought here on the hand cart?'

'Yeah. Brown the maid?'

'Wally, that was my mother. My very own mother. I still can't believe it.' She took his arm and guided him towards the door leading to the back room. 'Look, there she is. She's sleeping. I'm going to build her up with love and care and good food, then we'll catch up on all the things we never got a chance to do. Fourteen years' worth.' She clasped her hands delightedly. 'Oh, Wally, I'm so happy.'

Caught up in her utter delight, he spontaneously threw his arms around her and hugged her tightly. 'I'm so happy for you too.'

She beamed up at him. 'Thank you. Now let me go and you can put the kettle on whilst I hurry and get dressed. Then I've the fire to make, Daisy to get up and the breakfast to see to. Would you like some breakfast, Wally, or has your mother already fed you?'

'She's still in bed.' He grimaced. 'I couldn't eat anything, Tilda, me stomach's off. How's Ben's?'

She frowned. 'I don't know, he's still in bed too. He should be down soon, you can ask him yourself.'

'I will. It was me mother's treacle pudding. I reckon she must have put lead in it. Feels like it anyway.'

Tilda hid a smile. 'Whether she did or not, I shouldn't let her hear you say that.'

His grimace widened. 'Don't worry, I wouldn't dare. Besides, I don't want to change the good mood she's been in lately. She's a different person, Tilda.'

Half an hour later she a placed Ben's breakfast on the table. 'Go and hurry him up, will you, please, Wally, or his breakfast will go cold. Are you all right, Mam?' she called.

'I'm fine, Tilda dear. I wish you'd let me help you. I feel so much better after my good night's sleep.'

Tilda popped her head round the door. 'You'll stay where you are. Rest and plenty of food is what the doctor ordered and that's what you'll get. And lots of love, of course.'

Eileen smiled blissfully, then beckoned her daughter over. 'We do have to talk, Tilda.'

She went and stood before the sofa. 'Oh, we do, about lots and lots of things, Mam. But we've plenty of time. Come on, eat up your breakfast.'

Eileen cast down her eyes and plucked nervously at the blankets covering her. 'Tilda, I cannot stay here and be a burden to you. I have to go back to Mrs Riddington's. I have no money, you see, dear. All I possess is what I stand up in.'

Tilda fell to her knees and grabbed her mother's hands. 'Mam, you are never going back there, do you hear? I'm never going to let you out of my sight ever again. I don't know how you can even be considering it. You told me last night that she never paid you one penny in all the time you worked for her.'

'And she didn't. She said it was all owed back in rent for the room she gave me and for food and the damage she said I caused.' She smiled wanly. 'I had no fight left in me, Tilda, to stand up against her, and I was so worried I'd never get another job, what with my face looking so terrible.' She raised eyes filled with worry. 'Oh, Tilda,' she said gravely. 'The bill for the water closet. She's no intention of paying it.'

Tilda frowned. 'Why ever not?'

'It's a trick of hers. If I could have warned Ben I would have, but I never had the chance. I never knew when she was lurking around. What she does is pick on unsuspecting small firms who have never heard of her, gets them to do the work, then disputes the bill. Blames bad workmanship – anything she can. If the firm won't wear it, she threatens to sue and have their good name blighted. She always wins, Tilda.'

She shook her head in disbelief, then narrowed her eyes. 'Maybe she has in the past, Mam, but not this time she won't. What a nerve she's got! If you hadn't told me yourself, I wouldn't have believed it. Thank God you're out of her clutches.' Her eyes filled with love. 'I'm going to care for you from now on. If Mr Wragg, for whatever reason, is not agreeable to our both staying here, then I'll get another job and somewhere for us both to live. So put all worries on that score out of your head and you concentrate on getting better. Please, Mam?'

Eileen nodded. 'I will, Tilda. I have a reason to now, haven't I?'

417

Tilda reached over and hugged her tightly. 'Yes, you do. Now you lie back and have a rest.'

Eileen sighed reluctantly. 'All right, dear. But I really do feel so much better now. Before you go, I'd just like to ask you something. It's about Ben . . .'

'What about him?'

'Where does he figure in all this? He seems such a nice young man.' She looked at Tilda hopefully. 'Are you and he . . . ?'

Tilda knew what was coming. 'What, me and Ben McCraven?' she exclaimed, aghast. 'Mam, we're just workmates. "Friends" would be stretching it. We met just by . . .' Her voice trailed off. 'Mam, whatever's the matter? What did I say that's upset you so much?'

Eileen caught her breath, fighting hard to compose herself. McCraven was the last name she had expected to hear. She hoped, prayed, that she'd heard Tilda wrongly. 'What did you say his surname was?'

'McCraven. Why?'

She stared transfixed at her daughter for several long moments. 'Er . . . nothing, Tilda.' She forced a smile. 'I thought you said something else.' She took a deep breath. 'Met by what were you going to say?'

'By chance, Mam. He came by the cottage one night out of the blue and I fed him. It all started then.' She laughed. 'We can't seem to get away from each other.'

'Why did he leave Scotland? Did he tell you?'

The urgency in her voice was not lost on Tilda. 'Is his reason important, Mam?'

'No, no,' she replied hurriedly. 'I just wondered, that's all.'

Tilda shrugged her shoulders. 'He's never actually spoken about his past to me but so far as I know he's looking for a longlost relative. I don't think he's had much luck, though.'

He wouldn't, Eileen thought, because the so-called longlost

relative she gravely suspected he was seeking was already dead, thank goodness.

How cleverly fate had played its hand. Fate alone had brought them together, two unsuspecting people who could never have realised that their lives were already linked. And it was best they never knew. Too much sorrow had already been caused, too many physical scars were still slowly healing, all inflicted by a man who could not possibly have possessed a soul. From his grave Eli was still reaching out and affecting their lives. No step forward could ever be taken until the past was finally buried. Somehow she herself would have to find a way to let Ben know that the person he was seeking was already dead. She had to put a stop to this young man's wasting any more of his life.

'Are you all right?' Tilda asked.

Eileen smiled and patted her daughter's arm. 'How could I not be all right, Tilda? I have my dearest wish come true.'

'Ben's not there, Tilda,' Wally interrupted, heading through the door.

She rose, frowning. 'Isn't he?'

'No. His bed's all rumpled like he left in a hurry.'

'Oh. Hurry or not, it's not like him to go out without his breakfast. I wonder where he's gone?' She frowned. 'Are his things still there?'

Wally nodded.

She sighed, relieved. 'Well, there's no point in wasting his breakfast. I'd better eat it.'

Seated at the table, Wally grinned. 'I bet it's something to do with the houses.'

She raised her head. 'Pardon? What houses?'

'Oh, er ... ain't Ben mentioned them?'

'No. And you'd better tell me, Wally. What houses?'

He gulped hard then proceeded to explain what had happened the previous night.

Tilda listened intently. 'You say this was all your mother's idea?'

Wally nodded. 'It surprised me un' all, Tilda.'

'Mmmm,' she mused. 'But whether it's a good idea or not, Ben can't do anything without Ted's say so.' A suspicion suddenly struck her. She scraped back her chair and rushed into the back room.

'Everything all right, Tilda?' her mother asked.

'Yes, yes, everything's fine,' she replied, diving behind the armchair at the side of the chimney breast. Prising loose the brick, she put her hand inside and pulled out the leather wallet where the business money was kept. Her heart thumped wildly. Except for two white pound notes, three gold sovereigns and some loose change, the wallet was empty. All the money they had made over the time they had been at Wragg's had been inside that wallet. How much the figure came to she wasn't sure without checking the books, and out of that money outstanding bills for materials had still to be paid, but regardless it had totalled a fair amount, at least two hundred pounds by her reckoning.

She felt sick. Besides herself only one other person knew where the money was kept: Ben.

Replacing the wallet and the brick, she rose and smiled briefly at her mother as she passed by towards the kitchen.

'Are you sure there's nothing wrong?' Eileen asked.

Tilda paused by the door. 'No, Mam, everything's fine,' she forced herself to say.

Chapter Thirty

Later that morning Tilda realised she was going to have to leave her mother on her own, just for a little while. There was one very important errand she felt could not wait, especially in view of what Eileen had told her. And Tilda needed to keep her mind occupied. Ben's whereabouts and the missing money were causing her grave concern. She hoped with all her being that he had taken the money to purchase the houses; the alternative, that he had stolen it, did not bear thinking about. She decided that if nothing was heard from him by nightfall then steps would have to be taken. She had no other choice. Until then she would try her hardest to carry on as normal.

She stopped the perambulator before the wrought-iron gates of The Larches and stared through them at the grand gabled house at the end of the short drive. So this was where her mother had been kept a virtual prisoner for the past fourteen years. All thoughts of Ben were swept from her mind as she pictured her own mother at Mrs Riddington's beck and call, day and night, not receiving a penny for her hard labours. That in itself was bad enough, but on top of that her own husband had cruelly disfigured her and separated her from the one being she loved and who loved her. It had been a nightmare with no means of escape.

A steely glint flashed in Tilda's eyes. Those years of hell that her mother had lived through could never be eradicated but she herself could do something to make the years remaining a different matter. Reaching up, she unlatched the gates and pushed the perambulator through.

The bell clanged loudly and she stood back and waited. Presently a young woman in a flimsy pink housecoat answered the door. She looked Tilda over disdainfully. 'It's about time you arrived. We're in chaos here.' She noticed the perambulator and a happy Daisy doing her best to pull the hair from her doll. 'Is that yours?'

Tilda nodded.

The young woman frowned severely. 'I don't think Mrs Riddington's going to like this. Still, at the moment she's desperate so you'll have to do. You'd better go round the back.'

'I'll stay here, if you don't mind,' Tilda said curtly. 'Would you tell Mrs Riddington that Matilda Penny from Wragg's the builders would like to see her.'

'Oh, you're not the new maid then?' she said, disappointed, then sniffed haughtily and stood aside. 'I suppose you'd better come in.'

She led Tilda through a broad sweeping entrance hall, carpeted thickly with red Axminster. Water colours and oil paintings adorned the flock-papered walls and elaborate vases filled with dried summer flowers set on several marbled-topped occasional tables. Tilda refused a seat, preferring to stand.

Presently Margaret Riddington glided down the stairs. 'What is it you want?' she snapped, walking towards her. 'This is most inconvenient.'

Tilda took a deep breath. 'I've come to collect the payment for work that was done, Mrs Riddington. The end of the month is not convenient for us.'

'Oh, isn't it? Well, that's too bad because all my bills are settled then. But I'm glad you're here because it saves me a letter.' She pushed out her chest and folded her arms. 'I'm far from happy with the standard of workmanship. The closet keeps blocking, the cistern is crooked and there are holes in the plaster. The whole job is so below standard a child could have done better. In view of this I am withholding payment,' she said smugly.

Tilda did not bat an eyelid. 'I'm sorry to hear that, Mrs Riddington. If you'll please let me assess the work then I can give you my views.'

'It's not convenient.'

'Isn't it? Well, I'm afraid I have no option then,' she said, producing a large screwdriver from her pocket.

Margaret eyed the tool, confused. 'What do you propose to do with that?'

'Take the water closet back.'

'Pardon?'

'It still belongs to Wragg's, Mrs Riddington. Until you pay for it, that is. You appear not to want to pay for it, so I'll take it back. I have the hand cart outside,' she lied, hoping Margaret Riddington did not realise. 'I'll try not to leave too much of a mess.'

'What? But that's preposterous!'

'It's the law, Mrs Riddington. Goods supplied remain the property of the supplier until payment for said goods has changed hands.'

'But I have a houseful of visitors,' she snapped, eyes darting towards three guests descending the stairs.

'I'm sorry, I cannot come back. This way, is it?' Tilda said, pointing past her.

Margaret Riddington's face reddened in fury. She was beaten and she knew it. 'Stay there,' she barked. 'I'll get my cheque book.' She leaned over, thrusting her face to within inches of Tilda's. 'You can be assured I will not be using Wragg's again.'

'I'm sorry to hear that, Mrs Riddington. And I won't accept a cheque. They can be cancelled. Cash, please.'

'Cash! I don't keep amounts like that in the house.'

'Oh, I'm sure you do, Mrs Riddington. If not, I'll take goods to the value.'

Margaret's fists clenched in temper.

'Anything wrong?' enquired a middle-aged man dressed in tennis flannels.

She smiled sweetly at him. 'No, nothing, Robert. Enjoy your game.' She turned back to Tilda. 'Stay here.'

Minutes later she returned and slapped a handful of notes into Tilda's hand. 'Now sign this receipt and get out,' she hissed.

Tilda counted the money, put the notes in her pocket and signed the receipt which she handed back. She smiled at Mrs Riddington. 'There is just one other matter...'

'What? I've paid you, what more do you want?'

'My mother's wages.'

'Your mother's wages? But I...'

'Does the name Brown mean anything to you?' Tilda interrupted.

'Brown! Brown was your mother?' Margaret narrowed her eyes. 'I owe that woman nothing. She walked out on me, leaving me stranded. She knew I had guests.'

'You owe my mother at least ten shillings a week for fourteen years, Mrs Riddington. Three hundred and sixty-four pounds to be exact. To be charitable we'll call it three hundred pounds, allowing for food, uniform and breakages. I doubt my mother broke much, and two uniforms over fourteen years would have cost you hardly anything. Judging by her health the food you allowed her was hardly enough to keep a dog alive. So I think I'm being generous, don't you? I'll have the three hundred in cash, please.'

Tilda felt her legs shaking and fought to appear calm. It wouldn't do for this woman to see that her nerve was breaking.

Margaret Riddington stared, stunned. She opened her mouth to retaliate but Tilda stopped her.

'If you don't pay what you owe my mother, I will very loudly inform all your guests exactly how you treat your staff, then I will put it all around Leicester. I hardly think that will look very good, considering your husband's profession.'

By the redness of her face and the bulging of her eyes, Tilda thought Margaret Riddington was about to burst a blood vessel. Without a word she turned and marched away. She returned shortly afterwards and thrust an envelope at Tilda. 'There's twenty pounds in there. It is my word against your mother's that I paid her no wages. I will stand up in court and call her a liar. Now take it or leave it because you'll get no more.' Grabbing Tilda's arm she marched her forcibly to the door. 'Now get out,' she hissed pushing her out on the doorstep. Before Tilda could respond, the door was slammed shut in her face.

Swallowing hard, she raised her head proudly. At least she had secured the money for the water closet and something for her mother. If she was honest, she'd achieved much more than she had expected. She wanted to jump up and down with joy, she felt so good. Running down the steps, she grabbed hold of the perambulator handle. 'Come on, Daisy,' she said, laughing happily. 'Let's get home.'

Chapter Thirty-One

The walk back took Tilda much longer than she'd expected and the chilly December afternoon was drawing to a close by the time she arrived home. She was just about to turn the pram inside the yard when Wally burst out of it. He was grinning all over his face.

'Wally,' she cried, catching hold of his arm. 'Is Ben back?'

'Oh, he's back all right, Tilda. And won't you be in for a surprise!'

She wasn't listening to him. The only thought in her mind was Ben. Joy fought with relief. His return meant he hadn't stolen the money – and she felt joy because ... Tilda was too naïve to realise what her feeling of joy was trying to tell her. 'Right, I need to speak to him,' she said brusquely.

'You'll have a job, Tilda, he's gone out again.'

'But you've just said he's back?'

'Well, he was and now he's gone out. About an hour ago.'

'Where to? Oh, never mind. He never tells anyone where he's going. He's so annoying, that man. I pity the poor woman who marries him.' She heaved the perambulator into the yard. 'I'll see you, Wally. I have to get Daisy in and see to my mother.'

His eyes twinkled in merriment. 'I'll see you later then. I'm coming for dinner.'

Tilda frowned. She couldn't remember inviting him. 'All right. But I don't know what we're having.'

I do, thought Wally, smiling to himself.

As Tilda opened the kitchen door an unexpected appetising aroma reached her and she could not help but sniff it appreciatively. As she closed the door behind herself, her eyes fell on her mother, busy at the stove.

'Mother!'

Eileen turned and smiled happily to see her. 'Hello, Tilda dear. It's cold out there, isn't it? I was getting a bit worried about you as the night started to draw in.'

'Mother, you're supposed to be . . .'

'Get your outdoor things off and I'll mash you a cuppa. I was just about to make one for . . .'

'Mother,' Tilda scolded. 'You promised me . . .'

'Hello, Daisy,' Eileen said, tickling the child under her chin while purposely ignoring her daughter. 'Why don't you give her to me?' she offered, holding out her arms. 'Whilst you go and say hello to . . .'

'She's too heavy for you, Mam,' Tilda cut in. 'And she's quite capable of walking.' She stood the child down and Daisy promptly toddled out of the kitchen. 'Mam, when I left you this morning, you promised me you'd . . .'

'I hope you like cottage pie, Tilda?'

'Er . . . yes, I love cottage pie. Mother!' she snapped exasperatedly.

'Yes, dear?'

'You're supposed to be resting.'

'I have rested. I slept all night for the first time in years and I didn't get up this morning 'til well after nine. Now, Tilda, please stop fussing, you'll wear yourself out.' Eileen smiled tenderly. 'I am glad you're back, I did miss you. Did your day go well?'

Smiling in defeat, Tilda shook her head. 'Oh, Mam, what am I going to do with you? And to answer your question, I did have a good day and I hope you think so too.' She delved into her pocket and pulled out the envelope. 'This is yours, Mam.'

Eileen wiped her hands on her apron, the one Tilda usually wore. 'Mine? What is it?'

Tilda stared round. 'Where's Daisy?'

'Oh, she'll be with her father,' replied Eileen, ripping open the envelope. 'Oh, Tilda!' she exclaimed, clasping the banknotes to her chest. 'This can't be mine.'

'Yes, it is, Mam. That's where I've been. To see Mrs Riddington. It's not all I hoped to get but at least it's something.'

Tears of joy filled Eileen's eyes and she threw her arms around her daughter, hugging her tightly. 'This something, Tilda, is more money than I've ever possessed. I can't believe Mrs Riddington gave it to you.'

'Neither can I.'

'Oh, Tilda, Tilda! There's so much I can do with this. I could . . . I could . . . Oh, I'll be able to take you shopping.'

Tilda smiled at her mother. 'Mam, it's just a thought but why don't you use some of the money to visit a beauty parlour and let them style your hair so that it covers the scar? That way you won't have to wear that cap any more.'

Eileen nodded thoughtfully. 'I might do that. Would you come with me if I did?'

'Mam, you don't need to ask. I'll go wherever you want me to. Except,' she said, laughing, 'back to Mrs Riddington's.' Suddenly she froze, frowning hard. 'Did you say Daisy would be with her father? Did I hear you right?'

'Yes, dear, you did.'

'Ted Wragg? *That* father.'

Eileen smiled teasingly. 'Why, how many fathers has Daisy got, dear?'

Tilda stared. 'Ted! Ted's here?'

'Yes. I've been trying to tell you that since you came through the door.'

Throwing off her coat, Tilda dived into the back room and abruptly stopped in her tracks. The furniture had been moved around to make room for a large cumbersome wheelchair which was parked by the fire. Ted was sitting in it, a blanket tucked firmly around his legs and Daisy perched on his knee; his head was bent, one cheek pressed against hers. They were both asleep.

Tilda tiptoed over softly and stared down at him, smiling.

Her presence roused him and his eyes flickered open. 'Hello, Tilda, lovey. I expect I'm a bit of a shock?'

'Oh, Ted,' she said, kneeling down in front of him. 'Not a shock, a wonderful surprise. So this was what Wally was trying to tell me. But how did this come about? You never let us know the hospital was sending you home.'

'They weren't. Well, not just yet. As you know, they wanted me to go to some sort of convalescent home. But there seemed no point, Tilda. If I'm ever gonna walk again it'll happen come time, whether I'm in hospital or not. Besides, I'm sick ter death of being poked and prodded. I just needed to be home. When Ben explained the situation here . . .'

'Ben! Explained? When . . . when was this?'

'This morning. Turned up at the crack of dawn, he did. Lots he needed to talk to me about, he said. You know, Tilda, he made me feel real needed. I haven't felt like that for such a long time.' He eyed her sharply. 'Eh, yer can take that stricken look off your face, gel. He's told me everything.'

She gulped. 'Everything?'

Ted nodded, smiling warmly. 'You know, when all's said and done you've both managed better than I'd hoped and there was bound to be the odd mishap. The building trade is a cut-throat business. You can't turn your back for one minute. I admit losing that money by such devious means is something we could have done without. But, well, the business isn't quite bankrupt, and for that we have ter be thankful.' He patted her hand. 'You've earned yerself a bonus.' He grinned. 'Mind you, if Ben gets those houses, you might have to wait a bit for it, 'cos it'll use up practically all we have.'

A sparkle lit his eyes. 'Ben was so excited he even brought the money with him so if I gave the go ahead he could go straight round and clinch the deal. Whyever I didn't think of doing something like that before is beyond me. That's where Ben is now, so let's keep our fingers crossed. But if we don't get those houses, we'll try for some others. This is just what I needed, Tilda. Something to get me blood rushing again.' His eyes filled with sadness momentarily. 'I know it sounds daft but I can feel Maud giving me her blessing.'

'It doesn't sound daft at all, Ted.'

Eileen came through carrying two mugs of tea.

Ted sniffed hard. 'Thank you, Eileen,' he said appreciatively. 'I was just about to tell Tilda about our arrangement.'

Her eyes darted to her mother then back to Ted. 'Arrangement?'

'Ben's telling me about your mother being here was what really made my mind up about coming home. It took a bit to convince the doctor but I wore him down. Well, let's face it, what's the point in having two lovely ladies at my disposal and doing nothing about it? That right, Eileen?'

'That's right, Ted.' She sat in the chair opposite and took her daughter's hand. 'Ted's asked me to help care for him. Get him on his feet again. The hospital has sent instructions on some exercises he can do and I'm to see he carries them out.' She looked at Ted. 'But I still stand firm on taking no money. Room and food is all I'll settle for. After all, you're paying Tilda to care for Daisy and there's only so many wages a business will stand.' Eileen patted the envelope inside her apron pocket. 'Especially in light of this, Tilda.'

'We'll see about that, Eileen,' Ted said firmly.

Tilda eyed her mother. 'But you need to rest yourself. This won't be too much for you, will it?'

'Helping out here will be nothing like the work I did for Mrs Riddington. And I need to do something. I'm not made to sit around all day. Now that *would* finish me off! She rose. 'I'll go and see to the dinner. When you've finished your chat with Ted, Tilda, maybe you'd like to set the table?'

Tilda watched her leave the room.

'What's the matter, Tilda?' asked Ted.

'Pardon? Oh, it's hard to put into words, but it just feels as if I've never been apart from my mother. We've just slipped so easily back together.'

Ted smiled in understanding. 'Look after her, Tilda. Make every moment you have with her special. You were meant to find each other again. Most of us don't get that second chance.'

'I know, Ted, I'm one of the lucky ones.' Her eyes grew misty. 'I lived without my mother long enough never to forget that.'

An hour later they were all sitting round the table looking at each other expectantly as they waited for Ben. It was well past six. Daisy had already been fed and was playing happily on the peg rug in front of the fire with a pile of wooden bricks. Her father, his wheelchair pushed up to the head of the table, was watching her. 'She's clever. Don't you think's she's clever? Look at the way she's piling those bricks.'

Eileen laughed. 'Well, what do you expect, having a builder for a father?'

Ted grinned proudly. 'Eh, that's true. I never thought of that.'

'Are we gonna be eating soon, Tilda?' Wally whispered. 'I'm starving, and I'm meeting Elsie at eight. I daren't be late or she'll set her brothers on me.'

Tilda laughed. Elsie Battle was a shy seventeen-year-old and when Wally had proudly brought her round to be introduced, the girl had blushed scarlet. Tilda had taken to her straight away, knowing without doubt that should Wally settle for her, he'd make a wise choice. She had felt honoured to note that her approval of Elsie had been important to him. Tilda just hoped that Wally's mother didn't frighten Elsie off.

'Her brothers wouldn't hurt a mouse,' she said, slapping Wally playfully on his arm. 'Softies, the pair of them. Give Ben another few minutes.' She frowned thoughtfully. 'You don't think he's gone to the pub, do you? It'd be just like him to do something thoughtless like that and us all sitting here waiting for news.'

They heard the back door shutting at that moment and all eyes turned in that direction.

'It's Ben,' Wally announced as though none of them had guessed the fact themselves.

He sauntered in, stopped in the doorway eyeing them all, and said: 'Are yous waiting for me? Good, I'm starving.'

I don't believe him, thought Tilda. 'Well, Ben?' she demanded.

He eyed her innocently. 'Well, what?'

'Cut it out, smart arse,' Ted snapped impatiently. 'Tell us what happened.'

A slow grin spread over Ben's face. 'We're in business.'

Ted thumped the table triumphantly. 'Good lad, you got 'em!'

'Yippee!' whooped Wally, waving his fist in the air.

'That's wonderful,' cried Tilda.

'I'll get the cottage pie,' said Eileen, rising.

Daisy accidentally knocked over her piled-up bricks and wailed loudly in temper.

Ben pulled out his chair and sat down.

'Did you have to haggle much?' asked Ted.

'The owner snatched my head off when he saw the cash. He never thought he'd sell them. He's arranging to see his solicitors and the deal will be finalised next week. Then,' he said, rubbing his hands together, 'we can start.'

Ted eyed him thoughtfully. 'How much cash d'we have left then, lad? I reckon we've some juggling to do. I noticed from the order book you've a couple of jobs lined up next week and I expect materials will have ter be bought for 'em?'

Ben nodded. 'And we need some blocks of lime for the pit. We're running low.'

'Yeah,' chipped in Wally. 'And ironmongery. I used the last of the six-inch nails yesterday repairing a window frame in Gladstone Street.'

'Six-inch nails in a window frame?' Ted queried.

'The wood was rotten, Ted. I had to replace the bottom completely.'

He nodded . 'I see.'

'Oh, I nearly forgot,' piped up Tilda, swallowing a mouthful of food. She jumped up from the table and rushed into the kitchen, returning with a wad of notes which she set in the centre of the table. They all stared, surprised.

'Where's this come from?' Ben asked.

'Payment for the water closet,' she said proudly.

He stared at her, dumbfounded. 'Yous went and collected this and she paid yous? Cash! Just like that?'

She nodded.

'I'm impressed, Tilda.'

'Thank you.'

'Damned clever idea, that.' Ted smiled at Ben. 'And the

money from that job will make all the difference. We can pay cash for some of the materials instead of getting them on tick, and negotiate a good price.'

Eileen stared around at them all. 'Is anyone going to eat this dinner or are you trying to tell me my cooking's terrible?'

They all dug in.

For the next hour all the talk was of plans for the houses, of when they would be able to inspect them in detail and assess what work was required, and the probable cost of the materials needed. It was a happy gathering, each member of the party in their own separate way honoured and delighted to be a part of it. Each knowing that without their commitment the venture would not succeed, each prepared to give it their all.

It was Eileen who drew the proceedings to a halt by noticing that Ted was showing signs of fatigue and reminding Ben that they still had to sort the front room into a makeshift bedroom for him until the time came when he could make his own way up the stairs. Wally, forgetting his date with Elsie, threw himself wholeheartedly into the job, as did the others. Daisy got under everyone's feet and finally Tilda saw the wisdom of putting the child to bed, much to Daisy's dismay. Her displeasure could be heard for half an hour afterwards.

After tucking Ted comfortably in bed and leaving Tilda chatting to him, Eileen made her way through to the kitchen to make him a drink.

Ben followed her, taking his coat from the back of the door. 'I'm off for a pint,' he announced, pulling it on.

She smiled at him. 'You deserve one after all you've done. That was a wonderful thing you did, fetching Ted home.'

Ben shrugged his shoulders. 'I didn't plan it that way. It just kinda happened.'

'Not many things in life are planned, Ben. Not good things

anyway. You didn't plan on finding me, did you? I don't know how I can ever thank you. To be reunited with my daughter was a dream I never thought would come true and it pains me deeply to think she thought I was dead for all these years.'

He scratched his ear, embarrassed.

'Still,' she continued, 'that's all over now. It's what remains of the future we have to concentrate on. I'm going to try my hardest to make up for lost time.' Eileen suddenly saw this as her chance to speak to him. 'What about your own parents, Ben? Do you see much of them?'

He eyed her for a moment. 'They're both dead,' he said coldly.

His tone made her flinch. She hadn't considered that his mother might be dead too. Her heart reached out to him. 'I'm sorry,' she said sincerely. 'Is that why you left Glasgow?' She noticed him look quizzically at her. 'Tilda must have mentioned that's where you came from. I have heard that life up there is harder than here, if it's possible. Not many jobs to go round. Left to start a new life, did you?'

He nodded. 'Something like that.'

She patted his arm. 'Looks to me like you're achieving it.' She picked up a mug from the draining board and set it on the table then took a deep breath. Well, here goes, she thought, praying that her plan worked. 'I met a man from Glasgow once. Not a nice character at all.'

Ben's eyes narrowed. 'When was this, Eileen?'

'Oh, let me see,' she said casually. 'It was before I worked for Mrs Riddington. I was still recovering in the hospital. Yes, that's right. It was just before I left. A man was brought in. He'd been badly hurt in a fight.' She fixed her eyes squarely on him. 'Knife wounds, if I remember rightly.' She watched the colour drain from his face.

'Eileen, do yous remember this man's name, by any chance?'

He was fighting to keep his question casual but the urgent tone in his voice came through.

'Yes, as a matter of fact, I do,' she said, spooning sugar into the mug. 'Only because the name he gave was not his real one. They found out his true identify afterwards from a newspaper article hidden in his pocket.'

Ben caught hold of her arm. 'What was his name, Eileen? What was it?'

She pretended to think. 'It ... it was Duggie Smilie.'

She saw him sway. Grabbing his arm, she guided him to a chair and sat him down. 'Ben, what on earth's the matter? Did you know this man?'

He raised his eyes to her. 'What happened to him?' he asked hoarsely. 'Please, Eileen, can yous remember if he recovered?'

'No, Ben. No, he didn't. He died. He was buried in a pauper's grave. That's all I know.'

A wail of anguish came from him and he buried his face in his hands. Eileen stared at him, deeply distressed for the pain she was causing him but realising it had to be done.

'Ben,' she said gently, pulling a chair next to him and sitting down, 'what was this man to you? Please tell me?'

He eyed her blankly, then his whole body sagged. 'He killed my father, that's what he did, and sent my mother to an early grave.'

'I see,' she said softly. 'And is he the reason you came to England?'

He slowly nodded.

'I see,' she said again. 'Well, whatever you had in mind for him, someone else beat you to it.' She sought his hand and held it tightly. 'Whatever this man did, he wasn't worth ending up on the gallows for. I'm sure neither of your parents would have wished that, Ben.'

'No,' he whispered. 'But I badly wanted to avenge them. The

thought that he was alive somewhere and my folks both dead drove me insane at times. I just wanted to find him and . . . and . . .'

Eileen knew exactly what Ben had wanted to do, having had similar longings herself for fourteen years.

'Ben, it's over. Duggie Smilie is dead. You have a life to live. You must get on with it now.'

He stared at her searchingly. 'Yous are sure he's dead?'

'Ben.'

He shivered. 'All right, Eileen. All right. I believe yous.' He rubbed his hands over his face. 'I've not told anyone aboot this. Tilda, Wully . . .'

'I won't mention it, Ben. You have my word.'

He smiled briefly at her. 'Thank you.'

Eileen patted his arm, rose and busied herself with the tea. This young man needed to be left on his own to think. But that was not to be. Tilda walked in.

'Want a hand with that tea, Mam? Oh, hello, Ben, I thought you'd gone out for a pint?' She eyed him. 'You look pale. Are you all right?'

He raised his eyes to her. Suddenly an overwhelming sense of freedom flooded through him as the burden of his vow to his dead parents lifted. He took several deep breaths. Eileen was right. It was over. The way for him now was forward. He could go wherever he wanted, do anything he liked. He was surprised to realise that he didn't feel cheated, just greatly relieved.

'I'm fine, Tilda. Never felt better. I am going for that drink.' He smiled warmly, then stared thoughtfully at her. 'Yous wouldn't like to join me, would yous?'

His offer shocked her. 'Me?'

'Yes, Tilda. Why don't you go with Ben? I'll watch Daisy,' her mother offered.

Before she could reply a knock sounded on the kitchen door

438

and Maurice popped his head round. His face lit up on spotting Tilda, then turned quickly to Ben. 'You've left the gates to the yard open again,' he said. 'I had to come that way. Couldn't mek anyone hear me at the front.'

Ben grinned sheepishly. 'I'll lock them on my way out.'

'Off for a pint are yer?' Maurice asked.

'Yes. Er . . . fancy coming along?'

'I think I will. Oh, that reminds me. I saw Jeanie on my way here. She told me to tell yer not to be late.'

Ben groaned. 'Oh, I forgot aboot that. We've time for a quick one first, though.' He turned to Tilda. 'Some other time, eh?'

Maurice froze. What did Ben mean by 'some other time'? Some other time for what? Was there something going on that he didn't know about? He shook himself mentally. He was so smitten by Tilda he was imagining things.

He turned to her and smiled. 'All right for Sunday still?'

'Sunday? Oh . . . yes. I'm sorry, a lot has happened here and it slipped my mind. You haven't met my mother, have you, Maurice?' She turned proudly to Eileen. 'Mam, this is Maurice.'

Eileen put down the teapot and accepted his proffered hand.

'Pleased to meet you.' Maurice smiled. 'I didn't realise Tilda had a mother.'

Eileen hid a smile.

Tilda's eyes lit up. 'Maurice, would you mind if my mother joined us on Sunday? Oh, and we could take Ted in his wheelchair. He's home, Maurice, isn't that good news? I'm sure the trip out would do him good.'

'Tilda,' Eileen politely interrupted, 'if you made arrangements with Maurice, you don't have to feel obliged to include me.'

'No, Mrs Penny. I'd like it if you joined us.' And he was sincere. He'd welcome the chance to get to know Tilda's mother. She seemed a nice woman, nearly as nice as her daughter.

'That's settled then,' said Tilda, smiling. 'What about you, Ben?'

'Yes, Ben,' chipped in Maurice. 'Why don't you bring Jeanie with you?'

He shook his head. 'Thanks for the invite but I've other things to do. Right, come on then, Maurice, let's be off.'

When the door had shut behind them, Eileen stared thoughtfully at her daughter. 'Just friends, you said?'

'Pardon? Oh, yes, me and Maurice are good friends. He's a nice man, is Maurice.'

Eileen smiled to herself. She hadn't meant Maurice.

In the early hours of the morning Eileen rose quietly from the bed she was sharing with her daughter and made her way to the window. Drawing the curtains aside, she stared out. A frost had fallen and all the neighbouring roofs glittered white in the moonlight. She smiled. Never in her lifetime could she remember feeling as happy as this. The baleful legacy Eli had left behind had finally been lifted. She herself was reunited with her daughter and Ben was no longer wasting his life searching for the man who had caused him so much pain. In her own way she had repaid her debt to Ben. Eli no longer had a grip on any of them. She wondered what the man himself would say or do if he was alive, and shuddered. Eli's evil had known no bounds.

She turned and smiled across at her daughter. Maybe, though, there was still some good to come from Eli's actions. Maybe fate was still playing its hand, but maybe it needed a little shove in the right direction just to make sure . . . She stood in thought for a moment, wondering what she herself could do.

'Mam.'

She turned to see Tilda looking across at her. 'It's all right, dear, I couldn't sleep. I'm just so happy to be here. I'm still reeling from the shock.'

Tilda smiled sleepily in the darkness. 'So am I, Mam. Come back to bed, you'll catch your death.'

Eileen walked back and climbed inside, pulling the covers around her. She sought Tilda's hand. 'I love you, Tilda,' she whispered softly.

'Oh, Mam, I love you too.'

The trip to see the Christmas tree in the Town Hall square was a great success. The tree was magnificent, dominating the entrance to the Town Hall. People from all walks of life meandered around enjoying the atmosphere.

Grabbing a moment to herself whilst the others were inspecting the ornate lions guarding the fountain in the middle of the square, Tilda wandered towards the tree and gazed up at it in awe. Memories of past Christmases filled her mind. She saw herself at the rickety table toasting the air with her tin mug of warm water, her father lying in a drunken stupor on the straw mattress in the corner of the room. She remembered another Christmas tree and how she had wandered into the shop just to gaze at it and the assistant had treated her as though she was scum. She shuddered, momentarily closing her eyes.

She felt a hand touch her arm. It was Maurice.

'Are you all right, Tilda?' he asked.

She smiled. 'I'm fine.'

He looked relieved. 'I thought for a minute yer weren't enjoying yerself.'

'Oh, I am, Maurice, I am. How could I not be? Thank you for asking us to come.'

'Oh, it's my pleasure, Tilda.' His eyes swept around. Everyone else was occupied. Now was his chance to ask her the question he had been building up to for weeks. He took a deep breath. 'Tilda . . .' He saw her eyes fix on someone across the square and frowned. 'What is it, Tilda?'

'Pardon? Oh, nothing, Maurice,' she said, bringing her gaze back to him. 'I just thought I saw Ben. But I didn't.'

Maurice's face fell. So his instinct had been right. Tilda Penny's heart belonged to another, whether she realised it or not. His own heart sank.

'You wanted to ask me something?'

He shook his head. 'No, Tilda, it was nothing,' he said forlornly. 'Nothing at all.'

Chapter Thirty-Two

From the moment the documents were signed, giving owner-ship of the row of houses to Wragg's, a buzz of excited activity overtook the builder's little yard as everyone pitched in to do their bit.

Ted was in his element, drawing up plans to modernise the houses with his wheelchair pulled up to the table. He also began making plans for the expansion of the business once the houses were completed. Tilda took over the ordering of the materials and the supervising of the deliveries, whilst still caring for Daisy. Eileen kept them all fed and the house warm and clean, helping out elsewhere whenever she could.

The heaviest burden fell on Ben and Wally who crawled into bed each night exhausted, both wondering how long they could keep up the normal running of the business as well as renovating the houses, but both knowing that, given time, their hard work would be worth it.

On the first morning Tilda stood by the door and handed Ben his sandwich tin. 'There's enough in there for both you and Wally. Good luck. Ben.'

He nodded. 'Luck's not what's needed, Tilda. Just hard graft.'

'Yes, granted.' Impulsively she took the horseshoe off its nail. 'All the same, take this with you.'

To please her he took it. It was still badly buckled but shone now from constant polishing. It confused him to realise he was pleased to think she had kept something he'd given her.

'I'll hang it by the door of the first house,' he said gruffly.

'What will yer do with your share when we get it, Ben?' Wally asked one night weeks later as they made their way home.

'Haven't thought,' came the blunt reply, which was actually a lie. Ben had been mulling over several different ideas, one being that as circumstances had changed, he might now return to Scotland. Things were different now he hadn't the burden of finding Duggie Smilie on his shoulders. Added to which he would have a few pounds in his pocket. He could start a little odd job business of his own. He'd plenty of experience. When these houses were finished his job here was done and his commitment to Wragg's over. He suddenly thought of the horseshoe Tilda had given him which he had nailed up in one of the houses. Maybe it had brought them luck after all. 'What about yersel'?' he asked Wally.

'Buy me mam summat I reckon. I might get her one of them gas stoves. She's always hankered after one.'

'And what about Elsie?'

'Elsie?' Wally blushed scarlet. 'Oh, I'm gonna marry her, Ben.'

He laughed. 'Now why doesn't that surprise me, Wully? In the circumstances, maybe yous should use the money to get your own place? Unless you fancy living with your mother or her's?'

Wally grimaced. 'Oh, I don't, Ben, no. Yes, you're right, maybe a little house is what I should be looking for. Maybe I could get one of ours for rent when they're sold. Wadda yer reckon?'

'I don't see why not. You could be first in the queue asking the landlord.'

'Will yer be me best man, Ben?'

He stopped in surprise. 'Me?'

'Well, you are me best friend.'

'Am I? In that case, I'd be delighted. If I'm still here.'

'You're thinking of going back to Scotland then?'

'Just thinking about it, Wully. Just thinking. Once these houses are finished, Ted'll be able to afford to take on someone else qualified, same as yous.' He slapped Wally on the back. 'Yous won't have to be carrying me any more then, will yous, Wally?'

'I've never minded, Ben. Besides, I ain't had to carry yer for a long time now. Took to this job like a natural, you have.'

Ben smiled. 'All the same, there'll be nothing to keep me here once the houses are done.'

Wally eyed him thoughtfully. 'Tilda'll miss yer.'

'Tilda?' he said, surprised. 'Oh, I don't think so, Wully. Anyway she'll be too happily married to Maurice to notice I've gone.'

'Oh, but her and Maurice aren't...'

'Wally,' Ben interrupted, 'I told yous before. I'd be the first to congratulate her. She deserves to be happy.'

Somehow Wally wasn't convinced Ben was telling the truth but decided it was best not to say anything.

They arrived at the yard gates. 'I'll put the hand cart away and lock up if yous want to get home?'

'All right, Ben, if yer sure? I just want to crawl into bed. I think I'm too tired to eat me dinner tonight.'

Ben smiled. 'Me, too. See you in the morning then.'

'Yeah, night, Ben.'

Rose was waiting for her son and pounced as soon as he entered the door. 'How's it going then, Wally? Reckon the work'll be finished soon?'

'Oh, hardly, Mam, we've still loads to do. Ted is insisting that it's all done proper and that's only right. Why are you asking?'

Rose turned her back on him, her eyes glinting wickedly. 'Only taking a motherly interest, son. That's all. Now sit yerself down, I'll just get your dinner.'

'Daisy, stay away from the water, there's a love,' Tilda called to the child. She linked her arm through her mother's and took a deep breath. 'Oh, smell that air, Mam. Spring's on its way at last, thank goodness.' She looked lovingly at her mother. 'You look a picture in that hat you bought from Dakin's.' Her eyes twinkled merrily. The cloche hat more than complemented Eileen's shingled hairstyle which hid practically all her scar. Tilda felt her mother looked quite glamorous. 'I think Ted thought so too by the way he looked at you when we left earlier.'

'Now that's enough, Tilda dear,' scolded Eileen.

Tilda looked out across the Abbey Park and smiled happily. 'Do you want to sit down for a moment?'

'I'm fine, dear, I'm really enjoying this walk. Oh, on second thoughts, go on then. My legs do ache just a little.'

Together they walked towards a bench and sat down, both drawing their coats around them.

'Daisy's enjoying her freedom. Look at her little legs go,' laughed Tilda.

'She is a lovely child. Reminds me of you at that age.'

'Does she? What sort of child was I, Mam?'

'The best.'

'Oh, Mam. I suppose that was a daft question. All mothers think there's no child like their own.'

'That's right, dear. And you'll think the same when you have yours.'

'It takes two, doesn't it, mother? I have to find a man first and I can't see that happening somehow.'

Eileen shook her head. 'Why do you undervalue yourself so badly, Tilda, dear?'

She sighed sadly. 'Oh, Mam, when you look at me, you don't see me as I really am.'

Eileen frowned. 'Don't I? I think I do.'

'No, you don't. I'm plain, Mam, and I have a withered arm. I've no illusions about myself.'

'Tilda, the world is made up of all sorts of different people. When I look at you, I see the same as everyone else. Someone who is kind and caring, someone who has spirit. And you have a lovely smile that lights up your face.'

'My plain face.'

'Oh, Tilda. What do I have to say that will convince you otherwise? There are many people who see your worth and not your plainness.'

'Ah, see, you've admitted it. It doesn't worry me, you know. I'm quite happy with the way my life is now. I've got you, a job, friends. I have a future, Mam. What more could I want?'

'But is it enough?'

Tilda stared at her mother thoughtfully. To have someone fall in love with her was something she dare not hope for because she knew it would never happen. A picture of Ben came to mind unexpectedly. All her instincts told her that although he now appeared settled, and for some unexplained reason his quest to find his longlost relative had apparently ended, Ben would go once the houses were completed. He had never intended staying in Leicester, and despite what he had achieved here, would no doubt want to be on his way one day soon. She realised suddenly she would miss him dreadfully and hurriedly pushed all thoughts of him away. What she had now would have to be enough. At one time it was far more then she'd ever dreamed of having.

'Yes, it is, Mam,' she said firmly.

Eileen smiled wistfully and patted her arm. 'Love sometimes has a funny way of showing itself. Remember that, Tilda, dear.'

Tilda stared hard at her. 'Are you talking about Maurice?'

'You tell me.'

'He's a lonely man, Mam. We just enjoy each other's company, nothing more.' She smiled thoughtfully. 'Anyway, since I introduced him to Mary, those two seem to be getting on quite well together. I know she's still married to Paddy, but . . . well, I'm hoping something might come of it. They really are suited. Maurice has taken to the children too. They're like the family he never had.'

'Yes, that would be nice for them both,' Eileen said sincerely. 'But I really think it's time you concentrated on yourself instead of other people.' She patted her daughter's arm. 'Now we ought to be going. Daisy is beginning to tire, and you have to take those sandwiches up to Ben and Wally.'

'Yes, I have. And talking of Mary, I want to pop in and see her on the way back. Although she's managing well, all things considered.'

'I thought you'd just told me Maurice was keeping his eye on her? Mind you, Mary does have a lot to thank you for, dear, and I don't just mean for introducing Maurice.'

Tilda lowered her head. She had been appalled the first time she had paid a visit to Mary's, intending to see how the woman was getting on after their encounter outside the gates of the yard. The house was not just untidy, it was dirty. Tilda herself had had less than Mary in the cottage in the woods, but at least it had been clean.

Gently coaxing Mary, Tilda had set to and helped her scrub the house from top to bottom. She bought some distemper and painted the walls, and from the second-hand shop purchased some sheets and blankets and other bits and pieces, telling Mary she could pay her back when she was on her feet again.

She had also advised Mary on how to get the most from her money. Because of what she had done, Mary now had a lodger and his money was helping to keep the family together. All in all, Mary was a much happier woman. In Tilda's eyes that was payment enough. To have helped someone who desperately needed it had given her such pleasure.

She smiled at her mother. 'When the houses are finally finished, maybe you and I could take a trip to see Fanny? You'd like her, Mam. In some ways you're very much alike. And Eustace. You have to meet Eustace.'

'I'd like that, Tilda. But lots of things could happen between now and then. Let's wait and see, eh? You might have concerns of your own to occupy you.'

Tilda looked across the grass to check on Daisy. 'Come on, Mam, we'd better get back,' she said, helping her mother to her feet. 'And I bet I have to carry Daisy all the way home. I never used to like pushing that heavy perambulator around but I wish I had it with me now.'

Chapter Thirty-Three

It was several weeks later when Ben pushed Ted's wheelchair around the corner and positioned it across the road from the houses.

'Well, what do you think, Ted?'

He stared speechless. The last time Ben had pushed him round to Denman Street the work had hardly started. Now, apart from tidying up and gathering the tools still scattered around, it was all finished.

'If the inside looks as good as the outside, then you've done a better job than I even dared hope for. We'll sell these, lad, no bother. And for a good price un' all. In fact, I've already got a buyer lined up. Chap called Randall called ter see me last week. Heard through the grapevine what we were doing, had a look and liked what he saw.'

'Did he? I never saw him.'

Ted laughed. 'Too busy working, I'm glad to say.'

Wally came out of the front door of one of the houses and grinned broadly. 'Done yer proud, Ted, ain't we?' he said, walking across the road.

'More than proud, lad. You've earned yer bonus.'

'I've heard so much about this bonus, Ted, I wonder if it exists,' laughed Ben.

'Oh, it'll exist all right, you cheeky beggar. Now push us over the road and let me get a better view.'

Back at Wragg's yard Ted unscrewed a bottle of beer and filled some glasses. 'Everyone must have a drink,' he ordered the gathering.

Tilda eyed hers hesitantly. Her mother pulled her aside.

'A drop of beer to toast our success won't hurt you, Tilda. Listen, my dear, I know what's going through your mind. Your father took drink to excess and then he was violent with you. Don't let that memory spoil things now. People like him, I'm glad to say, are the exception. So pick up your glass and join in the toast.'

Tilda sighed. 'You're right, Mam.' She leaned over and kissed her on the cheek. 'Thank you.'

'Cheers!' everyone cried, glasses clinking.

'Here's to the next lot,' piped up Ted, at which everyone groaned.

'Would everyone like to sit down?' Eileen suggested. 'Ted has something to show you.'

'Oh, what?' asked Wally.

'Just wait and see,' Ted said, grinning.

They all sat down except Eileen and stared at him expectantly. She moved to his side. 'Right, when you're ready, Ted. Just take your time.'

He nodded to her. Slowly he inched himself to the edge of the chair, planted his feet flat on the floor and started to push himself upright. They all held their breath. It took several long moments for him to stand up. Once shakily upright, he clasped Eileen's hand and together they walked six steps across the room, turned and walked back. Ted sank thankfully back into his chair before raising his head in triumph. 'Well, has no one anything to say?' he demanded.

Tilda jumped up and clapped her hands ecstatically. 'I can't believe what I've just seen.'

'Me neither,' said Ben, joining her.

'Well done!' cried Wally.

'It's all thanks to Eileen. Whilst you've all been out of the house, we've practised the exercises the hospital gave me to strengthen my legs. I took my first step last week but I wanted to wait until now to show you all.'

'Well, I'll be blowed,' gasped Ben, pretending to be annoyed. 'This afternoon yous made me push you in your wheelchair when yous could easily have walked.'

'Hardly all that way,' laughed Ted. 'But we're working on it. Ain't we, Eileen?'

'I'd better be off home,' said Wally. 'Me mam'll be waiting.'

'Not seeing Elsie tonight?' Tilda asked.

'Yes, later. Goodnight then.'

'Goodnight, Wally,' they all answered.

'I think I'll go for a pint,' Ben said, rising. He walked towards the door, stopped and looked hesitantly at Tilda. 'Are yous seeing Maurice tonight? If not, maybe you'd like . . .'

A knock sounded loudly on the door. Ben frowned, annoyed, and went to open it. Jeanie stood there.

'You never come to see me these days, Ben, so I thought I'd come and see you.'

He forced a smile, trying hard to look pleased to see her. He ran his hands through his hair and looked straight at Tilda. 'I'll say goodnight, then.'

'Goodnight,' she replied softly.

Eileen just smiled to herself.

Outside in the street Jeanie linked her arm through Ben's and eyed him excitedly. 'Ben, take me to see the houses. I've heard they're ever so nice. Just a peek, please?'

'But it's too dark . . .'

'Oh, you must have some candles. Please, Ben?'

He sighed heavily. 'Oh, all right. Just a quick look. And

453

yous must be careful because we've still some odd materials lying around.'

Jeanie looked up at him adoringly. 'But how can I not be safe with you to look after me, Ben?'

He ignored her remark.

Inside one of the houses, Jeanie stole around candle aloft. 'Oh, Ben, it's a little palace,' she enthused. 'This would make a lovely home, and it's only round the corner from me mother. I can just imagine a table there and a clippy rug by the fire. Oh, and one of those gas cookers in the kitchen. Oh, and Ben...'

He was staring at her, shocked. He hadn't realised until now that Jeanie had marriage in mind. She was a nice enough woman, would make someone a decent wife, but himself?

'Oh, what's this?' Jeanie asked, unhooking the horseshoe from the nail.

Ben glared at her. 'Put that back!' he snapped.

'Why, what's so precious about it? It's only an old horseshoe.'

'It might be to you, but just put it back. And we'd better be going.'

Hooking the horseshoe back on the nail, she turned and pouted at him. 'Oh, not yet, Ben.'

'Now,' he said, reaching over to take her arm. He hustled her towards the door and took the candle from her, blowing it out. 'I've remembered, I got things to do.'

'What things? I thought you were taking me for a drink?' She frowned at him. 'You're not still seeing that Brenda Brownside, are yer, Ben? You can't be, I warned her off. I told her I'd flatten her if I saw her hanging round you again.'

'Jeanie, I'm not seeing Brenda. I'm not seeing anyone. For Christ's sake, I've been too busy.'

'Well, there's summat up.' Her eyes narrowed. 'It's got summat ter do with that horseshoe, ain't it? You were all right 'til I mentioned that.' Her face fell as realisation struck. 'Ben McCraven, you can't be serious?'

He turned towards her after locking the door. 'Serious about what?'

'She gave you that horseshoe, didn't she? It was her. That Tilda.'

'No, Tilda didn't give it to me. Just leave her out of this.'

Jeanie placed her hands on her hips. 'No, Ben, I won't. I saw the way you were I looking at her just before we left tonight. You must be mad! Why, she's ugly, she is, and she's got that arm. Folks 'ud think you'd taken leave of yer senses if you . . .'

'If I what, Jeanie, eh?' His face reddened in anger. 'I've told you to leave Tilda out of this. You've no right talking about her like that.'

'Haven't I? I have if she's trying to take you from me.'

'Jeanie, Tilda can't take what wasn't there in the first place.'

'What d'yer mean? We've bin courting for months now. Me mam's bought me some sheets for me bottom drawer.'

'Well, you'd better give them her back then! I'm not for marriage, Jeanie, with you or anyone. Besides, I'm leaving as soon as this deal with the houses has gone through and I get my money.'

Tears filled her eyes. 'Oh, no, not leaving?' she gasped. 'But, Ben, you can't. I love yer.'

He stared at her remorsefully. 'Then I'm sorry.' He took her arm. 'Come on, Jeanie, I know for a fact that I'm not the only one you've got yer eye on. What about Archie Grimmell?'

'Archie Grimmell?' she replied, sniffing hard. 'He's all right I suppose. But he ain't you.'

'He's got a good job, which is more than I'll have in a few days' time. What money I get won't last long on the road.'

'Yer really going?'

He nodded vigorously. The thought of marriage with Jeanie had finally made up his mind for him. 'Yes, I am.'

Chapter Thirty-Four

Ted counted out the money and passed the notes across the table to Ben. 'You've earned every penny, lad.' He sighed heavily. 'Are yer really sure about leaving? I could find yer plenty of work, yer know. This is only the beginning. Look . . . er . . . if it's something more that yer after, a partnership or something, maybe we could work something out.'

Ben took the money and put it in his inside pocket, then he picked up his bag. 'No, it's not that, Ted, but thanks all the same. My time here's finished.' And that was true. Ted was home and on the mend, the houses were completed and Tilda had her mother. And Maurice. 'I never intended staying in Leicester. I'm heading back to Scotland.'

'Well, if yer sure, lad, I wish yer the best.'

'Thanks, Ted.' Ben turned to face Eileen and held out his hand. 'Take care of yersel'.'

'I will, Ben, I will. Are you not going to wait and say your goodbyes to Tilda? She won't be long, she's just popped to the shops.'

Ben already knew this. 'No.' He was quite firm with his answer. Saying goodbye to Tilda was something he couldn't face for some reason. 'You say my goodbyes for me.'

He was aware of the look that Eileen was giving him. 'Is there something the matter?'

'Not with me, Ben. Well, you'd better get going. It'll be

dark soon.' She caught his arm. 'Remember, dear, not everything happens by chance. Some things we have to make
happen for ourselves.'

As she watched him depart, Eileen shook her head.

As Ben let himself out of the yard gates, he collided with
Tilda.

They stared at each other silently.

'You are going then, Ben?' she asked finally.

He nodded. 'It's best that I do.'

'And you weren't going to say goodbye?'

'Well . . . it's been said so many times before.' He grinned.
'You'll be glad to see the back of me.'

'And you me.'

He held out his hand. 'Goodbye then, Tilda.'

She accepted it. 'Goodbye, Ben.'

She watched him walk off down the road. He didn't even
turn and wave.

With a heavy heart, she walked across the yard.

Eileen who had been watching the proceedings from the
kitchen doorway, shook her head as Tilda approached. Fate
surely did need a shove. She just hoped it wasn't too late.
'You're just going to let him walk out of your life? You're not
going to do anything, Tilda?'

She eyed her mother quizzically. 'I'm sorry, Mam, I don't
understand.'

'No, you don't, do you? You love the man, Tilda. Can't you
see what's been staring you in the face.'

She sighed heavily. 'Oh, Mother, Ben and I were only ever
just acquaintances. We were thrown together. Well, now it's
over. He's gone wherever he's going and I'm . . .'

'Yes, Tilda?'

'I'm going for a walk.'

She about turned and headed back across the yard.

Head bowed against the March wind, she trudged aimlessly. All she could think of was Ben and how much she would miss him. No, more than miss him. She froze in her tracks. Her mother was right. She *loved* him. 'Oh, God,' she groaned, flattening herself against a wall. It had crept up on her and she hadn't even realised it was happening. But regardless of how she felt, she could never expect Ben McCraven to look in her direction. She was a fool even to think of it. She should be happy with the way things had turned out. But suddenly going on without him seemed unthinkable.

A year ago he had come into her life just by chance and in that time they had seen so much through together. She owed all her new circumstances to him, and now he was gone. Distractedly, she rubbed her withered arm then wiped away a tear. Suddenly she felt desolate. Taking several deep breaths, she raised her head and realised her aimless wandering had brought her across the road from what had until recently been a row of slum houses. She sighed heavily. Only yesterday she had helped Ben and Wally give them a final sweep out and brought a shine to the windows before Ted had handed the keys over to the new landlord. She managed a smile. Wally had secured the end house for himself and Elsie, and they were so happy. She wished she could feel the same.

She suddenly remembered the horseshoe. It was still hanging on a nail by the kitchen door in the middle house. Ben had given her that horseshoe. She would ask Ted for a key tomorrow and get it back. She would keep it safe. It would always be a reminder of Ben. Not that she would ever need to be reminded. The likes of Ben McCraven were not easily forgotten.

She forced herself away from the wall she was leaning on and brushed down her coat. She hadn't realised how long she'd been out. It was growing dark. Come on, Tilda Penny, she silently scolded herself. You have things to do. People will be worried about you. A year ago she had no one to return home for. Now she did. For that she must be thankful.

As she was about to walk away a door opened in the middle house, alerting her attention. Instinctively she slunk into a doorway and watched. She gasped in shock to see Paddy O'Malley emerge, followed by a smartly dressed man. They stood on the cobbles outside and shook hands.

'Thank you, Mr McCraven. Tell Mr Wragg I was sorry I never got to meet him. Some other time maybe,' the man said, putting a long brown envelope into his pocket. 'I'll be taking possession tomorrow.' He stood back and scanned his eyes along the row of houses. 'Got myself a bargain here, all right. Soon have this place filled up with tenants.'

The man departed and a grinning Paddy walked back inside and shut the door.

Tilda's mind whirled. Why had the man called Paddy 'Mr McCraven'? What was Paddy O'Malley up to? It was something terrible, her gut instincts told her.

Without giving it a second thought, she stole across the road to stand outside the middle house, peering in at the window. The front room was empty. She stood for a moment and frowned. What on earth should she do?

She glanced up and down the street. Not a soul was in sight. By the time she managed to fetch someone, Paddy could be long gone. There was nothing else for it. She would have to tackle him herself and find out what he was up to. She ran as fast as she could around the back of the houses until she reached the one Paddy had come out of. She stood and listened. She could hear movement inside. She put her hand on the door knob and turned it.

Ben leaned back against a stile and stared down the expanse of road twisting away in the distance to disappear amongst trees.

He exhaled loudly. He had travelled quite a distance in just over an hour. It was surprising how much ground could be covered when travelling alone, with no one to hinder his progress. This was what he had wanted. So how come he didn't feel happy? Why did the road stretching ahead seem forbidding rather than inviting? If he was honest with himself, he didn't even know where he was headed. He stood for several moments, staring blankly down the road. Then it hit him. He was lonely. For the past year Tilda had been constantly by his side. Suddenly he missed her and yearned for her company.

He raised his eyes and studied the darkening sky. If truth be told Tilda Penny had filled his thoughts from the moment he'd left her standing by the gate. It had taken all his will-power not to turn back, nor even wave. Damn her, he thought. He didn't even like her.

But he did. Somehow, without his realising it, Tilda Penny had got under his skin.

He felt angry with himself for letting this happen. He just wanted to walk away and get on with his life. But how could he when the loss of her left such a big void? All that they had been through together flashed through his mind – and it had all begun when he stood at a fork in a road and made his choice as to which route to take. Chance had led him to the cottage in the woods. But was it chance? Could it possibly be that he was supposed to meet her? After all, that chance encounter and what had subsequently happened had finally led to the discovery of Duggie Smilie's demise and the lifting of his burden. Without that chance meeting he could have wasted the rest of his life on a futile search.

He turned his head and stared back down the road he'd just travelled, running his hand through his thatch of red hair. How was Tilda? he wondered. 'Oh, don't be stupid, Ben McCraven,' he muttered. Of course she was all right. He'd only been gone an hour. Tilda had so many people to watch out for her now. Her mother, Ted, Maurice. He grimaced. He didn't like the thought of her ending up with Maurice, not at all. He was a good man, quiet and capable. If she settled for him, she would always have bread on the table, he supposed. But would she be happy?

Suddenly the thought of her with Maurice turned his stomach. 'Oh, God,' he groaned. Then, like a bolt from the blue, the truth hit home. He loved her. Loved all that she stood for. The thought of not seeing her again was unbearable. The shock of realisation nearly sent him reeling backwards over the stile.

Regaining his composure, he sighed despairingly. Eileen had known, and so had Wally for that matter. But after the way he had treated Tilda, how could he expect her to care for him in the same way as he did her? It was too late now. He couldn't go back.

Picking up his bag, he made to resume his journey then stopped abruptly as he suddenly remembered the horseshoe. Take it for luck, she had said. It was still hanging up on a nail in one of the houses in Denman Street. If he had it with him, it would be a reminder of her wherever he went. Not that he would ever need reminding. The likes of Tilda Penny he would never forget. He could go back and get it and no one would know.

'You all right, mate?'

Ben jumped and stared at the man addressing him. 'Er . . . yes.'

'D'yer want a lift?'

Ben eyed the cart. Where on earth had it come from? He hadn't heard it approaching. 'Where yous headed?'

'Leicester.'

He had to ask the question. 'Do you usually travel this road?'

The man stared at him quizzically. 'Well, no, I don't. I came to a fork in the road and thought this way 'ud mek a change. Why?'

Ben smiled. He knew he was meant to go back. Everything he wanted was back at that little builder's yard in Leicester. He just had to hope it wasn't too late. He jumped aboard.

Holding her breath, Tilda opened the door. She didn't know who was more surprised at her entrance, herself or Paddy. They stared at each other, shocked. Paddy was first to gather his wits. He hurriedly swept the pile of notes he was counting into a carpet bag and snapped it shut. Grabbing the bag, he straightened up and grinned across at her wickedly.

'Well, you're the last person I expected ter see. Come in, why don't yers?'

'What are you doing?' she demanded, advancing.

'Doing?' He laughed, a sound loud with contempt. 'Counting me gains. And I've gained a lot. All thanks to Wragg's. And it was so easy! I've ruined him, that's what I've done. I've ruined you all.' He wagged a finger. 'That'll teach Wragg to turn up his nose at me. And as for that Scottish bastard... Wouldn't work with me, he said. Well, he'll regret that decision. I did warn him, he can't say I didn't.'

Tilda's heart raced wildly, fear of the unknown mounting rapidly. 'Mr O'Malley, what have you done?'

'Mr O'Malley? Oh, I like that,' he said smugly. 'Everyone 'ull call me that in future. When you're rich, they do, don't they? And I am rich. It's all here,' he said, patting the bag. 'Two thousand, two hundred and twenty pounds, give or take. You never let me finish counting it.'

'How much?' she gasped.

'To be shared with me. That right, Paddy?'

His eyes darted over Tilda's shoulder. 'Oh, 'ello, Rose. You're early.'

Tilda spun round and stared to see Rose Skuttle walking through the door. She was holding a suitcase which she let drop to the floor.

'Looks ter me like it's a good job I am. What's she doing here?' she demanded.

'Dropped in to wish us luck, Rose. That right, Miss Penny?'

'What have you done?' cried Tilda. 'What have both of you done?'

'Took what we deserved,' hissed Rose. 'Ted was a fool to put the likes of you in his house and set that Ben over my Wally. But the biggest mistake he made was turning me down. I'd have made him a good wife. He'll be sorry now.'

'Tell her it all, Rose, she might as well know. Tell her how you impersonated her.'

'It was you,' Tilda cried, astounded. 'Why?'

'Had to have money to finance our plan. Documents don't come cheap.'

'Documents? What...' The truth suddenly dawned. 'You've forged deeds to these houses and sold them. That's what you've done, isn't it? But to get that much money...'

Rose giggled gleefully. 'Yeah, you've got it. Not once but five times. Now ain't that clever? And we'd have done more if we'd had more time. Ain't that right, Paddy?'

'But that's fraud,' Tilda whispered, appalled. 'You'll go to prison.'

Rose laughed harshly. 'Us! Oh, no, *we* won't go to prison. We used Wragg's and McCraven's names. We'll be long gone by the time it's all discovered. It'll take some doing, convincing the authorities you lot ain't behind it. We're really good at this impersonating lark, ain't we, Paddy? Mek a good couple, don't yer reckon? Anyway, it was me who gave you the idea about the houses in the first place. I deserve a reward.'

Tilda stared, horrified.

Paddy eyed Rose angrily. 'It was me who told you first, Rose, don't forget that. And I managed quite well on me own before you came on the scene,' he bragged. He eyed Tilda wickedly. 'Never knew it was me behind that delivery scam, did yer? Would've done well fer meself if you hadn't put a stop to it. In a way this is all your fault.'

'Mine!'

'I'd planned to keep that going for just a while longer, mek what I could then clear out. Well, you cottoned on and stopped the deliveries. Which annoyed me, see?'

'Ben was right,' she gasped. 'He said it was you.'

'Clever boy then, ain't he? But not so smart as me.'

Tilda's mind was racing frantically. She couldn't let them ruin Ted like this. Or blacken Ben's name.

Rose was growing impatient. 'We've told 'er enough, Paddy. Let's split the money. I've a train to catch. I wanna get away from here.'

'But what about Wally? Your son, Rose. What's all this going to do to him?'

She turned on Tilda. 'I couldn't give a damn. Wally's old enough to tek care of himself.' She stabbed a finger in the girl's chest. 'Me. I have to think about me.'

She turned back to Paddy. 'Well, are we...' Her eyes widened in shock. 'What a' yer doing with that, Paddy?'

'This, Rose?' Menacingly he waved the length of metal he'd retrieved from his inside pocket. 'Yers didn't really think I was going to share the money with you, did yers? If yers did, you're a bigger fool than I thought yers were. If she hadn't turned up, I'd have gone before yers arrived.' His eyes darkened. 'Now get out of my way, both of yers.'

Rose roared in fury: 'No, you don't, Paddy O'Malley! That's

half mine, that is.' Screaming, she threw herself at him. Her unexpected attack caught him off balance and they both landed on the floor, the bag and the length of metal flying from his hands.

It happened so quickly Tilda was too stunned to move. There was a sickening thud as Rose's head smashed against the floor. Tilda jumped back, appalled.

'Oh, my God,' she murmured, clasping her hand to her mouth.

Paddy reared up and turned to face her. 'You next,' he hissed.

Terrified, she stepped back and her feet touched the bag. She spun round. Instinctively she bent and grabbed it.

'Give that to me,' he snarled, advancing on her.

'No!' she spat. 'This is not your money.' Her heart thumped so painfully she thought it would burst. Her eyes darted frantically. She had to get out. But he was nearly upon her and between herself and the door.

A thought struck her. It just might work. Mustering all her courage, she held the bag towards him. 'Come and get it then, Paddy.'

A grin split his face. 'Now there's a good girl. I knew you'd see sense.'

As he approached, she held her breath, swung back her arm and brought the bag crashing against the side of his head. Immediately she ran for the door.

A look of utter surprise filled Paddy's face as his legs buckled. 'You bitch!' he hissed. 'You shouldn't have done that.'

Gulping, she yanked the door open, fled outside and raced round the side of the house. Her whole body shook. She could hear Paddy cursing behind her.

Several people stopped and stared but all she could think of was getting back to the yard. There Ben would... Then she remembered he'd gone. Oh, God! her mind screamed.

The yard was in sight. As she ran she looked back over her shoulder. Paddy was almost upon her.

'I'm warning you,' he cried breathlessly, 'drop that bag!'

He lunged for her, the tips of his fingers catching her shoulder. She stopped, spun round, and kicked out one leg. She caught him right on his shin. He reeled, stumbling backwards. Not waiting to see the outcome, she belted for the yard door. She pushed her weight against it and prayed frantically it wasn't locked. It yielded and she jumped through, kicking it shut behind her. Holding her breath, she inched backwards, praying that no obstacles blocked her path, eyes seeking out the best place to hide.

The door banged open and Paddy came through it. 'I know you're in here! Now give me that bag and I'll let you go.'

She froze. He was so close she could hear him breathing.

Suddenly the kitchen door opened and her mother came out. 'Who's there?' she shouted. 'Tilda, is that you?'

Her heart thumped. Fear for her mother's safety erupted. Go back inside, she wanted to scream.

Thinking no one was there, her mother retreated and the door was shut behind her. Tilda gasped thankfully.

Unexpectedly the moon came out from behind a cloud and illuminated the yard. Paddy spotted her instantly and a wicked grin spread over his face. 'You can't win, Tilda. Now give me the bag,' he coaxed. 'I won't hurt you. Hand it over like a good little girl.'

'No,' she whispered, shaking her head. 'It's not yours, you're not having it.'

Without taking her eyes from him, she took several hurried steps back. Something wobbled beneath her feet and she nearly lost her balance. She looked down and gasped in horror. She had walked across the plank spanning the lime pit! The milky white harmless-looking liquid glistened innocently back at her. Tilda froze. One wrong move and she could topple right into it. She had been warned often enough. She knew then she was going to die. But she would sooner that than give Paddy the bag. She raised her chin, eyes flashing defiance. 'If I go in, the bag goes with me.'

His face fell alarmingly. 'Don't be stupid.'

'Oh stupid, am I? We'll see about that.'

He eyed her for a moment. 'Then have it yer own way.'

She gulped as she watched him bend to take the plank in his hands and tip her over. She shut her eyes tight and waited.

Suddenly all hell was let loose. Paddy didn't know what hit him. The next thing he knew he was pinned to the ground, his face thrust within inches of the white substance. His eyes bulged in terror.

Tilda screamed, wondering what was happening.

'Tilda, for God's sake, don't move!' a voice commanded.

She caught her breath. 'Ben? Oh, Ben, is it really you?'

Yes, it's really me, Tilda. Just don't move. I'll be with yous in a minute,' he said, acutely aware of the danger she was in. He shook Paddy's head hard. 'I should put yous in there,' he hissed. 'But you ain't worth it.' His eyes flew back to Tilda. 'Are you . . .'

'I'm all right,' she assured him. 'What's happening?'

'Stop asking questions. Just make sure yous don't move.'

'I daren't move. Oh, Ben, Paddy and Rose . . .'

'It's all right. It's all under control. Yous just concentrate on keeping still. There'll be time to talk later.'

He wrenched Paddy upright just as the kitchen door opened again and Ted hobbled out. 'What the hell's going on?'

'Get the police,' Ben cried. 'And hurry.'

Wally stepped through the door in the gates. 'What the . . .'

Ben's head turned. 'Oh, Wully, thank God! Take hold of O'Malley and don't let him go.'

468

Wally rushed over and roughly grabbed Paddy.

Ben leapt towards the pit and held out his hand. 'Now, Tilda, just come towards me slowly. Are yous listening to me?'

'I can't, Ben! My legs are shaking too much and I'm frightened about dropping the bag.'

'Sod the bag, Tilda. It's you I'm worried about. Just look at me and put one foot in front of the other. Don't look down. For Christ's sake, don't look down!'

Her eyes were fixed on him. 'My legs won't move Ben.'

He stepped on to the plank. 'All right, hold tight, I'll come and get yous.'

She gasped. 'No, Ben, you might fall in.'

'Then we'll both go together.'

Her jaw dropped. 'You would risk death for me?'

His reply came without hesitation. 'Yes, Tilda. Yes, I would. And I suppose you want to know why? It's because I love you.'

'You love me! Oh, Ben,' she uttered, astounded. 'You really love me? Really? Me?'

He gazed at her tenderly. 'Yes, really, Tilda. More than anything in the world. And if anything happened to yous, I couldn't live without yous. Now give me your hand.'

'Oh,' she cried ecstatically. 'I love you too. I didn't realise 'til you went away.' Without another thought she flew down the plank and fell into his arms.

Crying out in shock, he crushed her against him. 'Tilda, that was a stupid thing to do. Yous could have been killed.'

She looked at him adoringly. 'Oh, Ben, I knew I wasn't taking any chances, with you there to save me.'

And One For Luck

Lynda Page

Grace Wilkins and Bessie Rudney have been neighbours for over twenty years but it takes the outbreak of the Second World War for them to become friends. Bernard Wilkins doesn't like his wife or their daughter mixing with the Rudneys; and the more time Grace spends with Bessie, her six boisterous children and her loving husband Tom, the more she realises what has been missing from her own loveless marriage.

As the war takes it toll on Leicester, and one by one the menfolk leave to join the fighting, Grace finds comfort in helping others. First, Clara Smith, her reclusive neighbour with a tragic past, needs her support; then hundreds of evacuees come to town. Among them are Londoners Madge Cotting and her waiflike children Jessie and Tony, whose welfare causes Grace serious concern. Each day, as she takes on another new challenge, Grace realises that her daughter has been right all along – it's time to break out, really make something of her life, and possibly find true love, before it is too late . . .

0 7472 4855 9

HEADLINE

Any Old Iron

Lynda Page

Kelly McCallan has more than her fair share of worries. Her mother is dying and needs constant care; her father has returned to Leicester from the Second World War but is an emotional wreck; and her brother, Mickey, has turned to a life of crime that is putting the whole family at risk.

Kelly's boyfriend, Rodney, and his sister, Glenda, know that she's scared of what Mickey might do next. But they turn a blind eye to her fears – with disastrous consequences for them all. When Kelly has lost everything she holds dear, she and Glenda pick up the pieces and start again. And one man, in particular, is there when Kelly needs him most: Alec Alderman – a kind and gentle rag-and-bone man. But Alex has problems of his own . . .

'If you want an enthralling saga, read Lynda Page' Martina Cole

'You'll be hooked from page one' *Woman's Realm*

'Full of lively characters' *Best*

0 7472 5505 9

HEADLINE